MASSES
&
MOTETS

JEFFREY DESHELL

MASSES & MOTETS

A Francesca Fruscella Mystery

FC2

TUSCALOOSA

FC2 is an imprint of The University of Alabama Press

Inquiries about reproducing material from this work should be addressed to
the University of Alabama Press

Book Design: Publications Unit, Department of English, Illinois State
    University; Director: Steve Halle, Production Assistant: Hannah
    Kroonblawd
Cover Design: Lou Robinson
Typeface: Adobe Jenson Pro

Library of Congress Cataloging-in-Publication Data

Names: DeShell, Jeffrey, author.
Title: Masses and motets : a Francesca Fruscella mystery / Jeffrey DeShell.
Description: Tuscaloosa : FC2, [2019]
Identifiers: LCCN 2019007163 (print) | LCCN 2019009382 (ebook)
    | ISBN 9781573668842 (E-book) | ISBN 9781573660730 (pbk.)
Classification: LCC PS3554.E8358 (ebook) | LCC PS3554.E8358 M37
2019 (print) | DDC 813/.54—dc23
LC record available at https://lccn.loc.gov/2019007163

To Lynne Tillman

"I pray to God to rid me of God."
—Meister Eckhart

MASSES
&
MOTETS

INCIPIT

I

This incipit has no privilege, no outstanding value, no control. It's not before, above, outside or beyond any text.

It's simply another prayer. Another sermon. Another crime.

II

I will write this in the first person, because faith, perhaps more than anything, is *personal*.

I will confess to not being comfortable telling stories about my stories. Nor writing about my faith.

III

I don't know what I have faith in. How could I?

What is the antonym, the negation of faith?

Doubt?

No. Knowledge.

IV

This novel is an attempt to work with the music of Pierre de la Rue (c. 1460–1518). Sometimes known by the name Peter van Straaten, although there exists much confusion as to whether van Straaten was a completely different person. Pete of the street.

De la Rue composed thirty-one individual masses, with over sixty motets and chansons known or implied.

De la Rue is known for his exploration of the lower register. His *Requiem* Mass requires not one but two *oktavists*, that is, *basso profundos* who are comfortable with pitches as low as contra Bb.

When La Rue's *Requiem* was transcribed in 1931, the transcription was raised a full fourth, to accommodate modern singers.

I took from La Rue his four-part choral writing and the structure (and titles) of a few masses and songs.

V

The music gave me a way into theology. And vice versa. The music and theology allowed me to think of a narrative that doesn't rely on the constraints and teleology of psychological realism or the constraints and teleology of Hegelian phenomenology. La Rue's music and the accompanying negative theology suggested a narrative and language prior to or outside the jurisdiction of psychology and phenomenology.

VI

The beauty of theology is that it might always remain unverifiable, unaccountable. Open.

This should be our unceasing prayer. Hopefully unanswered.

VII

In psychology, the other is located internally. In theology, the other is external.

VIII

The detective as witness. In this case, of a certain male hysteria.

Requiem
INTROITUS

"Pray without ceasing."
—I Thessalonians 5:17

Pseudo-Dionysius tells us, "We must begin with a prayer before everything we do, but especially before we are about to talk of God" (*Divine Names* Chapter 3). What is prayer? Our Lord tells us often how to pray—"Our Father who art in heaven," (Matthew 6:9–13) and when to pray—"pray without ceasing" and even what and whom we should pray for—"And whatever you ask in prayer, you will receive, if you have faith" (Matthew 21:22) and "Therefore, confess your sins together and pray for one another" (James 5:16). Our Lord, in his wisdom, even tells us how *not* to pray—"When you pray, you are not to be like the hypocrites; for they love to stand and pray in the synagogues and on the street corners so that they may be seen by men. Truly I say to you, they have their reward in full" (Matthew 6:5, see also Luke 18). But this doesn't quite answer the question, my brothers and sisters: what is prayer?

Prayer is language. And language is prayer. Prayer is language directed toward God. And language is prayer directed at both God and man. In the beginning was the Word (John 1:1); we all know this. And Christ was the Word made flesh (John 1:14). We all know this as well. Our language is a transubstantiation from the Word into the word, from God into Christ, from heaven into earth. Our language is also the paschal, as passing over from word into the Word, from Christ to God, from earth to heaven. Our language is a constant repetition of these gifts, the aleph and omega of Christianity, the virgin birth and the resurrection of our Lord. All language is prayer, and we must pray without ceasing, in our hearts, with our minds, and with our tongues.

This knowledge illuminates three dangers. The first danger is the problem of blasphemy. If I have said above that all language is prayer, how can that include blasphemy? I have two things to say to you: first of all, I say to remember that language is directed to both God *and* men, so that when men hear curses, God might hear praise. We cannot presume to know what God hears. Secondly, do non-believers blaspheme? Wouldn't this be a waste of breath? In fact, most "non-believers" do nothing but pray when they attempt to blaspheme God. What men call blasphemy is perhaps a purer prayer, a prayer unencumbered with human sense, untainted by human expectations and knowledge, a language incomprehensible or misunderstood to all but God. The Beast of Revelation is a possible exception to this, but the Beast and the Whore of Babylon are finally defeated by the Word of God, *verbum Dei* (Revelation 19:13).

The second question you may have with this knowledge is the question of origin. Where does language as prayer and prayer as language originate? If, as is usually thought, prayer comes from man and woman, from our hearts, how can it reflect the divine

Word? Can we, full of sin, possibly be holy enough to speak to God? And should we use the same tongue, the same mouth ("Give ear to the words of my mouth," Psalm 54), the same language that we use to speak of insects, of animals and of the filth of the world, of ourselves—in short, our sins, weaknesses, lusts and degradations—to speak to our Heavenly Father? If we answer that certainly prayers come from us, from our hearts, then how can we possibly think that we are blessed enough to speak to the Divine? Even the most pure among us, the Holy Father in Rome, has sinned. Think of the tremendous distance separating God and ourselves, and how small and inadequate our own sinful voices must be. How can we possibly be worthy to speak to God?

And if prayer does not come from us, if prayer is a gift from God, "Every best gift and every perfect gift is from above" (James 1:17), then we have a strange condition, a circle, in which God presents a gift only on order that we use it to praise him. What kind of gift is this? Do we honestly believe that God presents us with the gift of prayer only to have us "regift" it back to Him? What kind of small God needs His gift returned?

I say to you now that language and prayer come from God, as all things come from God. I say to you now that language and prayer come from us as well, at the same time. Language pre-dates us, but we take it into our hearts to fashion it to express our deepest thoughts. Language is indeed a gift from God, which we form to make our own, which in turn we give to God in prayer. "One thing God has spoken, two things I have heard" (Psalm 62:11). This is the dual nature of language. Yes, language and prayer come from God, but the words "come" and "from" no longer have the same meaning. And neither does the word "God." But I will speak of these things in other places.

Finally, you ask about silence. Is silence prayer? Or is silence the lack of prayer? Our Christ gives an example: in Matthew 27 when our innocent Lord Jesus Christ was accused by the chief priest and Pharisees, he responded with silence, "*nihil respondit.*" And when questioned by Pilate, again he answered with silence, "*non respondit.*" These silences were not silences, these silences were full of language and prayer, these silences signified *everything*. Silence is at the heart of prayer: silence is pure prayer. Silence asks for nothing, silence does nothing, silence represents nothing, silence degrades nothing, silence is nothing. In the nothing of silence, we speak to God, uncorrupted by the concerns of the world, uncorrupted by the concerns of ourselves, uncorrupted by any image of God. And in silence, God speaks to us. In silence, we avoid the hypocrisy of public prayer. In silence we approach the true nothing that approaches the silence of God. This is the prayer we must pray ceaselessly, the prayer of silence. In silence, we are one with God.

But beware. Even silence can become lyrical, can become impure and fallen. My words to you, my silence to you, perhaps falls back into lyricism: that is, my words and my silence are directed from me toward you and not toward God. That is the danger of prayer. That is its duality, its constant hypocrisy. That is its eternal, inescapable irony. May God grant us the ability to pray in *true* silence. May this be the prayer we speak before God. Amen.

It was a quiet Sunday morning. But hot, already seventy-some at six-thirty. I'd been having trouble sleeping: failing asleep immediately but then waking at four thirty and only maybe dozing until six forty-five when the alarm pushed me into the day. I wasn't drinking—a couple glasses of wine with dinner—so it wasn't that. Thoughts of mortality, maybe, but I'd suffered those since my son was born. Age.

Both my body and my head felt heavy, thick, like parts of me—heels, wrists, butt, shoulder blades and the back of my skull—had liquefied in the night and settled in pools where my skin met the bed. I considered rolling over to shut off the alarm before it rang, but the Sunday gravity kept my limbs pressed firmly back. I'd thrown off the top sheet sometime in the night, so I lay stiff, completely exposed to the early morning. I thought suddenly of Dehmel, I don't know why, in a similar position, slaughtered in the Oxford Hotel room. And of Lowenthal's destroyed head. I had never been so wrong. Never. I felt strangely detached from all the victims, even Benderson. Which is to say I felt no guilt. I did feel bad. For being so wrong. And for Benderson being so wrong. And I suppose I sympathized with Dehmel, whom I knew least, and so who possessed the greatest innocence. Or at least likability. Maybe not: she married the fuck Lowenthal in the first place. What kind of woman would do that? I know what kind of woman would do that. And crazy Zemlinsky, who pled guilty to murder two of Sixto and the gardener, to avoid any charges with Benderson. Everyone was happy to keep a lid on that. Zemlinsky would most certainly rot in Cañon City. But girlfriend had stones; I had to give her that. Benderson got a full-dressed funeral.

I felt bad not for them, but for myself. Benderson's death affected me, sure, but it affected me mostly for how it affected *me*. When he was killed a part of my life was amputated. Truth be told, I had little affection for the current version, but the past

Benderson, the former Benderson, the Benderson whom I loved and who loved me, that Benderson I missed. But how could I have been so wrong? I needed to let it go.

I had to get up, get some coffee in me, see if Nicholas needed a ride anywhere, see if Hector needed anything. Work was slow, a couple of assaults and gang shootings, but victims were surviving, and I was consulting, not leading anything at the moment. Which was probably a good thing. So this Sunday was free. It would be too hot to run, unless I left soon, and I wanted to read the paper and take my time over my coffee. I'd hit the gym later, try to get the flab off my arms. One, two, three—up.

I sat on the edge of the bed and yawned. I looked down at my chest: my boobs seemed not so much sagging as disappearing. I didn't miss them. I yawned again and thought about my mother. Two mastectomies and dead at fifty. Never saw her grandson. I was having a harder and harder time picturing her. A quiet, uncomplaining woman, ambition and joy hidden or stifled by an often cruel husband. Said cruel husband was seeing out his last years in a Lakewood facility, visited regularly by his grandson, who liked to practice on the large Steinway Model B the Harmony Pointe Nursing Center had somehow acquired. Maybe I should go see him today. Take the grandson and some booze. Maybe. Okay, time to get up, take a pee, and get some caffeine.

I preemptively killed the alarm, went to the bathroom, avoided the mirror above the sink, sat on the toilet, then put on my thin robe and padded downstairs to the kitchen. Coffee smelled good: Hector must be up. He was sitting at the kitchen table, his face behind the *Post*, steam rising from his triple-sized McIntosh mug. He put the paper down when he heard me. "*Hola.*"

"*Hola.* Everything okay?"

"Everything's fine. I've been up since five. Too hot to sleep."

"You going to Mass today?" I asked as I poured myself a cup of coffee and added half-and-half.

"Went last night. Then went to the Legion with Maxie and Big Pedro."

"Stay out late?"

He shook his head, glanced at his paper. "Eleven-thirty. Big Pedro's old lady's sick. Something with her belly. Could be cancer. Daughter's coming up from Santa Fe."

"That's too bad. How old is she?" I sat down across.

"Same age as him I think. Seventy." Coffee was good, strong. "Maxie says 'hi.'"

I looked at the headline: A SCORCHER! I looked across at Hector, who quickly dropped his eyes. "Why you trying to set me up with Maxie?"

"He's fun and he's got bucks. Could do worse."

"I ain't in the market. Besides, he's ten years older than me."

"Eight."

Last fucking thing I needed. "Read your paper."

He lifted his right eyebrow quickly, like he was flicking off a fly. It was a gesture I recognized from his son, my dead husband. The day now seemed to stretch before me without much pleasure, interminable and hot. Hector took a bite of toast and set it down carefully on his plate. "You got plans today?"

"Nothing really, why? I was thinking about visiting my dad."

"That'll cheer you up." He picked up the paper and angled it so he could both read and keep my face in sight, but he had to tilt his head so far back to read through his lower bifocal lenses that his necked popped loudly. He frowned and raised the local section up to his face.

"No, it won't cheer me up," I sighed. I thought of my father's stringy white hair, the smell of piss and disinfectant, the swollen ankles of his catatonic roommate. I hoped the AC was working. How long had it been since I last visited? Before Memorial Day. April? March, definitely March. Christ. I'd try to get there well before noon, so I wouldn't have to eat lunch with him. And bring him a bottle of something.

Would that be the way I'd go out? I'd rather do a Benderson. Except for the dumpster part. And the naked part. And that wouldn't be fair to Nick. Not that lingering in some hell-home would be all that great for him either. I picked up the front page and started to scan.

I could barely hear my cell ringing softly in my bedroom.

He preferred staying in and eating Sunday dinner by himself. Since the Germans came (there weren't enough Poles to make a difference), the after-Mass meals had become tedious, the conversations dominated by theological gobblydygook or legal hair-splitting rather than light talk of wine and football. Here, he could focus on his food and not have to think about questions of transubstantiation, statutes of limitations or the woman's pill for the following morning. At home he could concentrate on the delightful sensation of very young cow cooked quickly with fortified wine, butter and pine nuts, and not have to pause to pretend to listen to Father Vertov's stuffy and incomprehensible theories, to smile thinly at Monsignor Belavaqua's attempts at humor or nod at Cardinal Green's arguments about preteen boywhores. What did they know anyway? They never left the City. He was, as that American said, boots on the ground.

Here at home he could be alone with his chop, his string beans and his wine. He could take off his shoes, sit comfortably in his shirtsleeves, listen to music if he so desired and think or not as the mood struck. He wasn't listening to music, nor was he thinking much. The veal was good, not dry like at the Secretary's, although he would have liked a few more pine nuts. This was an exceptionally good wine, a 2001 Case Basse Brunello. He smiled to himself as he thought that he'd finish the bottle, yes, likely before dessert, which would then require a finé before bed. The beans, however, were not crisp enough, no, not all. He'd have to say something to Father Benoit. He took another bite of veal. Perhaps the perfection of the veal compensated for the deficiency of the beans, and if he were to chastise Benoit for the latter he'd have to praise him for the former. The veal was delicious, with just the right amount of vermouth. Sweet vermouth. He'd rather not speak to Benoit unless he had to. But he liked string beans and very much would like to avoid a repetition of this particular experience. They were edible, yes, but not enjoyable. And it would be most unfair to Benoit to let him believe his kitchen was pleasing in all respects when it was not. He would have to say something tomorrow. He would mention the success of the veal as well.

He poured another glass of wine. Dabbed his lips with his napkin. He'd glimpsed the Holy Father earlier, walking with Beautiful Georg in the Apostolic Palace, his head bent and his arms clasped behind his back. Beautiful Georg gave him a tiny, nervous smile, and his Heavenly Father seemed to have closed his eyes. No matter: he was doing God's work. Let not the left hand know what the right was doing. The recognition came from God.

From whom all blessings came. Including this meal, this meat and this wine. He put a small morsel of veal in his mouth and kept it on his tongue. This was a beautiful gift, from Christ the Lord, and he was not worthy. No, he was not worthy to receive such a wonder, such a perfect morsel, such a delightful bite. From God to the mother cow, then to the young calf, from the Tyrol *butteros* to the truck drivers, to the butchers and then to Father Benoit, and the dairy farmers, the wine and spice merchants, the grocers, all to his table and then to his mouth. All under the watchful eyes of Jesus. A gift to him and to him alone. He moved the morsel around with his tongue and bit into it with his right molars. The juice of the meat mixed with the butter and spiced wine, ah, an intimation of heaven, just this side of perfection. He was not worthy to receive such a bountiful gift, and he closed his eyes and bowed his head ever so slightly in gratitude and amazement.

He chewed slowly and swallowed, then opened his heavy lids and swallowed again. Another sip of wine, exquisite. *Ad coenam vitae aeternae perducat nos, Rex aeternae gloriae. Amen.* He set his glass down and quickly made the sign of the cross in front of his face. Perhaps grappa after the Brunello. He'd received a present of a couple of bottles of homemade *grappa gialla* from his friend Monsignor Guzman, a Jesuit. The Jesuits had everything. They were always so smart and polished. He sighed. He'd done fine for himself, for a poor but curious country priest. He was educated and ordained by the Dominicans, and brought to the Vatican by Father Ciavonne, for whom he did a few small favors, three years before John Paul II died and the Austrian installed. A couple of small ones would help him sleep.

God's gifts. And God's work. Food was one of God's gifts. So was wine. And sleep. And Redemption. And to help pay for this, he did God's work. As best he could. But it was not really payment. How could it be? It was more acknowledgment of the Grace of God. "My grace is sufficient for you, for my power is made perfect in weakness." He was weak, but his weakness allowed God and his power to work through him. He smiled and took another bite of the veal. It was not payment, no, for the gift was too great to ever be repaid. His work was a reminder, to himself, that he could never repay God for His gifts and blessings. His work was a prayer, a prayer of weakness.

He yawned. The wine and the heavy meal were having an effect. He took a forkful of the beans into his mouth and pushed his plate away. Besides the sogginess, they were sauced with too much vinegar. He swallowed with some difficulty. These too were a gift from God, he supposed. More butter, and perhaps lemon rather than vinegar, would be an improvement. And certainly the cooking time halved: this is not England, Father Benoit. Although being French, he should know his way around les haricots verts. Belgian, not French. Perhaps that explained it. He was finished with the wine, and grappa would be wasteful. He recited the Ágimus tibi gratias and made the sign of the cross.

He yawned again and loosened his collar. It was stuffy in his small sitting room where he took his meals: the drapes were heavy and the small table fan ineffective. He was pleased he had an air conditioner in his bedroom. He would sponge himself with cool water before his compline. He looked at his calendar: St. Benedicta of the Cross—Jeremiah 31:31 and Matthew 16:16–23. "And I say to you that you are Peter, that upon the rock I will build my church." He smiled. His cell phone signaled the receipt of a text message. And almost immediately his landline began to ring.

Hail Mary, full of grace, the Lord is with thee. But is the Lord with me? It doesn't feel like anybody's with me. Not with this terrible, terrible pain. I don't get no sleep, Lord, hardly no sleep at all. I don't know how I can stand it, Lord, how I can stand it. Bayer, Tylenol, Advil, none of it works, Lord, none of it. I talk to the doctor and the doctor, she's a woman, she just looks at me. Maybe the priest will listen, maybe the father will have some ideas. My neck hurts so bad, I can barely drive to church, Lord, barely drive the six blocks to Mass. One of these days I'm going to end up in Saint Joseph's hospital, dear Lord.

I'm sorry, Lord. I know you're my savior and my personal salvation. I know you sent Your only son, our Lord Jesus Christ, to die for my sins. I know you sent Your most holy servant, Saint Madron, to intercede for all those in pain, Lord, some with pain worse than mine. I know you don't allow more than we can bear, Lord. And what is my little pain compared to Yours, Lord? It's nothing.

In the name of the Father, the Son and the Holy Spirit. Amen. There's no holy water. It looks like I'll have to cross over to the other side, and I can't see any little red lights on over here. It's so quiet here, so peaceful. It looks like hardly anybody's here. There's an altar boy straightening the missals, but nobody else I can see. I like to say my confession before Mass, that way I can take communion with a pure soul. Mr. DeMarco, rest in peace, used to moan and groan every single Sunday. "Why can't you wait for eight-thirty mass once in a while? Even God ain't up this early. It'd be nice to sleep in and have a nice Sunday breakfast every so often, wouldn't it? I mean a man has a right to ask for that." I slept like a baby back then. It was hard for me to get up. I loved Mr. DeMarco, Lord, You know that, but I didn't always love the foolish things that came out of his mouth.

I do love this church, this I do. All the beautiful stained glass, praise You Jesus. Look at Jesus over there, rising to heaven, surrounded by those beautiful angels, isn't that a sight this early morning. The light just takes my breath away, Lord, streaming through that blue and white. It hurts my neck to look up that high, but isn't that a sight.

All the doors are closed and the little red light is on, so I'll have to wait. There's no nameplate on the door. Hmmm. I'll just sit in this pew. I don't mind waiting. In the name of the Father, the Son and the Holy Ghost. Amen. I'm not going to kneel, Lord, if that's all right with you. There's not another soul around. Oh, what's this on my glove? Lipstick. I hope that will come out with some bleach. I can keep my thumb over it like that. I do hope I can get that spot out, maybe put some Shout on it first. I've had these gloves forever, simple white cotton gloves. The simplest is always the best. I have another pair, one for winter, thin leather Mr. DeMarco, bless his soul, gave to me for Easter a year before he died. But these white cotton ones I've had forever. I don't remember getting lipstick on them before. The light is still on. That person must have a lot to talk about.

I don't have so much to talk about. You know that, Lord. Not that I'm perfect, far from it, I'm a sinner and unworthy of Your Holy Grace. But my sins, they're tired sins, Lord, small and tired. I don't think I have a mortal sin left in me. Not that I'd want to Lord, not that I'd want to offend Thee. And the fathers, they don't want to hear the same old same old, how I complain too much, how I'm vain and selfish, and I want a new Sears toaster and a trip to Hawaii this Christmas, and I don't do for others nearly as much as I should, Lord, and I don't respect the memory of our dearly departed Mr. DeMarco, my husband of forty years, not because I don't miss him, Lord, but because I can't remember him the way I used to. I'm sorry, honey, but it's true. Those good fathers, I must bore them to tears. Especially that old one, Father Philip, the one who always gives me three rosaries to say. I think he's sleeping half the time. I don't like that young African, Father Antoine, who breathes through his mouth. You can hear him before you get in the booth. I wonder who's in there now. It's odd that they didn't bring a nameplate. All of the other lights are off, and I see the door's slightly open.

They're really taking their time, Lord. It's already a quarter to six. Usually they close up at six so people can get ready for Mass. I'm not sure there'll be enough time for me.

Maybe if I walk by, someone will hear me and hurry it up. There's usually never anyone here this early, that's why I come. I've never had to wait this long before. Oh, oh, my neck. The other booths are empty, I can see that. Is there anyone else around who could help? I could ask that altar boy to see if he could find another priest, but that would likely take too long. I could wait until next week, I suppose. I'm going to get up and walk past.

I can't hear anything. What's that on the floor? Someone must have dropped their wallet. I'd better pick it up and give it to the deacon. There're so many sneak thieves around everywhere, even in church. That's why they have to lock the collection boxes. I could give it to that altar boy, but lead us not into temptation, Lord, lead us not into temptation. I wonder who it belongs to. Willem Martinez it says. Colorado driver's license. He looks like a crazy, like a drug addict. Four dollars. Blessed are the poor, for theirs is the kingdom of heaven. Maybe he's in confession now, that's why it's taking so long. I can't hear anything, though. I shouldn't stand up here like this, going through a man's wallet.

Did someone spill wine on the floor? This church is usually so clean. Who's been drinking in the confessional booth? Maybe someone snuck in and passed out last night. This isn't right. There's no noise, not a sound, and something's spilled on the floor inside. I wish I'd brought my other glasses, but I don't think it's wine. I'll knock. Lord, forgive me. Father, are you in there? Is everything all right? Father? Lord, this isn't right. The door's not locked. Jesus, forgive me.

It's dark in here. Oh God, oh God, oh Lord, oh Jesus Christ! I can't speak, I can't breathe. He has no face! No sound, no sound. Lord Jesus, he has no face! Oh God!

KYRIE

"He who has ears, let him hear."

—Matthew 11:15

Last time we spoke, I suggested that silence could be a pure prayer, released from the concerns of the human, fallen, language of Babel. Silence and perhaps even blasphemy. It is good, yes "it is good that one should wait quietly for the salvation of the Lord" (Lamentations 3:26). There is so much that silence can do: silence can foster awe before God—"Let all flesh be silent at the presence of the Lord" (Zechariah 2:17); silence can indicate a submission before the Lord—"and so amazed were they at his reply that they fell silent" (Luke 20:26); silence can provide freedom from all the world's noise and earthly distraction—as Mark teaches us in the story of Jesus's transfiguration (Mark 9:2–8); and silence can prepare us to commune with God. In silence and solitude, we approach the holy space of Our Lord Jesus Christ.

Silence can be an invitation, an invitation to the Lord, for it is only when our mouths are shut that our ears are open, as the old saying goes. Silence truly is a gift from God, allowing us the space to prepare to listen to his gentle voice. Some of us even try to formalize our silence, incorporating it into rituals that often serve to purify our souls and bring us closer to the Lord our God. But silence can be an invitation to evil as well. Sometimes, in the absence of God and the word made flesh, silence opens the self up to sin, to sinful voices and craven desires. Nature abhors a vacuum, and evil can rush in to fill the perceived absence of God's grace. We are not all Jesus who can withstand the temptation in the desert. Sometimes we need the Word of God to protect us from Satan's toils.

And sometimes silence can signify indifference, lack of concern, selfishness and death. Sometimes we remain silent out of fear. Sometimes we are afraid to speak up, afraid to rock the boat, afraid to witness to the Glory and Grace of Our Heavenly Father. Jesus exhorted his disciples to "go therefore, teach all nations: baptizing them in the name of the Father, the Son and the Holy Ghost" (Matthew 28:19). But we don't always accomplish this. We don't always try. Who has time for this? Sometimes we remain at home, on our couch, concerned only with our own salvation, our own immediate needs, spiritual and otherwise. Sometimes we ignore the suffering of our fellow human beings, of our neighbors, of our friends and even of our families. Sometimes we ignore the sin in the world, the constant stream of lust, greed, murder and stupidity. ~~It is a sin to say nothing when we see our neighbors murdering their unborn, when we see our friends surrendering to lust, when we see spiritual violence celebrated in entertainment for even our youngest children. Our own community has suffered tremendously because of silence, because of the failure to speak out, the failure to witness when so much damage was being done to those placed in our trust. It is fair to say that this internal silence has done far~~

~~more harm than any external forces could ever do~~. It is a sin to remain silent in the face of the filth of the secular world, a filth that not only corrupts our worldly existence, causing immense and widespread physical suffering, but a filth that also works, with its distractions and temptations, to endanger our spiritual survival. Breaking the silence, in the face of this onslaught of sin, is not only our duty unto Christ, it is a vital tool for our very survival as followers of Christ and members of His Holy Catholic and Apostolic Church. This silence, this failure to witness, comes not from God, but from our own depravity and sloth.

Silence has its dangers: silence can readily turn wicked, indifferent, afraid or cunning. And yet silence can also open the space of prayer, of genuine interaction with self and with God. How do we know which silence is which? How do we know whether our silence is holy, the silence of the Apostle James and of Marguerite Porete, who writes, "For He alone is my God, about who one does not know how to say a word" (*Mirror of Simple Souls*, 232)? Or if our silence is the silence of indifference, of laziness and self-concern, of fear and estrangement from our God. How can we tell? How can we listen? How can we learn to read silence? How do we know if the silence is the mark of life, of the possibilities to turn away from the world to gather a cloud of forgetting below us in order to hear more precisely the sweet word of God? Or if this silence is the silence of the grave, of separation from God and our Savior, and a turn inward, a turn to our mortal selves and to our mortal sins? How do we acquire the ears to truly hear the silence of God?

For next time, I will talk about a specific silence, a particular silence, a silence that is at once singular and universal. It is the silence of death. But more specifically, the death of who we are celebrating, the particular death of our *Nuestro Padre*.

It had been awhile since I'd visited the Cathedral of the Immaculate Conception, Denver's monument to virginal reproduction in the heart of downtown, sandwiched between a McDonalds on one side and the City Grill on the other, with the Nob Hill Inn (Happy Hour 8–11 a.m.) across the street. I showed my ID to the uniform outside, covered my shoes with those paper hospital boots, put on the thin rubber gloves, and went in through the side door. I briefly wondered where they held Mass that morning as I carefully made my way across the polished marble floor. The smell—incense, cold stone and furniture polish—brought me back to the feeling of my starched bleached communion dress and the dry taste of the wafer as it dissolved in my mouth. I saw a guy in a tracksuit talking with two other uniforms and an older lady to my right. I recognized Detective Maldonado, who was talking with a priest near the far confessionals. He saw me and motioned to the left, where the klieg lights shown brightly from a doorway. A couple of other uniforms milled about the closed front doors of the nave. The crime scene hazmats were scurrying around, examining, measuring, recording. I didn't see the medical examiner.

As I said, it had been awhile since I'd been inside the cathedral, indeed any church or house of worship. I had attended the two or three service funerals here, but had shown my face only outside in the parking lot and then at the gravesite. Same with the ceremonies at the other churches and synagogues: I'd hover around in full dress but I didn't go inside. Not since Roberto died. I ignored Benderson's send-off completely.

It had been even longer since I'd been in a confession booth. Before I got married. If I had to choose, confession was always my least favorite sacrament (other than extreme unction, I suppose. And ordination). I was always kind of freaked out about telling my sins to some old man behind a screen. Bless me, Father, for I have sinned. My last confession was three months ago... It feels good to do this with my nipples, Father, I don't know why.

The booths had changed, modernized, with small red lights above indicating occupancy and heavy wooden doors replacing the purple velvet curtains. From the corner of my eye I could see a uniform approach me, notebook in hand. I waived him away. I wanted to see the body fresh, with as little preliminary information as possible. I didn't want to fall into patterns before I'd gathered my first impressions. That was my mistake with Lowenthal: I'd too quickly solidified my interpretation and closed off other possibilities. I motioned for Maldonado to join me. One of the CS suits was videotaping the body and the scene, while another watched from the doorway. I tapped that one on the shoulder and after he turned, I said in a louder voice than I wished, "Can I get a look?"

"Yeah. Medex hasn't been here yet. How you doing, Detective?"

"I'm all right. And you?"

"Can't complain."

"This a bad one?"

"See for yourself." The videographer lowered his camera and slid past us and I stepped inside. Maldonado followed.

No mouth, lip, eye, cheekbone, forehead, chin or nose were discernible. Nothing—except the position relative to the body, a single tattered left ear and a few scattered teeth—marked this, this mess, as a former face. He was on his back, his arms stiff at his sides. He was dressed in black, his white priest collar ostentatiously untouched, its purity offensive amidst the carnage. Both heels of his good shoes rested about a foot and half above the floor on the wall near the door. He was slim, not tall, about five seven or eight. A thick splattering of blood (and I assumed brains and facial tissue) decorated the white wall opposite the door. There was a large pool of blood et cetera underneath his head. The spray was relatively contained, suggesting that he hadn't been shot from an angle (i.e., from the chin or the top of the head) but had met the projectile or projectiles frontally. A metal chair was pushed in the corner opposite the body, and the padded kneeler was extended under his left arm. His legs had been positioned posthumously so that the door could close: it was unlikely that whatever final reflexes his destroyed brainpan could muster could manage to lift both heels up to the wall to achieve the present arrangement. I kneeled down to take a closer look at the head. I could see small black pellets embedded in bone and tissue. The enclosed space smelled heavily of cordite and meat.

"Where's medex?"

"We're having a hard time reaching him. His assistant's on the way."

"Shotgun. Close range."

Maldonado nodded. He looked pale.

"Any ID on him?"

"CS didn't find anything."

"We'll need some way of identifying him. Dental charts might not be that useful. Or at least that quick. Any preliminary ID?"

"Father Duquesne said it might be a Father Vidal." He shook his head. "What kind of *pendejo* kills a priest? With a shotgun to the face?"

"In a confession booth."

He nodded again. "In a confession booth." My knees started to complain, so I stood up.

"There was a wallet found just outside the door. The lady who found him picked it up."

"But not his."

"Some lowlife. Willem Martinez."

Hmmm. I looked around, trying to see if there was anything else. CS would do a better job on the cellular level, but I wanted to let these initial impressions reverberate: I wanted to be open to the possibilities of different modalities, polyrhythms, various tonalities. The bare white walls, excessively illuminated. The folding metal chair and kneeler, the dark wooden screen. The blood and tissue, bone and brain. What had once been the location of a man's thinking and dreaming, singing and whispering, praying and doubting, now dispersed, scattered and spattered. In a small room of repentance and forgiveness. The transgression here was deep and violent. I started to feel that rush, that shiver at the base of my spine. It was like the moment when I first started to play during a recital, the first few bars of Bach's Invention no. 1 or Mozart's Sonata no. 14. It was almost sexual this feeling, thrilling and transgressive. I stepped outside the booth and Maldonado followed. I peeled my gloves off and tossed them in a Denver Police Department wastebag. Philips and the videographer rushed in to the room behind.

It was a tragic thing, but Alitalia was barely a functional airline. Even in Magnifica Class. The food was nearly inedible, the seating uncomfortable, and the service uncaring. And the near company—a mannish woman from California who only looked up from her furious notebook scribbling or computer typing to stretch her arm across his face for another gin and tonic—was unbearable. Across the aisle, a dark young man in an expensive British suit kept his sunglasses and earphones bolted to his head. The one stewardess he had tried to speak to, whose accent and thick ankles suggested a fisherman's daughter from Crotone, had too little time for even the most basic courtesies, and had given him a glass of Primitivo (Primitivo!) rather than his requested Sangiovese. The male stewards, while seemingly more competent, were somehow blind to his presence, although he wasn't a slight man.

He could never manage to complete any work on airplanes. What could he do, study his notes? It was wise, in his capacity, to keep written communication, indeed all communication, to a minimum. He'd prepared his plans, his thinking, weeks before and had gone over these preparations carefully in his head before leaving his apartment. He had a few scribblings but kept them locked in a safe in his office. He preferred using the time on the airplane to clear his head with conversation and trivialities (and no more than two glasses of wine), which allowed him, when he landed, to see the situation more clearly and with less anxious prejudice. He could then meticulously compare the situation on the ground with the preconceived contingencies in his head. In his own good time. But here were no convenient trivialities to fill the time. He considered a third glass of wine but was put off by the earlier Primitivo error. He gazed at the newspapers and magazines, but after reading a long article about his beloved Lazio in *La Gazzetta dello Sport*, he could find nothing additional to hold interest. He fiddled for some time with the entertainment system, but recognized few of the offerings. He finally tried to ignore everything and sleep (with the aid of half an Ambien), but his body knew the time was incorrect. And the airplane bed reminded him of a coffin. He got off the plane at John Kennedy tired, stiff, unsettled and in a blackened mood.

Which worsened badly in the airport. The passport queue was crowded and slow, and he got in the wrong line to pick up his luggage and recheck it. He became confused and was forced to ask a small black woman in a light blue uniform for help. Evidently, this was a serious insult, resulting in narrowed eyes and sneered, incomprehensible invectives. He allowed her to finish her curses before walking away. *"Excusi, excusi signora."* Oh America. "How can we sing the song of the Lord in a foreign land?" He dozed fitfully on the plane to Denver and woke up dehydrated and disoriented—with a painful knot on the left side of his neck—just before landing.

A young Capuchin monk with a very thin beard met him at the top of the stairs before the baggage. "Greetings, Reverend Signelli. *Spero che tu abbia fatto un viaggio piacevole."*

"Good day. Speak English please." Cough.

"Of course. I hope your journey was a pleasant one. Archbishop Aguilara sends his regards. He is traveling. Abbot Pascal will welcome you at the rectory."

Cough. "It was not a pleasant journey." Cough. An abbot? He was not surprised that the archbishop merely provided his regards: this was not an official visit, and publicity was to be avoided. But sending an abbot bordered on the edge of *affronto*. Conley was the auxiliary bishop, a Jesuit, and was no fool. And Cardinal Doherty, it was said, liked his wine. But he had no knowledge of the Capuchin, Abbot Pascal. Those stairs... he was having a hard time catching his breath.

"Did they warn you about the altitude, Reverend Father? We are a mile above sea level, and the air is thin. And dry: you need to drink water constantly."

"You are right; my mouth has no moisture. Where do I collect my suitcase?"

"This way, Reverend Father. Let me take your bag and get you a bottle of water first."

"A cup of cold water, yes. You are too kind." Cough, cough.

"It is a very sad day for our diocese, a very sad day indeed." The monk shook his head as he took the small bag at the Father's feet. He stood and their eyes met. His large brown eyes were surprisingly hard, almost cold, and their expression seemed to violently disagree with his words. "It is difficult to comprehend how such gruesome violence can originate with our fellow man. We are all confused, Reverend Father, confused and shocked."

"Brother...?"

"I am Brother Lanzarote, Reverend Father, Ignacio Lanzarote. I have been assigned to make sure you are provided with everything you need during your visit."

"Where do you come from, Brother Lanzarote?"

"Madrid." Lanzarote motioned the direction for the father to walk, then followed a step behind. He reminded him of a certain old waiter, an ancient *paisano* who used to serve the *branzino* at La Verenda. He didn't think he liked Mr. Lanzarote, the waiter.

"Your Italian is very good."

"I studied for three years in Rome."

"Oh. *Americano del Nord? Romano Maggiore?*"

"*Athenaeum Pontificium Regina Apostolorum.*"

He frowned. This was a complication. The *Athenaeum* was a Legionary college and the differences between Legionaries and

Capuchins were great indeed. Although Lanzarote now wore the hood, he might still have loyalties to that crazy *Nuestro Padre*. He would have to be extremely careful around this waiter. Cough cough. "Could I have some water, please?"

Hector put down the newspaper—the news was so goddam depressing—and got up and poured himself another cup of coffee, then made his way downstairs. This could be a big day. David Rivera, who had made some big money with Pepsi in Pueblo and real estate in Boulder, was coming to audition some gear for his ski *haus* in Breckenridge. He'd gone to high school with David's older brother, Benny. David had good ears, knew what he wanted, and wasn't afraid to spread his cash. This could mean six figures. He'd installed both his home theater and his man cave two-channel in his Gold Coast mansion, but this wasn't a slam dunk, as David had hired Lucas at Denver Electronics to do his son's house in Westminster; all wireless control zones, computer files and solid-state crapola, all designed for convenience, for fingertip access to the entire world's music, all engineered to suck the life out of the musician's sweat and blood. He knew David liked turntables and tubes, so hopefully that's what he'd want in his ski *haus*. That's what he'd set up in the big studio, anyway.

He went around to a small fridge near his workspace and checked that he had beer, wine and seltzer water. He knew he'd stocked it yesterday but wanted to reassure himself. He should have gotten some champagne to celebrate but didn't want to count his chickens. He cocked his head, listened to see if he could hear any sounds from Nicholas stirring above. He'd need some help schlepping and placing the Auditorium 23 Hommages and the Sonus faber Aidas, which were almost 400 pounds each. Plus, Nicholas had good ears, the good ears of the young, and could help make sure the room was ready. But Nicholas was still asleep.

He liked this time of the day, alone, a cup of strong coffee in his hand, early enough to avoid traffic sounds and the necessity for AC, surrounded by all the gleaming metal, glass and wood instruments of musical reproduction. He could listen at times like these, really listen to the music, listen and try to improve, always improve, what he heard. He walked into the big studio and turned on the two small corner lamps.

He set his coffee down carefully on the end table by the couch. This was the tube room, where yesterday he'd swapped out the less expensive kit, keeping only the premium amps, preamps and turntables. He moved slowly, methodically, powering first the turntables, phono stages and then the two DACs, then the preamps, and finally the power amps and integrateds: he kept the power conditioners always on. He really liked the glow of the tubes, especially from the big 845s, the brilliant orange and yellow light smoldering through the grey metal of the plates. The room warmed quickly: the 845s and KT 150s put out a lot of heat. He needed some music to get the right electrons flowing, give the glow of the tubes something to do. He walked to the record cabinet on his right and picked up the first album he saw, Andy Warhol's tomato red *Cross* on black matte background, the Anonymous 4 singing Hildegard von Bingen's *The Origin of Fire*. It was a beautiful cover, no labels, nothing visible except that cross, redder than blood, redder than anything imaginable, redder than red. He was not one for modern art, nor medieval music, but that image had struck him, and he was intrigued when Francesca had given it to him for his birthday, right before Lucy had passed. He had found some comfort in the music during his daughter's hospitalization and death, and now the music had become inseparable from memories of that time. Not in a bad way: there were very few moments in the day he was not thinking of Lucy, his dead wife, or his dead son. No, the music provided some background sweetness to that time, a riff that he would never escape. The haunting plainsong of Bingen he now found indispensable.

The simplicity and purity of the female monophony was a great recording for showing off gear, like the Audio Note ONGA-KU Integrated, with the 845s and silver-wired transformers, that could reproduce those voices, especially the timbre and decay, with amazing clarity and presence. He took the record from the sleeve, cleaned it carefully, and set it gently on the Artemis Labs SA-1 turntable with matching Schröder Reference tonearm and van den Hul Gold Frog MC cartridge. He pushed the rocker switch of the power supply and the platter began rotating. He gently, gently lifted the tonearm and placed the stylus down on the groove. There was no sound. He thought he'd connected the Artemis to the ONGAKU and then to the Aidas, but something was wrong. He checked the volume on the Audio Note, and the knob was set at three o'clock, which meant he should be hearing something. He then checked the input and saw that it was turned to AUX. He twisted the volume to zero, then turned the input to PHONO, then gradually increased the volume pot. He sat down on the couch.

As the exquisite voices filled the room he looked at the image of the cross in his hands. He'd buried two children, a girl and a boy, plus his wife, in a small cemetery in Walsenburg. Three crosses. There was something wrong there. Two children, two children—that wasn't right. There was something mean and cruel about burying a child, something inexplicable and disorienting. What kind of God would do that? What kind of God would ask that? What kind of sin did his sweet Lucy carry with her? She was only four. He didn't like asking these questions, not because it felt disrespectful—quite the contrary—but because, by asking, he was implying there was someone to ask these questions to. Someone who could say, Well, Hector, Lucy had to die at the age of four because... And then explain it to him, rationally and without emotion, why a four-year-old girl, four years and two months, had died of cancer of the blood. And why a thirty-year-old man, in the prime of his life, with a wife and child, had to be killed by a suspended license drunk whose alcohol level was three times the legal limit. It was a striking image, this cross. But what did the image help when faced with those all-too-real crosses in the Walsenburg dust? There should have been something he could do. The music played on, quietly, solemnly, inevitably, while he held a reproduction of Warhol's red *Cross* in his hand.

He liked this part, with the four voices all climbing the register in unison, almost like Coltrane and Cannonball, together but distinguishable. But something was off. The soundstage was constrained, and the attack was sloppy and ill-defined. The Aidas obviously were too close together.

PSALMUS

"As the deer pants for streams of water,
so my soul pants for You, my God.
My soul thirsts for God, for the Living God.
When can I go and meet with God?"
—Psalm 42

Last time we spoke of silences, of the many different silences, of the good and evil possibilities of silence. In its most pure and holy form, its form nearest, if we can speak in such inadequate terms, of the cloud of unknowing which perhaps is the approach to God, silence is the sign of longing, the space of almost pure desire, of, as Psalm 42 so eloquently puts it, a thirsting or panting for the Living Waters of God. The Hebrew is *ta 'a rōg* גרַעַת, which means pants, yearns for, longs for with a passion that our Latin's *desiderat* can't but approximate. This silence, this stillness, this quiet, where the stag prepares to drink, where he thinks of nothing but slaking this great consuming thirst, this is the holy silence which is a gift from God.

But this is not the silence I wish to speak of today. And I realize that to speak of silence is strange, at first hearing. But silence itself speaks, and that is its danger.

The silence I wish to speak of today is the silence of the grave. The silence of death. It is the silence of one particular death, one unique death, the death we are gathered here to commemorate. To celebrate. To mourn.

This is one particular death, yes, as all deaths are particular, the death of the Most Reverend Marcial Maciel, LC, founder of the Legion of Christ. We will have time later to remember his accomplishments, to gather his friends, to recall and celebrate his life and his love, to bring back to mind the incredible *charism* with which he touched us all, young and old, rich and poor, healthy and sick, Latino and Anglo, European, African and Asian. I want to talk about silence first, the silence of our recently departed, the silence of *Nuestro Padre*.

I spoke earlier about how each death is a singular event, unique and incomparable. But that's not quite exact, is it? In a certain way, all deaths are unfortunately analogous. All of us here, all of us in pastoral care, who minister to the sick, the dying and bereaved, we know death and we know how similar deaths are. All are different, yes, with different actors, settings, circumstances etc., but all are the same, too much the same. Everyone dies too soon. Lives have infinite variety but death, deaths are similar. In hospitals, care fa-cilities, even in home beds, we watch the loved one breathing, more or less lightly, then suddenly they are not. Sometimes there is pain, but not always. Sometimes there is a noise, a groan or a sigh, but these are but minor accessories. There are violent deaths, that is unfortunately too true, for sometimes the injured do not die in bed but meet our Lord in a pool of blood on the cold ground. Some of us have witnessed these deaths. But still, I say to you, that these deaths too are alike. There might be more pain, and therefore more noise, but the poor earthly body is breathing, perhaps struggling but breathing nonetheless, perhaps screaming or crying but, yes, breathing, and then the breathing stops.

And when we reach a certain age, and our friends and colleagues begin to die, we get too used to attending funerals. Mourning quickly becomes a duty. While it is true that each of us dies but once, all of the deaths we witness are unfortunately too much the same.

And every single death, every death in the world, always carries with it the death of another, the passion of our Lord Jesus Christ. No one dies alone, and death is not final. These verses in 1 Corinthians are one of the most important in the Bible: "O death, where is thy victory? O death, where is thy sting? Now the sting of death is sin: and the power of sin is the law. But thanks be to God, who has given us the victory through our Lord Jesus Christ" (1 Corinthians 15:55–57). We have victory over death in Our Lord Jesus: the death of Our Lord has transformed each human death into victory. Victory and salvation. The death of Christ changes *everything*.

And so when we talk about the death of the individual, we are talking also, always, about the death of Christ. His death alone is incomparable, remarkable, unique and exceptional. But I want to focus, as much as I am able, on *this* particular human death, the death of Father Maciel, the death that has created such a void, such a silence in our lives today. For we owe him that. Yes, I would like to talk of the death, and the life, of Father Maciel.

But in talking *of*, I cannot talk *to*. I can talk *about*, but not *with*. In talking of, I am enveloped in silence: to my speaking, a silence answers, a silence of loss, a silence of mere memory, of a voice or presence having been removed. Father Maciel cannot respond to my words, cannot laugh and say, "Let us move on to more important business." No. In talking to *Nuestro Padre*, there is now only silence. We say that the dead have been *silenced*. This silence always is a silence of the past. This is the silence of death. This is not the silence of our Lord, the silence of longing, of prayer and holiness, of solitude and solicitude. Our Lord's silence is the silence of the desert, of hope, of clearing (and indeed temptation), the silence of the future. The silence of the desert of our Lord is a silence directed toward unknowing and the unknowable, a silence lifted toward the indefinable and unspeakable. The silence of the grave, on the other hand, is a silence turned inward, away from the other who is no more and into our memories of him. In dying, the other person moves from his existence as an other being, as an other entity, moves from the person we can talk *to* and *with*, moves into ourselves, our memories, our souls. While we know that this death is only a transition, that Father Maciel has left us to be closer to, to be *with* our God and Lord Jesus Christ, for his friends remaining on earth he lives now only *within* us. He is part of us, he *is* us now. He can no longer surprise us, as he used to do, with that smile of his, that smile that came from his eyes and sometimes took a moment or two to reach his lips. He can no longer delight us with those elaborate and generous gifts, those perfect presents, those small miracles that arrived from out of the blue and showed such penetrating and joyful insight.

Death brings a bad silence. The silence of Father Maciel is now really *our* silence: it belongs to us, comes from us and returns to us. This silence, the silence of the grave and of death, comes not from the Lord and does not open unto the Lord. No, this silence comes only from ourselves and opens only into our own memories. This silence is bound up in meaning, this silence has too much to say. This silence is no silence: it speaks to us, shouts to us of sadness and loss, of memory and death, of finality and absence. This is the sting of death, death's victory. This silence returns us to ourselves, it is selfish, narcissistic and vain. It is no opening unto the Lord: in fact, it prevents such an opening, for it fools us into thinking our silence, the silence of death and the past, could be the silence of sincerity and holiness. To say again: the silence of the grave is a circular, solipsistic silence, a silence that comes not from the Lord but from ourselves, and it reaches not out and up but back and down, back into our own egos and memories. Glory be to God. Amen.

I walked a few feet away from the confessional and stopped behind one of the wooden pews. I looked at the altar, recessed in shadow, and then up at the stained glass, pale and washed out, above. I then looked down, to the various cops and techs milling and buzzing, talking and examining. It always surprised me, the number of people who worked on a case, the sheer industry and complexity of the murder-solving business. Gone were the days of Sherlock, Watson and a couple of foaming beakers, replaced by hazmat suits, full spectrum video, organic chemistry, physics and ballistics, advanced medical technology, cutting-edge data mining and surveillance instruments and techniques, not to mention a small battalion of lieutenants to manually or physically examine A, B and C, and an army of uniforms under them to manually or physically examine A1, B1 and C1. And let's not forget Schlaf and the other bosses above, the various press and press officers to one side, and the DA and his assorted minions to the other. I ran my fingers along the smooth wood of a pew back. I could feel Maldonado to my right, slightly behind. All these people, all these man-hours present and to come, all these emails, phone calls and data searches, all this energy and expense, all this work, all orchestrated to try to recreate a moment or two of history, a moment consecrated, made important, by the premature death of a single human being.

I don't work well with others. I never have. I've always preferred solo recitals to ensembles or, God forbid, accompaniment. I don't like trios—the piano often chords and arpeggiates while the violin sings and soars—or duos, four hands, none of it. It's not about the attention, it's not about being relegated to the background, because there's a lot of interesting things that can happen in the harmony. It's about being distracted, it's about having to listen to others in order to hear the music. It's about having to rely on these other players, their skills, their timing, their moods, their tastes, their souls, for lack of a better term, in order to hear and then to anticipate and to play. It's not about ego, or it's not only about ego. It has to do with trust, granted, but mostly it has to do with the desire to really hear the music, to hear the music purely, without distortion or distraction, without detraction or embellishment, without any other getting in the way.

This character trait has never served me particularly well. I wasn't good enough to attempt a solo career (that was evident rather early), and I've made a few rather glaring (some might say spectacular) errors as a detective. But it was always *my* career, and they were always *my* errors.

I turned to Maldonado. "What do you think happened here, Detective?"

He shrugged.

"I think there are a couple of possibilities. Maybe three. First of all, this could be a passion killing. It takes some real anger to stick a shotgun in someone's face and pull the trigger. Let alone when that someone is a priest. In a church. But priests don't generally excite such passions; priests generally don't go around screwing people's wives."

"No." I wondered how Catholic Maldonado was: we both knew what I was going to say next.

"But they do screw. At least a few of them. This could be some revenge killing, some child wronged sort of thing. That might explain the extreme violence and perhaps even the setting. In the confessional. We'll need a positive ID on the victim and then a thorough, and I mean thorough, profile. I'm not talking that Illuminati Da Vinci bullshit, but the Catholic Church can be difficult to work with. We will need a file on the deceased."

"We have the wallet. Maybe the killer wants us to know who did it."

"I'm not convinced about the wallet. Second possibility, which is close to the first, that there is some sort of symbolism involved, that this is an attack not on this specific priest, but on this specific church or diocese. Or on the Catholic Church as a whole. This is a big church downtown. We'll have to do some digging about this parish and this diocese: have there been any reports of abuse? Has anyone been recently transferred in or out with allegations, rumors or suspicions of abuse? Again, we'll run into resistance."

Maldonado murmured into what looked like a large smartphone, "Was the hate directed toward this priest specifically? Or was it directed at this church? Or just the church in general?"

"The third possibility I can think of is robbery. Is anything missing from the church? Have any of the collection boxes been broken into?"

"I spoke with Father Duquesne, who told me he looked around after we were called. The congregation was dismissed, and he didn't notice anything immediately." He smiled at me. "I don't think they have collection boxes any more. At least not in the cities."

"Get him some uniform help and ask him to check more thoroughly."

"There's another possibility. One of his fellow priests."

"Father with a grudge. You're right. But how many own a shotgun? Where did this guy live, anyway?"

"If it's Father Vidal, he lived in the rectory. In the back."

"You seal it?"

"Uniforms: soon as they got here. No one in or out."

"Good. What about Mass this morning?"

"Father Duquesne sent everyone to Holy Ghost or Saint Ignatius."

"What did he tell them?"

"Plumbing issues."

"Send a couple of uniforms to each."

"Already done."

"Speaking of plumbing, I'm surprised the press aren't here yet."

"Duquesne's pretty sure it's Vidal. Recognizes the shoes."

"We'll need more than that. Rush the prints through. And one more thing. Make up a list of all violent sex offenders and have a uniform check for alibis. See if any have been recently released or relocated. Also, anyone with a violent history of crimes against churches or clergy. This will take some time, I know."

I heard a clacking to my right and turned to see a youngish woman in white surgeon scrubs walking forward from the side door. As she approached, I saw black cycle shorts and a bruise-colored purple-and-red cycle jersey underneath the white. The staccato was caused by the inability of the white hospital booties to effectively muffle the noise of bright orange bicycle shoes meeting polished marble flooring. She carried a black leather backpack slung perfectly over her right shoulder. She stopped in front of me and demonstrated what someone must have told her was her "killer" smile.

"Hi. I'm Dr. Collero, the new assistant medical examiner. Sorry about the getup, but I was told this was urgent." She looked behind me and the smile faded. "Body in there?"

I nodded and she moved past me without hesitation.

As soon as it was a decent hour, he'd ask to be removed to better accommodations. A nice hotel. This was unavoidable. While he'd slept through compline, he woke up at the beginning of the third nocturne, well before lauds. And while this wasn't completely the fault of his room, he felt trapped, like he was physically bound by the thinness of the dormitory walls (proven repeatedly by audible evidence of his left neighbor's gastric distress) and the closeness of the air. Not to mention his own reserve and discretion. The bed was comfortable enough, with adequate pillows and blankets, but there was further space only for a small chest, a sink and a crucifix on the wall above his bed. The door to the water closet was a flimsy plastic accordion-like contraption, and there was no tub or shower. He'd insisted on anonymity, and it was obvious that his attempt to arrive and remain beneath the cloak of the night would make him far too miserable to be effective.

He'd not been capable of much yesterday and it was already Wednesday. He'd need to speak with Malachi today and find out why the priest was dead. He sat up in his bed and made the sign of the cross, *Requiescat in pace*. He yawned. His mouth was dry, like linen, and his head ached dully. He remembered his pills, for his kidneys and his blood, and then remembered he'd forgotten to take them the day before. He sat there on the bed, both hands gripping the edge of the mattress, his head bent down and his back slouched forward. He would need water to take his pills, especially the blood pills, which were the size of a ten lira coin. There was a glass near the sink. He preferred bottled water, Solé if possible, or Lauretana. He remembered the water from the pump from the dirt square of his dear Provvidenti—tepid and smelling heavily of chalk—that he avoided whenever possible, preferring to walk a kilometer down the hill to the well at Saint Antonio's, where the water was cold, clear and sharp, like the face of Father Bruno. He hadn't been back to the hill country in what, six or seven years, when he helped bury his young cousins, the twins. *Requiem aeternam dona eis, Domine et lux perpetua luceat eis: Requiescant in pace. Amen.* Such waste. He wiped a tear from his eye. Sentimentality was a sign of age, of weakness. Sentimentality and living in memories.

He had realized for a while that he was not the hard man he once was. His soul had softened as his blood thickened. He hated Milan, but had always admired Gattuso, the Rhino, numero 8, the way he would crush your ankles then help you up with a smile. More than Gentile, who appeared too cynical and controlled, Gattuso tackled with his heart. And the way he protected the pretty boy, Pirlo, like a *cane corso*. He shrugged: he was no longer Gattuso, protecting the skillful, punishing the wicked. No, he was an old man who desired bottled water and a larger bedroom.

Perhaps he too should hang up his boots. He rubbed his brow with his right hand, then looked up: perhaps I would better serve You, Oh Lord, in a small parish in Molise, not too far from Provvidenti. I would be quiet, Oh Lord, peaceful and serene, and I would blend into the stones, Oh Lord, and try to help the poor when I could. He hesitated and then looked down at his feet. You are everywhere my Lord, everywhere, but You feel far from me tonight. Perhaps I left You in Rome, eh? Or perhaps You remained in Provvidenti, near the well. Perhaps it was I who left You in Provvidenti. He carefully turned, then supporting himself on the bed, kneeled on the thin carpet, his elbows on the mattress. *Pater Noster, qui es in caelis, sanctificetur nomen tuum. Adveniat regnum tuum. Fiat voluntas tua, sicut in caelo et in terra.* I have tried to do Thy will, my Lord God, Thy will and the will of the most Catholic and Apostolic Church. *Deus ultionum Dominus: Deus ultionum libere egit. Exaltare qui iudicas terram: redde retributionem superbis.* You are the God of retribution Oh Lord, and I act through Your will. His thirst grew, and the kneeling put some pressure on his bladder. And he wasn't sure God was listening. Not tonight. Maybe Blessed Mary would listen. *Ave Maria, gratia plena, Dominus tecum. Benedicta tu in mulieribus, et benedictus fructus ventris tui, Iesus. Sancta Maria Mater Dei, ora pro nobis peccatoribus, nunc, et in hora mortis nostrae.* Amen.

His heart felt heavy and alone. He knew better than to presume to ask for signs. God's shining forth would come: a carved rosary from a cardinal, a bottle of Chianti from the Secretary, a note from Beautiful Georg, or the osso buco from the Osteria del Gall. And once, even, a slight nod from His Holy Eminence. And the fact that still, in hushed telephoned whispers, he was given tasks, that was the most obvious sign of all. These were signs from men, true, but they were men of God, sanctified by the Church: if the Holy Eminence nods then God must be nodding too. Perhaps. He yawned deeply. He was not as foolish as to confuse the ways of God with the ways of men. And he remembered the Austrian from before, where he was not His Holy Eminence, but God's Rottweiler.

This was not the Rottweiler's *negotium*, this was his. His left knee began to ache, and he shifted it slightly on the carpet. He had been given this task, yes, but maybe he'd carried it out poorly. Maybe this had been a mistake. A man had died, and God must be displeased: God's will was never murder. He thought back to his conversations with Malachi. He hadn't suggested such violence, he was sure of that. Such an act had never occurred to him. He had made it clear that it would be best for all concerned if the book, an evil book certainly filled with slander and lies, was returned to the Church, where it could not be used by the Church's many enemies. That is what he had told Malachi, and Malachi understood such things, such necessary discretion and restraint. This was an important business, but there was never mention of harming anyone in the return. He had not forbid anything, true, but only because he didn't imagine he needed to.

He tried again *Deus ultionum Dominus: Deus ultionum libere egit. Exaltare qui iudicas terram: redde retributionem superbis.* God was distant tonight, a mere dot on the horizon of a desert.

#Myfirstmurder. Of a priest no less. Shot in the face, is that true? Need to confirm, need to confirm. Who's sniffing? Who's thirsty? Channel 4? Not on Twitter? Post? Never say shit until the next day. 9? Slow and stupid. Still silent out there. Gotta find who's at the scene. S'up. Whose there? News? Fruscella and Maldonado. medex 2. PDH. PDH? Kidding? He's 110. Not this 1, assistant. Name? Dunno. Hot tho. Any media? TV, rpts, any? 9 just pulled up. Small or big? Vehicle, van, small or large? Large. Here's 7. And 2. 7 big 2 small. Getting crowded. Confirm vic and COD? Priest gunshot. Confirm? No. Where r u? Near door. Get closer confirm vic and COD. Find out. Ah, there we go CBS Denver Unconfirmed reports of a shooting in Denver Basilica Cathedral. And here's 9 Jim Schue Breaking: Shooting downtown Denver church we're on scene. Hey Andy. No comment just now. As soon as I get more info you'll more info. I got no info. Ok. Ok. Bye. And again. Hey Charlotte. Yeah, no rest for the wicked. No, I got nothing. You'll be the first. Bye now. Vic = Priest. Others? No. COD? SHOT-GUN!!!! Well, well. A priest shotgunned in the Denver Basilica. #Priestshotdeadinchurch. Confirmed? No. Get more intel. Who's that? Ok. Hello Vernon. Yeah, I got nothing yet. Not on the down low or the up high. You bet. Later. I need some help. Hey Jerry, it's me. Time to go to work. Yeah I know what time it is. Check this: a priest shotgunned downtown. Not confirmed. Yeah, in the ca-thedral. The one on Colfax, block away from the City Grille. That big white thing on the left. Who's working Data today? Can you give her a call, see who's wanting what? Hold on, got another call. Fox. Fuck 'em. Anyway, see what you can find. Fruscella. Yeah. I know, huh. And don't you know someone at the medex? PM me. And soon. Yeah, yeah this is big. This is huuuuge. Later. Schlaf, I'd better answer. Hello? Yes sir. I did speak to her sir, and yes, it seems as if we are on the same page. Right. Nothing goes out without her say-so. Yes, sir, they are calling. I understand. Yes. Yes. Good-bye sir. Fuck. That woman is NOT going to make my life easier.

#saltydriedup. Dead priest. Shotgun in confessing room. Need more. Confessing room? That doesn't sound right. Text to Fox: Can confirm nothing. WLYK. Who's this? Hello? How did you get this number? No. No. Goodbye. KWGN reports suspected shooting in Denver Catholic Cathedral downtown. More to come. CBS Denver is facebooking photos. Gramming, Snapping fuck. I need something here. C'mon c'mon, answer. I need something here. Detective Fruscella, this is Lieutenant Clark again. Please call me when you get a chance. It's urgent. Does she text? Detective, urgent, please call immediately. Let's see, age 52, promoted in 2000 and again in 2008, primary on Solano killings, Lassiter murder and Drees kidnapping and murder. Oh, primary on Lowenthal case, the Secretary of Death. Heard something about that, have to ask Jerry. Maybe take Seal out for a drink. To do, check on Lowenthal rumors w/Jerry and Seal. Not exactly photogenic, is she? #saltydriedup. That's a better shot. I do like those big eyes, though the hair needs work, makeup too. Strong face, maybe too strong. Could use some height. Hi Charlotte. Still nothing. Hey, you remember the Lowenthal case, right? Who did that for you? She got a file you can send? Before I was here. Thank you. I won't forget it. The Gmail address, not the police one. Thanks. AP what the fuck is AP doing? Breaking early morning shooting in Denver Cathedral. Hello? Yeah I just saw it. Who's the beat? Nothing confirmed. I tried. Later. CNN not on it yet. Small favors. From the J-Man Data desk on the deep deep denial lots of buzz re Argentine passports. Name Jerry name? Yes! Andrea Vidal. Andrea? Thought it was a priest. More? No. Okay Andrea who are you? Facebook, LinkedIn, psychiatrist in Boston, Instagram, YouTube, Soundcloud, Pinterest, okay I get it I get it, Andrea Vidal Denver Basilica no no "Andrea Vidal Denver Basilica" there we go. We welcome the Reverend Father Andrea Vidal to our Denver diocese Father Vidal, who was born in Buenos Aires Argentina, comes to us from Mexico City, and will join our administrative staff. So Andrea is a priest. #priestswithgirlnames. Who knew? What's the date here? November of last year. Less than a year. CNN! Hello? Yes, this is Lieutenant Clark from the Denver Police Public Information Office. We cannot confirm anything at this time. All information requests and news briefings will come through this office, yes. As I said, we cannot confirm or deny anything at this time. Yes, this is the number to use. And that's the email, yes. I don't. No, I don't have a guess. Thank you. Jerry will dig this. CNN bro CNN. Who's gonna retweet? Perez? Who's the assistant medex? Where's that file? CBS Denver Sources inform us at least one dead in Denver Cathedral shooting. Sources? Who the fuck is talking to them? Who's talking to media!!? I need to get down there now. Need more eyes. C'mon dude, who's talking out of school? Definitely I'll have to go. Should have been there already. Agricola where are you? Jerry you know a hot assistant medex? Waiting, waiting. Jerry? No, ask Katie. Going to church. Any more from Data? No. CNN huh. Cool. I need some more eyes. Katie, wake up wake up. We got a killed priest. No shit. Office time, girlfriend. Get him off you and get some clothes on. Yes, please shower. Hey, you know any hot assistant medexes? Yeah, he's like eighty. Agricola texted PDH, so I assume we're talking female. One of the uniforms I use to keep me in the loop. All right. I'm going down to the crime scene. Call me when you're online. Please hurry. Make sure I got all my shit, iPad, all three cellies, do I need my Air, yeah let's go.

OFFERTORIUM

"Do not besot yourselves with wine; that leads to ruin.
Let your contentment be in the Holy Spirit;
your tongues unloosed in psalms and hymns and spiritual music,
as you sing and give praise to the Lord in your hearts."
—Ephesians 5:18–19

We spoke of silences, last time, and the dangers of a silence that is not of God, not of the joyful Holy Spirit, but a silence of death and mourning. And how are we to tell the difference? How can we know the silence of God from the silence of Death? How can we—as we remember Father Maciel—know if the silence we hear comes from ourselves or from God? How, as we contemplate the death of our Lord Jesus Christ every Good Friday, and indeed with every individual death, how can we know whether this silence is of Our Father or from our own misguided souls? How can we tell if our silence is prayer, an opening of our hearts into the grace of God, or if our silence is deafness, a closing and hardening of our hearts, a slothful turning inward to our egotistical concern for our selves?

Perhaps we might say that 'I know my own heart. I know that I am sincere, that I am truly listening to the silence of God.' And

I would reply to that: 'Do you know your own heart? Can anyone know their own heart?' Proverbs 16 tells us "The plans of the heart belong to mortals, but the answer of the tongue is from the Lord. All one's ways may be pure in one's own eyes, but the Lord weighs the spirit." Even though we think we know our own hearts, God alone can see into our innermost being and know who we justly are and what we are actually doing. Can we ever be certain the plans we are making are plans from God and have nothing to do with our own self-interests and egotistical concerns? Can we ever really detach from ourselves and say 'Yes, I am certain I am doing the will of God?' Of course not. Any time we say 'I,' we are not saying God. And the second verse repeats this: we can fool ourselves, but we cannot fool God. "The Lord alone" weighs our spirit. And let me say to you: it does not matter how good we think we are. It does not matter how pure, how holy, how filled with the Holy Spirit we believe ourselves to be, we are always, always, always mistaken, always wrong about ourselves. We can never know. Let us never forget Jeremiah 17:9: "The heart is deceitful above all things, and desperately wicked: who can know it?" Romans 8:27 answers that for us: "He knows us far better than we know ourselves, knows our pregnant condition, and keeps us present before God."

God alone can know our hearts. God alone can know us. God alone can know whether the silence we hear is the silence from Him or the silence from ourselves. God alone can know whether the silence at the heart of prayer is a true silence or whether it belongs to the world of Babel and death.

We cannot know our own hearts. We need to think carefully about what this means. I must confess, I do not know what it feels like to feel strong with God. Ephesians 6 tells us to be strong with our Lord, to "put on the full armor of God, so that you will be able to stand firm against the schemes of the devil." The closer I get to God, the less I matter, the less I exist. God does not give me strength, the strength of self and ego, no, but gives me His armor to fight wickedness and sin in the world. God gives me the strength to disappear, the strength to be absorbed into divine communion with Him. God gives me, us, the strength to negate our own desires and egos, the strength to give up the strength that belongs to our own will and preoccupations, and "become like little children," Matthew 18:3. The closer I am to God, the less I am. So those who can say 'I know my own heart, and I know I am close to God. And God is responsible for my success. I would never have become the great man I am if not for God. I know God and I know His will and I know what must be done,' for those who can say such things, they say to me that they know neither God nor themselves.

We are unknown unto ourselves. We know ourselves as little as we know God. This is the beauty of God's grace. To be certain is not to have faith. This is not the death of the self, but the true possibility of the life of the self in God.

This negation, this true possibility of the self that can exist only in the detachment from self, this is ecstasy, in the original meaning of the word. Ecstasy comes from the Greek word ἔκστασις, which is a combination of the word *ek*, which means 'outside', and *statis*, which means 'to stand.' Ek statis, then, means to stand outside oneself. This is not necessarily the ecstasy of mystical states or other types of ostensible intoxication: we do not have to speak in tongues or dance around like the followers of St. Vitus. No, this ecstasy, this standing outside of itself, can be quiet and invisible. It can take place in the darkest of nights, in the most silent of times. It is a true standing outside of yourself: not in order to see yourself, to become even more conscious of yourself, and not even as a way of losing yourself. No, the ecstasy of God's love is a way to become *indifferent* to yourself.

We will see what Luke has to say about such ecstasy when we meet again. Glory to God in the highest. Amen.

"So tell me about this wallet. William Gonzalez?"

"Willem Martinez."

"This Martinez got a sheet?"

He checked his phone: "Yeah, nothing major, all possession. Pled out, never served time."

"Address legit?"

"Couple uniforms checking now."

"What do we know about our father here? If the ID holds up."

Maldonado read "Andrea Vidal, age 50, Argentine national, born in La Plata, Argentina, in 1960, educated at *Universidad Nacional de La Plata, Licenciatura* in 1981 in Theology, *Facultades de Filosofía y Teología de San Miguel*, PhD in Theology at the Pontifical Gregorian University in Rome, 1985. From 1987 to 2008 was assigned to the admistrative offices of the Legion of Christ, headquartered in Mexico City. Resigned from there last year."

"What did he do in Mexico City?"

"Says here General Director Administrative Staff."

"What was he doing here so early in the morning? Hearing confession? Preparing for Mass?"

"Father Duquesne, the parish priest, said Vidal heard confession but never celebrated Mass."

"So what,was he hearing confession at four a.m.?"

"According to Duquesne, Vidal often came here early before Sunday Mass. It seems he liked to make sure everything was ready, spic and span. He also, according to Duquesne, enjoyed the cathedral. He'd come here often."

"Surviving family?"

"Mother, two brothers."

"We need a warrant for his room?"

"Duquesne gave permission. Wants to cooperate fully. Crime Scene's in there now."

A uniform approached me, hesitantly. "Press is here, Detective. *Post*, Channels Four and Twelve."

"Keep them out." My phone rang. It was from the precinct. "Hello?"

"Detective Fruscella? I'm Lieutenant Clark, from Public Information. I'll be assisting you in your communication with the press. Are there any reporters at the scene?"

"There are."

"Have you spoken to anyone yet?"

"I have other things to do."

"I'm sure you do, Detective. I'm emailing and texting you my contact information. Please direct all inquiries to me, and please say nothing yourself. I'd like to meet this afternoon to discuss strategy, say four o'clock back at the fort?"

"This is the first day of a murder investigation, Lieutenant, so I'm not exactly sure when I'll have free time."

"The more you work with me, Detective, the less you'll have to work with the press. Now unless you enjoy the exhilarating give-and-take of formal press conferences, or the thrill of thinking on your feet during misheard questions and misquoted responses shouted back and forth as you walk from your office to your car, I suggest you allow me to handle some of this for you. It is, as they say, my job. By the way, do you tweet?"

"What?"

"Do you have a Twitter account? Or Facebook?"

"No."

"I'm glad that hasn't changed. We'll see you at four."

Okay. How old was he, twenty? My phone beeped to indicate a text message, and then another ting for an email. I put it quickly in my front pocket and turned back to Maldonado.

"I want to find out what this Vidal did in Mexico and here. Can we get a phone number for the Mexico City office? And yes, I'm aware that it's Sunday. Get Lorcano on it. And is Duquesne in charge here? Who was supposed to say Mass?"

My phone rang again. Again, the precinct. "Hello."

"Fruscella, Schlaf. Anything I need to know?"

"Unidentified male Caucasian, shot in the face. Prelim ID a Father Vidal, 49, Argentine national. I'm going to try to confirm ID, time of death, and more about why he was here."

"Jesus Christ, a priest. Who's with you?"

"Maldonado."

"Good. Talk to Nehdjaru yet?"

"No, his assistant. In bike shorts."

"Excuse me?"

"Nothing."

Silence.

"Keep me informed, Detective."

"Will do, sir, will do."

A slight pain in his back was joining the pressure on his bladder and discomfort in his knee. It was hunger, yes, and thirst, these pains, and the jet lag, yes, all of these together, yes, these were the causes of his inability to sleep. But what kind of servant of God allows small bodily discomforts to produce such weariness of the spirit? Would he be James, or Peter, asleep in the garden? The flesh is indeed weak. He swallowed hard and touched his dry lips with his dry fingertips. Then he bent his head again.

Ave Maria, gratia plena, Dominus tecum, benedicta tu in mulieribus. Et benedictus fructus ventris tui, Iesus. Sancta Maria Mater Dei, ora pro nobis peccatoribus, nunc, et in hora mortis nostrae. Amen. His heart was empty tonight, empty and alone. His profession—and what was his profession exactly: soldier? counselor, helper? servant? banker?—had no special saint, and he was somehow put off by both the Sicilian Agatha and Father Nicola, the purse thrower, the saints of Molise and Provvidenti. He remembered especially the festival of Agatha, where he and his brothers watched Father Bruno carrying the primitive wooden figure, with the two slashes of vivid red indicating the amputation of her breasts, holding his gaze and fluttering his stomach. He always felt much closer to Mary, but tonight she was elsewhere, keeping away. Sometimes he was a purse thrower himself, but he was no saint. He swallowed again. He was not even sure he was useful to God.

Ave Maria, gratia plena. His work, his work, it could be a lie. And since he had no children, no wife or family, if his work was a lie then he was a lie. His complete life. Had he been holy enough to be certain he was listening to God and not to Satan? Had the signs of success been mere lies, sent from the Deceiver himself? And even if he had truly served the Church, the Church was made up of men, human men, fallible men, sometimes selfish or shortsighted men. And men were not God. The Church could be used by Satan too, God forbid. Some of the things he had done, some of the purses he'd thrown, he had misgivings, doubts. He had paid people not to speak. He had arranged priests to move from parish to parish, from diocese to diocese, to avoid the circulation of falsehoods and destructive gossip. He had shamed two nuns into leaving their orders. The enemies of the Church were many and their threats required rigorous diligence, this was true, but had he battled these enemies alongside the Holy Spirit or in legion with the worldly interests of man and the Beast? Did his successes glorify God? Did his successes please God? Did his successes come from God, from whom all good things flow? Or were they even successes at all?

Dominus tecum. Sister Berenice, a Daughter of Saint Paul, was a shrill, pushy woman, modern, with no sense of history or tradition. She was Italian, but Milanese, and she reminded him of that woman who read the news on RAI 24, Lucilla something, the blonde-haired woman with the very long legs. Sister Berenice belonged on the television, pushing microphones into faces of footballers and describing the traffic. She had spoken to civil authorities, against specific admonitions, and had spoken both to the police and to the international news agencies, interviews of lies and slander, confused rants of accusation and defamation against a priest, his bishop and his diocese. He remembered reading her lies and slander in his office in Rome and having to sit, he was so angry and light-headed. He had made the telephone calls immediately,and taken a flight to Trieste that day to make sure his wishes were understood. She had appalled him when he had interviewed her, the way she had strolled into the chamber with her expensive shoes and light blue suit that was nothing like a tunic, the way she had leaned forward in her chair when she answered his questions, the way she had looked at him fully with strength and anger in her clear brown eyes. He had done the correct thing with Sister Berenice.

He was not sure he had been correct with Sister Kiara, a tall, stooped, very thin Cistercian with a long pale face. She had not gone to the police or to the press, only repeatedly to her various superiors, who finally contacted the *Congregatio*, and he had been dispatched. She would not look at him as she sat across a table, her frightened eyes darting to and fro, finally coming to rest on the hands in her lap. "I saw what I saw," she kept repeating, "I saw what I saw." I saw what I saw. I saw what I saw. He had tired quickly of her meekness, her obstinacy, her trembling and her deference. Her black scapular, contrasting against the white of her tunic, coif and veil, had also severely annoyed. She had soon begun to weep. He didn't think she was lying: she believed she actually had seen the unspeakable acts she had inarticulately reported. Despite, or perhaps because of her humility, he had not tempered his letter to her archbishop. She was susceptible to deceit, he had written, and was prone to the hallucinations. Moreover, her refusal to listen to the counsel of reason was proof of her errors. Her soul was weak, he had concluded, and required ministry and care before she could return to God's service. He had done as he was instructed: Sister Kiara was discredited, and the father in question, Father Belhomme, was removed from Ireland and retired to a Benedictine monastery in California. Sister Kiara soon left her order, he was told, and remained silent, contacting neither the Garda nor the press.

Benedicta tu in mulieribus, et benedictus fructus ventris tui, Iesus. Was this a success? Did the winnowing of Sister Kiara and her tears please God? This tall, stooped, reverent creature posed little threat. Her accusations were vague and confused, and her stubbornness in repeating them added nothing to their credibility. She saw what she saw, yes, but what she saw didn't happen. He did not know what had happened to her after she left her order.

A thought chilled him: what if she had told the truth?

The Aidas were sounding like shit: they were strangling the voices. They were too heavy to move without help, so until Nicholas came down, he'd be better off switching to other loudspeakers, like the squat Voxativ Ampeggio Due single drivers. Nicholas had hooked up the speaker switch to an iPad, but he could never learn crap like that, so he got up and manually changed the signal to the Dues. That was better. The voices regained their balance and presence, and a sense of intimacy with the music filled the room. The attacks were more precise, and he could almost hear the breath moving back and forth through the four throats. These were excellent loudspeakers, extremely expensive, but the doped single drivers sounded breathtaking with the simple no-feedback circuit. One power tube per channel, one driver, one melody, simplicity creating beauty. He'd emphasize that to Rivera.

He sat back down and sipped his coffee. He was getting old. His hearing was getting old. Business was not good: he kept the shop open only because it gave him something to do, not because it paid for itself. It had been awhile since he'd made a big sale. Most of his current business was replacing blown tubes or otherwise tweaking and maintaining systems he'd installed years ago. Small was the way to go now, hidden, wireless, invisible, mobile. No one wanted big-ass tubes, 400-pound loudspeakers or vinyl albums cluttering up the feng shui. No one wanted fidelity, high or even mediocre, no, they wanted cheap, compressed files and lots of them for their earbuds and iPhones, their private soundtracks, the incidental music to their self-absorbed lives. Everyone loved music, but no one listened to it.

He wasn't that fucking old. Maybe he should hook up a solid-state amp in the studio to give Rivera some choice. He had a D'Agostino that was musical and powerful, and worked well with the Hommages and the Magicos, but was too powerful for the Ampeggios he was listening to now. He'd ask Nicholas what he thought, seeing as he'd been the one moving it from the south studio. He'd try it with one of the smooth Audio Note preamps, as the tubes of the preamp sometimes softened the glare of the 250 watts of transistor power. He wondered what kind of rooms a ski *haus* would have. He imagined tall ceilings and lots of wood and glass, with white people gathered around in tight pants and bright sweaters, drinking clear cocktails and chatting in hushed tones. Would the $7000 Artemis table, the $4000 Schröder tonearm and $2500 van den Hul Gold Frog cartridge into the $140,000 ON-GAKU and the $100,000 Ampeggios be appropriate? Probably not. And would Rivera really want to cart all his LPs up to Vail, no Breckenridge? Probably not. And would he want to bias those big 845s every couple of months or so, not to mention adjust the table speed and clean the stylus and other upkeep tasks? Probably not. He should have probably thought about this before.

Yeah, he'd get Nicholas to bring the D'Agostino in, and then even the darTZeel Danologue with the Boenicke B8s. That might be a sweet little system, if Rivera didn't want to go whole hog. Actually, he could set it up in another studio, keep this one for the heavy hitters, seeing how the darTZeel and Boenickes would only run about $20.5K with cabling. He didn't think Rivera liked CDs, but he'd offer to help put his vinyl on a computer disk. Nicholas knew how to do that. That was a good plan B.

He picked up the album cover again. There was no printing on the cover, no markings, nothing but the red against the black. On the back, it was all black, with small white writing on the left-hand corner: "anonymous 4 hildegard von bingen the origin of fire." A slick four-page insert held all the liner notes.

The image was joined to the music, which was joined to his daughter, which was joined to his daughter's death, which was joined to his son's and then to his wife's death. The cross of death. The music of fire. He liked that he couldn't understand the words, that they were just musical notes to him, devoid of any extra musical meaning. He had no idea what they were about, as he had avoided the inner sleeve—was surprised he still had it—or any other reading about the composer or her music. While he did love the purity and simplicity of these a cappella voices, he hadn't made other purchases of the composer or the singers, nor had he searched out sacred music, music by women composers, or medieval music of any kind. No, this was a gift from Francesca, a singular gift, and while he found it indispensable in a way, its very indispensability made it unrepeatable.

If he did have to describe it, he'd say there was a longing in the voices, in the notes, some sort of plea, maybe even a prayer. It wasn't joyful, not celebratory certainly, and it didn't sound like praise, like Bach, for example. It was plaintive: full of separation and sorrow. And fear. Or maybe he was just projecting, inserting his own heart into the notes singing to him from centuries ago.

Lucy had been dead how long now? Twenty-one years. She had been their surprise, their miracle baby, for Daddy was forty-nine and Mamma forty-six when Dr. Yeager shook his head and said to them both, "you are most definitely pregnant." It wasn't an easy birth, not for Bella certainly, whose age made her "high-risk," and who was made to attend weekly fetal heart rate monitor sessions, and semi-weekly targeted ultrasounds, as well as a barrage of other tests. But her birth went smoothly (cesarean), and she was a beautiful baby, with chubby arms and legs, and a shock of black hair that grew and grew. There were no problems for two, almost three years. But then she started sleeping a lot, needed three naps a day, and they took her in for tests. They should have taken her in earlier; he'd always believed that.

SANCTUS

"If anyone comes to me and does not hate his own father
and mother and wife and children and brothers and sisters,
yes, and even his own life, he cannot be my disciple."

—Luke 14:26

I would now like to speak of one of the most difficult passages in the entire New Testament, Luke 14:26: "If anyone comes to me, and does not hate his own father and mother and wife and children and brothers and sisters, yes, and even his own life, he cannot be my disciple." We have to ask ourselves, what can this mean? Is Jesus Christ asking us to hate our families, our children, our parents, our own lives? Both the Greek and the Latin are unambiguous: the Greek is μισέω, *miséo*, to hate or detest, the Latin *odit*, from *odi*, to hate. There is no textual ambiguity here, nothing lost in translation. Jesus Christ is telling us that we must *hate* our families, *hate* our brothers and sisters, *hate* our children and parents, indeed hate our very own lives, everything that is dear to us, in order to come to Him. We must love our enemies (Matthew 5:44) and hate our families. Is this what Christ is telling us? Is this the truly radical nature of Christ's thought, to hate those who are dear to us and love those who are strange or do us harm? Did Jesus hate his family? Did Christ detest his mother? Did he hate his own life? If Jesus hated his own life, then what would it mean that he gave it for us? What kind of gift would that be? It can't be a sacrifice when you give up something you hate.

It's much more than misunderstanding, or non-understanding. I can be comfortable with not knowing, in the mysteries of faith (τὸ μυστήριον τῆς πίστεως, *mysterium fidei*, 1 Timothy 3:9), but I can't be comfortable with Jesus who tells me to hate my family and myself. It seems like the worst kind of contradiction to think that the very greatest commandment save one is to "Love thy neighbor as thyself" (Mark 12:31) and that we must also hate our families, our neighbors and ourselves. How can we do this? What can Jesus mean by this hate?

I remarked earlier that ecstasy means "to stand outside." Let us look at something even more fundamental than ecstasy: let us look at existence itself. The words are very similar: '*ex*' meaning out and '*sistere*' to stand or to take a stand or to cause to stand. To exist, therefore, is to stand or to cause to stand out. Out from where? Or, a more important question: out from *whom*?

To exist means to stand out from God. Our existence is nothing but standing apart. We possess nothing in the world but this existence. Everything else—homes, cars, clothing, jobs, health, brothers, sisters, parents and children, seven sons and three daughters (Job 1:2)—everything we could possess or think we could possess, all can be taken from us. And we would still exist. The one possession that neither the world nor the enemy of man can take from us is our existence, our ability to say "I," our power to stand apart from God.

This may appear to be difficult to think, but I believe it to be true: we, in order to exist, must stand apart from God. Also, and one perhaps needs the patience of Job to follow this line of thinking, God chooses this separation—if we can say anything about what God "chooses." God determines that we are to stand apart from Him: otherwise, all would be God. This is the gift that God has given us: He has effaced Himself so that we may exist. God has given up being everything, has removed himself by creating us. Simone Weil writes, "God could create only by hiding himself. Otherwise there would be nothing but himself." God, in His perfect love, has allowed us to be, by retreating from us and vacating His ever presence.

By creating us, by hiding and separating from us, God has given us the gift of life. What can we do with this gift, this existence? We can do but one thing: give this existence back to God. We have nothing else to give. Our possessions are contingent, our talents temporary, our circumstances provisional. Even our families, our very children, are but dust in the wind. I can't help think of Abraham here. But we must *choose* to give our existence back to God, which means we must choose to give our existence back to God *in time*. Not in our time, not in our own sweet time, as it were, but within time. By withdrawing, God has cleared out a space so we can be, so that we can say "I." Our lives, then, should be dedicated *to the process* of closing this distance, *to the process* of returning to God. Any sort of immediate union, a union outside of time, is impossible. We can not simply decide, in the now, without work (or pain and suffering and joy) to enter into the presence of our Lord. We can be "born again," yes, but to be born is but a first step: to be born is not the goal.

It is our gift to God to negate our own "I," to collapse this space of existence, to work ceaselessly and tirelessly to give ourselves over to Him completely and utterly. Now how are we to do this? How can we negate our "I"?

This is what Luke means by "hating our own lives." If life means separation from God, we must hate this separation and do everything we can to lessen it day by day. If existence means separation from God and placement in a world of things and people, plants and animals, also separated from God, we must hate this world and seek to destroy it. Not destroy it outwardly, externally, objectively, no, because these are God's creations, but destroy the world of things and other people *within ourselves*. We cannot be attached to the world, we cannot love the things and people of this world and love God. We cannot want to be, to exist with the things of the world, with the plants and animals, the food and drink, the clothing and cars, the comforts of home, yes, even the people of this world, our family, our brothers and sisters, mothers and fathers, yes, even our children, we cannot love God if we are attached to the things and people of the world. If we desire these things of the world, we cannot negate our own I, and we will remain forever separated from God. Another name for eternal separation from God is Hell.

This sounds very strange, doesn't it? Luke is telling us if we do not hate, we will end in Hell.

Per evangelica dicta, deleantur nostra delicta. Amen.

The rectory was accessible from a narrow hallway behind the altar. Accompanied by Duquesne and a couple of uniforms, Maldonado and I walked slowly, past the two closed doors on either side, and into a small reception area, with three-foot-high cathedral windows on the left and three smaller square windows on the right that opened out to a parking lot. The early morning August light, striped by the metal bars outside the windows to our left, streamed brightly through and harshly illuminated a beige desk, too large for the space, that intruded from the left wall into the middle of the room. Behind the desk, the far wall featured a large oil painting of Jesus on a turquoise cross inlaid with rubies. A smaller portrait photo of Pope Benedict in virginal white hung above an adjacent doorway. After the dimness of the cathedral, the light irritated. We stopped, and I turned to Maldonado.

"That it? The rectory?"

"Yes, ma'am."

I moved forward toward the door.

"Excuse me, excuse me." Duquesne wheeled around to face me. We were nearly the same height. "I am sorry, but the rectory is, umm, we, you are prohibited from the rectory proper. It would upset the fathers most severely. Not to mention the archbishop, if he were here."

"Unless your archbishop has a police force," I said, as I made to brush past him, "I believe I have jurisdiction here. A crime has been committed not seventy yards away, and I need to search the apartment of the victim. If you hold this up and insist I get a warrant, I will, but then I'll get a warrant for every room here, and I'll search every nook and cranny. You might be able to avoid that, at least for now."

"You don't understand: it's not the warrant that worries me. The fathers here expect a certain privacy, a certain amount of sanctuary free from worldly concerns. They, we, have become used to this privacy and sanctuary. Your presence, a woman's presence, will violate the rules and the spirit of the rectory. It has always been this way."

"What? I am a detective with the Denver police force. I am investigating a murder. And I don't have time for this." Feisty little fucker shifted to block my way.

"I understand. And we do want to cooperate all we can in order to help solve this terrible, terrible crime. And I mean no disrespect, Detective, truly I don't. If your presence in Father Vidal's room is required, let me suggest a compromise." He smiled. "I will ask all the fathers who are still present, and most have already left for their pastoral or liturgical duties—thank goodness the archbishop is in Asia—to gather what they need and to vacate the rectory. This will take ten, fifteen minutes at the most. I would have done this earlier but I did not imagine that you personally would try to gain entrance."

"Is this Catholic law?"

"I do not know the specific canonical or doctrinal rulings. It is the way we've done things here, at this rectory, for as long as I've been here. And I'm sure for a long time before that. And I'm fairly certain this is the tradition at most, if not all, other rectories in the United States. Not to say the world."

"I'm sorry, Father, but I need to see for myself where our Father Vidal lived. And I don't have time to wait for all of the other good fathers to clear out. In fact," and I turned to one of the uniforms behind, "I'd prefer if no one cleared out. Please ask everyone to remain on the premises. We'll have some questions for them."

I turned and walked past Duquesne, who pivoted back, pulled out his phone and began to dial. I stopped and looked at Maldonado. "Where's Vidal's room?"

"Two fifteen. Second floor."

I pushed open the heavy steel-and-glass door and noticed immediately a thick metallic odor, a smell of men, old men, old men too long left alone, left alone not for lifetimes but for centuries, centuries where they developed rituals of beauty, cruelty, hope and exploitation. Like most masculine spaces, the air suggested discipline and self-control combined with laziness and self-indulgence. I recognized the familiar trace of poverty—an odor of sweat, cheap food and unwashed bedding—but oddly there was something of voluntary deprivation here, not of want but of meanness. No wonder they didn't want me here: they were ashamed. Ashamed? Or guilty?

I heard faint music, sounded like mariachi, and hesitated as Maldonado pulled his phone from his jacket pocket. "Maldonado. Okay. Nothing around huh? Yeah. Hold on." He looked at me, "This is Kinney and Lyng, checking Martinez's address. There's no such address as 5420 Osage: Osage stops at 52nd, two blocks away."

"Have them check transposed numbers, nearby numbers. Make sure there's no mistake. And then have Data pull up his info, his sheet and previous addresses. Contact FBI and State Po: you know the drill. I'll be up in Vidal's room."

"Do we have a suspect, Detective? A person of interest?"

"We have a dead priest, a wallet and a bogus address. I'm not sure about anything else."

What if that Sister Kiara's weeping, stammering, unintelligible, insistent story were true? He'd never yet considered the possibility. Father Belhomme had witnesses, other priests from the school, who had guaranteed his presence at a retreat many miles away. He'd taken it without thought that Sister Kiara was mistaken and was seeing things that weren't there. It was true that Belhomme was traveled, that much he had gathered, but, as was usual in his duties, he was not provided with full information regarding the histories of those he was to help, to defend, extricate or make obscure. He hadn't particularly cared for the man—a stocky, middle-aged MSC who, convinced of his own charm, chatted nonstop and smelled heavily of cigarettes—but never imagined that he could have achieved the opaque acts Sister Kiara had tried so doggedly to describe. Belhomme was a man of God. What then was Sister Kiara?

Sancta Maria, Mater Dei. I have tried to protect the Church from her enemies, Oh Mary, I have tried to protect You from the liars and evil-sayers who would drag you down into the muck. Had he taken enough care? Decisions had already been made, true, and he had gone not to pass judgment but to ease what had already been determined. And what could he have done, even if he had believed her? Father Belhomme would still be in California, and Sister Kiara would have earned even more distrust and annoyance of her mother superior, her bishop, the Dublin archbishop and the CDF. If he had believed her, that would have likely caused more trouble. The interviews would have multiplied, the tears would have multiplied, and the descriptions, with each repeated telling, would have become more incomprehensible and fantastic. Sister Kiara would not have prospered under such scrutiny. And Father Belhomme, Father Belhomme would still be in California.

Both of his knees, as well as his back, were now beginning to cause greater discomfort. He had done what he was told, without notice or noise. He was without blame. That was not true. He had written his letter so that Sister Kiara was made to appear guilty, infinitely more guilty that Father Belhomme. And she was not, she was not guilty; of all those he had met in that task she was the least guilty of all. He was guilty. He was mistaken. He had failed God. And if he had failed Him once, he could have failed Him always. The infinite guilt was his. The infinite failure.

His complete life wasted. No, that could not be. Oh Jesus, Mary, it could not be. He had faithfully served God and his Church, had done what he was told, had kept the rumormongers and blasphemers at bay. His tasks had been difficult, sometimes nearly impossible, but he had done his utmost to defend the purity of the Church. And if he was mistaken in his past, what of his future? Where would it end? His dream for a tranquil prebend outside Provvidenti was absurd: he was exceptionally unfit for such pastoral care as he found country quiet and the sins of others equally distasteful. No, he would continue this, this mission, go where he was needed, do what was required, until he went to live with the nuns at the *Residenza Garbatella* and wait for his mind or his kidneys to fail.

Mary, where are you, where are you? What have I done?

Ora pro nobis peccatoribus, nunc, et in hora mortis nostrae. Amen. The hour of our death. What will be the hour of his death? He shifted his weight from his greater sore knee to his less sore knee. His kidneys could fail and he could die. Perhaps this general discomfort and sleepiness was a sign, a harbinger of a heart attack or stroke. His meals, his food had replaced the cigarettes and cigars he enjoyed when younger, and without the exercise he'd become heavier. Still, his father had lived, fat and happy, until ninety, the stubborn *stronzo*, his mother until eighty. He maybe had another fifteen, twenty years. Did he? He needed to sit up, get off his knees and rest his back. His kidneys, his kidneys were his weak spot.

He had to take tests, his urine for sugar and blood. His doctor had told him dialysis was not out of the question, maybe sooner, maybe later.

And after his fifteen, twenty years? How long in purgatory would he suffer? And who would offer prayers for him to reduce that time? Perhaps his brother, Giacammo, and his friends from the congregation, Fathers Annuncio and Zancredi. But perhaps he'd outlive them. What then?

What if everything about his life had been a lie, an error? What if he were to spend eternity exiled from God's sweetest grace? What if he were to be burned for all time in eternal and infernal hell, his skin searing under unimaginable flames, his mouth thirsty forever for the sweet water of Our Lord Jesus Christ? How could he bear the scourges of the demons or the sulfur-laden air, or the molten lake of fire? What if his name were not written in the Book of Life but the Book of Death?

The voices hovered around an elongated D, then up to an F, where the record skipped, like it had done for a few times now. He'd let it play: it only had a couple of minutes left on that side now. The record was getting old too.

They should have taken her to the doctor earlier.

"Hey, Popi."

He turned and saw Nicholas in the doorway, long and lean, barefoot in athletic shorts and a Broncos T-shirt, a huge cup of coffee in his hand. "You drinking coffee now?"

"Yeah."

"Leave me any?"

He shrugged and smiled.

"C'mon in here. Sit down for a second." He patted the seat next to him. "I need you to help me move those big Aidas farther apart, and we need to stick those Hommages way in the corners. But come here. What do you think of this?"

"This music?" Nicholas sat down, his long legs splayed out in front of him. He needed a shower. His feet needed a shower.

"Yes, this music."

"My mom gave you this, right?"

"Yes. It's ending soon: what do you think of the setup?"

"It's a triode, right? What cabling you using?"

"Nordost for the speakers, Audio Note interconnects. I got some AN, Nordost, Black Cats and PranaWire in everywhere else."

He nodded his head. "Sounds good, Popi. How's it do with strings? And bass?"

"I don't know: I just put this on."

Nicholas rose and walked over to the record shelf. "We got something new the other day, real good midrange and bass. Mobile Fidelity recorded. Here we go."

"Nothing heavy, okay? Too early in the morning."

"Nah, this is great. You'll like this." He watched as Nicholas gently lifted the tonearm and placed the Bingen back in its sleeve. He didn't recognize the new cover, dark brown and black background with numerous painted figures. Nicholas washed the black disk carefully. "It is heavy," he commented as he placed it on the platter and carefully set the stylus in the groove. He walked back and handed Hector the cover.

The room burst into sound, the stately strings and an undertone of harpsichord. Vivaldi. "I know this."

"*The Four Seasons*. Salvatore Accardo. Doesn't this sound like spring, Popi? Listen to that bass. Even on the single driver." A solo violin began dancing, and was soon joined by another. "Listen to that tone. He plays a Stradivarius." The full orchestra returned with a flurry of bowed bass. The solo violin played nimbly above. The orchestra quieted now, and the beginning theme returned. Nicholas had closed his eyes and was gently swaying his head to the music. It was clichéd, or at least he'd heard it a number of times before, in a number of different contexts. But it was exquisitely done. Hector looked down at the cover in his hand.

It was a somber painting, with angels dominating the top center and a woman offering her white breast for a grey-bearded man to suck in the right foreground. To the left of the woman he could see the feet of what looked like a corpse, carried through a doorway by a worker whose face was hidden by shadow. The bright, naked back of a man centered the bottom left, and it looked like he was grabbing onto the cloak of a rich-looking figure standing above him. There were two men center left doing business of some sort, while a bearded man drank water behind them. He looked closer at the angels above. One teenage angel was holding another, who appeared to be trying to reach out to the earthly figures below. Above the wrestling angels he noticed a Madonna and child, with baby Jesus looking amused. Strange.

"You like that, Popi? That painting?"

"I don't know." The music abruptly stopped, and he spoke louder than he meant to.

"We studied it in AP Art. It's by this guy Caravaggio." The music started in again, bouncy, stately, repetitive. He liked the way the riffs first appeared loud and stately, then were repeated much softer and gentler, with the harpsichord more audible. The solo violin entered again, with a sweeping arpeggio, playing off and against the melody of the upper strings.

"It's an odd painting, Nicholas. I'm not sure I understand it."

"It's called the *Seven Acts of Mercy*. It's supposed to show all of these acts of kindness."

"What's this woman doing here?"

Nicholas chuckled. "Her name is Pero."

"*Perro? Dog?*"

"No, not that *perro*. Pero and her father Cimon. In Rome, Cimon was a prisoner, and he was starving to death, and so Pero would go in every night, and, well, feed him. So that's one of the mercies, feeding the hungry. She also visits the imprisoned, which, by the way, is another mercy. Two for one."

"Caravaggio, huh?"

The music stopped again and then began with a slow, melancholy introduction, with the harpsichord providing both grounding and trills. The upper strings took over, in unison, speeding the tempo and intensifying the tone, making it nearly ominous. First *pianissimo*, then *forte*, then back to *pianissimo*, the threat, or at least the possibility of danger, becoming louder with every repetition.

AGNUS DEI

"Saying, I will declare thy name unto my brethren; in the midst
of the church will I sing praise [Greek, "*hymnēsō*"] unto thee."

—Hebrews 2:12; quoting Psalm 22:22

We spoke a few weeks ago about the two kinds of silence, the
silence of the grave and the silence of God. I would now like to
speak of the holy silence, the silence of Our Lord, the silence that
allows the possibility of a genuine opening to the possibility of
God. To be more precise, I want to speak today of preparing for
the true silence of prayer. It is this silence, and this silence alone,
that allows us to speak to God. And it is through this silence, and
this silence alone, that we can perhaps hear God's voice speak to
us. This true silence, the silence of God speaking, is the sound of
grace. It cannot be earned or achieved; it is a gift, undeserved and
unanticipated, from God. While it cannot be earned or hurried, we
can perhaps prepare to receive it.

To begin with, let us turn to the writings of His Holiness,
Pope Benedict XVI. His Holiness is writing about Pseudo-Dionysius here: "God cannot be spoken of in an abstract way; speaking

of God is always—he [Pseudo-Dionysius] says using a Greek word—a 'hymnein', singing for God with the great hymn of the creatures which is reflected and made concrete in liturgical praise." In order to prepare for the gift of God's silence, His Holiness is telling us we must sing, hymnein. What can this mean? How can our singing prepare His Holy silence?

The Bible is full of singing and music, both Old and New Testaments. The Psalms, of course, are a central piece to both the Jewish and Christian traditions: "Let us make a joyful noise to the rock of our salvation" (Psalm 95:1), and Paul, in his letters to the Corinthians, Ephesians and Colossians, recognizes the importance of music, partially as a way to unite the members of the early church in "teaching and admonishing" (Colossians 3:16), but also as a way of praying, of "singing with gratitude in your hearts to God." It is this understanding of language as prayer that we are interested in here.

We must remember that the language of experience, the words we use when we talk of our everyday concerns, our lusts and our desires, our objects and images, our hope and fears, these are all woefully inadequate to use when we speak of or to The Most High. Should we try to speak to God with the same language we use to call our cow (Eckhart "Deutsch" 16b)? All of this worldly language, all of the various nouns, verbs, adjectives, adverbs, prepositions, conjunctions, exclamations, etc., all are inadequate, or even sinfully inaccurate, when used to speak of Our Lord God. All the nouns we've been using, even the words like "God" and "Lord," these are untrue, because they come from *our* language, *our* thinking. Our catechism, following God's revelation in Exodus, tells us that God's name is YHWH, I Am Who Am. It goes on to say that "Out of respect for the Holiness of God, the people of Israel do not pronounce his name. In the reading of Sacred Scriptures, the revealed name (YHWH) is replaced by the divine title 'Lord'" (CCC 209). Just as nouns are inaccurate, so too are verbs. Is the "speaking" of God the same as the announcer on the news or the bus driver? Does God "hear" us as our child or the butcher? Of course not. God can hear and speak to us, but only His hearing, speaking and knowing is so much more perfect and true that the actions are incomparable, and for us to think that our words can name His actions is sadly misguided.

Can we say even that God has attributes? Is He good? No, for goodness is a human attribute, and we cannot begin to comprehend whatever "goodness" God may possess. Can we say that God is angry? No. Pleased? No. We know when people act pleased, when our children are pleased when they are given a toy or a piece of candy, or when our boss in angry when we fail to finish our work in a timely manner. But is this possibly comparable to God? No. God does not even act mercifully in this way, for we can have no experience of God's mercy, for these words "mercy" and actions "merciful" are words and actions of humans, and God's actions cannot be defined by such language. These words, all words, have no meaning when it comes to God.

Just as our language of experience fails whenever we try to apply it to God, so does the language of concepts: the philosophical or theological language remain erroneous when speaking of God. Idolaters confuse God with things, theologians confuse God with concepts. Our Holiness recognized when he wrote that "God cannot be spoken of in an abstract way." In other words, all of our abstract speculation, all of our philosophizing about what can and cannot be said of God, this too is inadequate to truly approach Our Lord. Everything I have said, everything written by our church fathers, even the words of Our Holiness, all come from below, and all are only, or not even, mere feeble approximations, mere insufficient metaphors or shadows of the true being that is God. This language, and this silence, comes from us, and this language is closer to the language and silence of the dead than it is to the language and silence of God.

Music is a way of preparing approaching the silence of God. Jesus himself tells us, in Hebrews, to sing: He quotes Psalm 22 when he says "I will declare thy name unto my brethren; in the midst of the congregation will I sing thy praise" (Hebrews 2:12).

The word *hymn* is a translation of the Greek *humnos*, ὕμνος, which means sacred song. Singing is neither mundane language nor conceptual language. Singing is a way to bypass the experiential nature of language, the mundane, everyday language we use to communicate with others in this world. We don't sing to the butcher or to the television repairman. At the same time, singing is a way to also bypass the intellectual jargon, the abstract theological speculation and philosophizing. I will not suggest that music is a synthesis of the mundane and theological, rather I believe that music is a way out of or around both the worldly and philosophical. Music is a way toward God.

Singing is the language of ecstasy. By singing, we travel out of ourselves: we bypass the mundane language of commerce and computation, and we refuse the conceptual language of speculation and philosophizing. By singing, by music, we can begin to approach the true silence that is God's grace.

In the name of the Father, the Son and the Holy Spirit, Amen.

What was the difference between shame and guilt? A long, narrow, wine-red hallway stretched before us, closed wooden doors on either side, ill-illuminated by four dim sconces. Shame was universal, guilt was particular. Shame had no cause, guilt did. I walked slowly past the closed doors and thought about my old Italian grandmother and her friends at Mass, heads covered with toques, platter hats and pillboxes, mantillas or light veils. Guilt or shame? Or simply tradition? I felt like unpinning my hair, maybe undoing the second button on my blouse. I almost wished I'd worn a skirt or my one nice cocktail dress or maybe even seven veils, throw a little leg at the closed doors and the dank sheets. I was too old: I should have brought the bicycling medex with her tight Lycra shorts and clickity-clack shoes. But God knows what lifted their tents, maybe Maldonado would feature tonight in late-night prayers and solitary cassock rubbings. Anyway, according to the news, once we reached high school, we were all too old.

At the end of the hall, a partially opened door only partially obscured the view of a stainless steel refrigerator and white kitchen cabinets. A small illuminated exit sign came into view on the right. A green staircase icon was helpfully centered on the wooden door beneath the exit sign. I placed my right hand on the vertical tubed door handle and began to pull. I stopped. I turned back to the dark hallway of closed doors.

I was already sick of the smell, the stink of women-hating, the miasma of overt and unbroken repression, sexual and otherwise, the unmistakable and inescapable taint of child rape and denial. They were all guilty. Guilty as sin. I closed my eyes to steady myself. The faceless priest as a sacrifice, an eye for an eye, a face for a face.

A life for a life.

I had to be careful here.

I opened my eyes and turned to Maldonado. "Wait until we get a TOD and positive ID, but I want everyone who lives here questioned, gently, about where they were when our vic was killed. They were likely sleeping or praying alone, but ask anyway. Ask if anyone saw or heard anything unusual. Use plainclothes, not uniforms, and do it here, and do it discreetly, and if you have any trouble, let me know about it before you even mention continuing the interview downtown."

"Got it."

"And luck of the draw, only involve men, male officers here in the rectory. That's between us."

He nodded as I pulled the door open and climbed the stairs. I don't know why I did that.

The second floor hallway was a replica of the first, without the kitchen and the front vestibule: 220, 219, 218. I began to walk up the hall, past the closed wooden doors and murky yellowish sconces. There was no sign of life. It was warmer up here, hot. I wondered if the good Lord provided individual AC. A door at the end on the left was partially open, and light spilled from the frame.

I walked quietly and listened, strained to hear something, anything behind the doors: a cough, a murmur, a radio, a mumbled prayer, anything. Either the rooms were vacated or the good fathers were well versed in practicing silence.

I reached the door and stopped, changed my latex gloves, and hesitated on the threshold. Despite myself, despite my years of police training and experience, and my decades of education and, well, living, despite everything I'd worked for and become, I still felt like I was about to violate some ancient and irrefutable law. All my earlier enthusiasm and energy had dissipated, been sucked out by the too-red walls and the closed wooden doors. I didn't belong here. I wouldn't be able to find this priest killer.

I wasn't sure I wanted to.

I heard a cough and then a faint—a very faint—humming coming from inside the room. Was it? Yes it was: *Gretchen am Spinnrade*. One of my faves. I opened the door and walked in.

The humming stopped as a gowned and masked tech turned to me from the left, where he was examining a large new-looking architect's desk, one of those where you stand and work. I nodded at him, then surveyed the space. The inner sanctum. The room was about ten-by-twelve. Most of the light was provided by the far wall's three square windows, two-by-two, with white rolled-up shades. A made twin bed with an ugly orange bedspread was pushed up in the left corner below two of the windows. Directly in front of me against the right wall was a low chest of drawers upon which rested a clear glass water pitcher and two glasses. A matching blonde armoire stood tall on the left, next to the desk. I could see a small wooden chair next to the left wall between the armoire and the bed. A table lamp with a foam-green glass base and a large cream shade balanced on the seat of the chair. The walls themselves were pale yellow drywall, without decoration. I moved into the center of the room and slowly pivoted. A three-quarter-length mirror in a dark wood frame hung from the door, and a darker, almost black crucifix hung above. The room was warmer than the hallway. If there were clues here to the person who was once Father Vidal, they weren't obvious at first glance.

And what if there were no books? What if he would simply cease to exist, all consciousness annihilated? He remembered Father Patterson, a hale and hearty American with eyes full of wonder, who came to the Vatican after years in the American farmland, what he called "the sticks." Patterson had been at the Vatican three days when, during lunch, in full view of perhaps seven Italian cardinals, he had dropped, face-first, into his risotto Florentine. He was sitting next to Patterson on his right, speaking with Father Zancredi, when he heard a sharp thump at his back. He turned and witnessed Father Patterson's face, cheek resting on the half-cleared Wedgwood plate, the previous wonder in his eyes replaced by surprise and what looked like a deep and infinite disappointment. There was no transcendence visible, no beatific welcoming of the embrace of light. One minute he was there, perhaps enjoying the arborio and fresh spinach, thanking Jesus for the texture of the rice, the heaviness of the fork, the thickness of the napkin, thinking himself very fortunate indeed to be placed in the midst of such beauty, surrounded by a near-perfect union of the celestial and worldly. And the next minute, the next second, what? What could he have been thinking, just before he ceased to think? Just *as* he ceased to think? Did he realize he was dying? Not everyone quickly noticed, and the murmured conversations and noises of enjoyment took some time to cease. One of the cardinals, Clemente, rushed over with his oil, put his ear to Patterson's mouth, gently cupped his neck and lifted his face from the food, then turned his shoulders and set his body on the floor. Fathers Frankel and Biggio slid out of the way. No one else moved. *Per istam Sanctan unctionem et suam Piissimam misericordiam.* It was only when one of the Vatican doctors arrived with a *soccorritore* a few minutes later that whispering and movement resumed. He was surprised to find that he was standing against a marble column three meters from where he had been sitting.

It could have been him, face in the risotto, but it was not. Not that time. To be there, one minute, sitting and eating, one minute, one second, one second, one second, and then not. What could be thought, in the solitary second before death? Did he comprehend a moment or two before? And then what of the intervening time? Was there hope? Joy? There was no joy in Father Patterson's eyes, at least that he could see. No, the expression of Father Patterson was not one of loving anticipation, not one of triumphant victory, and not one even of defeat; it was the expression of being removed irrevocably from the match.

This was blasphemy and error. He believed in victory over death. Death had no sting, death was but the shedding of the world and the beginning of a new eternal life in Christ.

And how many seconds, how many beats of his heart, remained for him? How many more heartbeats before that *one*, the last? That one, unique moment, a moment unlike any other, the one moment not followed by another. The moment without doubt, *this* is the very last. He counted to himself, now, now, *now*, now. This, *that*, always *that*, would not be a moment of peace. He would not feel anticipation *now, now, now, now*, but an indescribable sadness, *now, now, now, now*, a despair so profound that his mind could only faintly approach. Now, now, now, now, *now, now, now, now*. He believed, with all his heart, that with God's grace and mercy he would pass from this world and enter into a perfect communion with God the Father, Jesus Christ the Son and the Holy Spirit, the Blessed Virgin Mary and all the angels and saints. But back deep in his mind, an echo of the now, now, now, now he could not contain, and the now now now now threatened all.

It wasn't the despair of having to leave this life behind, nor was it the uncertainty, the inability to imagine what God's pure love and communion would be in the next life. No, it was somehow the terror of that single moment, that unique and timeless now, a time outside of guilt, penance and redemption, a moment somehow beyond the grace and love of Jesus Christ. This is what he saw in Father Patterson's eyes. And what of Father Vidal, who was killed, murdered in the Confessional of the Basilica in Denver? What had he been thinking, that very instant before his life on this earth had stopped? What was in the expression of his eyes? Did they wear the same expression as Patterson's? Was there sadness? Anticipation? Forgiveness?

He felt something move from deep, deep in his stomach, something thick and dry, gathering slowly, slowly in his lower stomach, a desert moving up, up his stomach to his diaphragm, where it hesitated, gathered more force and mass, then up, up, crawling slowly up his esophagus, so dry and large, up, up, up to his throat, he couldn't breathe, so dry, he shivered, so dry, like a desert, flowing up, up, he was choking, choking, from the very back of his throat a sound both neither scream and sob escaped and he heard it as if it came from far away. He clasped both hands over his mouth.

No, no, no, he could not think, he could not think *that*. He breathed heavily through his palm. This was Satan talking to him. This was his confusion and the travel hours, his lack of food and water, the new surroundings and the thin air; all were affecting his thoughts. The devil knew his weaknesses. He groaned and struggled to his feet, the mattress sagging deeply as he used it to push his knees up from the floor. The room seemed shrunken, almost coffin-like.

He would not die well.

Ave Maria, gratia plena, Dominus tecum. Benedicta tu in mulieribus, et benedictus fructus ventris tui, Iesus. Sancta Maria, Mater Dei, ora pro nobis peccatoribus, nunc, et in hora mortis nostrae. Amen. But he would not die now.

Surrounded by some bunnies, and it ain't fucking Easter. There's 2, 4, 9 and Fox, and CNN and Telemundo, okay, and Charlotte from the *News*. Doesn't Frankie write for *HuffPost*? F murder at dwntn cathedral MSTA. OK. I guess we're good. Cap straight, tie knotted, smile on, you can do this bro, you can do this. No comment yet, I've only just arrived. Let me talk to the primary and I'll try to have something for you on my way out. No, I don't know. Detective Fruscella. It's a sad day for our community. I don't have any information about that. Let me talk to her first. I have no information at this time. I do. I will say this: all Twitter, Facebook, Pinterest, Reddit and Instagram, whatever, all information will come from my office and my office alone. Eye contact. All official interviews or statements will come from my office and my office alone. Everything not from my office is rumor and likely incorrect. Any information that does not come from my office and is published or otherwise disseminated can do great damage to our investigation, and can severely hinder our ability to apprehend the responsible parties. Now, if you all will excuse me. Flash the badge, duck under the tape. Don't forget the boots and gloves. Cap off. That went well. I should have brought Katie with me, impress the press with the long-legged assistant. Let's see where that hot medex is, or if 'Cola's just shining. Thirsty AF. Where is the fucker, anyway? Sergeant, is there a uniform here by the name of Agricola? No idea, huh? Is the medex still here? She's with the body? Just follow the lights. Thank you. And do you know where I can find Detective Fruscella? Thank you. Never been here before, I mean, why would I? Last time I was in church was for Dee Dee's wedding in Boulder. I wonder if the body's bagged yet. That must be it on the gurney. Shit just got real. Dude was a priest. Should I cross myself or something? Probably should check out the site. Maybe later. Which one's the medex? The one with the Sidis? Them's nice shoes. Wish she'd take that hood off. There we go. Good haircut, nice face. Looks fit, but hard to tell in that gown. Keep her close when doing pressers. Maybe get a *Westword* feature. I gotta find the Fruscella. This will have to be quick. Excuse me. Penny Collero. I'm Lieutenant Clark of the Public Relations Office of the DP. I wonder if we could speak later today. After the autopsy? Coffee? Great. Daz Bog near Comanche? Sure. Around two? Here's my card. Lots of media out there, be careful. Thank you. Maybe update the FB, let people know I'm in the house. Fifteen new messages, six IM's. Cool.

There she is. Serious RBF. This is not going to be easy. Healthy hair, could use a style, the long straight brunette doesn't work with grey streaks, Morticia. Detective Fruscella. Detective. I'm Lieutenant Clark, Public Information Officer. We spoke on the phone. Lipstick okay, a little eyeliner, could use some primer. I just need a couple of minutes. I understand that, but I'll be as brief as possible. Thank you, thank you very much. Buttoned up cream blouse, navy vest with matching slacks, good looking pair of flats. Aware but not fussy. First of all, let me remind you that any official communication regarding this case must come from myself or my office. We need to keep the public informed, we need to keep the media out of your way so you can do your job, and we need to ensure that we protect the integrity of the case. My job is to relieve any media pressure or presence so you can do your job. Not a big fan of the resting bitch face, though: sexy when you're twenty, after forty, not so much. But I'll need to give them something now, throw them a bone. Can I tell them there's a single victim? I won't divulge, but have you made a positive ID? Cough, cough, Andrea Vidal. Was he a priest? No, I'll stick with the single vic and method of death. Is Data searching for next of kin? You'll need to keep me in that loop. Gunshot wound? Shotgun? No, no need to divulge now. Age? Thank you. Okay. That should be enough for now. Detective, please answer your phone when I call, it will save us both a lot of time. Do you text? On your phone? No? I will call you later, but I don't think we'll need to meet face-to-face this afternoon. Thank you. And please don't speak to the media. Like I say, that's my job. And maybe visit a salon: at least get it layered.

That didn't go so well. Maybe a B- or a C+. Let me sit down here. Twitter opened. BREAKING: DPD can confirm homicide Denver Basilica. Male victim, age 49. No suspect info. at this time. Should I tag it? Not yet. What else Jerry got going? UPDATE: LoDo Let-Out. No evidence found of shootings at Vinyl. @Broncoswin—we did interviews, no evidence. BREAKING: Hit and run on 3000 block E Granada. Injuries nonlife-threatening. No suspect info. at this time. Same old same old. Copy paste for FB, Reddit.

Nothing from Good Charlotte yet. It is Sunday morning. Should I go out now, face the paparazzi? Give Jerry a call? Find 'Cola and spill about my coffee date with Dr. Penny Collero? No, work before pleasure. I do wonder who's been squealing to the MSM? Last thing I need is a leak. Jerry. Wasup? Get Data to check out next of kin for Vidal. Official request, just trying to be helpful. You saw it, right? No names yet. Naw, she's gonna crack my *huevos*. Get her P1 File, regular channels. I dunno, bro, I just want some info, see em aaii, you know. Looks *can* kill. No, they're outside. I gotta go. kay eye tee.

Nuestro Padre, Literal Father, Our Father Who Art in Hell, Our Father of Abuse, Our Father Who Fucks His Own Children, Our Father Who Brings Hell to His Children, Our Father of Lies, Our Father of Hypocrisy, Our Father of the Forced Hand Job, Our Father of Anal Rape, Our Father who Sucks the Cock of Teenage Boys, Our Father Who Raises Money, Our Father Who Injects Heroin, Our Father Who Injects Morphine, Our Father Who Snorts Cocaine, Our Father Who Rubs Cocaine on His Cock, Our Father Who Kisses the Pope with Adolescent Semen on His Breath, Our Father of *Millionarios de Cristo*, Our Father Who Betrays the Gospel, Our Father Who Betrays Youth, Our Father of the Private Vows, Our Father Who Used His Children, Our Father of the Stuffed Envelopes, Our Father of the *Opera Carita*, Our Father of Plagiarized Prayer, Our Father of the Two Faces, Our Father of the Sideways Glance, Our Father of the Forefinger to the Lips, Our Father of Mendacity, Our Father Who Fooled the *Regnum Christi*, Our Father Who Fooled the *Athenaeum Regina Apostolorum*, Our Father Who Fooled the Legionaries of Christ, Our Father Who Fooled the Diaconate, Our Father Who Fooled the Presbyterate, Our Father Who Fooled the Episcopate, Our Father Who Fooled the Doctrine of Faith, Our Father Who Fooled Pope John Paul II, Our Father Who Fooled Pope Pius XII, Our Father Who Fooled General Franco, Our Father Who Fooled Cardinal Micara, Our Father Who Fooled Msgr.

Alfredo Bontempi, Our Father Who Fooled Msgr. Polidoro van Vlierberghe, Our Father Who Fooled Cardinal Angelo Sodano, Our Father Who Fooled Cardinal Joseph Ratzinger, Our Father Who Fooled Cardinal Eduardo Somalo, Our Father Who Fooled Msgr. Stanisław Dziwisz, Our Father Who Fooled Carlos Slim, Our Father Who Fooled Franc Rodé, Our Father Who Fooled Mel Gibson, Our Father Who Fooled Thomas Monaghan, Our Father Who Fooled Rick Santorum, Our Father Who Fooled Father John Neuhaus, Our Father Who Fooled Plácido Domingo, Our Father Who Fooled Mary Ann Glendon, Our Father Who Fooled William Bennett, Our Father Who Fooled Flora Barragán, Our Father Who Fooled the Graza-Sada families, Our Father Who Fooled Blanca Gutiérrez, Our Father Who Fooled Norma Hilda Baños, Our Father Who Fooled Me.

Damned be your name
Your punishment come
Your soul be shunned
By earth as well as heaven
Give us forever
Freedom from you
We will never forgive your sins
As you ignored innocence entrusted
Lead us not anywhere
And deliver you from our memory forever
Amen

COMMUNIO

"Away with the noise of your songs!
I will not listen to the music of your harps."
—Amos 5:23

Silence, music, prayer, language, death, life, heaven, hell; where does all this leave us? What can we know? What can we do? What can we do today, right now, on this earth, if God will not listen to our songs?

Jesus tells us what we are to do, in simple, straightforward, unequivocal language: "And thou shalt love thy God, with thy whole heart, and with thy whole soul, and with thy whole mind, and with thy whole strength... And thou shalt love thy neighbor as thyself. There is no other commandment greater than these" (Mark 12:30–31). There is no ambiguity here, nothing to misunderstand, misinterpret or confuse. The greatest, the most important, the fundamental requirement to follow Our Lord Jesus Christ is that we love God with our whole being and we love our fellow humans as we love ourselves. This is the absolute focus of Jesus's thought. Nothing else matters: not status, money, the keeping of ritual, chastity, obedience, holiness, good deeds, discretion, learnedness, kindness—nothing. Without the love of God and our fellow human beings in our hearts, our faith is useless, barren, hypocritical. Without the love of God and our fellow humans in our hearts, in our whole beings, we cannot be followers of Jesus Christ. Without the love of God and our fellow humans in our hearts, our songs will go unheard.

And we all know, love is the most difficult thing to do.

I will speak today on the difficult task Jesus gave us when he said we must love God "with thy whole heart, and with thy whole soul, and with thy whole mind, and with thy whole strength." Perhaps some other time we can discuss the task of loving our neighbor as ourselves.

And how are we to love God? You may say, and you would not be completely wrong, that loving God is the easiest, most natural thing in the world. How effortless it should be to love He who has given us earthly life and who has sent his only son to grant us eternal life. How could we not love God in his generosity and goodness? But what do we love when we say we love God? I Corinthians 8:6 tells us "Yet for us there is but one God, the Father." In loving God, we love our Father (who art in heaven), our kind, generous, tender Father, Πατήρ, *Pater*, *Abba*: we can see him, feel his caresses on our cheek, hear his praises (and reprimands) in our ears. We love God as a child loves his father: what could be more natural than that? But if we think about this and are honest with ourselves, we know that our experience with our father is far removed from our experience with God.

Our God is not our Father. Or rather, the figure of the father is merely a metaphor, an approximation, an image that we use to help us think about and love God. There is only one person in all of history who did not use this term as a metaphor, as a figure of speech, and that person was Jesus Christ, whose father *was* God the Most High. Jesus did teach us the *Pater Noster*, that is true, but as a parable, an allegory so that we childish sinners can have some image or idea of the relationship between God and his created beings. And Jesus too was bound, while on earth, by the limits of human language.

Some may say that they hear God's voice, feel God's presence, that God touches them. While I cannot be certain they are mistaken, I do believe, honestly, that they are using metaphors, figures of speech to try to express in everyday language what transcends the everyday, what can't be contained or approached by the everyday. We insert images between ourselves and who can't be imagined, between our sinning childlike selves and the unimaginable God: we create a beneficent Father, white-bearded and kind, in order to try to love Him. But that is not God. How can we love what we cannot see? How can we love what doesn't exist? And I don't mean "doesn't exist" as in He is absent and unreachable. But I mean that He doesn't exist like we exist, like a dog or table exists, like anything we can see or touch or imagine exists. And the first thing we ask of our beloved, if we are not insane, is that they exist. Love needs reality.

This is our problem with loving God. This is our impossible task. And make no mistake, Jesus understood its impossibility. Jesus knew what he was asking: to give ourselves completely to what we can't see, what we can't know, what we can't understand or even imagine. This is what it means to be Christian. This is what it means to *believe*.

So I repeat: what do we love when we love God?

Another way to put this: what is the reality of God?

I would answer that distance is the reality of God. In order that we exist, God must not. God moved away from us, abandoned us, even (although this too is an inexact image, a mistaken figure of speech), in order that we would have enough space to be. This is the one and only experience of God we can be certain of: if we exist, He is distant from us. And so the reality of God, as I've said, is distance. And I've also said that love needs reality. And so we must love God's distance. We can love nothing of God other than this distance, this separation, this severance.

As I've reminded you, our job as Christians is to work, within time, to close this distance, to end this separation and to ultimately reunite with God. But this is not to be completely accomplished within our earthly lifetimes. Even Jesus didn't reunite with His Father while alive. Remember our Lord's passion and his lamentable cry on the cross: *"Eli, Eli, lama sabachthani?"* that is, My God, My God, why hast thou forsaken me? (Matthew 27:46). These were the very last words the human Jesus spoke.

And there are some, it is true, who believe they have nearly bridged this gap, who are convinced they are within the divine light and are now so close to God, they can hear His voice, can feel His presence, indeed, can almost touch Him. I believe, with all my heart, that either they see nothing but their own desires and egos or they are using false images in order to express this inexpressible distance. I can understand both temptations and have succumbed to both myself.

I say to you now that we must love this distance with our entire being, even as we try to abolish this distance and reunite with God. This distance is what we have of God, what we can be certain of, what God has given us in His divine mercy, wisdom and grace. This distance is the reality of His love, and we must experience it and love it in return. No other love for God is possible while we still exist.

We send our song out into the unimaginable distance. We "praise him with the lute and lyre." And God listens. He listens. In the name of the Father, the Son and the Holy Spirit.

With the fingertips of my right hand, I gently opened the armoire door. Not much. One pair of light wool knit black trousers from Mossimo (Target?), one pair of dark blue cotton Dockers, one pair of dress slacks from M&S Collection, a stiff black suit jacket without a label, and two cassocks, one heavy and one lighter, both without labels. Everything was carefully hung on wooden hangers. Beneath, a neatly arranged pair of black Thom McAn Oxfords, a pair of black low top Converse sneakers and a pair of black leather Aldo sandals, slightly worn. A medium-sized suitcase occupied much of the right side. I pushed against the case: it felt empty. I'd go through these things more carefully after the techs were finished, but our good Father Vidal seemed relatively unburdened by worldly possessions. I closed the armoire, turned and took a couple of steps to the chest of drawers. The top drawer on the left held only the priest's underwear and socks, and I quickly rifled through his patterned Fruit of the Looms. In the right I found an Argentine passport with the photograph of a handsome dark-eyed man, Fr. Andrea Arturo Vidal, LC, an H-1B US visa issued the previous August (the numbers matched, but the visa photo, which was seven years newer than the passport's, showed more grey hair and more lines around the mouth and eyes), and a number of entry and exit stamps from the US, Argentina, Mexico and Europe; two plain wooden rosaries, a small *Roman Missal*, a pair of cheap cuff links, a half a package of Starburst, a small flashlight, two keys on a key ring, two white clerical collars, a quarter, two dimes and three pennies and an AA battery. In the right drawer below I found four Arrow white cotton button-down shirts, a pair of Levi's jeans, black swim trunks with a tag from H&M, 20 Euros, and two white cotton laundry bags with "Vidal" in Magic Marker. The drawer next to it was empty. I pushed that drawer closed, turned and walked over to the desk. The tech stood and I noticed his name tag, Straat.

"Straat. You know Schubert?"

I could see him smile through his mask. He looked about sixteen. "I love Schubert."

"Finding anything?"

"Plenty of prints. They all look similar."

I turned and looked around. "Tidy guy. Looks pretty neat."

The desk was bare, except for a closed book in the right corner and a few colored Post-its pasted along the top edge. I leaned over to look. The book was thick, with "Latin Vulgate, Douay-Rheims, King James" printed in embossed letters on the cover. On a light blue Post-it I could make out "Jeremiah 5:22," with "fear and abandonment" scrawled beneath. On the pink one next I read "2 Samuel" with "*in extenso*" beneath and on another pink one I read "Weil *metaxu*." Not the greatest handwriting for someone so neat. I took out my notebook and copied the notes. I'd check the biblical passages quickly. I didn't know what "Weil *metaxu*" meant.

"Did you get pictures of these yet?"

"Murphy did. He was called downstairs, not sure when he'll be back."

"Did you dust the desk and book?"

"There's no paper here, no notebook or anything, just this Bible and these three Post-its: where's the rest of the pack? And I don't see a computer. I don't even see a pen or pencil. Have you run across anything?"

"No."

"Is there another room?"

"There's a bathroom behind you. We gave it a quick look, but then Murphy was called downstairs. I didn't see any computer or paper or anything like that."

I looked around the room again. There wasn't much here: nothing on the walls, nothing on the floor, nothing but cheap, nondescript clothing, no photos of anything or anyone, no letters, no personal mementos or objects, no cell phone or music player or electronic device of any kind, no address book, no artifact or document that showed he had any contact with another human being. And the shoes. The shoes downstairs looked expensive, the clothing up here was not. Who was he? What did he like? There was no clue about who or what he was. Other than the verses from the Bible. And obviously the fact that there wasn't much here, that he hadn't left much behind, that could tell a lot. Maybe.

What kind of life could you have to leave so little behind? This wasn't a question of poverty: this was a question of erasure.

L'Homme Armé

KYRIE

Friday of the Nineteenth Week of Ordinary Time, 2005

After all, I remain. This is not a boast of triumph, but an admission of failure, of profound disappointment. I am largely ignorant of Descartes, but I sense in the *Cogito* the possibility of a similar disappointment, something of the absolute limitation of man. After all this, I am. *Ergo sum. Apres tout, je suis.*

It is strange that it is my very existence that causes this feeling of abject failure. It is because I have survived that I have, in a sense, died. Dead to God, I remain in this suspended state, neither here nor there, *Limbus Infantium.* Unrecognized, unrecognizable, as if unbaptized, I hang on, now without momentum, now without belief. Separation, suspension, the alpha and omega, the curse of the I am.

To no longer be able to think what will become of me. To simply and eternally think, I am. The Limbo of the child, with no past and no future, no suffering and no joy, no time, oh God, no time. Pure innocence.

My innocence impure. I have consciousness, consciousness of the infinite separation. I am not a child, but a suddenly old man tainted with memories, memories of hope, the cruelest imaginable. *Limbus Patrum*, where the aged and decrepit sit and mumble about the old laws and sacrifices, the time when there was clarity in obedience, when you knew where you stood. The God of rules, covenants, deals, of an eye for an eye, of anger and remorse, of endless shall-nots and begats. All written in stone: you knew! Useless now, this aged uncapitalized god, broken, rent, existing primarily in memory, or the theater of memory, archaically acted in reproduced costumes, inauthentic masks and dead languages. An entire belief reduced to local color and ill-remembered stories.

But the *Limbus Patrum* is reserved for the holy pre-Christians, and I am neither. My original sin was washed away at six weeks, along with that possible excuse. And my unoriginal sins, my many many unoriginal sins, both venial and mortal, both of commission and omission, have stained my soul beyond cleansing. Possibly even beyond redemption. Who can say?

To be denied Limbo: where does that leave me?

Here.

Redemption's opposite: betrayal. To be betrayed by a single man, by men, by humankind, this is not extraordinary. Betrayal is constant: any contact with human beings cannot help but end, sooner or later, in betrayal. This is no dark night, this is not cynicism or self-pity. One expects to be betrayed by one's brothers and sisters, children and parents, friends and teachers, superiors and parishioners. The lack of betrayal, betrayal deferred, that is what shocks.

Still, one does not expect to be betrayed by God.

It took Jesus thirty-three years to realize that to exist means to be betrayed: it has taken me almost forty-five.

Jesus fucked everything up. There was nothing wrong with life before, nothing wrong with the relationship between God and man. There was no lack, no need to come down and meddle. The God of Abraham was an angry father, capricious but not inexplicable, vast but not infinite, powerful but not unerring. You followed the rules—you ate this and not that, you wore this and not that,and you did this and not that—that was how you got along. And you wandered, without a homeland, subject to the good or ill will of your hosts. But there were no mysteries. There were warnings, admonitions and regrets, irrationality, but no mysteries. And there was music.

But then Jesus came down and put an end to all that. Jesus told us to love our God, our God who is so far away. How can we love what we cannot see or touch, what we cannot even comprehend? We can love Jesus, but that is not the same thing as loving God. We can love Jesus, but He too is curiously absent. He is not now: He is either in the past—dead and has risen—or in the future—He will come again. But He is not now.

Asking us to love our neighbor as ourselves. But how are we to love ourselves when we are separated from God? And separated not as the Jew is separated from the God of Abraham, as the child is separated from the absent father, but separated by an infinite gulf, the gulf between the finite and the infinite, between the particular and universal, between the image and the unimaginable, between the comprehended and the mysterious. When Jesus arrives God flees. Talk to My Son. But the Son is not here.

And when He comes again? To destroy hope totally? To destroy time totally? Or to repeat it? Where will God go then? What can be more infinite than infinity? And when He comes again, what can He say? Will He be embarrassed?

Whether He comes again or not, it will make no difference to me. Excluded from Heaven, Hell, two Limbos, and certainly Purgatory, I am now out of time.

This is not a dark night, for a dark night implies a dawn. There is no secret ladder, no Beloved awaiting me, no light to guide me.

To be so absolutely in despair. And therefore beyond it.

There is nothing to wait for.

This is my last entry. I write no more.

Maybe this sparseness wasn't unusual, maybe they all lived like this, with few personal possessions, with nothing to tie them down to the secular world. That didn't square with my knowledge, limited to be sure, of the Catholic clergy. I remembered, at seven or eight, being most impressed with my aunt Lissandra's frequent guest, Father Joseph, who drove a big Buick, ate a big meal, drank big red glasses of wine and smoked a big after-dinner cigar: there wasn't much in the world he had renounced. For all that he was small, maybe five-seven, and thin, one-fifty at the most, and he always brought a box of Russell Stover candies for my aunt. He once pulled a fifty-cent piece from behind my ear and gave it to me. I have no idea what happened to him. And maybe he did live like this, once the Buick was parked.

Still, something was off here. I needed more information. I looked around again, quickly, and then turned to Straat. "If you notice anything out of place, either something that should be here that isn't or that shouldn't be here that is, you let me know ASAP."

He nodded. "Will do, Detective."

I wanted to duck my head into another room to see if this stinginess was a custom of the rectory, but all doors were closed tight to this unclean female. Too bad my period had dried up years before. I held my breath as I hurried down the stairs, through the corridor and out of the closed rectory air. I found Maldonado on the telephone, pacing in the sacristy off the hallway leading to the cathedral. I breathed deeply.

He hung up. "Did you find anything?"

"Nothing. Didn't have much, our dead priest."

"Lived like a monk, huh?"

"But this isn't a monastery. How do these other priests live? I need to know that. Who's doing the interviews here?"

"Mullen and Wolff."

"Send them to me the minute they're finished." I started pacing as well. "What do we know about Vidal? He wasn't here long, right?"

"February last year."

"Did he have any friends here? Enemies? Where did he come from?"

"Mexico City."

"Who did he work for there? Did he have friends there? What is his order like? I need background, as much info as can be found. Who's on it now?"

"No one yet."

"Put someone smart on it. Someone who can speak Spanish and who knows their way around a rosary. And we need to check out this Willem Martinez too. What do we know, other than he liked to get high and his address was bogus? Put someone smart on that too, street-smart."

I looked around the room at the three sets of long, low wooden drawers flanked by two large closets. A framed print of Velásquez's

Christ Crucified dominated the far wall, indeed the entire sacristy, with that solitary white figure against the deep black background. I don't know much about art, but I knew that painting. Looking at the print, one could almost believe. There was the pleasant smell of incense, stiff linen and cedar oil. "Were you ever an altar boy, Maldonado?"

"No, ma'am."

"Me either. We went to Mass, when I was a kid, and I was confirmed, but after that, my family didn't press. Weekends were always busy, especially when the Broncos played, and I had concerts or recitals most Sunday nights."

I walked around those low cabinets to look more closely at the print. It was fairly big, about four feet tall and over two feet wide, and simply framed, with a glass overlay. I had seen the original in New York when I was in college, and remembered it as bigger, maybe twice as big, life-size. A short platform extended from the vertical beam of the cross, and Christ's feet were nailed to it separately. I wondered if that would be more painful than doing both feet with one spike. The bloody toes were elongated, and the toenails of both big toes needed trimming.

"What do we have here?"

"A murder. The murder of a priest."

"Passion or execution?"

"Passion most likely: his entire face was gone."

"What are the parts of a shotgun shell? The case, the shot and the wad, right? We know where the shot went, into our priest's face and head. But where did the case and wad go?"

"The shooter must have picked them up."

"But if this was a crime of passion, is that something he, I'm assuming it's a he, would do? After splattering the priest's brains in that small confessional, would he stop, search around for the casing and wad?"

"Maybe."

"And then drop his wallet"

"Maybe."

"And why a shotgun?"

"Maximum effect?"

"And no rifling marks. Difficult to trace."

I looked again at *Christ Crucified*. Nasty way to die. Certainly not the only innocent to be executed like that. And Father Andrea Vidal? How innocent was he? No one deserved a shotgun to the face. That was true.

"Get a team together, and we'll meet in an hour back at the ranch. I know it's Sunday, but we've got a murder."

This was a tight fit. Signelli bent low to fit his head beneath the ceiling, then swiveled his hips and buttocks awkwardly and heavily into the seat, dragging his legs and feet behind. The small car unquestionably registered his bulk. Malachi stared straight ahead, his back pressed against the upholstery of the far corner. Signelli breathed thickly through his mouth as he shut the door with too much strength. The car accelerated into the street.

"It's very warm." He shifted back and forth, trying to free a fold of fabric of his cassock from underneath his right thigh. His leg finally released, he turned his head with difficulty toward Malachi. "You look well, Father Malachi, very well: perhaps this country suits you. More sun than Dublin, certainly. But one must take care, yes, to cover the head, especially when accustomed to clouds and rain. Father Quist, did you know him? Father Quist, from Sweden, he had the cancer of the skin, in hospital five months last year. It was terrible. He returned to Stockholm. He is not an old man, Father Quist, not yet forty. No, what do you say, darkness in his skin, and bareheaded always in the hot Roman sun. It's important to have a good hat, one that protects the neck as well as the nose." He touched the back of his neck with the fingertips of his left hand. "Do you have a good hat, Father Malachi?" He quieted when he realized he had forgotten his own.

Malachi continued to stare at the headrest in front of him. "You need to wear that seat belt." Signelli moved to grab the harness, rotating his hips and shoulders stiffly, then turned again to search for the buckle near his right hip. He groped for it until he found it and finally inserted the tongue and snapped it in place. He leaned back, and keeping his shoulders straight, twisted his neck and head toward Malachi. "Perhaps it is not my business. Forgive me. You did not drive all this way to debate hats, did you, Father? And I did not fly from St. Peter's to warn you of exposure to the sun. We are busy men, too busy to waste time with such small speech. We need to discuss directly, face-to-face, this problem, or rather these problems, that we have. We can do this, yes?"

"Cigarette?" Malachi was looking in his direction but past him, out the window behind, as he held a pack of Chesterfields in his hand.

Signelli looked on with some surprise as Malachi shrugged and lit up with a small silver lighter. "No, no cigarette. I am not a smart man, Malachi, I'm sure you will agree. I am stubborn, si, but not intelligent. Ignorant, I lack imagination. I must confess, I am ignorant of the thinking behind this killing of Father Vidal. I cannot imagine why this was done. We are not men of death, Father Malachi, and murder is a mortal sin. So this must be an accident, yes, an error? You would never cause the death of another human, this I believe. There must have been a failure of understanding, something misapprehended, or something must have happened in the heat of the second. I tell myself this, yes, but I have never known you to make such a mistake, Father Malachi, I have never known you to allow such misapprehension or error. Never. And so I am confused, most puzzled. May I open a window?"

Malachi took a deep drag.

"Yes, and if, God forbid—and I don't believe this—this was not a mistake, not a case of misheard instructions or overzealotry or some other blunder, this only adds to my confusion. The sin is great, yes, and my imagination cannot connect you, the father I trust, to such great sin. Also, I cannot imagine what purpose it could serve, this killing of the secretary, Vidal. In fact, given the vital necessity of recovering the journal, I would imagine the death of its owner could only make that recovery more difficult." The car came to an abrupt stop, and Signelli extended his left hand to brace himself against the front seat, then sat back heavily. "And so I come to you, Father Malachi, very confused and very much in the dark. I am in the dark about the past actions, yes, and how such a tragedy could have occurred. I am also in the dark about the plans of the future. What penance can we do to atone for the guilt we bear in this accident, this tragedy? And what can be done to recover the journal? Everything about this business is obscure to me, Father Malachi, everything. So please, let me ask you plainly, old man to old man, one servant of God to another: Can you shed some light on this business? Can you tell me what happened, and what we are to do now?"

The car lurched forward as Malachi looked out the window and, exhaling, mumbled, "What's done is done."

Signelli sighed. "What's done is done? You can say nothing else? What's done is done? What have I said to deserve such an answer? Come, Malachi, we have too much history for an answer such as this. We are in this together, Malachi, we both desire the same thing. I need to know how you plan to obtain the journal. I need to impress upon you the importance of obtaining the journal: Rome will be most displeased if we fail."

Inhaling, "I gave no order to murder."

"The guilt is not directly ours. But we carry some responsibility, yes. I did not realize you smoked, Malachi. Did you smoke the last time I visited in Dublin?"

Exhaling, "The police have a suspect." The car made a sharp left turn and Signelli stiffened against the door.

"And so what's this guy doing here?" he pointed to the feet.

"He's burying the dead, Popi. That's an act of mercy."

Once again the solo violin soared above the accompanying strings, with a long vibrato held sweetly above a roiling sea of violas and cellos. Nicholas pointed to the half-naked man on the left. "And this is St. Martin, who's slashing his cloak with his sword and giving half of it to that beggar. Clothing the poor is an act of mercy." Hector wasn't listening to either the music or to Nicholas. He was looking at the feet, the feet of the corpse being carried out of the painting. They were large, unmarked but yellowish, and the man carrying the body held both ankles firmly.

It didn't really seem like mercy to bury the dead. Duty, obligation, respect, responsibility, yes, but not mercy. How could you *not* bury your dead? What was the alternative? And what difference did it make to the dead if you buried them or not? He wondered if Caravaggio had ever buried a daughter. Or a son. Or a wife. He was getting angry, and he didn't know why. Mary, she buried her son. But she didn't do it out of mercy, he was sure of that. And only for three days. And who did Jesus bury? Not his parents, not his disciples. Not even Judas. And he raised up Lazarus. He just couldn't see how burying the dead was an act of mercy. Not at all.

Or an act of faith. And what was faith, anyway, except the overwhelming wish to believe certain stories, the permission you gave yourself to indulge in certain narratives, the luxury of thinking that someone somewhere cares about what happens to you, that someone somewhere will keep you from being obliterated in death, that someone somewhere will give your life meaning. And this Caravaggio, did he believe the stories he painted? Did he believe in that someone somewhere, or did he just use it as an excuse to create and arrange these figures or as a way to make some money?

What stories did he believe?

He did have faith at one time, he supposed. He'd been confirmed, married in the Church, had all his children baptized. And buried. But he'd stopped going to confession and communion after Lucy had died and had stopped going to Mass altogether after Roberto, when he had started drinking, using Sunday mornings for recovery and afternoons for resumption and silence, sometimes with football added to the resumption and silence. What did some wet-behind-the-ears priest know about anything? He'd stopped drinking easily when Bella got sick and didn't pick it up again when she died. He didn't pick God up either. Although he did allow himself a beer or two now and then at the Legion.

He still didn't get the mercy angle. He believed enough to be polite to your fellow humans, to the people you came into contact with and who didn't do you wrong. But that was just common decency, not mercy, and you didn't need church or even a god for that. Most everyday people couldn't really afford to be merciful. Mercy was for the powerful; it was the opportunity for the strong to make themselves feel even stronger by pretending to curb their power momentarily. But even this mercy was designed to demonstrate their strength, to threaten you with their power by the powerful act of not using it. Mercy was for God, not for people. And Hector had little evidence of God's mercy in his own life.

The music was still playing, and Nicholas was still talking. "And this guy here, you can barely see him, see, behind here, in the dark? He's sick, and St. Martin is visiting him. Again, a two for one."

"How's burying the dead an act of mercy?"

"What?"

"These guys right here," he pointed to the figure holding the torch and the other carrying the body by the ankles, "how's this an act of mercy? If you believe in God, in that story, once you die, your soul goes to heaven, or hell, regardless of what your body's doing. And if you don't believe in God, or believe in another story, well, that doesn't matter either, you're just gone, *terminado*. And if you believe in reincarnation, I don't see how burying your body would work with that story. I can understand how visiting the sick or imprisoned or feeding the hungry," he pointed to Pero and her father, "might be merciful, although you have to admit, this is kind of bizarre. But I don't see how burying the dead is an act of mercy. The dead don't care."

"It's not an act of mercy for the dead, Popi, it's an act of mercy for the living."

The music quieted, with upper strings dropping out completely, the lower strings marking the time with quarter notes on the first and third beat, and the solo violin descending from a high F with a sixteen-note chromatic run until middle A, where it turned into a sweet *legato* passage of slurred eighth notes, dipping down to G-sharp below the stave. The speakers followed flawlessly, with thick texture in the lower strings, and the quick attack and accurate decay of the sixteenth notes of the solo violin. The bowing of the *legato* was particularly fine. He looked away from the album cover to the bank of tubes in front of him.

That was a nice sentiment, a smart idea coming from Nicholas. But Hector wasn't buying. He had buried Lucy twenty-one years ago. He had buried Roberto four years ago, and his Bella, three years, and burying them had been a sad duty that had torn him apart, not comforted him. He had buried most of himself in that cemetery in Walsenburg, and there was nothing in that that had helped him in any way.

What did he want?

He wanted his family to be alive.

The painting was focused on the living, with only the feet visible of the corpse. And Mary, Jesus, the angels, they were looking on, down from above, not acting, not participating, but looking on at the simple acts of human kindness. He looked back at the image. The painting was alive and all too human. There was no pleasure in Pero's face, nor embarrassment, just worry and fear of being discovered. And the expression of St. Martin, his head tilted to the side, showed a wondrous empathy for the men he was trying to help. Mercy was a gift, a gift outside the rigid system of self-interest, the usual sphere of human interaction. Hector realized that burial, burying the dead, was a process, not an immediate accomplishment. It was one thing to place bodies into the ground, cover them with earth and put crosses above. It was another thing to bury them.

Perhaps he hadn't buried his dead yet. He'd put them in the ground, true, but perhaps they were still unburied.

GLORIA

Feast Day of Norbert of Xanten, 2002

I was fucking her from behind, and I began to lose my erection. She wasn't unattractive, especially from that angle, her soft and doughy ass raised high, her spine shuddering in waves, her broad shoulders and neck dipping from the fulcrum of her elbows. I enjoyed her encouraging grunts as well, although when she twisted her face back to smile I immediately looked away. She was wet, dripping, and we had achieved a good rhythm. This was usually my favorite position: I like watching my dick as it comes out, the shaft and tip glistening depending on the light, hesitating aloft in the air, then reentering slowly, deeply, glans parting the labia lips; I like the way the top of my shaft and pelvic bone rub against the edge of the cunt, almost against the asshole; I often spread my fingers and palms wide against the buttocks, caressing and squeezing, opening and contracting, and gently work my thumbs down, sometimes inserting one into the cunt with my dick, sometimes caressing the rim of the anus; I like how deep I can get, how it feels like my cock is her second spine, penetrating up into her viscera; I like the feeling of tender assflesh colliding with my upper thighs and lower belly; I guess I like the almost complete control that position puts me in—I can hurry or slow down, change angles, use my hands to caress nipples or rub the clit, maybe even stick my thumb deep into her ass. One other advantage to that position is that I prefer not having to kiss a woman's mouth whose just been sucking my dick. It's a distinctive taste and smell, of faint mushrooms and wormy late fall leaves, and, if I've come in her mouth, harsh bleach.

When I'm *there*, when I'm really there and my cock feels like it can cut diamonds, it seems as if there is a muscle running from the base of my cock down to my prostate, up to the base of my spine, through my thighs and down to my knees. There's a heaviness in my balls, a thick, heavy liquid fire, and it's this heavy mercurial liquid, moving slowly back and forth, that creates my momentum. I'm almost always slow, the opposite of a rabbit, and from the back I can be as slow as I need. We had a good rhythm going, but something was beginning to fail.

I don't remember her name now even though it was just last night. She was a brunette, with short hair and lots of moles around her shoulder blades. Our *Nuestro Padre* was in the other room, with his "teenagers," boys who looked to me like they were on the north side of thirty rather than the south of twenty. They looked like twins, but it could just be that they dressed alike. I didn't know where Dollar Bill was. I hadn't taken anything, not even a hit off Dollar's spliff. She was high on Dollar's ecstasy and God knows what else. I don't think she was a pro, semi-pro maybe, would fuck once in a while for good drugs. Women can be like that: they don't need to be all there to fuck. In fact, it helps if they aren't. The room was fragrant: I'd come once earlier, and even though I'd taken a shower, we both were sweating heavily. There wasn't much sound, other than her soft grunts and the bed periodically complaining. But all of a sudden I started losing pressure. I was bareback, so that wasn't it, and she was tight enough, was very wet, but I started softening, my balls retracting. I became aware of the muscles in the back of my thighs, and when she grunted, it seemed like she was mocking me. I thought maybe I could tighten her, so I reached around with my left hand and felt around for her clit. She was bushy and shifted her haunch a little to allow my forefinger easier access, but her thigh was blocking my wrist's approach, and unless I shifted my weight forward, I could only reach the outside of her labia. I thought maybe a different angle might help, so I leaned back, raised my right leg from my knee to my foot and leaned forward, so I was thrusting down rather than horizontally. She responded eagerly, lowering her shoulders by spreading her elbows and raising her haunches to meet my thrusts. I felt a muscle in my lower back twitch. There wasn't enough friction, and I was now barely brandishing a serviceable utensil. I thought of the blowjob she had given me before and other cunts I'd been in. I thought of the few assholes I'd come in, and of the pricks who'd come in mine. A few names surfaced—Ramón, Brigitte, Tiffany, Jade, Hercule— but mostly nameless and discreet parts—a thick uncircumcised cock, a shaved cunt with small lightning bolt tattoos, a huge black- ish purple scrotum, an impatient asshole cleaned by my tongue. These thoughts didn't help.

I decided to focus on the task at hand. I sped up and shortened my stroke, not daring the long withdrawal, hesitation and slow reentry: if I slipped out now, I would have difficulty reinserting. I didn't care if she came or not. And I would feel no embarrassment, as her opinion of me mattered less to me than the opinion of the cricket to the windshield. No, I was still there and wanted to keep fucking.

I leaned back and looked down at her. I stared at the cleft of her buttocks and focused on the writhing knot of her tailbone. I imagined for her a scut of cartilage and fur and me grasping it with both hands. What were my hands actually doing? I don't remember. Probably gripping her hips.

As I write this down I'm getting hard. Harder than I was at the time. This has happened before.

I gazed down at her spine, just above where her scut would emerge. It was rhythmically dipping so her ass could meet my thrusts. My gaze moved up, past the small of her back to where her moles began just below her shoulder blades. There was some ambient light from somewhere, a streetlight outside or the moon, and the darkened moles sharply contrasted with her luminous skin. She gave a small grunt, and everything—her thrusting ass, her snakelike back, her dipping, mole-marked shoulders, her bobbing head, her animal noises, her slightly burnt smell—suddenly became ludicrous. What were we doing? With each thrust, coming became more and more impossible, as if I was doing the opposite of fucking. I became almost frenzied by the ridiculousness of this. I hurried my strokes, our bodies slapping together at stomach, ass and thigh, faster and faster as if I were trying to create mass through velocity, strength through speed.

I stopped and flopped out. She kept going for a few beats, as if she didn't notice my absence. I leaned back against the headboard and she quickly turned around. I shrugged. "I'm tired."

She reached for my shrinking and useless cock, no longer worthy of the name. Penis.

I blocked her hand away. "I'm tired."

"This is our victim, Father Andrea Antonio Diego Vidal, age forty-nine, Argentine national, arrived in Denver only last year. Found murdered, shotgun blast to the head, by person or persons unknown, in a confessional of the Cathedral Basilica of the Immaculate Conception this morning, August twenty-first, by a Mrs. Helen Threadgill of Congress Park. Time of death sometime between twelve midnight and five a.m. We'll know more once we get the medex report. Let's fill some of this in."

"Victim was highly educated, with a PhD in theology from a noted university in Rome. According to his supervisor in Denver, Father Duquesne, Vidal was multi-lingual, spoke Spanish, French, English, Latin and Greek. Again, according to Duquesne, he was more an administrator than a priest who served Mass. He was not assigned pastoral duties in this diocese, although he was allowed to give early morning Sunday confession."

"Was that the word Duquesne used, 'allowed'? He keeps saying that, keeps insisting that Vidal wasn't 'allowed' pastoral duties. Why? Was Vidal being kept from the public?"

"That was the word he used."

"Sex abuse. Sometimes priests are reassigned, given a desk job, a job where they don't meet the congregation. Could that be what was happening here? Where did he work before?"

"Mexico City."

"As an administrator. Says here he worked in the 'administrative offices.' Maybe he didn't have pastoral duties there either."

"For whom did he work?"

"The Legionaries of Christ."

"There's a lot of dirt here, ma'am, on the Legionaries of Christ. According to Wikipedia, this Legion of Christ was involved in numerous sex scandals, including allegations that the founder, one Marcial Maciel, quote 'sexually abused minors and fathered children,' unquote."

"And if Vidal worked for Maciel, then he might have known about this."

"Did Vidal work for Maciel? We need to find out. What's the chronology here?"

"It says here that Maciel died in 2008. He stepped down as director of the Legion in 2005 and was retired to Florida in 2006. New allegations came out in 2009. Six kids, possibly. Alleged abuse of boys, alleged drug use, alleged fraud. The Legion even admitted some of it and apologized to the victims."

"And Vidal left Mexico at the beginning of last year. About a year and a half after Maciel died and five years after he resigned as head of the Legion."

"Good, good, but we need more than a Wikipedia article, we need some real information, especially as to Vidal's position within the organization. Who's on that?"

"I am, ma'am. Detective Vitalsky."

"Progress?"

"I have a number of messages left with all various numbers I could find, but offices are closed on Sunday afternoons, and the home numbers I have aren't answering."

"You speak Spanish, Vitalsky?"

"I speak Spanish very well, ma'am. And I lived in Buenos Aires as a child."

"You a good Catholic, Vitalsky?"

"I'm a collapsed Catholic, ma'am."

"Excuse me?"

He stammered, turned a vivid shade of red. "Just a bad joke, ma'am. One of my brothers is a priest, a Franciscan. I know something about the Catholic orders and hierarchy and such."

I smiled. "Good. And it's not a bad joke. I might be a collapsed Catholic as well. Find out exactly what Vidal's duties were in the administrative offices. Was any money paid out? To the victims, after the apology? Anyone? We need intel on that."

"Do we have a motive? Could one of those abused boys have gone after Vidal? Maciel's dead, and maybe Vidal knew about the abuse."

"Or helped."

"Or joined in?"

"Maybe, maybe. Vitalsky, got your passport ready?"

"Ma'am?"

"I want you to go down to Mexico City for a couple of days. Given their recent scandal, and the sometimes reluctance of the Holy Catholic Church to provide information to civil authorities, mere telephone messages likely will remain unanswered. I'll get Schlaf to telephone the local po. I'll want as much intel as you can get on Vidal, the Legion, as well as the scandal and Maciel. Talk to the victims' lawyers and find out if they settled. There should be a flight tonight."

Vitalsky began to gather himself.

"Who've you been working with in data?"

"Richards."

"Who can take over? Needs to speak Spanish? Any good Catholics?"

No one raised a hand.

"That's sad. And Vitalsky, watch your expenses please. Anyone a Catholic at all? Elizondo, how about you?"

"I was raised Catholic, ma'am. Haven't been to Mass since I was twenty."

"You win. Vitalsky will brief you, but work with Richards. Find out all you can about Father Vidal from here." I turned to Maldonado. "We might need some help with all the Catholic stuff."

He shrugged, "The chaplain? Someone at the diocese?"

"No, I was thinking someone more independent. Maybe DU?"

"Regis?"

"That's a good idea."

"What? How do you know? Was it on the television? Can the man suspected be traced to us?"

"My man found a wallet at the scene, which he abandoned."

He thought for a minute. "That is fortunate, fortunate indeed. The police will place their suspicion on this other man, which will provide us with time." Signelli looked down at his hands, his clean and neat fingernails. Clean nails were important. "Father Malachi, I do not wish to supervise your business, but please tell me: with the secretary dead, how are we to locate the journal? And if Vidal has been murdered, won't the journal become an object of police investigation?"

Malachi gave a little smile, then turned away.

The car was stopped at a traffic light. He looked out the window, at the too-bright streets, the sun reflecting brilliantly off of the windows and the concrete. He noticed, through the glare, the people on the sidewalk in shorts and sportswear, tall, happy and busy, with a purpose or direction remarkable to his Italian gaze: dressing like they have nowhere to go, they walk as if they were late. He thought about sharing that observation with Malachi but decided against it.

The car proceeded through the intersection. He noticed the largest milk can he had ever seen, ten meters high, with the words "Little Man Ice Cream and Italian Gelato" on a big black-and-white cloth sign hanging from the top. He wondered how edible this Italian Gelato from this Little Man was. Certainly nothing could compare with his beloved *stracciatella* from his beloved Gelarmony. He was hungry: the breakfast had not tempted, he had accepted only coffee, and his body was still some hours ahead. He remembered the previous night with shame. He turned from the window toward Malachi.

"Is there any connection between the man the police are suspecting and Father Vidal? Could this man possess the journal?"

Without turning. "Don't know."

The back seat air was darkening with dense, grey clouds of thickening, almost solidifying smoke.

"Is your thinking that because the secretary is dead, his journal will not likely be discovered? Is this wise?"

No response.

"Doesn't the murder of Vidal necessarily involve the authorities, necessarily put this man and his possessions into the public eye?"

No response.

"If the journal is now found, won't the authorities keep it for their investigations? And then perhaps make it public? Isn't this the situation I told you we were trying to avoid?"

No response. He looked at Malachi in profile. His blue eye sparked through the smoke. It was not a laughing or dancing eye but an eye of calculation and cunning, surrounded by wrinkles and crow's-feet. *Malocchio.* Malachi's head was large and broad, his silhouette made greater by his nimbus of stiff white hair, expanding in numerous directions, unkempt and aggressive. He was not a big man and did whatever he could to increase the corporeal space his body described, from his shameless hairstyle to his flowing, overlarge cassock. *Pavoneggiarsi.* In Dublin, Signelli never saw Malachi without the violet *ferraiolo*, even when most inappropriate, like that Trinity College basement at three in the morning. The *ferraiolo* was now missing, but the hair, cassock and *malocchio* remained.

And for all the attempts at physical expansion, Malachi's language was guarded, contracted, terse past the point of rudeness and insult, as if each and every syllable cost incalculable physical and spiritual energy. Malachi's syllables were few and far between, and they often created more obscurity than they solved. And in the silence surrounding them, interpretations could be, would be, inserted.

He thought back to that cold, damp night in Dublin when he and Malachi had decided how best to proceed with Father Belhomme. He had always disliked Ireland: it had always seemed an outpost to him, stranger and wilder than even America, its populace primitive and its church near pagan. It was as if the people had just emerged from their tribal woodlands, blinking and dismayed in the bright sun of Christian Europe. They remained first generation Christians, cruel and severe, their zealotry to be envied and feared. He thought of the laundries, run by the Sisters of Mercy, where the unwed mothers would go, the Church's penance heavy on both them and their offspring. He was glad he was spared involvement with that. Many women died there, fallen or not. And even if fornication, concupiscence, was a mortal sin, God's mercy promised forgiveness. That was the whole point of Christ's sacrifice. These women should not have had to repeat the sacrifice of Our Lord. And their children? He thought briefly of Sister Kiara and her long Cistercian face.

Irish weather was damp and cold and grey. And the food, the potatoes and beer and overcooked meat, all lacked subtlety and texture. The cheese, the cheese was passable. He much preferred London, where civilization seemed more entrenched.

"What do we do now, Father Malachi?"

"What's done is done, like I said. We wait. *Is binn béal ina thost.*" The driver in front laughed harshly.

He looked over at Nicholas. He was trying not to be angry. "Do you believe this, this mercy, Nicholas?"

"What are you asking, Popi?"

"It's just this painting, this music. I don't know."

"You don't know what?"

"I don't know."

"That's what the painting and music make me feel too. Like I don't know. But in a big, gigantic way."

"So what you don't know, this doesn't frighten you?"

"No, Popi, not yet."

He didn't see Roberto often in his grandson, as he carried the eyes, the mouth and the posture of his mother. But at rare times in a few gestures—when he rubbed his nose or turned his shoulder or got up from the couch—Hector almost mistook his grandson for his son, and his heart was gladdened, if only for the moment that the visceral, unthought feeling took to change into the saddened realization that the feeling was mere memory, the incorrect superimposition of one distinct time and one distinct person onto another. One of those times happened now, and he saw Roberto, not Nicholas, look down with a bashful, furtive smile, his brown eyes darting.

The optimism of youth. The sadness of age. He looked back to the cover. He noticed a triangle of illuminated flesh created by the whiteness of Pero's exposed breast one-third of the way up the right edge, to the flesh of the angels center top, down to the beggar's shoulders and back near the bottom left. It was a crowded painting, with nine human figures, including the corpse, immediately visible, along with two angels plus the Madonna and child. And every figure was in action, gesturing. The flesh looked solid, substantial, tactile, as did the multi-pleated folds of cloth; the wine-covered fabric of Martin's cloak, the white and pale orange of Pero's dress, the white blouse and winding-sheet of the man holding the torch over the body. It was too full with all this flesh and fabric, too congested by this symbolism and drama: there was no room to step back, to rest, to breathe.

The music was busy as well, with the restless solo violin, the competitive upper strings and the lower cellos and double basses also adding their ideas to the mix. It was controlled, purposeful, flowery and perhaps too sweet. It was certain, somehow, confident in its repetition, and that all seemed so different from the sparseness, the patience, the delicacy of the Bingen.

"What do you like about this, Nicholas?"

"The music or the painting?"

"Either one."

"The music makes me happy, but also lets me think. With Mozart, I always think about how wonderful everything is, I always come back to the music and how everything fits together. And Bach, Bach is perfect. I admire Bach very much. But the perfection sometimes doesn't let me think. With Vivaldi, though, after I see the notes in my head, then I don't think about the music. I can think, but not about anything in particular. It's like you said, I don't know what I don't know. But I like that feeling, that feeling of not knowing. I sort of think about what I can't think about. I'm not making much sense."

"No, I understand. A little."

He put the cover on the couch between them and leaned back. Very soon after she died, he had difficulty picturing what Lucy looked like: she almost immediately became blurry, shadowy, insubstantial in his memory. And sometimes, then, when he'd look at photographs, he had some trouble recognizing her. His mind understood that this image of a little girl in a checked jumper and a straw hat sitting with Bella near a swimming pool was Lucy, but his heart took a few moments to be convinced. The presence of Bella didn't help, as he was never sure how much Lucy resembled her mother.

"And the painting? Is it the same?"

"I liked learning about the painting in school, about who everyone is and what they're doing and stuff. But that's just a small version: the real one is in Italy."

"What does the painting have to do with the music?"

"I'm not sure. Vivaldi used to work in the orphanage for girls, the Hospital of Mercy. Maybe that's why they chose it. It doesn't have much to do with the seasons, though."

He took another swig of his now cool coffee and wished for a moment he had something stronger to add to it. He didn't know what mercy was. Maybe it was just a hospital for girls. He thought of the jazz standard. He focused with difficulty on listening to that in his head instead of the music from the speakers. That was a good tune. Good old Zawinul.

CREDO

The Thirty-Second Saturday of Ordinary Time, 1972

For my confirmation tomorrow, my aunt Josefina, my father's oldest sister, has given me an expensive Catholic *diario*, with thick, creamy gilt-edged paper and a stiff and heavy bloodred cover. It has a light blue bound ribbon bookmark, which I find very impressive. On the right page, recto, is the calendar, the day of the week, the month and the day centered in black, with a short prayer for the day—it looks to be mostly lauds—along with a list of saints and their feast days. The prayers and the saints' days are written in cursive Latin script in red ink and are in very small print with wide, extravagant margins. The left page, verso, is completely blank, and that's where we're supposed to record our life and our thoughts, with the saints and the prayers looking across, guiding us. Whatever I write down, whatever I record on this left page will physically touch the Word of God and the names of His Holy Saints and Martyrs whenever I close the book. I wonder how honest I should be. That's probably what the Carmelite nuns have in mind: should I really write about Father Ignacio's bad breath or what might fill Eliana's sweater when these soiled and sinful words would be folded against the Lord's Prayer or the *Benedictus*?

I like how all the pages of the book are edged with gilt.

It's much too big for writing down and keeping appointments. And there doesn't seem to be a place to keep addresses or phone numbers. No, it's a *diario*, as a book of guidance and memory. I guess I'm supposed to look, first thing in the morning, for the guiding prayer and the saint of the day, *el santo del día* as Father Emmanuel used to say, and keep that with me as I go about my day. Then, when I come home at night, I'll record the day's events, my experiences and thoughts, all in the context of the Morning Prayer and the saints.

There's no lock. And it's too big to hide easily.

This is pretty cool. My favorite confirmation present. I got some cash from my brothers and sisters, and Mom and Dad got me that new backpack and the Nike Cortez sneakers, but I like this a lot better. It's so serious, such a serious object, so big and heavy, and beautiful, it must have been expensive. It makes me feel grown up. On the table among all the other stuff, it's impossible to ignore. It sure is nicer than every other book we have, except maybe the new Bible, the one that *Abuelita* gave to my father and mother when they were married, just because she didn't like the old Bible, the ratty New Testament that's been in Mom's family forever. I like the old Bible better, the cracked leather cover and the thin paper, the dried flat flowers pressed in some of the pages, the way it smells like lavender and leather oil.

After dinner, I take the *diario* to my room and open it, run my fingers across the paper and along the sharp edges, place my face deep and smell the cream of the paper and the blood of the ink, and practice placing the long ribbon bookmark between different pages. There's a printed circle on the first page, in the blackest ink, with spaces for my name, address and telephone number. I set the heavy book on my lap and feel its weight, comforting and almost protective.

What am I going to do with this? What will I write? There's that Father of the Church we're going to study next month, that guy that my dad likes, St. Augustine, and his *Confessions*, but I don't know much about those old writers. Why does anyone keep a diary? I have an excellent memory, so I don't need to write stuff down to be able to remember it a couple of days or even weeks later. And not that much happens to me anyway: I get up, go to school, sing in the choir, hang out with Miguel and ShirtTail, come home, practice my trumpet, wrestle around with my brothers, have dinner, watch some TV, do my homework and go to bed. I'm not fighting crime or anything or going to space or playing football with Sergio Villar. I'm twelve years old, what am I going to write about? And who's going to read it? Me, when I'm thirteen? Or fifteen? Or twenty? I seriously hope I have something better to do when I'm twenty than to read the scribbling of some snot-nosed twelve-year-old. I seriously hope I have a life by then, you know? Besides, writing is work, it's like being at school, and it's the opposite of living. You can't write and live at the same time.

I look at the verso side, the blank side, the wide expanse of cream-colored paper. I run my fingertips over it, and touching it, its weight and thickness, makes me think there's something there, a challenge or invitation: mark me up, fill me up, fill my pages. It's kind of like when I looked beneath Abril's skirt that one time at the playground or saw my sister Constanza get out of the bath.

It's kind of creepy, but kind of nice too. I mean, not my sister. It's weird.

I have no idea of what to do now. I can't just start writing. What does one put in a diary? How does one write one's life? I need some guidelines, some rules.

Okay. Rule Number 1: I will be absolutely honest. There's no point in lying. If I'm going to mark these pages, I will mark them with truth. Not for me, some me in the future or whoever's going to read this, but for these pages, for the *diario*. Diaries are not for stories, for made up fairy tales: diaries are books of life. I will respect the book and its heavy existence, its demand. I owe the book, and maybe even the nuns who made it, the truth.

But the nuns will never read it. Who might? My brothers? My sisters? My mother? Father? The fathers at school? If I'm going to write honestly, the truth, I will have to write without fear. I cannot write the truth and worry about who might read it. I close the book and lift it off my lap. It's large, huge, too big to carry around. And it opens easily: the blue ribbon is like an invitation. My brothers, especially Santiago, have no respect for my things. I'm going to have to find a hiding place for it. Someplace better than under the bed.

We're studying this composer Machaut, who wrote motets with the bass or tenor in Latin and the upper voices in French. Hmmm. Maybe I can do that. I'll write in different languages: Latin, French and Spanish and even English. I'm good in Latin, the language of Cicero, and that will keep all but my oldest brother, who's leaving for university in six months, and my father, who never comes in here anyway, from reading. I'm also good in French, which no one in our house except my oldest sister can read. And she can't read Latin. If I write in different languages, I can write without fear. I can write the truth.

"Let's turn our attention to Mr. Willem, not William, Martinez. What do we know?"

"Male, age forty-three, five feet ten inches, one hundred sixty-five pounds, brown hair, brown eyes. His home address is bogus. His rap sheet has seven items: public drunkenness, petty possession, a couple of times for patronizing a prostitute and once for pandering. Paid his fines for the possessions, sex charges dropped. Most recent arrest last April."

"U.S. citizen? Green card? Where's he from?"

"Not sure. We reached a dead end. We'll find out."

"Employment history?"

Silence.

"Food stamps? Disability? Social Security? Is he in the system at all? We gotta have prints from DMV?"

"His SS is as bogus as his address. His driver's license is real, but four years old. One of his AOs, Mouton, has since left the force. We're trying to reach another, des Prez. Otherwise, we're still looking."

"Gang affiliation?"

"None that we know of."

"Where was he picked up?"

"Last time, La Colina Bar and Grill on Colfax and Uinta. That was soliciting. Time before that, for possession, Plaza Liquors on Yosemite. Not too far away. Before that, January of 2007, he was nabbed at Popeyes Chicken, also on Colfax, for public drunkenness and possession. Seems to favor the Colfax strip."

"That's probably where he lives. What are the flops around?"

"There's the El Rio off Pontiac: meth-heads mostly. There's the Riviera off of Beeler, sometimes safe, sometimes not but mostly short-term. They're Aurora's problem, anyway. There's the Glenarm, on Glencoe and 19th, a halfway house for needle jockeys. And, of course, the San Sebastian."

The room chuckled.

"The San Sebastian. Didn't Two clean that up?"

"I was working Two then. We had plans but had to give up our task force to Six after that airman got killed in the let-out in Lodo."

"So it's still operational."

"Yes, ma'am. Crack, meth, junk, hoes, kids—anything you want at a steep discount. You can disappear there."

"And never be heard from again."

"Ain't that right."

"Still an SRO?"

"Yep."

"Two have anyone inside? Anything ongoing?"

"There was somebody there when I left. Gun trafficking. I could find out."

"Listen up. I'd like to find this guy, Mr. Martinez, and soon. Get his DL photo out to the uniforms, start at the Basilica with the good fathers. We know he was there. Go both uptown and downtown, and hit everything: stores, bars, gas stations, 7–Elevens. Hit the flops and shooting galleries. Leave the San Sebastian for now: it's not like anyone there will tell us anything anyway. Talk to Vice, call in some favors."

Two figures entered the room and stood in the back: Schlaf and Lt. Clark, who was thumbing his mobile phone. What do the kids say? Douche. I continued. "We need more info on both

Martinez and Vidal. We need to know especially if there was any connection. Did Vidal see Martinez in any professional capacity? Did he counsel him, give him confession, suggest any treatment or detox, loan him money, set him up with a place to live, etc., etc.? Do they have a history, either here, or in Mexico or Argentina?"

"Is Martinez a suspect? POI?"

"I don't know yet. Why was Mr. Martinez's wallet found outside Father Vidal's confessional the morning he was murdered? That's the question for now."

Two uniforms hesitated at the outer door, then awkwardly walked in and stood at the door, near Schlaf and Clark. "Officers?"

"Mullen and Wolff, ma'am. You wanted to see us as soon as we returned."

"Rectory interviews," Maldonado added.

"Right. Anything to tell us?"

Mullen or Wolff stammered, looked at his notebook, while Mullen or Wolff stood by. "We interviewed six fathers: Philip, Duquesne, Baca, Fraterelli, Dominguez and Bovic. Two more priests, a Father Salamanca and Antoine, were unavailable and rescheduled for this evening. Fathers Philip and Duquesne admitted to knowing the victim slightly while Fathers Baca and Bovic knew him only by sight. Fathers Dominguez and Fraterelli characterized their relationships with Vidal as quote colleagues unquote from Fraterelli and quote I guess you could say we were friends unquote from Dominguez. No respondents could offer any reason Vidal might be targeted, and no respondents could suggest other friendships or relationships Vidal might have enjoyed. Father Duquesne insisted that Vidal was not involved in any pastoral activity..."

Mullen or Wolff then read from *his* notebook: "Pastoral means the 'giving of spiritual guidance.'"

"'Pastoral.' I keep hearing that. Thank you, Officer."

"Was not involved in any pastoral activity other than that of hearing confession on Sunday mornings. Fathers Baca, Dominguez, Fraterelli and Bovic reported that Vidal rarely took his meals in the rectory. Fathers Baca, Bovic and Fraterelli…"

"Thank you. Mullen?"

"Wolff, Detective."

"Anything extraordinary? Anything seem odd to you, or stand out?"

"Detective? No, not really."

"Mullen?"

"No, Detective. Not really."

"Thank you. Please write up a detailed report and give it to Detective Maldonado. And Mullen, Wolff, what were their rooms like?"

"Ma'am?"

"Their rooms. Were they luxurious or poverty-stricken? What kind of furnishings? Were they comfortable or barren?"

"They were okay."

"Some were pretty nice."

"Father Baca's was nice. Two rooms had flatscreens."

"Fraterelli had a lot of books."

"Did they all looked lived-in? Or like hotel rooms? You know what I mean?"

"They looked comfortable, ma'am. Lived-in. All of them."

Schlaf and Clark turned and walked out.

He was not stupid and was suddenly annoyed and offended at being taken as such. He understood the Irishman was attempting to intimidate him, to blunt his questions and keep him in the dark—as to what purpose he did not know. He did not yet understand what Malachi wanted, and until he did, he wasn't sure how to proceed. He was hungry and tired. But he would not allow himself to be daunted, no matter how much smoke Malachi put into the air.

Malachi turned and stared, his blue eyes slicing through the smoke. "My suggestion would be for you to meet with the police officer in charge."

"What good would this do?"

"To offer Rome's cooperation. And to see where the investigation might be heading. They likely searched his room: maybe they found something."

"My visit is unofficial: what sort of cooperation could I offer?"

Malachi smiled a small smile and looked away. "Rome always has things to offer."

"I don't understand."

Malachi kept the small smile, then abruptly knocked on the window with his ring. "Take him back to the rectory," he said and without turning, "I'll be in touch."

He nodded and closed his eyes. He was furious. At what game was Malachi playing? Was he trying to provoke him? Why? He had always found Malachi trustworthy, but no longer. As the car made a sharp left turn, he opened his eyes and shot a glance at Malachi, his oversized white head surrounded by a nimbus of blue smoke.

He was suddenly dizzied by that smoke and thin air, the hunger and jet lag. His physical world was all too present: it enveloped him, pressed on his chest and head, overwhelming any possibility of thought, reflection, memory or plan. He imagined his lung constricted by fat, straining to circulate enough oxygen for his overworked heart. Breathe in breathe out breathe in breathe out. He needed to shed that image, to think clearly about what had been done and what remained to be done. Riding in the back of this automobile was making him nauseous. He felt as if they were floating a few feet above the ground, unmoored and adrift, susceptible to various vagrancies of the weakened atmosphere or to Malachi's cagey whims.

He needed solid ground to regain his equilibrium. The car mercifully stopped at a traffic light. He noticed building construction to his right and a small green park to his left. He looked behind him, unbuckled his seat belt, then opened the car door and, with some difficulty, exited. The sun and heat attacked him. He closed the door and looked at Malachi. The window opened.

"Aye. It's too hot to be driving around this desert of a city. I'll let you know about the meeting."

The sun was very hot on his forehead and made him wish for his sunglasses and *cappello romano*, both which remained in his room at the rectory.

"You'll send a car, yes?"

Malachi nodded, and as the car sped away he heard, "You need a hat, Father."

A car with a very loud radio sped past him. He crossed the street, away from the construction, with his right hand on his forehead to shield his eyes. Perhaps a coffee would help, something to put in his stomach and to place him more firmly on the earth. Perhaps it was not such a good idea to leave the car: he had no idea where he was or how to return to the rectory. A coffee or a bite to eat would be beneficial, of that there was no doubt.

But what of Malachi? How dare he treat him as some lowly errand boy or trembling old fool. They were the same age, he and Malachi, less than a month difference. And he wasn't stuck in some outpost parish in Sligo or Dublin or retired in the *arretrato* provinces of Arizona, no, he lived in the heart, the Vatican, and was sent wherever he was needed, wherever problems needed to be solved quickly and quietly. He had some plan, that *stronzo*, some scheme of his own. And a priest was dead, *Deus meus, Requiescat in Pace*, and that might not have been an accident. He wanted something, that bastard: he was using him. But what could he want? What could this priest, this Vidal, have to do with Malachi? He would not be Malachi's woman.

He noticed white lace curtains on his left, candles and unoccupied tables and chairs through the window. A *trattoria* perhaps? *Deo gratias*. Where was the entrance? He nearly stumbled over a green metal bench and saw a small awning with "Patsy's Entrance" in black letters. Neon signs informed him that "Patsy's is Open," and that "Peroni is Italy's # 1 Beer." He gratefully pushed open the wooden door.

It was cool and dark inside. A long dark wooden bar ran almost the length of the long narrow room on the left. The entrance to the dining room opened on the right, partially blocked by a sign that demanded that everyone wait to be seated. Two older men looked up from a conversation, and a younger man in a suit briefly raised his attention from his newspaper and meatballs. The bar smelled of garlic and *grissino torinese*, breadsticks, a smell he associated not with the kitchen of his home country but with approximations of it in Boston and New York. It was a smell that brought to mind plates heaped with macaroni and thick red *ragù* served with slightly sour wine; an American attempt at a Neapolitan meal. In spite of this memory, his mouth began to water. He walked up to the sign.

He had somehow been prepared for Bella's death, or perhaps the death of his children had numbed him, but he had met her passing with a kind of quiet acceptance, a grim stoicism that others might have confused with indifference but that he knew was closer to exhaustion. The shock soon dissipated, what tears there were had been dried rather quickly, and he had adjusted, welcoming his daughter-in-law and grandson to the apartment above his shop, spending his attention on helping with Nicholas, record collecting and hi-fi retail, and making the early weekend rounds with his buddies, one or two from high school and one or two from the navy. Some thought he should be grateful, deep deep down, that Bella had died relatively quickly and painlessly, without involving him in extended emotionally and financially expensive caretaking. He seemed freer, and no one blamed him. He missed her terribly, of course. They had been together almost forty years. She was always the adult in the room, always the one who thought ahead and planned. But he buried some of her with Lucy, the better part of her humor and joy. She carried her sadness heavily, obviously, they both did, and the two of them, Roberto was out of the house by then, lost much of their laughter and spontaneity. At first, she became obsessed with Roberto, what he was doing, who he was seeing, but that gradually shifted into a frantic busyness, a continuous cleaning, rearranging and remodeling, often abandoned midstream. The melodrama of grief. Finally, a silent lethargy settled; into which not even a grandson could break.

She always loved their son though: Roberto's presence was the one thing that could put fresh clothes on her back or turn the corners of her mouth up just a little. And yet that too was taken from her. There was no doubt that the drunk who killed Roberto had also killed Bella. What did Nicholas call it? A two for one.

The music was relentless. He looked over at Nicholas, who, with his eyes closed and his head nodding, seemed to be enjoying it. But there was no time to breathe here, no time to rest or to think; it was mostly a flurry of notes, beginning high, with the solo violin or high strings, and then echoed low, until it would start again, and then again, until a fermata signaled the end of a section. And he always knew what was coming: he could anticipate, with surprising accuracy, the next riff and then the next. He'd heard this before, if not this exact piece then something extremely close to it. Maybe this belonged to some film or something he'd seen or something he watched on TV. Somehow the music was already familiar, the sounds coming from the loudspeakers merely activating what was already known, already *heard*, in his brain. And this familiarity was tedious.

"Nicholas." He opened his eyes and stopped bouncing. "You like this music, yes?" He nodded. "But isn't it, well, predictable? There's nothing unknown here, is there? No surprises? Do you find this tedious?"

"You expected that *glissando*, really?"

"Not always the solos, but the rest. It sounds like a car commercial."

"It's not Vivaldi's fault he's popular."

"All right. But even your old grandfather, a bad rhythm guitar player, can pretty much guess what's coming next. This ever get boring to play?"

"No, Popi, you can't think in phrases with Vivaldi; you have to think in notes. Individual notes. You have to slow your ear down, listen measure by measure, beat by beat, note by note if you can. If you anticipate, you'll miss the beauty, the rightness of his choices. Like the cello and violin duet coming up here, right here. I've played the piano transcription. Listen to the cello, that repeated dotted eighth; it should be an F, not an F-sharp. But it's that F-sharp that holds things back a little bit, and when everyone comes in, here, with sixteenth notes, the cellos on a D, but the two violins, not the solo, go to F-sharp."

"I'm not sure I understand."

"Sorry, Popi, that wasn't clear." He picked up the album cover and pointed to the shoulder blades and spine of the beggar. "If you want to draw, well, draw anything, you have to think in shapes. You don't think of this as a 'back,' not at first. At first, you have to draw lines, and then circles and ovals, and then see how these lines and circles and ovals all fit together. And then eventually, if you're good, you have shoulders; you have a back. But if you set out, right from the first, to draw a back, you'll never get anywhere. It's hard; it's like the hardest thing in drawing not to see a back or a face or a box of fruit. It's hard to hear the notes or a chord or even a measure and not the entire phrase. Especially with Vivaldi. But if you can slow down and not skip ahead, you hear how interesting his choices are. And you hear there's a lot of mystery there."

"It makes some sense with your drawing analogy. But I'm not sure I can hear it."

"It's probably personal, maybe too personal, you know? Not everyone can hear it; not everyone can believe it. It's like when you listen to that guy, John Coltrane. Not everyone will hear what you're hearing."

"You never can tell what Coltrane's going to do, though."

"I don't know. He's got modes, chord progressions, scales he prefers. He's got habits. And don't tell me after listening to his records hundreds of times you can't anticipate where he's going next. I've heard you playing along. Anyway," Nicholas stood up, "we should get to work, huh, Popi? Let's put on something you know, pipe it through the Hommages, and see where they need to go. You sit here and guide me, and I'll muscle them into the corners. Hand me the iPad: I think I hooked them up to number four. There. Yeah."

The music immediately became somewhat muffled, as if the orchestra was playing through yards of cloth. The gain seemed cut in half, both attacks and decays were muddy and vague, and the timbre of the instruments blended into one another, so you couldn't tell a violin from a harpsichord.

SANCTUS

The Thirty-Second Saturday of Ordinary Time, 1972

I open the book and turn the pages slowly, *miércoles junio 1, jueves junio 2, viernes junio 3...* Today is the 11th of November, and the diary began *enero 1*. I don't want to wait a month and a half. I'll forget about it by then. I'll begin tomorrow, the day of my confirmation, the day I'll take a new name, Antonio, the day I'll become a soldier of Christ. This makes more sense that waiting until *enero 1*. I don't like these numbers, this order. If I write the truth in order to respect the demands of the *diario*, I'm going to ignore its imposed system. I'm not going to adhere to the calendar dates; I'm going to refuse to follow its chronological structure. I'll begin where I want, and I'll go back and forward as I wish.

I look at the recto pages, the ones with the black and red writing, the block dates on top and the smaller red cursive of *la oración introductoria* and the list of the saints below. And the margins wide, dwarfing the surrounded print. I think about what it will mean to write honestly, to write about my thoughts, my sins, without lying and without leaving anything out. I know right from wrong, certainly, but the word "sin" always seems to blur that distinction. I believe, or more precisely *feel*, that I can do things that are wrong but are not sins, just as I can commit acts that seem right but are. My conscience and God's judgment have never been synchronized. That's all for now.

I'm having trouble thinking of anything to write.

Do I need to write in this diary every day?

I want to smoke. Not so much to have the smoke in my lungs, or to be with the cool kids, but to have something to write about. I wonder what it would be like, to write about something so strange, so foreign to myself, so bad for my health. I have a touch of asthma, and so smoking wouldn't be that great. But it would be fun to describe.

The cool kids, the smokers, go everyday after school to the president's statue in *Parque Sarmiento* to have a cigarette or two. I guess I'm friends enough with a couple of them, Cortez and Avalinni, to share small talk about Miles Davis and Jerry Gonzáles, but our orbits are different. So what do I do? I could go buy a pack to smoke on my own, but I heard that most corner stores won't sell to kids, and I don't want some silver-haired store clerk shaking his head slowly in front of giggling girls and frowning moms. I could ask Domi or Santiago, but I don't need that hassle. Or blackmail.

I can't think of anything to write. I got to do something. "Andrea took the thin cigarette to his lips and inhaled deeply. It was like he'd been smoking all of his young life. The way he smoked made him look older than his years."

Maybe. It might be cool to hang out with Avellini, although he likes Boca Juniors. Everyone goes to the park, which is the other way from my house. Damn it man, I'm going tomorrow. There's no choir practice in the afternoon, and if I don't actually do something, I might as well forget this diary business altogether.

The bell rang, and I hurried to the bathroom to try to avoid ShirtTail and Miguel, with whom I usually walk home. I had some vague lie about checking out the trumpets at Marcelo's Music, but I wasn't sure that would have deterred Miguel, and so instead of describing the thrill of inhaling tobacco, I'd have to nothing to write but the boring discussion of Kanstul versus Yamaha horns.

I waited ten minutes. Was that enough? I decided to wait another five, giving Miguel and ShirtTail the opportunity to wait for me awhile and then leave and also for the cool smoker kids to set up and get comfortable in the park. It was hot and I was sweating as I left the john.

I walked slowly, trying to notice the details, the world before my first cigarette. I saw Mrs. Batista on the corner near Harrods and she smiled, started to speak to me and then changed her mind and just stared. She probably wondered what I was doing there by myself. I straightened up and tried to look like I had business. I knew I would remember her black hair done high, her cat-eye sunglasses and her sleeveless white blouse.

I decided to increase my pace. I was already in trouble for not telling anyone I wasn't going straight home, and I was anxious to smoke the cigarette and get home to write about it. I walked fast through the big orange gate. I cut across a grass football pitch, the sun in my eyes and hot on my forehead, and saw Avellini sitting on the top edge of a bench, ciggy in his left hand, talking seriously to some kid from the upper grades. I didn't have a plan for how to approach him. I didn't want to butt in. Maybe this wasn't such a good idea after all. I bent down to retie my shoe, and the older kid magically walked away. Avellini saw me. I stood up. This was the dialogue:

"Hey."

"Hey. Isn't your house the other way?"

"You're right."

"So what are you doing here?"

"Looking for a smoke."

"You smoke? I ain't never seen you."

"Sure I smoke, once in a while."

"Long way out of your way for just a cigarette."

"I got stuff to do over here."

"So, you need a light?"

"I'm fresh out. Smoked my last on the way here. Can I borrow one of yours?"

"Marlboro Reds okay?"

"I love Marlboro, thanks."

And these were the gestures:

I shrugged. He frowned. I turned and looked behind me. He smiled. I nodded. He took a puff and flicked his ash down. I shrugged and nodded. He puffed and squinted. I smiled. He nodded. I shrugged. He stretched out his legs and reached into his pocket and withdrew a pack of cigarettes, which he held out to me. I took the pack, tapped one out and handed the pack back to him. I put the cigarette between my lips.

These were my feelings:

Hope, mild confusion, mild fear and embarrassment, hope again, excitement, cleverness, excitement and fear, gratitude and excitement.

Avallini held out his lighter and ignited the flame. I leaned over with my hands at my sides (I didn't want to appear too eager) and he moved the flame to the cigarette tip. I sucked.

My lungs exploded in coughing. I had just enough time to bring my right hand up to my mouth to keep the cigarette from shooting out. My eyes watered, and I couldn't inhale any air. A deep hack came up, and I bent double, trying to catch my breath. I heard Avallini laugh. The Marlboro was still between my lips as I tried to breathe a third time. My lungs felt seared. I removed the cigarette from my lips as a deep, barking, dry, hacking cough erupted from the center of my body. I could not catch my breath. Avallini, chuckling, slapped me on my back.

"Breathe, breathe, you're okay."

I had tears in my eyes.

I caught my breath, but another cough interrupted, a bit less violent. I handed the cigarette back to Avalinni.

I am writing this sixteen days later.

I will never smoke another cigarette.

I will never do a thing just to write about it.

I will not need to write in my diary every day if nothing noteworthy happens.

I got up early, dressed quickly and quietly and made it out the house without Hector or Nicholas waking up. I didn't want any questions, trivial or otherwise, and I wanted to avoid all newspapers and any other media intrusions. Another hot day. I drove with the radio off, got a latte at a Starbucks drive-through and tried to clear my head. We had a body, the body of a priest, his face destroyed by a shotgun blast. The method of murder, coupled with the chosen site, was significant, obviously, but its significance was still unclear. Although identification was found at the scene, I wasn't convinced that the wallet's owner was the killer: that would be too easy, too obvious. There was something else going on. The victim was a foreigner, a stranger, with possibly an illicit past, which might have provided a motive for his homicide. And what about that weird Pooh-Bah, the father who fathered those kids and molested the altar boys? With a shotgun? Some sort of raged revenge, directed at the institution rather than the individual? Or was it random? A Colfax PCP robbery gone wrong? There were notes here, snatches of melody and a few chords, but nothing was fitting together yet. Maybe today would provide.

There were a couple of reporters surrounding the gate to the parking garage, and I shook my head as I drove past. Wondered what Clark would say about that. When I got up to the case room, I wasn't the first one in. Maldonado was standing behind one of the female detectives, Lassus, looking at something on her computer screen. Sergeants Bull and Campion were comparing notes from their notebooks, and Detective Derore, unlit cigarette in his mouth, was furiously typing into his computer. I saw Elizondo in front of two monitors, looking into one then the other. Maldonado noticed me and waved with two fingers, then hurried across the room. I stopped and waited for him. He had on a nice grey suit, a blue shirt and a green-and-white striped tie, which clashed. "The Argentinian Consulate has been calling. They heard about the murder and want to know when we'll release the body. His family want to bury him back in Buenos Aires."

"I don't know. Do we have the medex report yet?"

"I think she emailed. I got something from them but I haven't opened it yet."

"Elizondo find anything new on Vidal?"

"He's digging. Vitalsky landed in Mexico City. He'll call or email when he finds anything."

"Anything on Martinez?"

"Not yet. We keep leaving messages with his AO."

I don't know why I left so quickly. Maldonado's irritating tie was no reason to run off. I wanted to be alone, maybe, but solitude could have been easily arranged by simply continuing to my office and shutting the door. I'd deal with the likely redundant medex report and the likely annoying Argentinian Consulate and hope for some new information soon.

Mullen and Wolff, the taller one looking all of sixteen, were chatting away near the coffee counter. One nodded and included me in the conversation. "The priests were all gone, place was deserted. I couldn't find anybody there. Finally, I see this cleaning lady, from Uruguay or something, had this thick accent. I showed her the picture of Martinez and she kept saying '*Sí Sí, asesinato, asesinato,*' like he was the one who was killed. Tried to explain that no, he wasn't the victim, but she kept repeating, over and over, '*asesinato, asesinato.*'"

"Maybe she meant Martinez was the assassin? Did she see anything?"

"No. Assassin is *el asesino,* different word."

"You sure?"

He nodded. "We're going back out this morning to interview the priests who weren't there last night."

"What's this cleaning lady's name?"

He looked in his notebook. "Valeria Canassa."

"What was she doing there on a Sunday night? Talk to Maldonado before you go: we should probably question her again."

There was no one behind the bar, and the muted red dining room held only a silent middle-aged couple and a lone man in a suit reading a newspaper. He welcomed the artificial coolness. He glanced around, searching for a waiter or someone to serve him. The man with the newspaper spoke without looking up, "Someone'll be out. Everyone's in back."

"*Grazie,*" he heard himself say. "Thank you." His throat was dry.

He sat down heavily on a stool at the bar. He searched around for a clock but didn't see one. He was very thirsty. Finally, a tall thin man with an overly bright purple shirt and black tie came out and began to pour a glass from a *fiasco* chianti bottle. He drank the glass down in one gulp. "Ray," the man with the newspaper said. "You have a customer."

Ray smiled. "Father. Welcome. Are you here for a late lunch?"

"Yes, yes, a late lunch. What time is it?"

"Almost two. Would you like to eat at the bar? Or perhaps a booth in the dining room?"

"A booth in the dining room."

"Of course. Please follow me."

He remained sitting. "May I have a glass of water please? It is very warm."

"Yes, of course. There you go." As he drank, the man with the suit from the dining room walked up to the bar, put his newspaper down and handed over his bill and credit card. The water was cold and tasteless. He glanced down at the newspaper: something about the Denver Broncos, a sports team, he guessed.

The man left without taking his paper. "May I?" he asked Ray.

"No problem. It's too bad about that priest who was shot, yeah?"

He nodded. He hoped to avoid such conversation.

Ray shrugged as he wiped the bar. "I didn't know him or anything. We get the Mount Carmel priests and sometimes the Italians from Louisville. Not so popular with the Basilica crowd. Where are you from?"

"Rome."

"Visiting Father Martinelli?"

"No. Just a tourist."

"Ready for your booth?"

"May I bring the newspaper?"

"Oh yes." He followed Ray though the dining room.

"Can I get you anything to start? A glass of wine? Cocktail?"

"I'd like more water, please. And perhaps some bread?"

"Yes, of course." Ray slid the menu gracefully across the table as Signelli sank deeply in the cushioned bench. "I'll be back with the bread and more water and to answer any questions you may have about the menu."

The menu boasted that all the macaroni was served with "Patsy's Original Spaghetti Sauce," likely a weighty *salsa di pomodoro alla napoletana* simmering since last Friday. He liked *capellini*, and maybe he could ask for just a little sauce, just to make it wet. And maybe some sausage as a *secondo*. Could he have sausage? What day was it? Wednesday, yes, he could eat meat. *Capellini*, with sausage afterward, with a glass of Sangiovese.

He folded the menu and placed it pointedly in front of him. He took a long drink of water, finishing it, the liquid cooling, *grazie Gesù, grazie.* Ray brought a basket of bread and another glass of ice water, setting them down carefully before him. "Do you have any questions about the menu?"

"No. I will take the *capellini*, with just a little sauce, please, on the edge. With sausage. And a glass of Sangiovese."

"Soup or salad?"

"Salad."

"Ranch, Italian, blue cheese or vinegar and oil?"

"The oil and vinegar, please."

"Anything else? Any appetizer?"

"*Grazie*, no."

Ray gathered up the menu and scurried off. He flipped open the cloth napkin covering the bread and placed a piece on his plate. It was American bread, white and thin. He unrolled his own napkin from the silverware and put it on his lap. *Benedic, Domine, nos et haec tua dona quae de tua largitate sumus sumpturi. Per Christum Dominum nostrum. Amen. Iube, domne, benedicere. Mensae caelestis participes faciat nos, Rex aeternae gloriae. Amen.*

He brought the bread to his mouth. It was feathery, insubstantial, and sugary, almost like cake. He chewed and swallowed quickly, keen to have something in his stomach. He placed another piece on his plate, broke a morsel off and chewed it more slowly. There wasn't much to chew. The bread dissolved rapidly in his mouth. He glanced at the newspaper, leaving it unfolded in front of him.

He ate rapidly, wanting to absorb the bread to weigh him down to the world. He still felt slight, itinerant, not floating so much but tentative, as if the gravity that attached him to the earth were temporary and unreliable. Such a state was making it difficult to think about Malachi and what to do. How dare he treat him with such disdain, such disrespect, *trattare a pesci in faccia.* And how much more difficult his task was now. The police were involved, and American police could be stubborn and intractable. What was he thinking, to expose this job to the eyes of the public?

He couldn't focus. He would eat, ask Ray to phone a taxi, then return to the rectory to rest.

Friday of the Octave of Easter, 1979
"Grace fills empty spaces but it can only enter where there is a void to receive it, and it is grace itself which makes this void."
Simone Weil—*Notebooks*

I have discovered grace. I know of no other way to explain it. I tremble as I write this. In Spanish, in my mother tongue. It came to me unexpectedly, the sweetness of absolute oblivion, the sweetness of His absolute presence. I am still overcome, still filled with the Holy Spirit, still filled with delightful traces of His all-embracing Goodness. There is no language for this. There are no symbols of His divine love.

I write to remember. I write to remember always, to remember that this union is possible, to remember that the self can be truly voided in order to welcome His Perfect Love. Oh holy night. I cannot contain my joy. I cannot contain my happiness in understanding that true ecstasy, the ecstasy that up to now had eluded me, is indeed possible and real. Grace is actual, possible and true. Thank You, Jesus. Thank You, Lord.

I need to be precise here, sober and somber. I need to control the words I use, so that the words do not replace the void of grace. But I need the words to remember, so I will be able to recall, in my moments of failure and despair, that such blessed emptiness, such divine voiding, is indeed possible and I have not spent my young life in vain. There is no formula here, no alchemical recipe that I can repeat at will. I understand. But still, to have a record of my oblivion, this is important.

It already seems like a lifetime ago, and yet it was mere hours earlier. Can this be right? I was weary after the heat and isolation of March and April and had a week before my exams, for which I was well prepared. I decided to take a trip not merely across the bay, to Montevideo, where I might meet up with someone I knew, but a little longer excursion up to Porto Alegre, where I had only been once with my father many years earlier and where the likelihood of meeting someone who might recognize me was greatly diminished. The trip was long, but I brought books, and soon I was hanging up my jacket in a small but comfortable room in Cidade Baixa, near the Rua Luiz Afonso. The room where I now write. The journey had tired me, but I wasn't sleepy, and I remember sitting on the bed and considering what to do: I could take a bath and call it a night, perhaps with the de Chardin I had to translate for my exam. But I had been reading and sitting all day, and my legs were restless. I decided to go out. To think now how close I came to remaining in that room, reading and studying, and thereby missing the sweet grace that was to follow. Oh Lord, thank You for my wandering, for the restiveness of my legs, for the energy I felt from being in this new city, alone and free. I looked at the full-length mirror on the door. I was thin, brown from the harsh sun and needed a shave. I want to the bathroom and washed my face, combed my hair, then changed my shirt into one slightly less rumpled. I put my coat back on, looked back at my abandoned satchel of books, locked the door and went out.

It was late, maybe one o'clock, but there were many people on the street, laughing, drinking and carrying on. A sharp chill was in the air, refreshing after the winter heat, and I was happy in my coat. I smelled meat cooking and realized I was hungry, as I'd had only a small *choripán* and a coffee on the ferry sometime around three. I thought I'd walk around a bit, get my legs some work and then duck into a bar to take something to eat.

I bought a beer from a vendor on the corner near where many couples were kissing against the walls. A bent old woman in a dark hood approached with an open palm, and I gave her a few *cruzeiros*, the change from my beer. The night seemed to burst open into possibilities, and I was happy watching the lively and beautiful young of the Brazilian street, drinking, kissing and appreciating the gift of life. I could see no sin, only innocence and friendly delight. A group of young women in Brazil football jerseys walked by arm in arm, eyes flashing, dark and beautiful, and I very much admired the ease with which they moved through the night, the gentleness with which they touched the world. I thought of how God's gifts can take many forms, including the sinewy smile of a beautiful black, and gave thanks for that brief glimpse of elegance and loveliness.

I am writing this to remind myself that last night, even before God's grace visited, even before my very self was voided into the night, was charmed. Music and laughter erupted from doorways, and the crowd of people on the sidewalk thickened. This is important. I remember, even before the miraculous events that I have yet to relate, that I was happy in my wanderings, that the night and the beauty surrounding prepared me or, more precisely, opened my soul up to the possibilities that followed. I know this language is inadequate.

I followed the sound of an accordion down a narrow alley, and came upon a group of people crowded around a small, elevated stage set up in an open garage where a tall, thin woman with short blonde hair sang in Spanish in front of a dark man with whiteface and a blue wig, seated and playing the accordion. The woman was exquisite, with thick black eyebrows and red red lips, and she sang in a deep, soft *cuyano* voice of betrayal and loneliness. I was always a fool for *cuyano* accents, and the way she moved, the way she leaned from the waist into the words of the *Chamamé*, fascinated, and so I finished my beer and made my way through the people to the front of the stage.

AGNUS DEI

Friday of the Octave of Easter, 1979.

She appeared older when I got closer, more thirty than twenty. Her eyes were open as she sang, but unfocused, looking out at the crowd at no one in particular. Her neck was long and unencumbered and seemed unnaturally white in the harsh lighting of the garage. She was wearing a short green dress of indistinguishable cut, and her bare legs looked thin and cold. She was wearing sandals, and her toenails were freshly painted the red of her lipstick.

I looked at her feet in front of me. Her ankles were very narrow and vulnerable, and her feet were long with pronounced arches, with a silver band on the big toe of her right foot. What was it like to paint her toenails that color and then to slip that silver ring over the knob of her big toe? And what did she think of her ankles? Was she proud of them? Did she believe them attractive, a good feature, to be emphasized with skirts and such? Or was she indifferent to them, thinking them unworthy of thought, simply a connection between leg and foot? They appeared so fragile. Did they bother, cause her any sort of pain or embarrassment? Her hips swayed slightly, but she didn't move that much.

The accordion and her voice intertwined, then separated and danced, a light, flirtatious 6/8. There was no guitar, but they didn't miss it: the accordion trilled with the right hand and kept the beat with the left. She sang of the river, and how her lover once went to the river and never came back. This was sad, true, but she was beginning to realize that there were perhaps other lovers. The accordion sang of something deeper and more mysterious than sadness, a dance on the very edge of melody where movement and note seemed almost random.

I couldn't take my eyes off her. She didn't move her feet much, only lifting up her heels, one then the other, in time to the beat. I tried to imagine seeing those ankles and feet in different contexts: at dinner in a long, flowing skirt, her legs crossed at the knee; walking on the Pinmar beach; sitting at a café in San Telmo, a stray cat around her feet; and yes, getting out of bed, surrounded by the whitest sheets. I forced myself to look away. I couldn't look away.

It was difficult to see her face, given where I was standing and the strange lighting bright on her neck. But as her ankles danced, I focused on the smoothness of the skin covering the thin bones,and the very high arch of her foot, the ball of her foot, the encasing of the heel in worn leather and how the thong of the sandal had rubbed a callous into the big toe of her left foot. I looked closely at the small, slightly oval circumference where her leg met her foot, and how supple and flexible it seemed, but too thin, too thin and tenuous, as if the structure was really too delicate to support the body, and could only do so temporarily, with tricks and deception. It was this provisional quality, this promise of imminent and inevitable collapse, that fascinated me, as it was there, between the calf and the foot, where her being, even soul, for lack of a better term, was located.

I don't want to go on, but I do wish to write, to remember, that these ankles, along with her soaring voice and the plaintive accordion, prepared me for what followed. Without the beauty and perfection I found at the mouth of this shabby garage, the truth of what followed, the truth of God's grace, would not have been revealed.

Just as the song ended, I heard a voice in my right ear, "Very nice, yes, but a bit skinny for my tastes." I turned reluctantly, annoyed about having to look away, to a pale unshaven face with dark circles around the blue eyes, a long nose, a high forehead bordered by spikes of silver hair and a missing bottom tooth on the left side. It was Chula, an old friend of my brother Santiago. This was exactly the type of encounter I hoped to avoid. I hadn't seen Chula in six or seven years, not since I started university. He was the polite one of Santi's friends, with courteous talk for my mother and gentle teasing for me. I had some vague memory of Chula wanting to take orders too, maybe the Benedictines, but washing out early or something. Out of the corner of my eye, I noticed the accordion player stand, and the singer back away from the lip of the stage. Applause followed, scattered and brief. I swiveled back toward the stage in time to see the singer pivot and walk back toward an unused drum kit, step offstage and into the darkness.

Chula laughed. "You have stars in your eyes, little Drea. Ana is beautiful, yes, but perhaps, oh, never mind."

"You know her?"

"We share a mutual interest."

"Where is she going?"

"That I do not know."

I didn't know what more to say. I would have liked to figure out a way to follow Ana. Perhaps she was singing somewhere else,or was going to a party or a restaurant. I didn't want to waste the night with Chula, but maybe he could help me.

"Do you have any idea where she might go? Is she singing someplace tonight?"

"No, Drea, no." He looked down, lowered his voice. "I have something better. Do you have any money?"

Ah, so that was it. He wanted to get high or something. I wasn't in the mood. "I have a couple thousand *pesos* and four or five hundred *cruzeiros* or so. Not much." I had more but wanted to be on my way.

"That it? No dollars?"

"No dollars."

He leaned closer to me. "Drea, I know you're not like your brother. Santi was always afraid, afraid of himself, afraid of life. I have something to show you, something to share with you. But we need more cash."

"What are you on about?"

He took my elbow and steered me away from the stage. "Let's walk." We moved quickly through an alley, and then out into a narrow side street, abandoned and poorly lit. He stopped next to chain-link fence and lit a cigarette. I was impatient. "What's up?"

He smiled. "You ever chase the dragon?"

"Heroin?"

"No, no, no. Smoke opium. Pure. With pipes. I know some Chinese guys."

"Some Chinese guys?"

He smiled again. "You asked how I know Ana. This is how I know Ana."

A good-looking black guy of about thirty was leaning against the wall near my office door, sipping from a Styrofoam cup. I usually don't like beards, but his goatee wasn't bad, flecks of grey, and it went well with his sharp face and close-cropped head. Sneakers, jeans, work shirt, leather vest, he slouched very well. "Detective Fruscella?" Deep basso profundo voice.

"Yeah?" Soft brown eyes, nice teeth. He stood up straight.

"Des Prez, from Vice, Second Precinct. I hear you want to see me. About Willem Martinez. Willie Boy, the Sergeant."

I opened my door and motioned him in. He had a slight limp. "Sit down, des Prez. Thank you for coming down." I closed my door and walked around my desk and sat. "Why the Sergeant?"

He sat down awkwardly and grimaced. "From *Platoon*. Willem Dafoe." He took another sip from his cup. "You're working the priest killing, I assume."

I found his folder, took out his DL photo blown up and slid it across the desk. "This him?"

He nodded.

"So you know Willem, the Sergeant?"

"I do. Willie's a party. I guess you could call him a facilitator. He loves to have a good time. A good time for Willie means getting high, loaded and laid. And the more the merrier."

"So Willie's a party? He deal drugs?"

"I've never known Willie to sell anything. He gives the shit away. He finds it, buys it and gives it away. That's not really dealing."

"If he doesn't deal, where's he get his money? He have a job?"

"Doubt it. I think his family's got bucks. He goes through it like it ain't never going to run out." Des Prez rubbed his right knee.

"Are you all right?"

"Fine."

"So how do you know Willie? Are you running him?"

"No. I busted him once for possession when we were doing that Colfax cleanup. He sent me a note couple days later, saying to check out a certain hotel room where a certain player was pimping underage poon...er, underage girls. I did. It was legit, so we keep each other in mind. A few favors now and then. But no, I'm not running him."

"Where does he live?"

"No idea." He rubbed his knee again and took a sip from his cup.

"How do you contact him?"

"I don't. I said I'm not running him. He disappears for months at a time, then'll show and party hard for a month, then disappear again. Sometimes I'll get a note—always about underage pimping or underage drug dealing, the nasty stuff—and sometimes I won't. Always typed on the back of a postcard and sent through the U.S. mail in an envelope. I don't know where he goes or what he does otherwise, but when he's in town, he likes to go off. I won't say he's harmless, but he's not really in my list of top ten problems, if you know what I mean. Not even the top hundred."

"Does he go to detox, maybe? The months he's not around, does he go to rehab?"

Des Prez shook his head. "Willie's not the rehab type. He doesn't regret anything; he's not running away or trying to forget. No, he likes what he's doing, is serious about it, like he's got a project or purpose or something." He chuckled, showed his white teeth, rubbed his knee. "Like it's his job almost. A job he loves."

"So you don't think he was meeting any priests for counseling or anything."

He shook his head. "Maybe he was, how should I say this, inviting one or two of the good fathers to one of his celebrations? What's the connection between Willie Boy and the priests?"

"That's exactly what I'm trying to find out. He bang with anyone?"

"Doubt it. Not his style."

"Does he have a potential for violence?"

"Willie's not harmless, but I've never had any trouble with him. His sheet's all drugs and whores, isn't it?"

I took a sip of my coffee, looked him straight and serious in his big brown eyes. "Any idea where I can find Willie?"

He hesitated for a while. "You might try the Satire. But I don't know where he lives."

"What have you done for him?"

"Detective?"

"You said you did each other a few favors, kept each other in mind. What favors have you done for him?"

"I never looked the other way, if that's what you're thinking."

I shook my head.

He sighed. "I haven't done much. A couple of years ago, I picked up some mail for him. From an old address, a place he didn't live anymore, a place that was going to be torn down."

"Was that on Osage?"

"Long time ago. Could have been."

"Was his driver's license there? In that mail you picked up?"

"There was a pile. I didn't look."

Hmm. "Where did you deliver this mail? Did you meet on a corner?"

"No. I gave it to the bartender at the Satire. I got a postcard from Willie thanking me about a week later."

"Bartender got a name?"

"I know him as Jimmy. He works days."

"Two years ago?"

He scratched his head, and then rubbed his knee. "Two years ago March, maybe beginning of April."

"When did you last see Mr. Martinez?"

"I last saw him last February. I heard he was in town in April but I didn't see him in person."

"How did you hear he was in town?"

"I'm not sure. Maybe from some guys at the Satellite I busted for X."

"Who does Martinez hang with when he's here? Besides Jimmy at the Satire? He got a crew? A girlfriend?"

"I honestly don't know, Detective. Whenever I've seen him, he's never alone, but I don't think he hangs with a regular crew. And I've never seen him with the same woman twice. But like I said, he's not a big blip on my radar: he doesn't sell, doesn't corrupt minors and usually doesn't cause a scene. Nobody complains about Willie; the opposite in fact. He just likes to try stuff."

I stood up. "Thanks for coming in, des Prez. I appreciate it. Call me if you think of anything."

He stood up and nodded. "You bet." He limped out.

He looked at the newspaper. He was not particularly anxious to read about the killing of Vidal. Italian newspapers seldom provided facts, and the facts they did offer were already known to those except the very stupid. And any newspaper, like this *Denver Post*, that allowed news about a sports team to occupy three-quarters of its front page did not inspire hope. He turned the page and looked, then turned the page again. It was on page five, a half-page article detailing the current state of the investigation.

It was now three days since the murder, and, according to the article, the investigation didn't seem to be progressing very successfully. The police were focused on a "person of interest," but as yet he hadn't been located. Just as Malachi had said. There were a few meaningless quotes from a Lieutenant Clark, who was not the investigating officer but belonged to something called the Office of Public Information. He detested such men, like Father Rubelli from the Vatican Information Service, a tall, unctuous fellow who smoked thin women's cigars and was missing his left arm. Such men were good only for giving shit the appearance of gold. Who was the investigating detective? Francesca Fruscella. A woman and an Italian. Maybe this was lucky? She wasn't Irish at least. He was tired of the Irish. He put another morsel of bread into his mouth.

He saw a flash of purple out of the corner of his eye and looked up to see Ray approaching with a wooden bowl of greens in his left hand, a holder for carafes of vinegar and oil hooked to the fingers of his right and a half-meter-long wooden pepper grinder, also in his right. He deftly placed the bowl on the table, followed by the carafes and straightened the grinder like a small aspergillum before him. "Would you like fresh ground pepper for your salad?"

He'd forgotten that the Americans served the salad before the *primo* and was disappointed that he'd have to wait for his *capellini*. "No, thank you." The purple disappeared quickly, almost magically. The bowl before him was mostly *lattuga iceberg* with a few leaves of *romana*. There were cubes of dried bread, a slice of pale tomato and thickish slivers of raw onion. No *scarole* or rocket to be found. But he was hungry, and he eagerly poured out a helping of oil along with a splash of vinegar. He mixed the greens and dressing with his fork, separated the onion to the side, then, spearing a few leaves, he took a bite of the salad. There was not much flavor to the lettuce, and the oil was thin and watery. It was, he supposed, better than nothing. He quickly folded another forkful into his mouth and chewed. The leaves were crunchy and cold, but there was little taste, no suggestion of the soil or the sun, of provenance or even of material. He cut a piece of tomato with his knife and included that in the next bite, which lacked flavor as the previous, the tomato adding only a slippery surface to the crispness of the greens. How could anyone eat such tasteless food?

The article continued on a following page. Some background on Vidal, a mercifully brief mention of the Legionaries and Maciel's scandal. It was unfortunate the archbishop was away: an official statement from the diocese might help discourage any journalistic reheating of Maciel's disgrace and the surrounding gossip. The tone of the article didn't betray any zealotry or even particular interest in the deep background of the murder, but perhaps his English was not good enough to grasp the curiosity of the writer. Two writers, a Samuel Brown and a Sylvia Brunjak. Vidal wasn't American, and a recent immigrant, so he would have no vocal advocate clamoring for justice, but even the smallest scent of dishonor from the Church often attracted crowds, like flies around *quinto quarto*, and recooked *la pajata* was often tastier than the original.

Malachi must know someone in the local police: how else could he arrange a meeting? The vinegar was harsh: stronger leaves might have forced it into the appropriate background, but these watery vegetables in his bowl were overpowered. He looked again at the police officer's name: Francesca Fruscella. It would be wise to obtain some information about this woman. He would investigate on the Internet when he returned to the rectory. He had some experience dealing with various legal institutions in Europe, and primarily, if not exclusively, these dealings had been with men. There were a few female *avvocatas* sprinkled here and there, and he remembered a *donna* judge in New York, but mostly the women he had come into contact with were either victims or secretaries. Never a prosecutor or *commisario*. Was she married, this Francesca? A mother? Perhaps a lesbian. She was likely not young. The image he was constructing of a middle-aged, pushy, unhappy American woman was not an attractive one, nor one who was easily susceptible to the influence of the Church. He was already beginning to dislike this Francesca.

His salad bowl was empty, save for the onions. He burped softly into his napkin: he had eaten too rapidly and that would likely cause him later discomfort. He thought of his neighbor of the night previous, the noises that emitted from his digestion that had startled and awakened him more than once. Then he thought of his own nocturnal outburst and felt shamed.

He turned pages of the newspaper but could find nothing else of interest. The article had been rather perfunctory, focusing more on the investigation than the victim, which was to be expected. There was no mention of the crime elsewhere: no comments by the columnists, no letters of grief, no *annuncio funebre* he could find. Father Andrea Vidal would not be missed in Denver, USA. Perhaps in Argentina. Not in Roma.

Friday of the Octave of Easter, 1979

I was looking for one thing and found another. Thanks be to God. For what I found was the sweetness, the joy, the terrifying separation, the absolute violence of Jesus's grace and love. I struggle to find the words, even in Spanish. I became nothing, a nothingness that opened to the space of the Lord.

I did have hope of seeing Ana last night, yes. But I was also intrigued by the promise of opium. I had never tried it before. And there was electricity in the night.

"How much?"

"For the two of us? Fifty American dollars."

I nodded.

There's no need to detail the twenty-minute taxicab ride, nor the long walk past a large hospital, silhouetted against a yellow moon. Conversation was stiff and soon died: Chula and I never had much in common, and besides, I was thinking about Ana and the bones and skin of her ankles. And her white neck. And we were both looking forward, I suppose, in very different ways, to what we believed would follow.

We came upon a darkened plaza, or maybe a parking lot, with junked cars scattered about, some with small campfires and vague shapes moving. It smelled like burned woodsmoke, cooking oil and plantains. A slight mist smudged the scene. Chula walked toward the center, hesitated, then bent over one of the fires and murmured to a child warming her hands. Chula stood quickly and walked into the shadows. The moon was soon obscured by a tall, looming building on the right.

I wasn't afraid. The entire night, I was never afraid. This was not due to any great strength on my part. I was not afraid because last night I could sense the real presence of Our Lord Jesus Christ in everyone I met or came into contact with. There was no evil surrounding me, only the deprivations of poverty, deprivations that sometimes force people into the extraordinary. But the extraordinary is not the same thing as evil. Or as sin.

We made our way to a low wall, and Chula followed it, and I followed Chula, the fingertips of my left hand lightly scraping against the rough cinderblocks. I heard low music coming from in front of us and could see flickers of light over Chula's shoulder. He turned and said something that I didn't catch. I noticed a sweet, sugary smell, barely perceptible against the night's damp mist.

We ducked below some tangled metal shape, visible only as a slightly darker outline, and came upon a small campfire, with what appeared to be an old woman sitting behind it, holding a stick in the fire. A few small flames would spark and then disappear behind her. The woman looked up, said nothing, then lowered her gaze back to the fire. The sweet smell was stronger here, not unpleasant. Chula turned to me, his back to the old woman. "How much you really have?"

"Dollars?"

"Yes."

"Sixty-three."

He held out his hand, and I took my wallet and handed over the American bills. He pivoted quickly and walked over to the campfire, where he kneeled down next to the woman. Chula spoke to her in Spanish, then switched to French and finally English. The woman kept shaking her head, saying "no, no," over and over again. Chula was patient, and he spoke for quite a long time, addressing or ignoring the woman's repeated objections. Finally she set her stick carefully down on the dirt and, after a while, held our her hand, which Chula covered with his own, transferring the money.

Chula stood, his face warmed by the fire and by anticipation. He motioned me to follow him with a flick of his head. We walked past the campfire and found a path through a small yard of bushes and tall weeds, then made a sharp right past what looked like a Volkswagen turned on its side, until we came to an old school bus surrounded by gravel. The door swung open as we approached, and a powerful torch illuminated Chula's face, then my own. Chula said something quietly to the light, which was quickly extinguished, and we climbed into the bus. Behind the driver's seat was a partition of wood, and a dim narrow hallway ran down the bus on the passenger side. A short, stocky man sat in the driver's seat. He held up four fingers, and Chula moved quickly into the hallway. We passed three doors, and I followed him into the fourth.

It was a little larger than a closet, illuminated by a bulb hanging from a cord draped over a screw set into the metal ceiling. A translucent red cloth had been thrown over the bulb to soften the illumination. The seats had been removed, and plywood had been placed on the floor, on which two thin mats were arranged parallel, each with a dirty-looking pillow leaning against the far metal wall. The walls on either side were made of old tin sheets painted various colors, haphazardly tacked to the floor and to one another. Between the mats, about a quarter of the way from the far wall, a rectangular tray held various objects of undetermined function. The room smelled of sweat and incense.

Chula struggled off with his coat, although it was just as damp and cold as it had been outside, rolled it up, placed it near the pillow and lay down on his back, his hands webbed under his head. I kept my jacket on and sat, back against the steel of the bus. I looked down at the tray but didn't know what I was looking at. I hadn't really expected to see Ana again, but I knew she wouldn't be in that bus anytime soon, and I was disappointed.

"Now what?"

"Flower smoke."

"What's that?"

"You'll find out, my friend."

COMMUNIO

The Memorial of Saint Francis of Assisi, 1995

It's only recently that I've considered audience. When I was young (was I ever?) I just needed to write. My memory has never failed: in fact, as I read over many of my entries, I am often able to supplement the incident and my reactions, adding a gesture or extending the dialogue or expanding on my thought processes and emotions. I can clarify things, adding to the naïve experiences the wisdom of additional distance and additional experiences: the arc often becomes clear only with time, and only by rereading and remarking can I discern the significance of events, the truth of this writing. Sometimes it seems as if I cannot control my pen: it's my duty to complement, elaborate, clarify. But I never cross out or contradict.

But not everything becomes evident or certain. There are still false roads, *cul-de-sacs*, mistakes and insignificance masquerading as consequence and vice versa. But, as I said, until recently it would have mattered only to myself. And to God.

There is the unavoidable question of blasphemy. I emphasize this as a question, unanswered, perhaps unanswerable. To put the problem simply: if I sin and write these sins down without guilt or repentance, isn't the act of putting these sins into language an additional sin? Perhaps even a greater sin? Wouldn't the recording of sin, coolly, without passion, after the fact, and in concrete language, be more offensive to God than to sin in the heat of passion, in the middle of the battle, so to speak, in real time? If sinning causes pain to God, wouldn't the description of this act be painful again? It would not matter that the pain initially was caused inadvertently, if the one who caused the pain, who committed the sin, did not know he was causing pain, did not believe he was sinning. To be almost proud of these transgressions, to not only commit them without guilt but then to record them without the shame: that is true pride, true blasphemy.

But is it blasphemy? Am I an apostate? Is my writing heretical—that is, does it attack God or faith? No, it does the opposite. Much of what I've done and recounted in my *diarios* has been with the express intent to negate my self and come closer to God. I do not deny God, ever. I worship our Lord God, His Son Jesus Christ, the Holy Sprit, and the Holy Catholic and Apostolic Church. My writing is a testament to my worship. These *diarios* are the story of a man who has dedicated himself, body, mind and soul, as completely as he could, to the Lord. As best he could. Is my writing imprecatory; does it curse God? No. My writing is one long prayer. In praise of freedom and grace. And is it contumacious? Does it express indignation or contempt? No, only impatience. And self-doubt. And wonder. By these criteria, the criteria of the catechism, my *diarios* are not blasphemy. But perhaps the catechism is limited? Perhaps I am reading incorrectly? Perhaps I'll never know.

I have done everything I can to write only to myself and to my God. I know neither. I write to find both. I do not understand the relationship between a writer and a reader, although I will guess that this relationship, like many (all?), is a relationship dependent upon desire. I will not begin to guess what God desires. What do I desire? As a reader? Or a writer? To not be read. To not be read by another. If I could keep my writing from God, would I? If I were to answer yes, wouldn't that suggest that I had secrets from God, that I possessed a self or an ego that wanted to remain apart from God, that desired an existence separated from God? But if I answer no, I keep nothing from God, doesn't my lack of shame at some of the deeds I've accomplished imply a great pride or ego? Isn't there the stain of contumacious blasphemy here, in that the prideful recounting of sin exhibits a real disdain for Our Lord?

I will need to be more careful with the concealing of the book and the veiling of any inculpating information. I will not be more prudent with the content. Never. I will not lie, either by commission or omission.

These questions haunt, but I keep writing.

It was just after nine a.m., too early for the Satire and Jimmy the Bartender. Perhaps I could gather some more background on the victim. I would avoid the Basilica for now and hope that maybe the Jesuits at Regis would be more welcoming. I stuck my head out the door, saw Detective Lassus and asked her to telephone Regis University and see if I could meet with someone in an hour or so to discuss Catholic organizations and administrative duties. Before I had returned to my seat, she buzzed and said that a Professor Randall Kirkpatrick, Chair of the Catholic Studies Department, had a class at eleven but could meet us anytime before. I asked Detective Lassus if she felt like taking a ride.

She carried herself well, did Detective Lassus, with simple dark blue suede Arche flats, slightly tanned hose, a navy blue pencil skirt and a white short sleeve blouse. The hose was a nice professional touch, because it was going to be hot again. She wore her dark hair in a French braid, which I might have minded but didn't. She drove fast and well, and we didn't make small talk.

A rather frumpy young receptionist nodded when I identified myself and asked to see Professor Kirkpatrick. We followed her down a modern but dimly lit hallway, doors all closed, until we reached an intersection and turned right, where an open door streamed light into the hallway on the far left. An unsmiling and unseeing student brushed past us, and the receptionist knocked on the open door and motioned for me to enter. "Professor Kirkpatrick: Detectives Fruscella and Lassus to see you."

Professor Kirkpatrick, a somewhat overweight man with the biggest double chin I had ever seen, rose to greet us. He was young, thirty-five maybe, and dressed in the black shirt, black pants, black shoes uniform of the urban priest. His face was clean-shaven and almost glistened. His second chin was neither sagging nor taut, neither jowly nor goiterlike, but almost natural in its pinkish health and vigor. It extended down in splendor, covering his throat, and reached down to his clavicle. His eyes were pale blue and serious, his hair longish and black.

I shook his hand. His body wasn't nearly fat enough to deserve that chin. "Detectives, please sit down."

"Professor. Thank you for seeing us. As you may know, a priest was murdered in the Basilica last night…"

He shook his head, "Terrible, terrible thing…"

"… and we are attempting to understand more of the victim's background and maybe to find a context for who might have wanted him dead, murdered in, well, that specific fashion and location." I remembered when boys in high school would stare at my boobs the same way I couldn't help staring at his chin.

"And you thought of me?"

"We are questioning the staff at the Basilica, of course, but I thought another, perhaps neutral or uninvolved perspective, would be useful." With my peripheral vision I noticed a dark red bookcase behind him and a matching desk with a closed Apple laptop in front. His desk was cluttered with papers, a telephone and opened books. There were no plants visible, and the walls were bare.

"And what questions might you have?"

"Father Vidal, the victim, belonged to the Legionaries of Christ, an organization headquartered in Mexico City. From our preliminary research, we've gathered this was a rather controversial organization. Can you give us any background on this?"

He answered quickly. "I'm sorry, I cannot. This is not my area of study. I assumed you had questions of theology, not inquiries regarding rumors about the Church."

I frowned, looked over at Lassus. She frowned too and shook her head. I turned back to Kirkpatrick. "We are conducting a murder investigation, Professor, and Detective Lassus made it clear to you that we need information regarding the victim's past."

"I did not speak to you personally. I am sorry you were misinformed." He abruptly stood up and held out his hand. "I wish you luck with your investigation."

I sighed and stood. "Is there anyone here who can help us? It's important."

He moved slowly around his desk and ushered us to his door and into the hallway. He brought his right hand to his mouth and then dropped it.

"Thank you for your time," I said to a closing door.

Lassus's neck was bright red. "I explained exactly what we wanted to his secretary: there was no room for misunderstanding."

"Did someone get to him? Tell him not to talk to us?" We walked to the intersection and turned.

"Did you see that chin?"

I chuckled. I usually don't appreciate discussions about the physical features of others and often display my disapproval quickly and unmistakably, but I found Professor Kirkpatrick a bit of a dick, worthy of any ridicule he and his chin elicited. "It was hypnotizing me: I couldn't keep my eyes off it."

The young frump was not at the desk, replaced by an older woman, I'd say fifty-five, with a soft smile and a silver '60s beehive. She sported a purple-and-green jeweled eyeglass chain around her neck, fastened to the earpieces of a pair of black cat-eyes. She wasn't a small woman, broad shouldered, maybe five-ten and one-sixty, with a floral print rose-and-lavender knee-length flare dress, a little tight on the top. I appreciated the fact that her outfit choices ignored both this century and her own body.

He had no idea what this book he had been asked to retrieve contained. He knew better than to inquire. He supposed it had something to do either with money—Father Maciel was wealthy and he knew wealthy people; embarrassment—Maciel was a drug addict, conartist and child molester who had powerful and potentially vulnerable friends; or some combination of the two. He guessed that Vidal was likely complicit in Maciel's sins but doubted his sins were so great to be unforgivable. The book was not worth his life.

Except that it was.

Perhaps there was blackmail involved. It was possible, even likely, that Vidal himself was of no threat. The fact that he had been reassigned to Denver instead of Africa or some other place more uncomfortable suggested a deal had been struck: to remain silent in exchange for the opportunity to live out his life still comfortably sheltered within the bosom of the Church. And the book was his guarantee, whereby Vidal would promise to keep it unread if left alone. But someone had thought the deal unfair. And that someone knew someone who knew someone else, and he had received a phone call. And then he in turn had telephoned Malachi.

He was in no mood or condition for such speculation. His mind was unnatural, his thinking jagged, the concerns of his body intrusive. And there were many obstacles to understanding. There was Malachi and the man Malachi had hired. There were the American police and their female investigator, Francesca Fruscella. And there was Vidal's background: secretary to that fraud Maciel. And finally, there was the crucial and overriding, ubiquitous and unbreakable requirement for discretion. For silence.

This was a great deal to pray about.

He looked up and saw the older couple to his left. He hadn't noticed before, but they were sitting diagonally across the table from one other, not directly. They were eating without noise, without conversation: every so often the woman would give a furtive glance to her husband, his head bent severely over his food, his arm stretched and bent on the table as if protecting his plate. There was something about their silence that signaled a worn intimacy, an unspeakable adherence to one another, a lengthy and habitual forced truce that would kill one within weeks of the other's death. Such was the choreography of dying attraction. The man raised his head to take a small sip of wine, and his wife hesitated, fork in midair... for what? Signelli didn't know. The wine was sipped, the glass replaced, the rhythm of feeding resumed. Her fork stayed there, suspended, waiting, waiting, until it rejoined the silent waltz of their wordless meal.

How would it be to live in such lengthy intimacy with another human being? A human being flawed, prickly and impatient or servile and self-effacing but above all, above everything, *there*, ever present, stubbornly, with whatever characteristics, extant, through months, then years, then decades of proximate coexistence. He had known a few people for many years: his confessor Father Zancredi, Father Mastroantonio, his brother Jacapo, Father Annuncio, there were a few others but no one with whom he shared intimate thought or habits. While he confessed to Father Zancredi, the relationship was one-sided, as he knew little of the father's own proclivities, desires, fears or behaviors. He knew that Zancredi was partial to Barolo and Sangrantino, didn't eat meat and was a fan of both Juventus and Aquinas, but these were peripheral, not essential, attributes. He could go months without seeing his brother, and then the conversation was often hurried, clumsy and short-lived. His mentors, Fathers Ciavonne first and later Father Diadosia, had died long ago. He kept up with few from seminary: many had emigrated, left the order or died. There was that Father Mastroantonio, who contacted him regularly to solicit his help obtaining a Vatican posting, but they had never been close.

His intimacy was with Jesus and His Holy Catholic Church. For this intimacy manifested itself most readily when he was physically alone. When he could free himself most completely from the distractions of the world, that was when he was able to enter into communion with the Lord Jesus Christ. In the darkness of solitude and prayer, that was the time when God would come to him. This was the intimacy that was consistent, trustworthy, vigorous and alive. Not the false and disappointing closeness of marriage or of fatherhood. He never ran out of things to say to Our Lord and never tired of Jesus's words of admonition or support. A wife would only distract. Until even the distraction grew cold. And a child or two: they would make solitude and prayer rare and difficult, until they fled. No, for him, he was happy in the Church, with his simple pleasures, opportunities for service and time for prayer. The alternative was unthinkable. *"Deus autem meus impleat omne desiderium vestrum secundum divitias in gloria in Christo Iesu."*

The old man abruptly sat up and pushed his plate away. The woman put her fork down and looked at the man.

Here was Ray with his *capellini* and Sangiovese.

"I asked for just a little sauce, and I brought you more on the side, in case you want more. We're famous for our sauce. I'll be right back with your sausage."

The Solemnity of Corpus Christi, 1982

I didn't write much in this original *diario*. There are a lot of blank pages and those beautiful wide margins. Once I thought that I wouldn't want the words of my sins to physically touch the words of Our Lord when the book was closed, and so I would write my sinful deeds and thought in the margins, on the same page of the prayers and days of the saints, adjacent but never touching. But at twelve, I didn't have many sins, and so the margins remained largely inviolate.

As did much of the verso as well. Everything's so scattered—given my aversion to chronology and following the system of dates—but it looks like I tried to keep up with it for a while at least; that's how I remember it and my memory's good. There's Latin here and Spanish of course and French but no English; my English was poor back then, my Italian nonexistent. But there's not much here, maybe twenty or so entries in all, and most entries less than half a page.

There's a lot I could add beneath what I did write and in the margins. I've since become an obsessive diarist. I didn't know anything back then. I didn't know that this kind of writing, the spiritual diary, is a tradition that goes back centuries: St. Augustine, St. Teresa, St. Ignatius, Catherine of Genoa, and these strange French ones of Soeur Jeanne des Anges, Armelle Nicolas, and Jean-Joseph Surin. I bought five A4 black Moleskines, unlined, when I started uni, and I've almost filled them up. I still begin writing always on the verso page, I still alternate often language from paragraph to paragraph, although I've added English and Italian to Latin, French and Spanish (and soon I might try Greek), and I still don't go in order: in fact, I try to go from one Moleskine to another, as randomly as I can. But now I write in the margins and in the margins of margins. I got the idea from studying the Talmud in my Judaism class, with all the interpretations and commentaries, and interpretation of the commentaries and commentary on the interpretations. I have five volumes of my personal Talmud, my own Mishnah and Gemara.

I'm going to Rome next week, to Pontifical Gregorian, to study for my PhD. Heavy and bulky as you are, I'm going to bring you with me, my dear *diario*, my originary text. And I'll buy you a nice fountain pen, a pen to write only in you, only on your thick, cream-colored pages, etched in gold. I will buy more Moleskines when I arrive, but I will keep you with me, as a souvenir and a reminder, a reminder of my Buenos Aires blood.

Lamentations

ONE

Friday of the Octave of Easter, 1979

An Asian woman, neither young nor old, with thin streaks of silver in her long black hair, slid quietly into the room, closed the door and sat cross-legged between us. She wore a light blue silk robe, cinched at the waist, and red satin slippers. She smiled and placed the long wooden box she was carrying next to the tray. Chula turned on his side to face her. She took a glass object in her right hand and with her left deftly lit a wick on the base, then returned the glass. All the while smiling. She then took a vial from one of the pockets of her bathrobe and poured a black liquid onto a large round copper spoon from the tray, after which she placed the spoon over the lamp. The liquid began to boil almost immediately, releasing that sweet, sugary smell I'd noticed earlier. We watched, and then she took thin wire and stirred the liquid, which now coagulated stringily around the wire. Expertly she gathered all of the black strings around the wire, and began to turn it slowly over the lamp, rubbing it occasionally against what looked like a whetstone, shaping it patiently into a small cone. She set the cone down on the edge of the tray still attached to the wire and removed a bellshaped bowl from the long box, along with a long, thick wooden tube or stem. Placing a small square of cloth beneath the bowl, she then screwed the bowl into the stem, about eight inches from the end, and looked up, motioning for me to lie flat on my side on the mat. Once I had done so, she handed the stem to me. Chula grunted, "She likes you."

She guided the bowl over the lamp and mimed for me to suck in through the stem. I did so, and she guided the bowl down to a few inches above the chimney and then grasped the wire and twirled it under the bowl. I continued to suck greedily but could feel or taste nothing. Once the pellet had been softened and shaped, she rotated the pipe gently so the hole was facing up and took the wire with the black cone on the tip and inserted the cone into the hole of the pipe. She then guided the hole to the lamp and motioned for me to suck. I did so and felt a warm, steamy vapor rise into my mouth and then my lungs.

A feeling of wonderful peace washed over me, starting with my chest and radiating outward to my head and limbs. Each wave that I inhaled brought more of this sweetness, more of this serenity: it was as if my soul, which was tense and twisted, was now beginning to relax into the natural ease of opening itself to God. I continued inhaling, but not greedily, as everything began to settle into a *natural*—I can think of no better word, perhaps *rightful* or *suitable*—pace and rhythm. I thought of Ana and those exquisite ankles, and yet it was somehow right that she was elsewhere. I shifted up on my elbow and looked at the woman watching me, waiting, the large copper spoon in her left hand. She sat there patiently, perfectly, beautifully, a small smile on her pale lips. My pipe was finished and I leaned back, rested my head on the pillow and closed my eyes. Colors danced slowly against my eyelids.

I held my breath in order to feel the rhythm of God.

After a time, I opened my eyes again, breathed deeply and looked over to the woman, who was busy forming another pellet with the wire and spoon. Her gestures were impeccable, no wasted or superfluous motion, and I felt more of my worry, my self, my I begin to melt away. She handed the pipe to me—our movements were perfectly choreographed—and soon I was tasting again the sweetest vapor and feeling the waves of this subtlest and quietest bliss wash over whatever of me remained.

I do not know how long this went on. I do know that time didn't matter, made no difference and that I was all the while both shedding and enjoying myself. But there was still me to enjoy and still selves to shed. In other words, I remembered feeling close to the nothingness that would open up to God, but this closeness was still a great distance, for there remained my ego, my I, my self to feel, and I had not yet reached the state of negation and nothingness that would truly accept God's grace.

After I finished another pipe, I lay back again with my eyes closed. The fact that I was still there, still thinking, nagged, but this feeling was nearly overwhelmed by the feeling of peace and joy. I was certain of God, but it was "certainty," "I" and "God," that was prohibiting the emptying necessary to true communion. Perhaps God did not matter.

The woman nudged me on the shoulder, and I opened my eyes and she handed me another. I closed my eyes and deeply inhaled. No, perhaps God did not matter. I felt a tingling on my thigh, almost like a caress. But everything seemed so far away and did not matter. I felt another caress, stronger this time, and I inhaled again and waited to understand if this was the drug or something actual. I felt the gentlest pressure on my crotch, unmistakable, and I opened my eyes to see the whiteness of the woman's crouched back, her spine lovely and sharp. I felt adjustment and caresses and then her fingers tenderly stroking my scrotum. I became aroused immediately. Or maybe I was always aroused, had always been aroused; it was more like that. I sucked on the pipe and could hear the crackle of the pellet in the bowl. I felt cold on my flanks and upper legs, and then my cock was surrounded by wet, warm, insistent softness. I heard Chula from a lifetime away. "You've had the smoke now comes the flower." The flower encircled, enclosed and encouraged, and it felt like my entire body was encircled by her lips, and my entire self was inside that gentle mouth.

I started to feel a blankness, something missing. Even though Spanish is the language from my family and childhood, I still cannot find the adequate words. This nothingness started high in my belly, just below the ribs. As I inhaled the smoke and as the flower drew me in, the gap, the void grew, slowly but insistently, spreading first upward to my lungs, then shoulders, then moving across to both upper arms. I finished the pellet, then let the pipe fall from my hands and lay flat, my shoulder blades flattening against the thin mat. I looked up at the crimson light, red like lips, like painted toenails, like the tendons of thin ankles, like the reddest flowers, like the blood of Jesus Christ, then down at the void now reaching up to my throat and flowing downward toward the woman's back, where she was now lying with her ribcage resting across my waist. The void, the nothingness, began to ascend her white back, and I closed my eyes. The void seeped into my hips, my genitals, my thighs. With eyes still closed, I touched my lips with the fingertips of one hand and caressed her spine with the other. After a while, the nothingness had reached my knees. There were no colors in my eyelids now, just a faint reddish glow. The nothingness (I wish I knew a better word) slowly began to move from my knees downward, and I moved my heels in to raise my knees up. I was not impatient. There was no time. I could now feel the nothingness descend slowly, slowly to my knees, my calves and then slowly to my ankles. I thought of the thin bones of Ana's ankles, the silver ring and red toenails, and suddenly, I wasn't, couldn't be thinking of anything, as I was emptied by and into the absolute nothingness of God's grace.

I don't know how long this nothingness lasted. When consciousness returned, I was alone in that small room. The overhead bulb had been switched off, the tray removed, Chula and the woman gone. I was cold, and a pale grey light illuminated the rectangular window. I was blessed.

I am certain of what happened and, for maybe the first time, certain of what I believe. I feel nearly unbound joy.

As we began to move past her, she shook her hair and said, "It's terrible about that priest, isn't it?" We slowed and Lassus turned. "I didn't take your call originally, and well, Professor Kirkpatrick, he can be, well, sometimes he's just too busy, too busy." She looked down, then her eyes met mine, then she looked away, behind us. She had something to tell us. We waited. She stared, then looked to her right. Then down at her hands. We waited some more. It was quiet in the office, almost silent: I could just hear the high-pitched whine of florescent tubes above. She looked behind me again, then leaned forward and loudly whispered, "Father Juan might be more helpful."

"And is Father Juan in today?"

She looked down at her hands again. She sat down in her chair and leaned back, keeping her gaze fastened on her hands resting on the desk. I am not a patient woman, but it seemed that it would be a mistake to interrupt whatever this was. She closed her eyes and rubbed her forehead with the fingertips of her right hand. Detective Lassus sighed heavily. The morning ticked by.

"Ma'am. Is Father Juan in today?"

She started and removed her hand from her face. "Oh yes, oh yes," she said in that stage whisper of hers. "I do believe he's in today. Please follow me." She rose quickly and turned gracefully around the counter. We walked down the same dim hallway but turned left at the intersection instead of right. At the first door past, she stopped and knocked loudly. "Father Juan?"

"Pásale."

The door was opened to a beautiful dark wood office that smelled faintly of cedar. Floor to ceiling bookcases occupied the left and far walls, and an antique desk, a darker shade of heavy wood, centered the room. Two red velvet and dark wood armchairs faced the desk. To the right, a large window dominated, with thick red curtains drawn about three-quarters of the way, allowing a rectangular panel of light to fall on the plush carpet and illuminate the entire space. A small man with a shaved head and white, bushy eyebrows over dark nearsighted brown eyes looked up from a book on the desk, then rose and shook first my hand, then Lassus's.

"Buenos días, las catedráticas. I am Father Juan, Juan Portillo. How may I be of service? First let me find my glasses."

"This is Detective Lassus, and I'm Detective Fruscella, from the Denver Police Department, Crimes Against Persons Unit. We are currently investigating a homicide, and we would like some background information on the victim. Professor Kirkpatrick agreed to speak to us but reconsidered. We're hoping you can help us." Father Juan stood and listened, his hands searching around his desk.

"To your right. By the big book."

"*Lo siento?*"

"Your glasses. To your right. Up. There."

His glasses were huge, thick black frames and thick lenses, and covered most of his face, including his eyebrows.

"Ah, *gracias, gracias.* Thank you. Please sit down. I apologize for assuming you were professors: it is obvious you are not students, and I've welcomed few police detectives to my office. Would you like a coffee, *profesoras?*" He sat and we followed suit. The chairs were extremely comfortable. He leaned forward and smiled, emphasizing the wrinkles near his mouth and eyes. He was older than he first appeared, perhaps around sixty. "Perhaps a *caffè corretto*, if it is not too early? An unfortunate habit acquired in Rome."

"No, thank you, Professor."

"I am no professor."

"I beg your pardon."

"*De nada.* But you have questions, *si*, about the priest who was killed in the Basilica?"

I nodded. "It seems the victim was involved in the Legionaries of Christ, and it seems as if this organization suffered through some scandal. Can you tell us anything about this organization?"

He looked up at the ceiling. Was he going to be another stonewall? He then looked at me and smiled, his face blurred by thick lenses. "The Legion of Christ is a clerical religious congregation, which means that its members are ordained priests and must take vows. There are two types of vows, simple and solemn, but their distinction doesn't matter in this case. Only maybe a little. The Legionaries of Christ, LC for short, was established in the thirties I believe by Father Marcial Maciel. It is a congregation that has come under some scrutiny, that is unfortunately true."

Again he paused. He moved his gaze to Lassus, who had been writing in her notebook. "Before the scandal, as you put it, the Legionaries were known for two things: the fantastic amount of money they raised and their, should we say, problematic vows. They are a very conservative organization and so have managed to solicit large amounts from donors who feel as they do, that Vatican II church reform has gone too far. Father Maciel was very charismatic and persuasive and was able to convince many people into supporting his Legion and perhaps looking the other way when his own irregularities began to surface. But the Legion has always been, I believe the English term is, 'a gold mine,' and it is not wrong to say that that perhaps blinded some in the Vatican regarding Maciel's sins." His voice, soft and deep, caressed. I wished I were back in school.

"The second aspect that has always characterized the Legion is the extraordinary vows their members are required to take. Each initiate is obliged to take vows of charity, humility and poverty. On the surface these vows do not appear to be suspect: many orders, especially those we call mendicant orders—those that subsist on charity—require similar promises. However, these particular vows were made not in reference to Jesus or to the Church as a whole, but to the Legion, or more precisely, to the *leaders* of the Legion. 'Charity' they defined as preventing any criticism of one's superiors, and 'humility' would prevent any aspirations to replace the leadership. These vows created an atmosphere of secrecy and unquestioning obedience, an atmosphere where Maciel's transgressions could flourish."

He felt good. He'd gotten some rest and had prayed lauds early and alone. It was Mary's Queenship Day, and that always made him happy, even with the ugly and disturbing story of Jephthah, the reading from Judges, that always strangely accompanied Mary's feast. The Hebrew God was a brutal God, testing Abraham with Isaac and accepting the sacrifice of Jephthah's unlucky virgin daughter. But now, after a refreshing shower bath and the bitter jolt of two espressos with lemon, his mind was focused and his body, for the present, undemanding, uncomplaining, almost unnoticeable. He looked at himself in the mirror as he shaved: the sad brown eyes with the surrounding puffiness tightened, the large Greek nose, the thin lips, the extended and wrinkled forehead (his worst feature), the white and black Caesar haircut. Vanity was not his sin, but he was pleased he looked intelligent, skilled, unavoidable. He smiled: yes, he was God's unavoidable servant. God's unavoidable servant's eyebrows were looking slightly untended. He hoped he could return to his Miska on the Via del Corallo in time to avoid an unsatisfactory visit to an American barber. He smoothed both eyebrows down and rubbed his forehead.

He had read some information on the detective, Francesca Fruscella, that arrived in an email from Malachi. Fifty-four, a widow with a teenage son, married to her job, *una gattara*. A former pianist in university. A few seemingly high-profile cases, local. Her face, from three different newspaper photographs, showed intelligence but frustration as well, perhaps bitterness. He had never heard the surname before, but her heavy eyes and thickened features suggested blood from the *mezzogiorno*, perhaps Molise or Calabria. She looked hard-headed, *testarda*, and often such women caused him trouble. This Detective Fruscella was possibly the worst of the old world and new: stubborn like a Calabrese and liberated like an American. He would have to be subtle here, be both forceful and understanding. With God's help.

He would wear his white cassock. He took it from the closet and examined it carefully, bringing it closer and further in front of his eyes, cocking his head and moving to examine it in better light. Spotless, yes, and the whitest of whites, like alpine snow: Benoit was handy with the bleach. He'd had Lanzarote iron it just after he arrived, and it was sharply creased, immaculate and flat. The white would intimidate, perhaps, but he hoped there was a remnant of respect for his office and his mission remaining in *la vecchia Americana* that would benefit. He set the cassock gently on the bed, then turned and looked in the mirror, patting his stomach. He used to be much thinner, even skinny, *magro*, that was true, *gambe di puledro*, legs of a colt. But years of wine, veal and macaroni had thickened and coarsened his flesh. He looked down: his legs were not presently those of a colt, or even a draft horse, but two worn Doric columns, heavy and immobile. But sometimes immobility was useful. Sometimes it was best to be heavy, consistent, unchanging like stone: *et super hanc petram aedificabo Ecclesiam.*

In his boxers and long black hose he felt uncovered on Mary's Feast Day, almost disrespectful. He crossed himself. *Salve, Regina, Mater misericordiæ, vita, dulcedo, et spes nostra, salve. Ad te clamamus exsules filii Hevæ, Ad te suspiramus, gementes et flentes in hac lacrimarum valle.*

This American, this *commisario*, how best to approach her? He had no time for patience: suddenly dangerous, Malachi was involved and both his motivation and timetable uncertain. He took a white T-shirt from the drawer, spotless and pressed like the cassock. The shirt was a bit tight over his torso. He thought of his doctor, the old goat Panzini, who smoked like a factory and told him to cut back on the risotto and to exercise. His football days were past, he found bike riding undignified, and the idea of playing *bocce* with Father Angelus or Father Hoffman was unpalatable. He walked every day from his apartment on Vicolo del Vicario to his office at Palazzo del Sant'Uffizio and often walked across the Ponte PASA to Emilio's or Baranto if he was feeling adventurous. True, he would then take a taxi home, but the initial walk was helpful.

He crossed himself and prayed, *In nomine Patris et Filii et Spiritus Sancti. Amen*, then slipped the cassock over his head.

Father Juan removed his glasses and began to chew on one of the arms. His eyes were unfocussed and directed down at his desk. I couldn't yet get a read on him: I was slightly surprised he was so forthcoming, but it seemed as if there was an undercurrent to his explanations, some deep harmony I wasn't quite hearing. He cleared his throat, replaced his glasses on his face and began again.

"Maciel's sins were multiple and serious. He fathered children from different women. He did support them financially, so at least there is that. He was a drug addict and used money from the Legion to buy drugs. He also molested young men, young no-vitiates, boys entrusted to his care. Although I am not God, that is the sin that must be the most difficult to forgive. You see why the vows he insisted upon became so important: the novitiate is taught from the beginning never to question the actions of his superiors."

"Even if his superior is molesting him?"

He nodded.

"You said that this gold mine blinded the Vatican into looking the other way. What do you mean?"

"There were rumors of Maciel's improprieties, especially his drug use, for many years, as early, if I remember, as the 1950s. He had enough influence that our Holy Father John Paul II point-blank refused to investigate all accusations, including those sexual abuse accusations. And only recently, and reluctantly, the Holy Office and Pope Benedict XVI have allowed the investigations to proceed."

"So the Church, the Vatican, protected this guy?"

"'Protected' is perhaps too strong a word. But you know En-glish better than I." He shrugged his shoulders. "Maciel had many friends. Including, at one time, His Eminence, Benedict XVI."

Up until then I had liked Father Juan, his charm and world-liness, his sonorous, smoker's tenor. But that shrug showed too much irony, too much detachment: it was the shrug that reminded me of Duquesne and all of his closed-door accomplices at the rec-tory. Too many sins had been committed under those shrugs.

"And this doesn't bother you? This enabling of rape?"

"It disturbs me, yes. But I do not, how you say, *tengo mi cora-zón en mi mano*, hold my heart in my hand. Failing to demonstrate *mi disgusto* is not the same as failing to feel it."

"So the Church sits back and does nothing while this priest rapes young boys?"

"That is not correct. Maciel was investigated, censured and forced to retire."

"After many years."

"The Church may be slow in policing its members in your eyes, Detective. But the Catholic Church is infinitely larger than the sins of Marcial Maciel. Or any of the other sinful priests. We will survive this."

"But will the boys?"

Father Juan gave a little smile and leaned back in his chair. "I am believing you did not come out all this way to debate me, Detective, on the questions of sexual abuse by Catholic clergy. You have some questions about a murder investigation, yes?"

"The questions might be related, Father. Perhaps, if the victim shared his leader's perversions, one of those boys might have decided to take justice into his own hands. This was a passionate killing, Father, not a robbery or an accident. Maybe Maciel was being killed *in absentia*. The murdered man was assigned to the Legion's administrative offices from?" I looked over at Lassus.

"1995 to 2006."

"Over ten years."

"The Legion's administration was rather large then, I believe. What were the victim's duties there?"

"We don't know yet."

"As I've indicated, the Legion considers providing information about itself to be 'uncharitable.' You might have some difficulty."

"We would appreciate any assistance, Father."

He chuckled. "Perhaps I can pick up the telephone and call my fellow *Opus Dei* spies, yes? This is not *The Da Vinci Code*. Detective, I am a mere priest. You overestimate me."

I rose and tried to smile. "Here's my card, Father. Should you hear from your spies or think of anything that might be of help."

He smiled, rose from his chair, returned his glasses to his face. "I hope I have been of some service."

"One more question, if you please. Why was Professor Kirkpatrick so reluctant to help us?"

He shrugged, a different shrug, a shrug suggesting not that the question was difficult but irrelevant. "Professor Kirkpatrick is new to this institution and perhaps wants to impress by demonstrations of loyalty. I believe it is nothing but the zealotry of the recently converted."

"Is there something you're not telling us?"

"There are many things I'm not telling you, Detective. But I have answered the questions you have asked as best I am able."

"That's a slippery answer, Father."

"Not at all, Detective. I have answered honesty and thoroughly while trying to avoid sounding disagreeably pedantic. If you have further questions, don't hesitate to visit or telephone. I do not know how to work my email. Goodbye, detectives." He gave a little bow to Lassus, then to me. He handed his card to us both.

It was ten-thirty. We might be able to reach the Satire by eleven.

TWO

The Solemnity of All Saints Day (Holy Day of Obligation), 1991
The Life of Saint Teresa of Avila by Herself
*Describes how doubts and questions begin to nag my soul and how I turn to
Saint Magherita of Cascia for guidance.*

Since I have graduated and been ordained, in these last three
months, I have been depressed, at a loss. This is why I have not
written much here: there are only so many ways to say I am feeling
great despair. My pen becomes heavy and I put it down. I bow my
head in exhaustion, not in prayer. This waiting, this wondering,
this uncertainty is distressing.

I have not yet been invited to Tertianship. How painful it is
to write these words and then to read them again, on paper, in
my own hand. There seems something irrevocable in these marks.
Oh Lord, please give me the strength to serve you through this
sorrow. Oh glorious Santa Rita di Cascia, plead before the divine
crucifix, speak on my behalf. Oh Santa Rita, so humble, so pure,
so mortified, grant me the ears to hear what the Lord commands
and the heart to follow his unique path for me and the stomach to
be able to follow what my heart knows is true, even if all the others

turn their backs on my way of serving thee. Oh Santa Rita, give my soul the strength to do what it knows it must do, even if it offends others, in the name of Jesus, Our Lord God and the Holy Spirit. Amen.

If I can detach myself and think of the problem rationally, then some of my distress is understandable. For a very long time, ever since I was a young child, I have been governed by a routine, an external timetable, a program that governed all activities. This agenda continued all through high school and then at university, then at the seminary following. At the seminary, I had very few minutes ungoverned. And so, now, for the first time since I can remember, I am free of chores. Here I am now, in this Roman limbo, with no appointments to keep, no classes to attend, no lessons to prepare or no exams to study for, no confessions to hear or souls to comfort, no there is nothing to give my days time, nothing to distinguish one hour from the next, one day from the next, one week from the next, one month. We will see they say. Not now they say. Perhaps next year they say. We will contact you they say. Let the Lord grant you patience they say. No, here they have left me to my own counsel.

And so I pray.

Oh, Saint Magherita di Cascia, my new patron saint, saint of lost causes and abused mothers, accept my veneration and devotion, accept my love and my praise. For you too knew what it was like to be spurned, first by your father who offered you, at the age of twelve, to an immoral fool, and then by the fool himself, who impregnated you just after the wedding and who beat and humiliated you, yes, whoring and drinking, insulting and infuriating his neighbors, until he was stabbed again and again. And you, oh wise and beneficent spirit, who then had to try to persuade your young sons to forego the vendetta against his killers, to return to a life of peace and Christian love, and when this failed, how you prayed day and night for some sort of reprieve, some kind of escape from the fate that awaited your sons. Oh, Santa Rita, your prayers were answered, when the Lord took the two boys before the boys could enact their sinful vengeance, damning themselves by murder. Did you pray for their deaths, Santa Rita? Their deaths that were their salvation? And then, broken hearted, you tried to enter the convent of St. Mary Magdalena, and they refused, they refused you! You had again to pay for your father's hasty decision, for your husband's filthy character, for the death of your boys. It was just you, alone, with your God and your prayers. How did you feel, Santa Rita? Did you have faith? You must have great faith, unimaginable faith. You again prayed and prayed, morning and night, your prayers humble yet resilient, prayers to your saints John the Baptist, Augustine and Nicholas of Tolentino, and they heard you, Santa Rita, they heard you, and didn't they lift you up bodily and gently, ever so gently, carry you up up, past the walls of the convent, and gently set you down, near the rose bushes, a miracle truly? And how sweet that must have been, Santa Rita, how sweet that must have felt, my love, for it proved not that you were right, no, for what use could you have of vindication? Not that you were holy or blessed to be favored so, because you knew that you were not. No, this garden miracle merely revealed what you knew all along, that your faith was not misplaced. Oh how beautifully sweet that must have been to receive the grace from God and his saints, the grace that says yes, yes, yes. Many years later you prayed to share Our Lord's suffering, and He allowed one of His thorns to pierce your forehead, causing a wound that bled but never healed. Oh how happy this wound must have made you! What joy this mortification of flesh, this mark of difference, this physical pain and misery must have caused. You were sharing Our Lord Jesus Christ's suffering! Once more your prayers had been answered with a perfection you couldn't have imagined. And if your flesh was mortified in life, Santa Rita, in death it is uncorrupted, and you lie there in your basilica, your body nearly intact.

I too bear a mark. But my mark is not as great as yours, oh Holy Saint. It is tiny, a mere pinprick compared to yours. In fact, it is not visible to physical eyes, only spiritual eyes. But like yours, it too comes from God, and it too sets me apart. It is why I have not been invited to enter into my Tertianship and be allowed to serve Our Majesty in the Society of Jesus. It is why I sit here in Rome, alone, with no opportunities to serve Our Lord through pastoral care or intellectual work.

I know my path is not for everyone, and I know that to some, it must appear fraught and mistaken. But just as others believed your path to be incorrect and wrong and how, through prayer and un- shakable belief you overcame the doubt and questioning, I too must pray, I too must keep my belief, I too must walk my path firmly and with faith, ignoring those who taunt me or misunder- stand, "for we walk by faith not by sight" (2 Corinthians 5:7). For some, like me, the path is through darkness into the light. But the darkness is vital.

The drive was easier than expected, and we parked in the Walgreens parking lot, across Race Street, about half-a-block away from the bar. I stopped at the corner and looked up at the large and famous vertical "Satire" neon sign, with the horizontal "Lounge" sign below, and beneath that "Mixed Drinks," with the white universal martini glass. It was a great sign. I turned to Lassus. "You been here before, Detective?"

She shook her head. "Not my kind of place.."

"It's a Denver institution. And it's not so bad. Pete the Greek bought it seven or eight years ago and cleaned it up, started serving food and stopped serving teens. Food's OK, but the margs are better. You should try it some night."

We pushed our way through the door and were greeted by the smell of green chili, disinfectant and spilled beer. Although rejuvenated somewhat, the place, at least in the morning, had not forgotten its roots, as the hard drinkers had surfaced, clumped along the long bar or separated solitary in the shadows, here to beat the lunchtime rush. It was quiet, a few murmurs here and there: people didn't go to the Satire before eleven a.m. to chat. Or to listen to Springsteen on the juke. People went because you could get two for one wells before eleven, and small drafts were ninety cents. There was no sign or anything; someone told you or you just knew. I forgot who told me. It would be a nice place to drink in the morning, if that interested you: it was cool and dark, the bar long, the customers incurious and the drinks cheap. Afternoon too. Hector used to come here once in a while, when he was early drinking. After his son, my husband, died. But he eventually stopped his morning booze and became interested in his hi-fi store and his grandson again.

We made quite the pair, Lassus and I, walking in. What would I think if I saw us? Lost tourists? Mother/daughter alcoholics? Mismatched lesbian couple? Cops? Definitely cops. I sat on a barstool about a third of the way down. Lassus kept standing to my right. A frazzled-looking bottle blonde in jean shorts with white tights, combat boots, two full sleeve tats and bright green eyes scurried by with two pitchers of beer, which she set on the bar in front of a couple of men in army jackets, then turned her head to us. "Help you?" The army jackets, a pitcher each, walked quickly to a table in the shadows.

"I'm looking for Jimmy the Bartender."

"You his mom?"

"Ouch. I was expecting something along the lines of 'I dunno who you're talking about,' or 'there's no Jimmy here' but to get all personal like that right from the drop, that's cold."

She smiled this luminous smile, and the frazzle disappeared, replaced by a radiance of intelligence and bemusement, a gracefulness that at once disclosed she was beautiful enough to dress as badly as she did. She took a bar rag and wiped in front of us, looked at me, then Lassus, still smiling. "If you're not his mom, then who are you?"

I removed my badge from my pocket and opened it for her. "Denver Police, Crimes Against Persons. I'm Detective Fruscella; this is Detective Lassus. Jimmy's not in trouble. We just have a few questions."

"You didn't need to show me." She pirouetted and walked to the door at the far end of the bar. "Jimmy. James. Somebody here to see you." She turned back to us. "You want anything to drink? Coke or something? It's hot out."

"No thank you."

Jimmy the Bartender shuffled in. He was youngish, maybe about twenty-five, and very very thin. He had rounded shoulders, and his thin cotton T-shirt hung loose over the bones of his frame. He wore baggy khaki shorts (it was impossible to imagine any clothing on him that wouldn't be baggy) and black high-top sneakers. He was as pale as he was thin, with no tattoos or other tribal markings, or visible needle tracks, marring his almost translucent skin. He had bleached his hair white and had gathered it neatly into a topknot, which gave him the appearance of some Kabuki parody, an albino Cio-Cio San.

"Hey," he said, not unpleasantly, through clean bright teeth.

"Jimmy? Jimmy the Bartender?"

He nodded. "That's what I'm called sometimes."

"I'm Detective Fruscella; this is Detective Lassus, with the Denver Police. Do you have a real name?"

"James."

"James? James the Bartender?"

"Jones. James or Jim Jones. Really."

"Jim Jones? Like the cult leader?"

"Like the rapper."

"Ok, Mr. Jones. Have you ever seen this guy?" I slid Martinez's photo across the bar. He looked at it quickly, then back at me. He looked at me longer than he looked at the photograph: he was obviously processing possible scenarios.

Finally, "Yeah. He comes in here sometimes."

"Know his name?"

He shook his head.

"Are you sure?"

"Yeah. He comes in sometimes, alone. Pays cash. Good tipper."

"Mr. Jones, this man's name is Willem Martinez. We want to ask him some questions about a murder. And we think that not only do you know his name, that you've done some favors for him. That's what we think. And because this is a murder investigation, we don't have time to dance around and play clever hipster games.

If you don't want to answer our questions here, we can give you a ride to the station and you can answer there. Maybe that would boost your street cred, I don't know. You probably wouldn't make it back before midnight."

"I ain't a hipster."

He looked in the mirror and carefully placed the *zucchetto* on his head. His newly washed hair was slightly unruly, so he removed the cap, combing his hair forward with his fingers before placing his cap on top.

For quite a while, this work was easy for him. For a little over thirty years he was adept at moving readily between different worlds, between the infinite permutations of the secular and sacred. To the earthly, he understood their environment, the mechanisms of power and efficacy, and comprehended the lure of various pleasures and pastimes, which, while he did not partake, he did not seem to judge. He carried with him the atmosphere of the spiritual, an air of distraction and detachment that made him all the more trustworthy and persuasive. And to the religious, he was seen as possessing extensive practical knowledge and experience of the material world, experience feared, admired and envied. This skill did not come naturally to him. It was only from God that this illusion of ease and ability was created and maintained. As a child and younger man, he was always both socially clumsy and extremely curious, and this juxtaposition served him well, for the awkwardness created the impression of innocence, of not ever belonging wherever he was, while the curiosity flattered and disarmed many who took pains to answer, explain and even help where normally they would ignore. This was not something he could consciously control, although he was aware of it. Thanks be to God.

But he was older now, and both his innocence and the curiosity had been all but destroyed by the work he did in Ireland. He had tried to compensate by energetic and meticulous planning—like a striker, Pippo for example, who loses his reflexes and pace and tries to get by on guile and guesswork—but for this case he didn't prepare with his usual care, instead contracting out much of the work to Malachi. This resulted in a murdered priest, *Requiescat in pace*, as well as trepidation and doubt, an unfamiliar uncertainty that worried and troubled.

But if here he could no longer rely on the appearance of innocence and his formerly energetic curiosity, nor extensive or even adequate planning, with the help of God he could still bring other characteristics to bear, most notably an unvarying and almost brutal tenacity. He understood that it was this tenacity, much more than any other quality or method, that had initially impressed his superiors, and it was this tenacity that now, thirty years in, kept attracting assignments. In Ireland, where he was stripped of his innocence and made to pay for his curiosity, and where even his faith was torn, he finished the job he was sent to do. The fact that the job he accomplished was too small for the situation was the fault of his superiors. The fact that his faith in the Church was severely shaken... he had no idea whom to blame for that.

He would see this through: he would retrieve the notebook. He sat on the bed and put his shoes on and tied them. This detective, this detective could be key. He looked again at what Malachi had sent him. She wasn't a fool, perhaps limited by circumstances, but her face showed intelligence, and her background suggested culture. How best to appeal? She would likely stiffen against any attempt at direct intimidation and scoff at overt flattery and familiarity. He had to be subtle here, clever. The white cassock was good, but he'd need something to break the ice. A gift, *un piccolo regalo*, perhaps. A bottle of wine? Not from the States, no. Flowers? Likely an error. She studied piano, but he knew nothing of music outside of the Church and not much inside to be truthful.

He once spent a month at the *Eremo di Montecasale* with the Capuchins in the mountains outside of Sansepolcro. He was there during the summer, recovering from the pneumonia he had caught from waiting for a contact almost forty hours in a driving rain during the Moro kidnapping. He remembered watching from his bed the intermittent stream of tourists and pilgrims walking uphill to follow the Tuscan trail of Saint Francis and his upside down cabbages. What was much more memorable, however, were the frescos of Piero della Francesca, especially *La Resurrezione* at a private home.

A book, a book of Francesca for Francesca.

He left his room, walked down the hallway, then the stairs, and came to the foyer. He had about an hour before the meeting. He saw Lanzarote smoking outside on the sidewalk. He opened the door and was greeted once again by a wave of dry heat. "Father Signelli."

"Father."

"I have been instructed to drive you to the meeting. A house in the neighborhood called Cherry Creek. Very expensive."

"Who gave you these instructions?"

Lanzarote raised his eyebrows. "I received a telephone call from Father Simmons, my superior."

"I see." Malachi wasn't going to attend.

Lanzarote looked at his cigarette, then at Signelli. "If we leave now, we will be early."

"I would like to go to a bookstore before the meeting. Do you know a shop in Denver where I can purchase a fresco book?"

"Pardon, Father, I'm not sure I understand."

"A book with frescos, paintings, a book of art. Where can I buy an art book?"

"There's a museum on the way, new art, contemporary. They probably have a shop inside."

"No, not new art, not that. Something more traditional, a master, an Italian. Piero della Francesca, do you know him?"

Lanzarote ground out his cigarette with his heel. "I am sorry, I don't know much about painting and such. Perhaps the main museum downtown would have this book. It is not too far out of the way."

"It's very hot again."

"Have you been drinking water, Father?"

He waved Lanzarote away impatiently. "Yes, yes. Let us go."

"Congratulations. What do you know about this guy? You know where he lives? Maybe you need to look at it again."

He looked down at the photo, grimaced sheepishly, then leaned forward. "Yeah, I know Willie. But I don't do favors for him. Some black dude dropped some mail off for him once was all. And I got no idea where he lives."

"What happened when the guy dropped off his mail?"

"Willie introduced himself one morning and asked if I'd keep his mail for him. Said it'd be a one-time thing. And would a hundred would cover the trouble."

"And?"

"Guy dropped it off. Couple days later Willie comes and picks it up. With the hundred. That's all."

"Did you look at it?"

"Nope."

Mr. Jones didn't strike me as particularly curious, so I let that one go. "When was the last time you saw him?"

"Couple months ago. I think it was a Thursday. He came in by himself, drank rum and Coke—two or three; I can't remember—and then ate lunch."

"Nothing else you remember?"

"He's a good tipper, like I said. Oh yeah, he often reads while he's drinking." Mr. Jones was pleased with himself.

"Reads? The paper?"

"No, he brings books. Sometimes two or three. He sits at the table over there" —he pointed to a corner table— "and drinks his drinks and reads his books."

"You recognize the books?"

He shook his head. "I'm not really a reader."

"What does he drink?"

"Different things . . . rum and Coke, martini, straight tequila. Always top-shelf though, no wells, even in the rum and Coke. Sometimes he buys the house a drink, if there's not too many here." Jones leaned back and scratched his left shoulder.

"He ever hang with anyone?"

"Nope."

"He ever call anyone on his cell?"

"Don't think so. I mean, it's not like I sit here and watch him."

"Does he come here a lot? Regular?"

"Naw. He'll show up for a day or two, three day in a row, then not show up for months, then maybe back for a week straight. Always in the morning. Latest he'll stay for is an early lunch." He looked around the bar. "Crowd changes for lunch."

"You never saw him at night?"

"Nope. Not in the afternoon, neither."

"If you wanted to get in touch with him, how would you?"

"I don't know why I would."

"Humor me."

"I don't know." He looked down at his feet. "Wait for him to come in here, I guess."

"And you have no other idea where to find him? Where he lives or where he likes to go?"

"Sorry."

"We'll just have to stake this out then. Maybe a couple of uniforms. You open at nine, right? Nine to two, you think, Detective Lassus?"

"They could sit at the bar so they wouldn't miss anything."

He looked up. "Good idea. We'll start tomorrow. Maybe we should call Pete, let him know."

"Thanks, James." We turned to go.

"No, no, no. Wait. I seen him once or twice at Voodoo Doughnut. He was having breakfast. It was early, like six-thirty in the morning. I waved to him one time but I don't think he recognized me, you know, because I wasn't behind the bar."

"Was he alone?"

"Yeah he was. I ain't never seen him with anyone."

"So he must live around here, huh? Breakfast at the Voodoo, hair of the dog and lunch here at the Satire. Listen, James, and this is important: do you have any idea where he lives or who might know where he lives?"

"That's all I got, man, honest."

"All right, James, here's my card. If he shows up, you let me know. Or if you think of anything else, you let me know. We want to find him, James." I slid the photograph back and put it in my pocket.

"Yeah, sure. You still going to stake out?"

"Maybe, but it won't be with uniforms. You won't know we're here. And neither will Pete."

I slid off the barstool and turned to go. The lunch crowd, with its noise, was beginning to arrive: doctors in scrubs from St Luke's, mid-level clerks from the capitol, bankers in suits from the local branches of Citibank, FirstBank and UMB. The drinkers, the quiet drinkers, were slipping out, focusing on keeping their buzz. A steel guitar blared and somebody—M-M-Merle? sang—"I'd like to hold my head up and be proud of who I am/but they won't let my secret go untold/I paid the debt I owed them/but they're still not satisfied/now I'm a branded man out in the cold." I looked back at the juke and the tattooed bartender, who was standing picking songs, gave me one of those beautiful bemused smiles.

It was hot out and bright. The wind had picked up, stirring up more heat and dust. "Should we go to this Voodoo Doughnut?"

"Cops and doughnuts: how can we refuse?"

"Our Mr. Jones was a bit shifty. You think he uses?"

"He *was* thin. But I didn't see any tracks, and his eyes were bright. I don't know. I'm more puzzled by Mr. Martinez." We crossed the street to the Walgreens lot. "Who brings books to a bar? What low-life always buys top-shelf? And Voodoo is pricey. Des Prez said he had money, but this isn't making sense. We have to find this guy."

My phone rang. It was the station. I hoped it wasn't that little fuck Clark.

"Fruscella."

"Des Prez. Got something for you."

"Yeah?"

"Precinct 3."

I hung up and turned to Lassus. "Doughnuts will have to wait."

THREE

The Solemnity of The Immaculate Conception of Mary (Holy Day of Obligation), 1985
Alphonsus Tostatus—*Paradoxa quinque*

God is.

God is not.

What a pitiful word, "is." What an inexact, pitiful word. To bring God down to the level of other existing things; can we make a bigger mistake? Can we make a more egotistical, a more damaging mistake, than to say or think that God *is*, like a house or new car, like a sheltering tree or a cool spring rain, like a stern father or displeased boss? Is God like us? How can God "be," if by being we mean to say existing in a world of thoughts, objects and feelings, real or imagined? How can God be, if He must, by his very nature, transcend such simplified human attempts at understanding such as being and not-being, presence and absence, nature and transcendence? To think that God "exists" is to think He can be comprehended; it is to think that *we* can comprehend him, and so it is to think that we are God. It is this thinking that can only prevent true belief. It is this thinking that makes any true "relationship" with God impossible.

Nor can we say that God is not, for the word "is," even in its negation, still places God firmly in what can be either present or absent, and God cannot be limited to such childish conceptions.

And what of the word God? This too is a mistake.

God is everywhere.
God cannot be approached.

God is not a destination, like the post office. I can't get closer to God through physical movement in space. I can't point myself in a direction and say I'm going to move towards God. I can't get closer to God through the metaphor of movement. The words "closer to God" have no meaning, either read together or separately. God is not defined or confined by space, cannot be thought of in spatial terms. God created space.

And God created everything within space. What has He not created? He has created everything, even our mistaken thoughts about things. What can I point to and say, "No, God is not there?" Disease, death, war, the suffering of young children—is God not there? If God is good, can God be where innocents suffer? Is the absence of God a sign of evil and sin? Is God in sin? Is God in hell?

God is everywhere. This I believe with all of my heart and soul. God is there when a twelve-year-old boy is raped, beaten and killed by his father. God is there, and God is here as I write this. God is there when the shrapnel bombs fall on the Palestinian mothers. God would not abandon his children. God is and is not. God is everywhere and yet cannot be approached.

And since God created everything, He also created time. He cannot be found *in* time but can only be found *through* time. God is not something or someone who can be obtained through diligent study or through great works of charity and kindness. God cannot be found through public worship or singing great songs of praise. God cannot be found in or through love, either the love of others or the love of self. God cannot be found even in the love of God.

God is withdrawing.
To rejoin God, one must cease to be.

God's greatest gift to us is that He withdrew His presence in order that we could exist. His grace is this withdrawal, this distancing, this vacating. These spatial terms are imprecise. Christ is a symbol of distance, of a distance that can be bridged. But in order for the distance to be bridged, we must cease to exist.

The ceasing to exist is not death. What I'm trying to put into words is a conscious, willful and deliberate negation of self. This negation of self opens the self up to perhaps close the distance between the self and God. The negation of self is the avenue to the possibility of grace.

The negation of self.
The negation of God.

Random or capricious negation is useless and perhaps worse: self-indulgent. This is sin. It does nothing to negate the self but, if anything, prevents any genuine ecstasy from occurring. This type of exploration actually strengthens the self, being, like the rebound of a motion, the constant return of the same.

What is necessary is a program of continuous self-negation, of constant and detailed attempts to achieve true ecstasy—spiritual, intellectual and sensual—and yet remain alive. Alive but not there. The question is this: how do I become nothing and live? This is no sin, but sincerity. This negation of self is not something we can accomplish on our own. To negate the self, we need God. But our images of God, of God the Father, God the King or God the Most High, are simply images that prevent us from truly seeing God. In order to negate our selves, we must negate our images of God. In order to negate these images of God, we must negate our selves. Pseudo-Dionysius says, "For by the unceasing and absolute renunciation of thyself and of all things thou mayest be borne on high, through pure and entire self-abnegation, into the superessential Radiance of the Divine Darkness."

This is my path: I will continue to dedicate my life to Jesus Christ by attempting, with all my heart, body, mind and soul, to negate myself as fully and completely as possible in order to be borne into God. My path is not one of light, no, but one of Darkness and absence, of separation, withdrawal and solitude.

"The man in union with truth knows clearly that all is well with him, even if everyone else thinks that he has gone out of his mind" *The Divine Names.*

In order to negate our selves, we must negate God.
In order to negate God, we must negate our selves.
In order to negate our selves, we must negate God.

Des Prez and Maldonado met us inside the door of the station, and after I sent Lassus back to HQ, they walked us through to one of the interview rooms. "We picked up Jarvis 'Buttercup' Flowers early this morning around one. Buttercup is the drug provider of choice for much of Cherry Creek and the Golden Triangle. He's boutique, not wholesale, more Whole Foods than King Soopers. We've been tailing him for almost two years. He retails to business folk, a couple of ballplayers, musicians, political interns, upper-crust housewives and husbands—mostly pills, coke and meth. He might know Willie because if Willie was really interested in A1 dope, Mr. Buttercup would be the man he'd see."

"What have you got him for?"

"At least three class three felonies, a couple of class twos. This ain't his first rodeo, so he's probably looking at at least twelve worth of time."

"Unless someone steps in."

"Always a possibility. Point is, he might be motivated to help you."

"Banger?"

"Not exactly, but he pays to play. Gangster Disciples."

"All right, let's talk."

"He's with his lawyer."

"Anybody we know?"

"Some youngster from Whitepool and Davis. Good firm, but they didn't send either Whitepool or Davis."

We walked in and sat down across the desk from Buttercup and his young-looking lawyer. I sat down and arranged his file and my photograph of Martinez in front of me. Maldonado sat on my left, and des Prez remained standing by the door. Buttercup's eyes were closed, and he looked asleep.

"Mr. Flowers. I am Detective Fruscella, and this is Detective Maldonado."

"Excuse me. Why isn't the video tape on?"

"This is an unofficial visit, regarding another case. We are currently working a homicide investigation, and we're wondering if your client could possibly assist us in that investigation. Your client's cooperation will be noted by your arresting officers." I slid the photograph of Martinez across the table to him. "Are you awake, Mr. Flowers?"

He opened his eyes slowly. "Tough night."

"Do you recognize this man, Mr. Flowers?"

He looked at it sleepily, then shook his head. "No."

"Are you sure, Mr. Flowers?"

"Yes. No."

"Mr. Flowers, my colleague here, Detective des Prez, he has a list of your clientele here: it's an impressive list, Mr. Flowers, an impressive list indeed. But although it is long, I'm guessing it's not comprehensive. In other words, I'm guessing there are people whom you've sold drugs to who are not on Detective des Prez's list."

"Don't know what you're talking about."

"Please bear with me, Mr. Flowers. As I said, I bet there are those in Denver you've sold drugs to who are not on Detective des Prez's list. And, furthermore, I bet some, maybe most of those not on Detective des Prez's list, like it that way, like not being on his list: in fact, I would bet that some of those would go to some trouble in order not to appear on Detective des Prez's list. The 'some trouble' I am speaking of might include harming you in some way, Mr. Flowers."

"Are you threatening my client?"

"Oh no, no. I am trying to empathize with your client, Mr. ?"

"Madelka. Simon Madelka."

"You see, Mr. Flowers, I can understand why you might be reluctant to admit a business relationship with any of your clients.

Part of your business code, Mr. Flowers, would have to incorporate a promise of confidentiality, like the attorney/client privilege or doctor/patient privilege . . . "

"Or priest/confessor privilege," added Maldonado.

"Or priest/confessor privilege," I agreed. "So you are wise to initially deny your acquaintance. However, these other clients not on the list, how would they feel should they suddenly appear on the list? Or, to be more precise, how would they feel if they were to suddenly believe they *would* appear on the list? We could release you, and then make a few arrests, letting it somehow accidently slip that we were acting on information you had provided."

Des Prez was experienced enough not to look at me after I said that, like I'd really fuck up two years of his work and let Buttercup go. I was just bluffing, hoping neither he nor his twelve-year-old lawyer would call it. They whispered together for a few seconds, but neither seemed to think I was kidding. I decided to press on.

"In fact, it seems to me, Mr. Flowers, the person depicted in that photograph might even be considered a freebie. If you would happen to let slip information regarding his identity and address, I really can't see how he'd learn about it, nor do I believe he'd be able to retaliate in any way. Unlike many whom you've done business with, eh, Mr. Flowers? You help us, you get the benefits of cooperation, and you really don't put yourself in any danger. Seems like a win-win, Mr. Flowers, a win-win."

More whispering. Then, finally, "Yeah, I know him. Willie the Sergeant."

"Did he buy from you?"

Silence.

"I'm not at all interested in any drug transactions, alleged or real. I need his address or how to locate him."

"I don't know where he lives, man. He'd come to me, or I'd meet him in a bar or something."

"You have a phone number or anything?"

Silence.

"They usually burn their phones," des Prez added.

"This is nothing, Mr. Flowers, this is nothing."

More silence. I looked at Buttercup and waited. He leaned back and closed his eyes. I gathered the file and made to leave.

"Stubby." Eyes still closed.

"Excuse me?"

"Stubby. Used to, um, party with the Sarge. Retired a couple years ago." He opened his eyes and nodded back at des Prez. "He knows who he is."

I looked back at des Prez, then stood. "Thank you, Mr. Flowers. Your cooperation will be noted."

The house was *brutta*, a mishmash of large boxes of stone, glass and wood, combined and arranged on the land seemingly by accident, looking like blocks thrown haphazardly by a child. The lawn was green and closely cut and seemed to go on for kilometers until curtailed by a high grey wall made of multicolored stones interspersed with what looked like bales of hay. He disliked modern architecture, as it reminded him always of Mussolini and that stupidity and crassness. As the car rounded a curve and reached the top of a low hill, he noticed a few trees of unknown species and what looked liked a swimming pool surrounded by white lounge chairs. The new angle did not improve the appearance of the house, as he saw that the sides and top of one of the cubes was made of what looked like corrugated iron, rusted and stained.

He tried to imagine the people who would occupy such a house. Who would feel comfortable in these geometric blocks, unnatural and false, mocking the grass and the trees and the horizon of the mountains? What kind of man would desire such alienation, such separation from what blended harmoniously and was balanced and pleasing? There was no evidence of children or of any other accident or carelessness. No, the disorder *was* the house, the childishness built in, and all spontaneity and whimsy drained by the forced illogic of the bizarre and jarring combinations. It was not a house to be lived in; it was a thing to be looked at. Looked at and then passed over, the eye restless and dissatisfied.

Perhaps he was getting old. But does age preclude judgment? Does experience insist on the suspension of all feeling and reason and the acceptance that which was insulting and base? What could he say to the people who owned this house? What common language could he share with ones who lived so blindly, their gaze limited so severely that they could see nothing of how the angles, colors and materials of where they chose to eat and to sleep clashed so violently with the surroundings, indeed with each other? What conversation could he have with someone who not only could endure such visual violence, but, given all the possibilities in the world—for the house was obviously fantastically expensive—would *choose* to build and inhabit such a visceral, aesthetic and even spiritual assault?

The house was distracting him. Theirs was the only car in the driveway, although he counted five garage doors belonging to a squat cube on the right. The sun was just beginning to set behind him as he opened the door to the hot and still night air. The smell of cut grass and dry ovenlike heat filled his nose. He looked at his watch: they were ten minutes early. Enough time to greet the owners, he imagined, and to perhaps sip a glass of wine, Verdicchio possibly? The bookstore had taken longer than he had planned and once again he was rushed, ill-prepared. He was not convinced this was wise, and the feeling of being manipulated began to grow. And he was not anticipating any joy from an awkward *Buonasera* with the house's owners.

Lights switched on as they approached. The paper bag with the book was heavy in his hand. Lanzarote opened his mobile, looked at it and pressed repeatedly into a panel on the right of the now illuminated door. He was puzzled at the purpose of such an elaborate doorbell.

"Are we not expected?"

"There is no one to expect us. I have the code for entrance. We are to use the house as needed."

"I don't understand."

Lanzarote turned and shrugged his shoulders. "These are my instructions. It was assumed you desired privacy." The door clicked and Lanzarote pulled it open, motioning ever so slightly with his chin that Signelli was to enter. "Please."

The foyer occupied the front cube of the structure, with stark white walls on three sides and glass on the fourth, to his right. The floors were dark wood parquet, shining in the brilliant light provided by a spherical chandelier above, looking like a single piece of cut crystal, about a meter in diameter. Recessed lighting spotlighted black-and-white photographs on the far wall as well as on the left. Except for a small wooden writing desk and a marble-topped side table, the room was without furniture. He moved to examine the nearest photograph: an old church, its whitewashed walls blurred and softened by the black dust surrounding it. The next photograph was identical, as was the third and fourth. Lanzarote closed the front door quietly.

He walked and then motioned to the far wall. "Please, Father, through that door. And then through the hallway to your left. There is a sitting room with refreshment. If you need the toilet, that is through the door on your right."

"You have been here before."

"Yes. This house belongs to a friend of the archbishop: he often allows meetings and hosts social gatherings for the raising of money. Sometimes, friends of the archbishop stay here: it is *de lux* as you see."

And yet he, a servant of the Vatican, was left to a tiny guest room of a communal and undercleaned seminary. He pushed the door open and more lights switched on. The hallway to his left was long and narrow, of pure white like the entrance, with the same dark polished floors. The walls were adorned with various crosses and crucifixes, all of different styles, ranging from a diamond crusted *crux gemmata* to a gold Celtic *pectus* on his left to a simple wooden cross of St. Peter, looking very old, on his right. He slowly followed Lanzarote down the hall, gazing at the artifacts on either side. They came to the end of the hallway, and Lanzarote opened the door, waited for Signelli to enter.

"That was easy."

"Yeah, it was. You'd think people would show a little more discretion. Especially in that line of work. So who is this Stubby?"

"Stubby's this old-school banger who managed the central Denver coke and meth trade for about ten years. His retirement was seven years in Cañon. He supposedly found Jesus in the pen." Des Prez looked at me. "He did all seven in Cañon because he didn't talk. That's also why they let him retire. He ain't Buttercup. Just saying, I wouldn't get my hopes up, if I were you."

"Where is he now?"

He chuckled. "He has a little condo in Highlands Ranch, believe it or not. I got his address and I'll give him a call, but you all should go on alone: Stubby's not too fond of me."

Highlands Ranch was a south suburb, the whitest in the Denver metro area. It was a planned community, which meant that you had to keep your lawn mowed and your house painted a specific shade of beige: fascism and racism combined in the name of property values. Stubby must have truly found Jesus, or at least a particular brand of Him, to be able to tolerate Highlands Ranch. But maybe it was a relief after Cañon City. Or maybe he had a good bud supply. I needed coffee.

The drive would take twenty minutes to an hour, depending on traffic. If I were in a slightly better mood, I would call the DougCo sheriff, tell them I was crossing the border into their territory to interview a witness. I was not in a better mood. I looked down at my phone and saw that Regis College had called. I-25 was thick, as usual, and full of foul-smelling trucks. The sun was bright and dry. Maldonado was drumming his fingers on the steering wheel. I decided to return the call. I turned the AC down and dialed.

"*Hola.*"

"Father Juan?"

"*Sí, sí.*"

"This is Detective Fruscella. I understand you've been trying to contact me."

"Ah, Detective, *buenos dias*. I have some information, Detective, that you may perhaps find useful. It seems that Father Vidal, *requiescat en pace*, was the *secretario* to the General Director, Father Marcial Maciel, from 2003 to 2006. Before that, he was a lower-level clerk in the financial administration of the order. My friend who provided this information also said that Vidal and Maciel were very close for a time, and he thinks Vidal was present when Maciel died in Florida but is not certain."

"Maciel was the guy who abused those kids and fathered children, right?"

"That is true."

"So, if Vidal was this guy's secretary, he might have known all about this, yes?"

He chuckled. "That is more your line of work, Detective. I save my speculation for other realms."

"Father, thank you very much." I shuffled through my purse, trying to find my notebook. "Father, one more thing. It says here that Father Vidal earned his PhD at the Pontifical Gregorian University. Can you tell me anything about this school?"

"Ah, *si*, P-G-U, an excellent school, one of the very best. It is Jesuit, you know, as is Regis. Many popes, including John Paul I, were students there and our current Eminence, Our Holy Father Benedict XVI, taught there for a while. It is strict, not easy to get in to. I studied there, many many years ago."

"Thank you, Father, thank you. You've been most helpful."

"Goodbye, Detective."

The traffic had thinned, and we were speeding along. I flicked the AC back up. "Juan says Vidal was the secretary to that order's founder, Maciel, the one who liked young boys. 'The gold mine,' as he put it yesterday."

"Is that why he got shot?"

"You tell me." I had to be careful here. I was all ready to think of Vidal as a pederast, a child-molesting procurer, working for Maciel, the definition of a dirty old man, both protected by the corrupt Catholic Church, an obsolete clan of other dirty old men with similar tastes. And while no one deserved a shotgun blast to the face, well, I didn't finish that thought.

I needed more info on Maciel: what was merely alleged versus what was proven. I needed this as neutral as possible. I couldn't ask Juan, and I couldn't trust the Basilica to tell me anything. I needed a good researcher, someone who knew at what he was looking. "Vitalsky have his meeting with the Legion this afternoon?"

"No, they cancelled again. Tomorrow morning supposedly."

"Email or text him and have him research the allegations against Maciel. Go to the newspaper archives, whatever they are. What were the charges, and what was proven? What did he admit? Was he convicted of anything? And was Vidal ever mentioned? I need something besides Wikipedia on this."

Maldonado nodded. "You want me to talk to Duquesne?"

"Yeah, maybe you should. When's the archbishop getting back?"

"He's in Asia, so not for a couple of weeks."

We rode for a while in silence.

FOUR

13th Sunday of Ordinary Time, 2002

Accounts 2000

01.01.2000

Credit Suisse	1287527803–13	$10.436.234
Hottinger & Cie	67–456834–28	$9.843.420
Banque Cantonale de Genève	34968395836464945	€13.429.890
Banque Julius Baer	45–92–19867	FS 1.342.235
Lombard Odier	785049A-123CBC	$12.345.000
UBS	52396–109872-ZXA-8376	$17.500.000
LGT Bank	GUADALUPE65*	FS 10.000.000
Swiss Bank*	Metaxu6791	$5.000.000
Totals		**$50.124.654**
		€13.429.890
		FS 1.342.235

Income (+$5.000)

Individuals

Mary Ann Glendon	$10.000
Plácido Domingo	$10.000
William and Elayne Bennett	$25.000
George Weigel	$10.000
Stephen McEveety and Mel Gibson	$100.000
Rick Santorum	$5.000
Thomas Monaghan	$2.000.000
William Donohue	$20.000
Dionisio Garza Medina	$500.000
Carlos Slim	$5.000.000
Hugo Salinas Price	$2.000.000
Roberto Servitje	$500.000
Alfonso Romo	$500.000
Moreno Valle	$500.000
Carlos Ruiz Sacristán	$750.000
Marta Sahagún	$100.000
Jonathan Morris	$200.000
Eduardo Somalo	$500.000
Stanislaw Dziwisz	$500.000
Angelo Sodano	€500.000
Francis DiLorenzo	$50.000
C. John McCloskey	$500.000
Chapo Guzman	$1.000.000
Servando Gómez Martínez	$500.000
Nazario Moreno González	$250.000

Organizations:

Opus Dei	€1.000.000
Communion and Liberation	€500.000
SSPX	FS 100.000
Knights of Columbus Mexico City	$5.000
Knights of Columbus New Haven	$5.000
Knights of Columbus Guadalajara	$5.000
Diocese of Dallas TX	$10.000
Diócesis de Salamanca	€250.000
Archdiócesis de Madrid	€1.500.000
Arcidiocesi di Napoli	€1.000.000
Archdiocese of El Paso	$5.000
Archdiocese of Laredo	$5.000
Archdiocese of Galveston-Houston	$10.000
Archdiocese of Guadalajara	$10.000
Archdiocese of Monterrey	$5.000
Archdiocese of Puebla	$5.000
Archdiocese of Tijuana	$5.000
Archdiocese of Yucatán	$5.000
F.S.S.P.	FS 10.000
Miles Christi	€200.000
Cancún-Chetumal Prelature	$500.000
Anáhuac	$600.000
Everest Academy Manila	$20.000
International Center for Integral Formation	$25.000
Notre Dame of Jerusalem Center	€5.000
Regnum Christi	€2.000.000
Grand Séminaire de Grenoble	$7.000
Priesterseminar Köln	€50.000
Ducal Georgianum	€50.000

Preister Seminar Regensburg	€5.000
Seminario Mayor Metropolitano del San Cecilio	€10.000
Priestseminar St. Beat	FS 250.000
Seminario Diocesano San Carlo	FS 100.000
Allen Hall Seminary, London	€20.000

Corporations

Carso Global Telecom	$100.000
Mexichem	$500.000
Urbi	$100.000
Grupo México	$250.000
Grupo Elektra	$75.000
Banco Azteca	$100.000
Total	**$9.140.000**
	€3.560.00
	FS 460.000

Donations under $5.000 indexed in Appendix B

Stubby was living in a condo complex called the Carlyle on the street Carlyle Park Circle in a subsection (according to the sign) of Highlands Ranch called Carlyle Park. His 'hood was across the highway from a massive Home Depot, and consisted of identical three-garage three-unit two-story townhomes, with light brown, pale green and watery yellow. repeated like one of Schoenberg's tone rows, into Carlyle Circle infinity. I did notice the anomaly of a Tattered Cover bookstore as we drove in and thought of the old joke about getting arrested smuggling books into Texas. I could possibly understand how someone would want to murder a priest with a shotgun, but I couldn't comprehend why anyone would want to live in a yellow-quartz townhome inserted between a peppermint-tea townhome and a mauve-beige townhome in the Carlyle on Carlyle Circle in Carlyle Park. I supposed you could see the mountains, far far away, from your bedroom window and tell yourself you were living large in colorful Colorado, but I'd almost rather be a dead priest than have to come home to this every night. We had passed a Starbucks just before the bookstore, but as much as I needed coffee, I didn't want to stop, remembering Persephone and her pomegranates.

Stubby's unit was mauve-beige. We got out of the car and the heat hit. Felt like over a hundred. "What's his real name?"

Maldonado looked at the file. "Anthony Erik Carpenter. Sixty-eight. Born in Las Vegas, Nevada."

"Vegas huh? So he likes the heat," was all I could think to say. Even with my sunglasses, the sun was intolerable. I shaded my brow with my hand as Maldonado rang the doorbell. A tall, thin, stooped man answered the door. He wore thick glasses with black old-school frames, a crisp white T-shirt, blue athletic shorts and flip-slops. "Yes?"

"I'm Detective Fruscella, and this is Detective Maldonado. We'd like to ask you a few questions."

He nodded, then moved aside to reveal a beige-gold carpeted stairway. "After you."

The temperature rose a degree for every step we took, so it must have been a hundred and ten at the top, a darkened sweatbox with only the faintest resemblance to a room where "living" would be one's guess as to its purpose. Through the gloom I could see the outlines of a TV, a couch and two chairs facing. The vague shape of a low table filled the space between the couch and the TV. I could feel sweat underneath my boobs and the small of my back. "I gotta keep the curtains closed because of the sun," he said behind us. "It's a little better in the afternoon, when I can open some windows and get a cross draft." He flicked an overhead light that cut the gloom and revealed a high cathedral ceiling, walls matching the carpet, and the couch matching the walls. A heavy chrome-and-glass coffee table separated the couch from the TV and chairs, an empty liter bottle of water standing near the center. It was better with the light off. "Sit down," he said as he moved to one of the chairs and turned it slightly. "Take the couch." A dog barked shrilly somewhere close. Stubby sat down and scratched his elbow. The couch was more comfortable than it looked, although when we sat, I noticed the faint smell of dog. "What can I do for you?"

Maldonado leaned forward and handed him Martinez's photo. "You recognize this man?"

"I don't know. You working on something?"

"We're homicide detectives, Mr. Carpenter. Do you know this man?"

"Yeah, that's what des Prez said; you were from Homicide. This about the priest?"

"Do you recognize this man, Mr. Carpenter?"

He stared at the photograph, scratched his chin and then his nose. He handed the photograph back to Maldonado. The dog started up again. I felt sleepy. "Yeah, I know him. Without the beard. Willie Martinez. The Sarge."

"Do you know where he lives?"

"No, I'm not sure. Somewhere near Cheesman."

"How do you know Mr. Martinez?"

He chuckled. I stifled a yawn. "We knew some of the same people, I guess you could say."

"Did you supply Mr. Martinez with any drugs?"

I could see his eyes narrow in the light. "Don't know anything about that."

I heard myself say, "I'm not at all interested in any sort of activity or commerce, illegal or otherwise, that may have occurred in the past between you and Mr. Martinez. We need to find him, and now. Please, Mr. Carpenter, what was your relationship with Mr. Martinez?"

"You think he killed the priest, is that it?"

We didn't answer.

He looked at me, then at Maldonado, then at the floor. I stifled a yawn. Carpenter was likely undergoing some sort of internal trial, with the voice of the *omertà* code of the gangster convict on one side battling with the voice of newly found Jesus whispering that killing a priest is going too far on the other. He had put his face in his hands, so I couldn't see his face, couldn't see the struggle. God it was hot. I felt like fanning myself with the file. I was having a hard time keeping my eyes open, and so I shifted on the couch, trying to jar myself back to attention. It almost seemed as if Carpenter were praying.

Finally, finally, he must have turned to me. His voice startled me. "You don't know anything."

And then, after a while, "Cherokee Apartments, across from Cheesman. Second floor. I don't remember the number."

The room was a cube was made of glass, with the exceptions of the parquet floor and the wall behind him from the hallway. The night sky was turning a deep *celeste opaco* and dominated the ceiling and the right panel, reminding him of his brother Jacopo's bicycle. A small floor lamp with a neon blue shade added very little internal illumination from the far left corner. It was dramatic, the glass walls and ceiling, much like being outside. As he proceeded, the wooden floor gave way to soft carpet, and he bumped his left shin against a low blonde table. A dark rectangular desk ran almost the length of the far wall, and as his eyes began to accustom themselves to the darkness, he noticed the shapes of two thick telescopes behind the desk. His white cassock seemed ghostly in the bluish gloom. Lanzarote floated deftly behind the desk, and the room gradually lightened. Signelli noticed a silver plate of cheese on the desk and two leather chairs on his left flanking the table he had stumbled against.

"Here are snacks, Father, and a drinks cart behind you in the corner." He turned to see a large silver cart laden with bottles. "I know little about wine, so I brought up a bottle of red and white: I am certain the cellar here is good, and I hope my choices adequate. You may adjust the lighting here." He turned back and saw Lanzarote pointing to a corner of the desk. "I will stay near the entrance, Father, to admit your guests. Is there anything else you can think?"

There was nothing else he could think. He nodded to Lanzarote, who glided past him soundlessly. As the door closed, he turned to the drinks cart. A silver bucket of ice held a bottle of San Pellegrino and bottle of Jacques LaTour Aligoté. He set his package on the floor, removed the cork, poured a large glass and drank half quickly. A bit minerally, but refreshing. He leaned down, picked up the bag and walked over to the desk, where he removed the book, wrapped in brightly colored blue-and-green giftwrap, set in on the center, and placed the bag in the corner near the lamp.

He sipped his wine. Where should he stand? Behind the desk? Or should he sit? At the desk or in one of the large chairs? This was more the set of a play than a functional room. He turned to look at the night sky, which was quickly becoming a purple, dusky slate. *Pater noster, qui es in caelis,* a dimming and receding heaven.

Propter quod placeo mihi in infirmitatibus in contumeliis in necessatatibus in persecutionibus in angustiis pro Christo cum enim infirmor tunc potens sum. He touched the cool glass wall with the fingertips of his left hand, his white reflection brightly mirrored. He focused his eyes on the grass behind and a thin solitary sapling fifteen or so meters from the wall. This was an indifferent place, neither sacred nor cursed. It was transparent and dead, too young, too new to reverberate either with God's low voice or with evil's mocking echo. The new world. It was as if God's illimitable love had not reached there yet, had not wanted to. Such thoughts were blasphemy, perhaps. God's love was there, and everywhere, present and powerful. *Pater noster, qui es in caelis.*

What would he see in this telescope? Could he see into heaven? *Non poteris videre faciem meam non enim videbit me homo et vivet.* To see God's face: what an awful and terrible wish. He wasn't ready to change tense, as Father Raymondo used to say. Not just yet.

His imagination was inadequate for such speculation. He leaned forward and tried to fit his left eye to the eyepiece of the nearest telescope, but no matter how he adjusted and squinted, nothing became visible. Just as well. He sipped his wine and turned. How best to approach the detective? The desk would create distance and perhaps strengthen his authority, while if they both sat in the leather chairs, there would be the illusion of friendly equality. Hmmm. Likely she would be fooled by neither.

He finished the glass and immediately desired another. What was his purpose here? What was his objective? To gather information on the status of the case, yes. And to inquire about Father Vidal's property, specifically any notes and records pertaining to his work with the Legionaries of Christ, records which might prove embarrassing and damaging to the Holy Church should they fall into the hands of the scandal-hungry press. Yes, yes. He would remind the detective that the property of deceased clergy pertaining to their ecclesiastical life or work was in fact property of the order to which the clergy belonged and reverted to that order. He would offer any assistance he could provide, yes, yes, yes. But how to best approach this?

He heard noises from the hallway as he grasped the cold bottle and poured. The Aligoté reminded him of the inexhaustible supply of Borgnano Pinot Bianco that Father Mancato used to share with him the summer he worked with the orphans in Cormons. It had been years since he'd thought about St. Fosca and those children, brown as the soil, always dirty, always hungry, always moving, like small bugs, kicking up clouds of dust. They would all eat their polenta early, about six in the morning, and then proceed to the sugar beet fields, where they would work until three in the afternoon. He had tried to avoid polenta ever since.

He sipped his wine and turned. "Father."

"*Ispettora*, Detective, please sit down. Would you like something to drink, some wine perhaps, or mineral water?"

R was twelve years old, going on thirteen. He was a dark boy, a mixture of Salvadorian on his mother's side and perhaps Puerto Rican, perhaps something else, on his father's. His mother was nineteen when he was born, alone, frightened but delighted with this boy who emerged from her womb with a full head of black bristly hair, skin the color of pancake syrup. She could do this, she was certain, with God's help. She could raise her beautiful son to be fine, upstanding and strong. And his eyes, his eyes were like shining black stars surrounded by the longest lashes she had ever seen. And she named him R, after her favorite saint, as a promise to God to raise him in the Church. Father M had assured her he would be welcome, regardless of his origin, that her sin was forgivable, perhaps already forgiven, but in any case it would not stain the soul of the boy: he would be baptized as soon as she was well.

He was a shy boy, hard to reach, and seemed to move within a space determined by a different relationship to time than most. When he was seven, his mother married J, a Panamanian who found Jesus in the California State Prison at Corcoran, and so R suddenly acquired a new father and two half sisters, older by ten and twelve years. A loved Jesus and *la grifa* equally and found it possible to devotedly demonstrate his love for both. R seemed to go on as before, thin-hipped and long-lashed, his movements somehow both furtive and deliberate.

Soon after marrying, J moved his family inland, chasing a night watchman job at a Staples warehouse. R and his mother had to say goodbye to the kindly Father M and hello to Father B, the parish priest, and Father G, the youth pastor. Father G was handsome, in that tanned Anglo sort of way, coifed blonde with big white teeth. He looked like a protestant, J thought, one of those slick *estafadors* on TV. It was difficult to know what R thought.

The first time, when R was twelve and a half years old, Father G took R by the wrist and placed his hand on Father G's lap. They were sitting in Father G's car, an old white Chrysler Imperial, and had both just finished large ice cream cones from Baskin-Robbins. R featured a streak of Cherry Chocolate Cake on his upper lip.

"Do you feel anything?" asked Father G. R didn't answer or move. "Do you feel anything here?" Father G rubbed R's hand on something inside of his slacks. "Or do you feel anything here?" and Father G leaned back and moved his hand from his lap to the place between R's legs. R looked out the window at a small yellow dog worrying a fast food bag near a rusted barrel. The dog was patient, relaxed, as if it were playing with the bag merely to pass time or to give R something to watch.

Father G took his hand from R and unzipped his pants. "Now you feel something, don't you," said Father G as he positioned R's hand on the base of his penis. "Make a circle with your fingers, like this. No, no, like this. That's it." He took R's wrist with the tips of two fingers and gently moved his hand up and down.

The dog was shaking the bag with its head. R could feel Father G's penis stiffening. The dog's shiver moved down from the head to the neck, through the torso and out the tail. "Do you feel that?- Do you feel that, son? That's the Holy Spirit making itself known. Thanks to you, my boy, thanks to you. Oh my beautiful boy, my beautiful R. Look at me, look at me please."

R kept his gaze fixed out the window. Past the dog and the rusted barrel was a sagging chain-link fence leaning away from the wind, and past that the dust partially obscured a slight hill, a solitary section of concrete wall and a once-blue portable toilet. The wind whipped the fast food bag away from the dog and against the fence. The dog gave a little bark, chased the bag, then changed its mind and ran in the opposite direction, quickly disappearing behind the car. "Come, Oh Holy Spirit, fill the hearts of your faithful. Look at me, dear R, look at me. This is the work of the Lord."

Before Father G dropped R off at home that afternoon, he told him how they were both doing God's work and that God's work was blessed, not to be discussed with anyone. And that if R were to discuss this with anyone, he, Father G, would be severely disappointed that R has chosen to disobey both Father G and God. Secrecy was sacred. Besides, he doubted very much than anyone would believe R anyway. Father G insisted that he accompany R into his house, where he greeted both J and the younger daughter, T. J thought Father G a little disheveled, given his customary impeccability. T thought R was more spaced than usual, but who could tell?

The second time also occurred in Father G's Imperial. They were parked at the same place, a cul-de-sac between two small hills surrounded by abandoned construction. Father G had taken four boys to a high school basketball game and had dropped the other three off. It was dark, and so there was nothing to see out the window, but still R turned away. Father G had brought some suntan lotion, and the car smelled like coconuts and bananas. Father G removed his fingers from R's wrist, and R let his hand drop. "You're not doing your part, son. You're letting me do all the work. This is not what God wants. I'm a priest: you need to believe me." They sat there for a moment, neither moving. Suddenly Father G moved his arm around R's shoulder and drew R's face to his. He began to kiss R lightly, gently on the forehead, the cheeks, the eyes, the chin. He moved his lips to the corner of R's mouth and drug his upper lip against R's bottom lip. Up close, Father G smelled like shampoo and incense. "Relax, my son. Enjoy God's work."

FIVE

The Feast of All Souls Day, 1991

The Life of Saint Teresa of Avila by Herself Two

Describes the continued course of my life and how the Lord granted me a great relief from my trials by bringing me a visit from the holy man, the Nuestro Padre, Father Marcial Maciel Degollado, and how he asked if I would serve our Majesty through him and the congregation of the Legionaries of Christ.

Something extraordinary happened last night, and I'm not sure what to make of it. I believe there is much of the work of the Lord here, but I will need to pray on it further. I will first try to write this down as neutrally and accurately as possible.

It has now been seven months since I graduated from the Pontifical Gregorian University and was ordained. But the Jesuits, my brothers, have abandoned me, leaving me here without an invitation to Tertianship or any explanation of my status. My questions are not answered and my calls not returned. This has left a great number of hours for prayer and for my as yet unsuccessful attempts to achieve a faithful Christian ecstasy. I believe I am on the right path, an unlit path, but true. No, I am not certain. Perhaps this is all a mistake.

Last night I journeyed out to walk and to clear my head: God alone was too much. I found myself in the Trastevere, in the

Piazza di San Francesco d'Assisi. It was late, just after midnight, and I desired company. I wasn't hungry, and I seldom drink, but I wanted to be in the presence of other human beings. The film house was just letting out, so I followed a group of ten or so university students, a bit younger than I, down the *Via Portuense*. They were all laughing and talking, flirting and holding hands, smoking, four men and five or six women. They sounded Roman, except one of the girls, whom they teased because her Brindisi accent was hard to understand. But she was the prettiest, with dark straight hair and a loping, athletic walk, and so the teasing was mild.

I followed for about twenty minutes, ten feet behind, and they never noticed me, or if they did, gave no sign. They went inside a young people's *osteria*, dark and cavelike, with cheap wine, American food and loud talk. These places are not for me, but I noticed a seat at the far end of the bar where I could perhaps have something to drink and not be noticed. I don't know what kept me from turning around and walking back into the night.

I ordered a beer, a Peroni, and sat. The group I had followed had disappeared into another room, and so I studied first the bartender, an older man of about fifty, a greying ponytail, a long German face, deliberate, almost underwater movements, and then a couple of blonde women sitting at the bar with very short hair, expensive looking jackets and black lipstick. I wondered what they could be doing: they were too well-dressed and handsome to be street whores, and they didn't fit my initial impression of the pub's clientele. Perhaps they were there to meet their dates.

An older, well-dressed gentleman appeared at the end of the bar. I was certain he was looking for the women, and I was interested to see their reaction. But he nodded slightly not at them but at me. Surely a mistake, I thought. He walked up and gently spoke in soft, perfect Italian, "Father Andrea?"

"*Si*, yes."

"Someone would like to speak to you."

"Here? Now?"

He smiled. "Yes, of course. Will you please follow me?" I took my glass as he turned and led me across the dark, crowded room and through a door on the far wall. This led to another similar room with loud music and few people, and again we walked out another door which led to an outside patio. This was strange: perhaps one of the whores I had employed had recognized me, or maybe Grigio, the man who sold me drugs, wanted something. Was I in danger? The patio was small, about five or six tables, and unlit. "Father Andrea," a friendly, high-pitched voice echoed from two dark shapes in the corner. I moved toward them and sat in a proffered chair. An older-looking man with glasses gracefully lit a cigarette and then a small lamp on the table between us. He leaned forward. His forehead was high, and his thick lenses reflected the light of the candle. "Father Andrea, I am Father Marcial Maciel, of the Legionaries of Christ. I am so very happy to meet you." I had heard of the Legionaries and Father Maciel: the Legion was very conservative and Father Maciel was very good with money. What could he want with me? "We have mutual friends, you and I." Mutual friends?

"From the Jesuits?" He leaned back into the darkness, the tip of his cigarette glowing in the gloom. His voice, while high-pitched and wet and full of lung, sounded kind.

"I know something about you and your situation."

"My situation?"

"Do not pretend to be stupid. I know you have not yet been invited to your Tertianship. You realize, of course, that it is unlikely you ever will be. No," he leaned forward and flicked his ash into an ashtray near the candle, "I'm afraid service to the Society of Jesus is not in God's plan for you." I couldn't speak, and even if I could, I didn't know what to say. Why did he know so much about me? And what was he doing in this *osteria* this late on a Tuesday night? He leaned back again, and I heard the man to his right cough. "I know something of why you won't be invited to continue and find your dilemma, well, interesting. You are, how do we say in English, 'at loose ends.'" He chuckled.

"How do you know all this?"

"That's not important." He leaned forward again, his forehead illuminated by the candle. "I do have some advice for you, my young friend. Although many disagree, I believe that faith is absolutely personal, between a sinner and God: it is much too important to be left to the advice or experience of others. Sometimes, if you find someone who understands and can empathize, this counsel can be wise and illuminating. But with the majority, with the religious as well as the world at large, you will find only mediocre minds and limited souls, shrill voices that are incapable of doing anything other than sanctimonious nagging. In our Father's house there are many mansions. Our relationship with Jesus is deep within us, and all the rest, the collar, the alb, the ciborium, the hymn, the nave, the transept, all of these are but medieval accessories, designed to impress the illiterate. God can see through such costuming to the true soul struggling within." He put his cigarette out in the ashtray and leaned back, disappearing completely into the darkness. "And the struggles of your soul, Father Andrea Vidal, they are genuine. And not unheard of."

I remembered my beer and took a small sip to wet my throat. I was at a loss. I was thrilled that a man of such power and influence had taken to me, yet was also wary of the attention. I had done nothing to deserve this, this scrutiny. But perhaps I was too mistrustful. His voice was kind, and he spoke as if he'd understood something my brother Jesuits did not.

He remained in the darkness. "I have a proposition for you, Father Andrea. I need someone who is intelligent and who knows languages to assist me. Will you join the Legionaries of Christ? To work on my personal staff, based in Mexico City? The Jesuits," he hesitated, "will not interfere."

We said our goodbyes and left. As we walked down the stairs, Maldonado called HQ to have the apartments staked out until we got there. "You know this place?" I asked in the relative coolness of the landing.

"No, not at all."

"Get someone to contact the owner, landlord, property manager or whatever. I want a list of tenants. I don't want to have to watch the whole complex, and I don't want to have to knock on every fucking door. I also don't want any mistakes here: we are *not* going to break down the wrong door and scare some four-year-old half to death because some marine wannabe can't tell a three from an eight. I'll drive."

The sun seemed even hotter and brighter than earlier, enveloping the entire pastel street with a detailed clarity that seemed akin to bleach. I would be happy to leave. My phone rang as I opened the car door, and I was grateful for the excuse to ignore either Schlaf or that asshole Clark from the PIO. I drove quickly as

Maldonado worked his phone and I ignored mine. Through extensive and often circuitous conversations with various departments and representatives of Mountain States Property Management Company of Golden, Colorado, Maldonado believed he had narrowed Martinez (whose name was unknown to documents and personnel) to two possible apartments: 206 and 218. Then, just as we turned off on Colfax, he thought he was pretty sure it was 218, as the name for 206 did check out.

"Good. Get the warrant?"

"Almost."

The Cherokee was an old Victorian on Humboldt. It was three stories, grey, with a concrete porch and a row of ten shiny new aluminum mailboxes next to a heavy wood-and-glass door. I drove around the block trying to find parking, and saw a couple of squad cars and the SWAT van, ordered by Schlaf I guessed, jammed into a tiny lot near a dental clinic. I found a bus stop, put the cherry on the dashboard and exited the vehicle.

It was cooler here, somewhat leafy, and the light was more forgiving, less transparent and oppressive. A couple of plain-clothes hurried up: a tall, sallow looking man with a ponytail, and shorter, dark Asian-Indian woman with an overbite and pretty eyes.

"You are?"

"I am Delaja. This is Farmer. No one in or out since we got here."

"I'm Fruscella; this is Maldonado. Back door?"

"Crissman and Delpino in the alley, with Lassus and Butorac."

"You check the mailboxes?"

"Yeah. No Martinez. Only a couple have names anyway."

"Close the street. Who's commanding SWAT?"

"I am. Captain Fay." A bulky white guy in full battle dress approached from the right and stuck out his hand. Four regular police officers materialized and joined us.

"All right. Fay, I want you and your team in support, *outside*. I don't want them in unless we call. Got that?"

"Detective, can I come with? I'll leave my team out here."

"OK." I turned to Maldonado, "What's the story with the tenant again?"

"Two eighteen is rented to one Corto Kirk, previous address unknown. Kirk's employer is listed as Handy's Landscaping, and previous employers are Coronado Moving and Atlas Van Lines."

I turned to Delaja. "Crime Lab here?"

She nodded. "They parked a couple blocks away."

"Is anyone here from the property manager?"

"Yeah, but he's in a squad car. Here are the keys."

"Do we know where two eighteen is located?"

She checked her notebook. "On the second floor. Two eighteen is to the right of that big window in front," she pointed. "There's a landing with stairs there and no elevator."

"How many rooms?"

"One bedroom, one bath, small kitchen off the main room, one walk-in closet. No balcony, fire escape on the right side."

"Everyone got photos?"

The six uniforms nodded.

I moved around to the back of the car and opened the trunk. "Everyone in vests."

I never liked this cowboy shit.

Up close, the Cherokee looked the worse for wear. The grey was hastily applied primer over brick. The heavy wood-and-glass door was maybe original but pockmarked and carelessly stained, with dark wood color smeared all along the edges of the frosted glass. We unlocked and opened the door.

The landing was painted badly using the outside primer and smelled of pot and burned bread. A darkened hallway on the left led to the rear of the building, with single doors on each side. To the right, stairs rose for a few feet onto another landing and then, accompanied by a picket railing painted an incongruous dull orange, doubled back steeply to the front.

"Tell the back door we're inside."

We made our way cautiously up the stairs, my weapon heavy in my hand, my vest heavy on my shoulders. Gravity was a bitch. We didn't stop at the first landing but climbed the creaking stairs, hugging both walls, to the second floor. We were likely surprising no one. I was sweating heavily.

She was shorter than he pictured. Her hair was dark and streaked with grey, swept back loosely in a mare's tail. She looked tired, her eyes especially, and it seemed as if her straightened posture was costing her some effort. He immediately felt some sympathy for this Fruscella and almost as quickly wondered from where such sympathy was coming. She was no *gattara*, no, but an exhausted provincial deacon wearily passing the collection plate to the three old women near the back.

"Thank you, Father. Water will be fine."

He poured some of the Pellegrino into a red wine glass and handed it to her. She gave him the slightest smile, held his gaze, then looked past him quickly, her eyes restless. They stood facing each other for some moments, sipping slowly at their glasses. "Please, sit." He motioned to one of the leather chairs and then moved slowly behind the desk. He kept his back to her even after he'd maneuvered to the spot near the telescopes, took a small drink of his wine and looked up again at the nearly black sky dotted with a few large stars. He could see his reflection do the same. God was in His heaven. He finished his glass.

He moved around to the grouping of low chairs and motioned for her to sit. She sat stiffly, erect, knees and feet together, her hands in her lap, her gaze directed somewhere just above his head. He set his glass softly on the table. He was in no rush. After a while, he motioned with his right hand. "This room, it is a strange room, yes? Like the set of a stage."

She made no reply but kept her gaze fixed, her face and body immobile. After a while she said slowly, carefully, as if she were considering each syllable, "You wanted to see me?"

He smiled, leaned forward. "Yes, yes, I wanted to see you. And thank you for agreeing to this meeting."

Without movement she answered, "I was asked to oblige. It was not my choice."

"We all have bosses, those we must answer to. But I did want to greet you, to have a conversation, to offer my cooperation."

She took a drink of water, shifted her weight slightly and crossed her ankles. "I am not sure what we have to discuss: I can share no information regarding an ongoing investigation."

"I am aware that you American authorities are closed with the details while the *caso* is being heard. But perhaps we can speak more generally, without the details?"

"I don't know how I can help you, Father. I'm not going to discuss this case."

He nodded. "But perhaps I can help you. I can remind you, for example, that the property of poor Father Andrea Vidal, *requiescat in pace*, the property pertaining to Father Vidal's priestly duties belongs not to his family but to the Catholic Church." He leaned back and intertwined his hands in front of his chest. "And I am guessing that much of this property is not relevant to his murder. And so, it would be appreciated if this property could be returned to the Church in a timely way."

She answered with that same measured tempo, as if she were reciting rather than speaking. "I can assure you Vidal's possessions will be released to the appropriate parties when the case is concluded."

He leaned forward again and spoke softly. "There exist documents the Church is most eager to recover. Documents which might prove slightly, should we say, embarrassing to the Church should they be made public, given the malicious scandalmongering of your press."

She brought her gaze down and looked him full in the face. "I have nothing to say, Father."

He smiled, took his glass by the stem and walked slowly to the drinks cart, where he poured himself another glass of the Aligoté. He moved around her quickly and sat heavily in the facing chair. As he sat, he gazed at the objects on the desk, first at the silver platter, then the gift wrapped book. "Would you like something to snack? Some cheese?"

"No thank you."

He took a sip of wine, then leaned forward and placed the glass on the table between them. He looked up and gave her a half-smile. "I understand you have a suspect."

She met his gaze but said nothing.

He broke off her gaze, looked down at his hands, then back up to her face. "Perhaps I've been misinformed?"

"Father, I've nothing to say."

He smiled. "I am not a bad friend, Detective. The Church, the Catholic Church is a very complicated organization. Some say too complicated. Some say it is not complicated but secretive. I do not know. I do know that it can help to have someone who understands what person to telephone. I can open doors. Perhaps can save time." He looked down and continued, as if talking to his hands. "For example, perhaps more information on Father Vidal's past, on his work with the Legionaries of Christ, would help your investigation."

"If the Church, the Vatican, has any information that would benefit this homicide investigation, I must ask that it be handed over with all possible speed."

"Oh, I am sorry: I've been unclear. This is most unofficial: I do not speak for the Vatican and certainly not for the Church. No, I am merely a private citizen doing what I can to help. I can represent nobody but myself."

"If the Church or anyone has information that pertains to a homicide investigation, then it must release such information in a timely manner or risk obstruction charges. . ."

"*La Chiesa non può essere minacciata.* Detective, you cannot threaten the Church."

Delaja had it right: 218 was in front to my right. I motioned with my head to the door and then with my left hand to the three other doors of the landing: I didn't want any surprises, innocent or not. A couple of the uniforms nodded. As I leaned against the wall and prepared to knock, Maldonado moved quickly around to the other side and banged on the door with his left hand. "Denver police!" he shouted. Dick move. What was that about? "Open the door." I'd have to talk to him about that. He knocked again. "Denver police."

Nothing. No sound from anywhere. "Denver police. Please open the door."

We waited. I motioned to Delaja, who held the keys. She unlocked the door quickly. "Careful, all," I said, not looking at Maldonado.

Fay went first, followed by one of the uniforms, and then Skinny (I had already forgotten his name). Weapons drawn, carefully and calmly, just like the TV shows. The apartment was dark, with lots of wood and an expensive-looking oriental rug underfoot. I made my way to the center of the living room. At first glance, the place was a lot nicer inside than out.

"All clear," from Fay. No surprise. We relaxed, holstered our weapons.

I started to put my rubber gloves on. "Thanks, Fay. You and your men can go now. Delaja, you and your partner can stay, but everyone else should stand down. Maldonado, get the Crime Lab up here."

The room was hot, the air stale. Thick wooden slats shaded the large window to my right. I moved to open them and saw they were covered with a fine layer of dust. The light admitted was soft and dappled by the window slats and the leaves of a tall tree near the street. I turned away from the window and looked into the living room. This was not the apartment of any low-life druggie I'd ever met. In addition to the aforementioned carpet, Persian if I had to guess and not from Design Within Reach, there was a worn dark leather loveseat that looked like an expensive Finn Juhl knockoff, a mahogany coffee table with hairpin legs and an antique drop leaf bar cart with a brass frame and wheels with numerous and varied booze bottles haphazardly arranged. A large floor-to-ceiling built-in bookcase dominated the wall farthest from the door. I moved across the soft carpet to examine the reading material: the books were neatly arranged, seemingly grouped by subject matter. The top four shelves featured religious books, from what I could tell, as many of the volumes were in languages other than English, with authors unknown to me. The bottom two shelves, well, there was a slight change of subject, with obvious titles and lavish cover illustrations: *A Beginners Guide to S & M*, with drawings and photographs, seemed well-read, as did *The Master's Manual: A Handbook of Erotic Dominance*. *Safe Word: A Guide to Masochism* included some marginal scribblings, although *The New Bottoming, High Protocol* and *Gorean Slave Positioning and Training* looked untouched. Most were in English but not all. I called Maldonado over. "What's wrong with this picture?"

"I don't know. Books are too neat?"

"No, look. The top shelf: four Bibles, and this looks like Latin, a bunch of commentaries, *Christ: A Biography*, *Lives of the Saints*, some deep religious books, not for the beach. Those are about two-thirds of the bookshelf, four out of six shelves, OK?"

"Yes?"

"And then on the bottom, pardon the pun, we have *A Beginners Guide to Sex with Drugs and Drugs with Sex*; *Fisting: Care, Responsibility and Trust* and *How to Bottom Without Pain or Stains*. An odd assortment, I'd say."

"Hmm. *Prostate Massage Made Easy, The Anal Sex Positions Guide, Fellatio 101.*"

From another room; "Detective, you should come here. You'll want to see this."

This could be anything. The bedroom was less lavish than the living room, dominated by a king-size bed with a small sisal rug in front, a light oak dresser with a mirror on the right and not much else. A full-length closet took up the left wall. A detective stood in the closet's mouth, his head twisted toward the bedroom door. As I got closer, I noticed a small dressing table inside the closet with two, no, three Styrofoam mannequin heads, each sporting long brunette hair.

Oh fuck. My first thought was that they were scalps. I hesitated, my stomach turned. "Wigs. Human hair, detective. Look." He presented a lock from the nearest piece. I swallowed. My breath returned. I touched the strands. I couldn't tell much through the rubber gloves. I didn't remember any cross-dressing books in the bookcase. "These are expensive, Detective. Remy hair, virgin I'd guess."

"Remy hair?"

"Expensive, the best wig you can buy. Virgin means undyed. I'd guess five hundred, maybe even a thousand each."

I never heard of any junkie with three grand in wigs. At least they weren't taken from some head now stored in the fridge. Nor from genuine virgins. These were too good to be mere props, weren't they? More like disguises? What kind of man who lived in the Cherokee apartments and drank at the Satire Lounge would wear thousand dollar wigs? And why?

SIX

The Day of the Solemnity of Saints Peter and Paul, Apostles and Martyrs, 2001
Angelus Silesius—*The Cherubic Pilgrim*

Ketamine, 50 mgs., time slow and sleepy
Underwater, the self quickens, hesitates, remains.
Ketamine, 75 mgs., I see my body
From far away, split but there, here, forever, always.
Ketamine, 110 mgs., K-hole
Separated from self, from God, from all, distance deceptive.
Ketamine, solitude, unbridgeable and constant
Soft and cold, the Other's touch nauseating, dishonest.

Psilocybe cubensis, the Latin wrong, before Christ
Before Europe, when God was many, everywhere and close
Quetzalcoatl, plumed serpent, bleeding and impregnating
Mushrooms as Eucharist, old blood, old dust, Amen.
Four dried caps, over two grams, taste dry, unclean, transgressive
As literal, pre-metaphor, body of earth, Christ flesh.

Impatient, nauseous, peripheral colors, peripheral others

Music somewhere, trumpet, the room too yellow, easy laughter, mirrors avoided.

Six dried caps and stems, three grams solo, sunny Cheesman Park

Inability to cease, the dread I am, relentless, indefatigable.

Nine dried caps with stems, four grams plus each, Ernesto, Just Bill,

A name I never learned with Su, afternoon Sancho's pitchers

Ernesto dances more giggles music too loud, Su and Just Bill gone

Nameless girl now looks young, thin, too fragile to be here.

Bill and Su return, Ernesto and I play foosball, approximate, asked to stop

Ernesto continues, asked to leave, Ernesto enraged, Nameless weeps

Cops threatened, Just Bill intercedes, I pay for Coors, sidewalk bright, hot

The Snug suggested, acclaimed, direction uncertain, Su left, me right.

The sun violent, blinding, reflecting off asphalt, metal, glass

Unbearable heat, dessicating, my flesh now brittle, inorganic

Following Su, forever it seems, through waves of heat and thoughts

I stumble, scrape my shoulder on bricks, Via Dolorosa loco tribus.

Snug cool, dark, with black drinks, laughter resumes, legs itch

Suddenly night, a broken glass, spilled beer, bleeding fingers, ruined shirt.

400 mgs. Mandrax, my fist buried deep

Inside someone, past the wrist, then oblivion, temporary.

500 mgs. mandrax, vague shadows, figures, tastes of salt

Monochromatic, a dark grey masking time-opening possibilities.

120 mg. molly, glasses of water

Childlike wonder, the world to be discovered anew

Seduction of seemingly pure beauty, imagery

Not spiritual, God lowered to earthly light, brilliant, mundane.

150 mg. molly, with water

Warehouse, loud music, human bodies, sea of angels

Bathroom blowjob, unholy mouth, sexless, anonymous
Smells of vomit, cum, sprayed chemicals, wet paper towels
We love you truly, the drug and I, whomever
And whatever you may be, on this the highest mountain.
Ecstacy, a fascination, a broken promise of nothing,
A small lamp glowing in the dark, proving only tragic resilience.

The closet was sparsely populated, with a couple of unlabeled light black wool suits, nicely cut; one deep blue cotton suit; three white button down shirts, also unlabeled; one ugly Hawaiian shirt from Tommy Bahama; two Izod polos, one pink and one deep purple; and a thick leather jacket, good leather, but again, no label. Three pair of shoes were arranged below, all on heavy wooden shoe-trees. They were black, one wing-tip, one cap-toed oxford and one plain oxford, from To Boot and Fratelli Rossetti and Oliver Sweeney. I didn't recognize the names, but I did recognize the quality, pardon the sexist cliché whereby all women love shoes. The leather was soft, the heels solid and the stitching fine: these were superior goods, beyond my price range. Who *was* this guy with the expensive fake hair and quality shoes?

I replaced the shoes and opened the top drawer of the dressing table in the closet. Socks, mostly black and all matched; underwear, mostly white and neatly folded, nothing that would tie him to the vic or to the Church. There were no half-burnt crucifixes, no Bibles with ripped-out pages (I checked), no newspaper clippings detailing the various and indefatigable Catholic abuses of the past years or decades or centuries. The movies were fond of that, although I had never met any killer with a clipping collection or scrapbook of obsessions. Most of the murderers I arrested were not that imaginative or else they had seen those same movies and were careful not to leave such obvious trails. Actually, almost all the killers I arrested weren't planning to kill that morning when they got up: it just kind of happened. Zemlinsky was one of the few exceptions.

Second drawer, T-shirts. White cotton short sleeves folded and stacked on one side, Hanes, and on the other the colored T-shirts, mostly black and dark blue, none with designs or logos, also Hanes or Fruit of the Loom. I took both stacks out, put them on the floor, and felt around the drawer. Nothing. I replaced the shirts carefully.

Last drawer: athletic clothes—Adidas and Nike shorts, black-and-white tube socks, generic, white-and-grey T-shirts. No sports teams, no beer, no bars or slogans, nothing but a small swoosh or that Adidas three-striped thing. Again, I felt around the empty drawer and found zero. I didn't see any sneakers in the closet. I moved on to the dresser against the far wall. There was a boom box on top, with various cassettes and cases strewn about: *Romantic Tango*, *Astor Piazzolla Tango in HiFi*, *Astor Piazzolla Interpreta Piazolla*, *Kanye West Late Registration*, *Diego Urcola Libertango*, *Los Tijuana Perros Pinche Perros* and some unmarked cases without tapes. Next to the boom box and tapes was an old clay incense burner in the shape of a square adobe hut with some incense ash inside. An empty rocks glass with no smell completed the accessories on top of the dresser.

The first drawer was full of drug paraphernalia, appropriate to the character of the Willem Martinez we'd initially fabricated. There were three old-school glass syringes, which I hadn't seen in quite a while, and reusable needles, clean and topped with plastic covers. There were a couple of charred bent spoons, a glass crack pipe, a small hash pipe, and six prescription pill containers, each with numbers written on generic white stickers attached to the sides: 5–22–6798 or 56–89–510–268. I opened one, with some trouble, and found six shiny unmarked blue pills. Dude did not like labels. Another contained dark brown powder, maybe heroin. I didn't open the others. There were also twelve brown vials, all unused and empty, rattling around loose, along with a few rubber tourniquets, wooden matchboxes, four green BIC lighters and three empty ballpoint pen shells. I noticed a small tin that once held Sucrets. Inside were four Plasticine bags, each with a medium-size crystal of what I guessed was top grade methamphetamine. There was also a squat glass jar half filled with change.

He looked at her again to see her reaction. She was still sitting stiffly, her posture rigid, her eyes tired. *Testa dura*, like a Calabrese. He licked his lips and fought down a yawn, wondered about the time in Rome. God give me strength.

"It seems," he began again, "as if we have started speaking on the wrong foot. It is not my intention to come to ask you to betray your regulations, to disclose informations you are uncomfortable disclosing; that is certainly not the reasoning behind my request to meet with you. No. I simply wanted to offer my help in securing researches that perhaps might help with your investigations. And to inform you that Father Vidal is—was—in possession of documents that the Church is most eager to retain. I am hoping we can count on your discretion concerning such documents, and on their timely release. That is all."

He waited for a few moments, looking for a nod, a frown, a shrug of the shoulders, but Fruscella sat without moving, her lips a thin line, her gaze locked to a point just above and behind his forehead. He sipped his wine.

"Fruscella. This is an Italian name, yes? Where are your people from?"

She took a small drink from her glass and looked back at him. "Campobasso. In Molise."

"*Nonni*? Grandparents?" She nodded slightly. "*Parla italiano?*"

"*So soltanto un po' di italiano.*"

"And your son, does he speak any?"

Her look turned colder, a look that could freeze beer. He had seen that look before in comfortable darkened offices of bishops as well as well-lit courtrooms, the look of absolute distrust and dawning suspicion from mothers to those who had allegedly damaged their children. This was the look at the beginning, the look when the unspeakable was not yet confirmed, where the unimaginable was still not possible. Later the look would change to one of desperate and unconditional hatred, a hatred so pure that it engulfed and overwhelmed even the future. Both expressions he had learned to respect. "Ah, no, no, this was only from a newspaper article, nothing more. Do not worry, Detective, I am only making conversation."

Silence.

After some time he smiled. "We are both tired, yes?" He stood. "It has been a pleasure to meet you, Detective, truly." She awkwardly placed her glass on the table before her and rose to her feet. He walked past her to the desk. "I have a small gift for you." He turned and handed her the present. "This is a book of frescos from the Italian artist, a true artist, Piero della Francesca. Like your name. Think of it as a gift from the old country. I do hope your regulations allow you to accept this?"

She smiled slightly and met his eyes, took the present. "Thank you."

"I took the liberty of including my personal card, with my mobile number, in case I can be of service to you. But I want you to look at the pictures, enjoy them. And if you come on a journey to Italy, maybe a holiday, I would be honored to show you a little bit of Roma."

She extended her right hand, which he grasped in both of his. "And perhaps I will see you again, before I leave." He released her hands quickly and made a slight bow. "Goodbye, Detective Fruscella."

For two years, May 1977 to March 1979, Father G raped R on the average of twice a month. Masturbation in the Imperial progressed to oral sex, once even in the sacristy, then mutual oral sex on a cot in the equipment storeroom of the parish gym, until finally Father G anally penetrated R in a series of hotel rooms off the 99. Afterwards, R always got ice cream.

When R's mother found blood in his underwear, R mumbled he had hurt himself on his bike. When questioned further, he looked down at the floor and said nothing. He was more careful after that, buying himself a six-pack of briefs and checking carefully to see that he was clean, and burying in a school trashcan any stained evidence of God's work.

In February 1979, on a Saturday after catechism, J gave R a ride home in the truck. "Father B wants to talk to all of us this afternoon. Hope you ain't in any trouble." R stared out the window.

Father B always looked busy. He was thin, dark and always had some part of his body in motion: his eyes would dart, his foot would tap, he'd scratch his cheek with the back of his fingers. Some didn't like Father B, as they found all that movement, all that kinetic energy irritating, almost repulsive. R could never quite listen to whatever Father B said, as his attention would always focus itself on whatever body part was twitching, vibrating or trembling at the moment. Father B always seemed as if he wished he were somewhere else.

He was there when they got back, his maroon Oldsmobile Cutlass ostentatious in the driveway. "I hope you ain't done nothing, *chico*. I hope you innocent as Christ." There were three of them sitting at the kitchen table: Father B, R's mother, and T. Father B stood quickly. "J, good to see you, R." he nodded. "Please, sit." They sat, R furthest from Father B. Father B folded his hands in front of him on the table and drummed rapidly in rhythm with both of his index fingers. He sighed and then sighed again. R heard a motorcycle accelerating in the distance.

"This is extremely difficult for me, extremely difficult." R could feel Father B's leg twitching under the table. "These, these rumors and accusations have put our parish in a precarious position. If false, they show a malice and malevolence toward our Mother Church that is dangerous, threatening and evil. And if true, may God help us, if true, they demonstrate how even the Holy Catholic Church is vulnerable to corruption by today's secular, anything-goes morality. Our enemies, our Great Enemy, will use these accusations, true or not, to sow discord among the holy and the faithful." When Father B stopped talking a small tapping was audible from his twitching leg. He abruptly sat back and brought the fingers of his right hand up to his chin and to began to stroke his thin beard. He closed his eyes and ran his right hand through his hair: one, two, three times while his leg continued to twitch. He folded his arms against his chest and tapped his ribs with all of his fingers.

He opened his eyes and looked at R. "I must ask you, ask you all, in the name of our parish, in the name of our Holy Church itself, not to repeat the accusations I am about to disclose. To anyone. As James tells us, 'the tongue is an unruly evil, full of deadly poison.' Do you all agree?" He was still looking only at R. The others made various noises and movements of assent. R focused on Father B's drumming fingers. Father B closed his eyes and sighed once again. He opened them, blinked rapidly and stared at R. "Two weeks ago, a boy of about your age, R, came to me with his father and accused Father G of touching him . . ."—he hesitated here, and the rhythm of his leg twitching and his fingers drumming continued—"inappropriately, on number of occasions. He described this inappropriate touching, I am sorry to say, in much detail. Such detail does not necessarily indicate credibility—the boy could possess an active, if corrupt, imagination, or there could be hallucinations involved. I do not discount the workings of the Archfiend, who is extremely powerful. But the accusations are, on their surface, plausible, and I believe it my duty to disprove them or, failing that, take the necessary steps to protect our parish."

"So why you here?" J asked.

"I am here because the boy in question indicated that he was not the only, um, participant in these activities; others were involved. Including R."

R's mother made a small noise with her throat. "No way," said T. R was mesmerized by Father B's tapping fingers. Everyone was looking at him.

"Is this true, R?" asked J, gently. "Did Father G do anything to you?"

R kept staring at Father B's fingers. No one said anything for a while.

"He took him to basketball games. Gave him rides home from school. They had a special project after catechism. Was anyone else there? Was there any supervision?" J's voice sounded too high and too loud.

Father B uncrossed his arms, ran his right through his hair once and folded his hands in front of his mouth. The only sound came from his twitching leg.

"R, did Father G do anything to you that he shouldn't have?"

R placed his hands on the table and began to slowly draw circles with his right hand. This went on for a time.

Quietly, suddenly, "He said it was God's work."

"What? What are you saying, boy?"

Barely audible. "He said it was God's work. What we were doing. He said God's work was secret." He looked at J, then Father B, then his mother. Then back down at his hands. Time passed.

"What did he do? Can you tell us, R?" said J.

R continued drawing on the table. Father B put his hands to his sides and rocked forward and back. "He put his penis in my hand. And in my mouth. And . . . " He stopped. "In other places." Another sound escaped from his mother's throat and she knocked her chair over as she hurried from the room, followed by T.

SEVEN

Thirteenth Sunday of Ordinary Time, 2002

Expenditures

Private Accounts 2000

01.01.2000

Credit Suisse	1287527803–13	$10.436.234
Hottinger & Cie	67–456834–28	$9.843.420
Banque Cantonale de Genève	34968395836464945	€13.429.890
Banque Julius Baer	45–92–19867	FS 1.342.235
Lombard Odier	785049A-123CBC	$12.345.000
UBS	52396–109872-ZXA-8376	$17.500.000
LGT Bank	GUADALUPE65*	FS 10.000.000
Total		**$50.124.654**
		€13.429.890
		FS 1.342.235

PAN (campaign for Vicente Fox)	$1.000.000 (UBS)
Amigos de Fox	$1.000.000 (UBS)
Manuel Espino Barrientos	$500.000 (CS)
Partido Popular	€1.000.000 (BCG)
Communion and Liberation	500.000 (LGTB)
Legion of Christ Seminary Salamanca	€400.000 (BCG)
Villa Rosa Woodmont CT USA	$50.000 (UBS)
Angelo Sodano	€1.000.000 (BCG)
Andrea Sodano	€100.000 (BCG)
Eduardo Martínez Somalo	€100.000 (BCG)
Stanislaw Dziwisz	€2.500.000 (BCG)
Norma Hilda Baños	$1.000.000 (LO)
Blanca Estele Lara Guiterrez	$1.000.000 (LO)
Eduardo Francisco Pironio (estate)	$500.000 (UBS)
Cardinal Roger Mahony	$3.000.000 (HC)
El Yunque	$1.000.000 (CS)
Televisión Azteca	$1.000.000 (UBS)
Université de Fribourg	FS 500.000 (BJB)
Roberto Formigoni	€500.000 (BCG)
Antonio Simone	€250.000 (BCG)
Instituto Cumbres	$100.000 (CS)
Josefita Pérez Jiménez	$100.000 (CS)
Roberta Garza	$500.000 (CS) REFUSED
Paulina Garza	$500.000 (CS)
Dionisio Garza Medina	$500.000 (CS)
Fr. Luis Garza Medina	$500.000 (CS)
Instituto Tecnológico y de Estudios	$100.000 (CS)
Raffaello Follieri	€500.000 (BCG)
Universidad Anáhuac México Norte	$100.000 (UBS)
Universidad Anáhuac México Sur	$100.000 (UBS)

Universidad Anáhuac Mayab	$100.000 (UBS)
Universidad Anáhuac Xalapa	$100.000 (UBS)
Universidad Anáhuac Cancún	$100.000 (UBS)
Universidad Anáhuac Oaxaca	$100.000 (UBS)
Universidad Anáhuac Puebla	$100.000 (UBS)
Universidad Anáhuac Querétaro	$100.000 (UBS)
Instituto de Estudios Superiores de Tamaulipas	$100.000 (UBS)
Instituto Superior de Estudios para la Familia "Juan Pablo II" Leon	$100.000 (UBS)
Universidad Francisco de Vitoria	€100.000 (BCG)
Università Europea di Roma	€1.00.000 (BCG)
Università Pontificio Regina Apostolorum	€1.00.000 (BCG)
Institute for the Psychological Sciences	$100.000 (UBS)
Universidad Finis Terrae	$100.000 (UBS)
Mexico City Police	$10.000 (LO)
Guadalajara Police	$10.000 (LO)
Madrid Police	€10.000 (BCG)
Denver Police	$10.000 (LO)
Tijuana police	$10.000 (LO)
Policía Federal	$500.000 (LO)
Policía Federal Ministerial	$500.000 (LO)

Maldonado appeared at the door in the corner of my eye. "We found some Schedule 1 narcotics in the refrigerator, Detective. Almost a pound of dried mushrooms and approximately eight small peyote buttons, according to the tech. There are also small amounts of what looks like hashish and a couple of baggies of high-grade marijuana."

"Yeah, there's a lot here too: some pills, some pipes and a vial of what looks like heroin, baggies of good meth."

"Martinez was a player."

"But was he? You were in Vice, weren't you? This is not a player's stash, is it? There's not enough to sell; it's all personal use quantity. And he seems to have the spectrum covered: hallucinogens, a crack pipe, meth, heroin, pills, hash, grass. What doesn't he have? You ever seen this variety, Detective? All for personal use? Dude was into *everything*."

"Maybe these are just his samples. Maybe his stash is somewhere else."

"Yeah, but des Prez never said he was a dealer, and I can't see him giving him as much rope if he thought he was selling."

"He did say he liked to party: maybe these are just his party favors?"

"No, des Prez said it was like Martinez had a project. Besides, if you were giving a party, would you provide meth *and* molly? Would you give some peyote over here and heroin over here? Hash *and* shrooms?"

"I don't know, Detective. I've never been to that kind of party."

"Me neither." I turned and continued my search. The second drawer was full of tape cases, some commercial, some homemade, some empty, some not. Like those near the boom box, they seemed to be mostly jazz and tango, Latin stuff, some Mexican rap. No classical that I could see. I'd let the tech guys go through these in more detail.

Before opening the bottom drawer, I stood and looked at myself in the mirror. My brow was deeply furrowed. I was having a hell of a time getting a handle on this Martinez. What kind of character owned the New Testament in multiple languages as well as an S&M manual? What kind of man studied theology and anal fisting? What kind of man used peyote as well as heroin? What kind of man had an expensive Persian rug in his one bedroom near-flop? What kind of man wore expensive shoes and tore the labels out of his bespoke suits? Could this kind of man kill a priest? Did this man kill the priest?

"Detective, we've found something."

I followed one of the techs through the living room and back to the entranceway. There was a closet to the left with the door opened and coats and jackets pushed to one side. A couple of small shoeboxes were scattered behind, near the front door. "We found this in the closet. Along with these." He first pointed to a medium-size safe, bigger than the kind you see in hotel rooms, and then to a large plastic storage container full of what looked like files or notebooks. "Can you open the safe?"

"It's not locked. The door's shut, but the locking mechanism wasn't engaged."

"What's in there?"

He leaned forward and took something from the safe, then held it up and handed it to me. "Just this."

It was heavy. A large book with a thick, dark red cloth cover, slightly worn on the top two corners. The pages were gilded on the edges, and I noticed a blue ribbon bookmark buried in the pages, attached at the top. I turned it over and examined the back. I didn't want to open it, not just yet. I kept turning it over in my hands, examining the outer covers. I moved back, then around the tech and Maldonado, and reentered the living room. I sat gingerly on the loveseat and set the book on my lap. I was still surprised by its weight.

I opened it carefully. The pages were thick, even through my latex gloves, and were a luxurious, off-white shade. The front cover was unmarked, and the facing page had three red lines with cursive letters below with the words "*nombre completo,*" "*dirección,*" and "*fecha.*" The lines were not filled in. There was no mark on either page, but I could vaguely feel and vaguely see the indentations made from the opposite side of the name page. Maldonado moved in to stand behind me. I turned the page.

He had slept, not soundly, and had taken only morning coffee. The meeting the previous night now seemed a waste of time, and the feeling that this entire task was slipping further and further from his control weighed heavily. He needed to request God's help. He needed a place to pray.

He didn't know if the authorities had finished examining the basilica, but he shuddered when he imagined stepping inside that place of murder, that desecrated house of prayer. A desecration for which he was, to some extent, personally responsible. The rectory had its own small chapel on the second floor, but the possibility of being joined by another supplicant in that space about half the size of the *Porziuncola* prohibited serious consideration. And he colored as he remembered that the time he had tried to pray in his small bedroom had not ended well. No, he had to go elsewhere.

Lanzarote suggested a church close to where he had picked him up after dinner a few nights previously. He waited anxiously in the rectory entrance. It was only nine-thirty and the sun was already oppressive, overwhelming. How could one live in such dryness? With no filter from the sun?

He looked up at the twin-domed spires with the rose window in the center and the blue-and-white statue of the Blessed Mary below. He read the plaque to the right of the stairs: "Italian Mount Carmel Church, Erected 1899, Rev. M. Lepore, Pastor." *In bocca al lupo*. He moved quickly up the eight or so concrete stairs to the large wooden doors. He tried the center door, but it was locked. Then the right, and finally the left opened. He nodded to Lanzarote, who sped off in the car. He would return in two hours.

He turned and entered the cool narthex, and as his eyes took some time adjusting to the scant light, he noticed various pieces of colored paper posted on the bulletin board on the right wall. He then made his way into the nave. It was a small church, not as big as it appeared outside, barrel vaulted with cream walls and ceilings, a burgundy carpet down the center and side aisles with severe oaken pews. Inside was plain, spartan and clean. He appreciated the light from the large stained glass on both sides, donated, he read from another plaque near the entrance, from an Elisabetta Falcone and Massimino Mastroantonio. His Mastroantonio was from Salerno, a fellow Dominican who served the Lord loudly, *metà del giorno*, visible to all. He desired to be a bishop, had always desired to be a bishop, and had not yet been made a bishop, which made him unhappy and caused him to serve all the more loudly. Mastroantonio contacted him regularly because he worked at the Vatican and believed some advantage, no matter how small, could be obtained. Perhaps he'd suggest a stained glass window, like his relative here in Denver. He dipped his fingers in the basin of holy water held by the statue of a blonde angel dressed in green, genuflected and made the sign of the cross.

He preferred the backs of churches, away from all the theater. God was everywhere, and in His house he liked the quiet God, the almost shy host, the God who leaned against the rear walls and spoke in whispers. He kneeled heavily in the corner of the back pew, his left knee immediately protesting. He bowed his head and closed his eyes. *Altissimu, onnipotente bon Signore, tue so le laude, la gloria e l'honore et onne benedictione.* He took his time with the "*Laudes Creaturarum*," luxuriating in the sweetness of the Umbrian like a childhood priest, Father Patti, used to do. Although he was Dominican, he loved this prayer, preferred it to the elongated Rosary, and he loved *Frate Sole* and *Sora Luna, Sor'Acqua* and *Frate Focu*, and especially *Sora nostra Morte corporale*, who came in at the end to remind everyone of the necessary humility. *Amen.* This was so much better than the *Obsculta, o fili, præcepta magistri, et inclina aurem cordis tui,* the Latin of obedience, or the *Laudare, Benidicere, Praedicare,* to praise, to bless, to preach. He stopped and listened in his heart. Nothing but noises from the construction outside. Perhaps God was not a Franciscan. He opened his eyes and sat back on the pew. He rubbed his left knee.

This was God's house, but God was not home.

The remaining, two men and a boy, all looked down. Both J and Father B knew that R was telling the truth. After a while, J spoke. "What happens now?"

Father B tugged his left ear, then slowly rubbed his palm over his mouth and chin. He scratched his neck under his collar. His leg started up again. He looked up at the ceiling, then at J. "I'll write to the bishop this afternoon. I'll remove Father G from his position in the youth ministry immediately: perhaps he is owed a vacation." He leaned toward J. "I must impress on you the necessity to keep this terrible, terrible knowledge inside the house, so to speak. We cannot provide our enemies with such damaging information."

"What about the boy? R and the other kid? Were there others? R, do you know if Father G bothered anybody else?"

R continued drawing circles on the table and staring at them. After a while he gave a barely perceptible shrug.

"The other boy mentioned only R," Father B said quietly.

J got up and opened the drawer to his left. He was looking for cigarettes: he really wanted a joint but didn't want to burn one in front of the Father. There was nothing in the drawer. No one in the house smoked tobacco. He sat back down.

"What about the boys, the children? What can you do to help the boys?"

"Father S has some counseling experience. I'll ask him to speak to R and the other boy. Separately, of course."

"That it?"

Father B sighed, then leaned back and folded his hands before his chin and bounced his knuckles softly against his lower lip. He focused his gaze down at R's hands, one lazily drawing circles on the table. He breathed heavily through his nose. J placed his hand gently on R's wrist, stopping his drawing. "Go watch TV."

Father B kept his eyes pointed toward the tabletop where R's hands had been. Soft dialogue from the TV wafted in from the living room. Finally, he sighed, stopped moving his hands and without looking up said, "I'm not sure what you mean."

J gave a little laugh. "You know where I was, Father, before I met R and his mother and we came here?" Father B shook his head.

"I was a guest of the state of California, in Corcoran State Prison. And you know who's the lowest of the low, the absolute scum of the earth? Below Charles Manson? Beyond Christ?"

"No one is beyond Christ."

"*Chomos. Chomos* are beyond Christ. At least according to the general prison population. And you know what *chomos* are? Child molesters."

"I wouldn't consider Father G a child molester."

"What is he then? Father G raped my son."

"We can't be sure of exactly what happened. And even if the boys are telling the truth, we need to handle this internally: it will do no good to broadcast this terrible mistake to the world."

"Rape is against the law."

"We need to work within God's law."

"I want him punished. I want him put in prison. They take care of *chomos* in prison."

Father B tilted his forehead, and slid his hand up to his forehead, where he began to drum on his forehead all five fingers. He then closed his eyes and rubbed his face downward three times with his hand. He leaned back and opened his eyes to the ceiling. He sighed heavily through his nose. He turned stiffly to J.

"I understand that's what you want." He lowered his voice. "But what does R want? Think of how he would feel to have to tell his story again and again. Think of the shame." J said nothing but met Father B's eyes until Father B looked away. He leaned toward J and lowered his voice even further. "We also don't know the circumstances about how much R resisted or struggled."

Smashing a priest was wrong, dead wrong. And J wasn't naturally the violent type. But the thought crossed his mind. Did more than cross—sort of lingered, looked around, had a drink. Father B saw that thought in J's face and quickly leaned back, ran the fingers of both hands under his collar and rubbed his hands together in front of him. "Of course, of course, there are no excuses for the sin that has been visited upon R, and for that we are all truly sorry. But I do not wish to compound the sin, either the sin against R, or . . ."—and here he sighed again and rubbed his temples with the fingertips of both hands— "the sin against our parish and our Holy Mother Church. By alerting the police we will be informing the secular press, thus inviting them to disseminate all sorts of twisted and distorted accusations against the parish and our Catholic Church. Think about how the press would treat R, how they would investigate, how they would ask questions of his classmates, his teachers, his mother. This would be to magnify, to multiply the sin committed against R and the other boy. I understand your desire that Father B be punished, and I say to you that he will be punished. But in God's house, in God's house he will be punished. And God's punishment will be a far worse punishment than any secular authority can impose."

EIGHT

The Thirty-Third Saturday of Ordinary Time, 1983

Thomas Aquinas—*Summa Theologiae One*

Question I: Whether negation of self by the individual will is possible, and if possible, whether said negation can lead to union with God through Jesus Christ.

Objection 1: Roman whores taste different from the whores in Buenos Aires. They were thin, beautifully thin, with no hips and shockingly black hair. They were slightly older than I, or at least that is what they both assured me in dialect I had trouble following. If I ever did know their names, I soon forgot them. We were always undressed. One had the whitest skin, like marble or expensive paper; the other was darker, with a dense forest of pubic hair, a thinner growth on his chest and belly and thick thatches under both arms. When I kissed them on their mouths, first the dark one, then the lighter, I got a mere hint of the sweet dissimilarity, of the unfamiliar mixture of new spices and new combinations; salt, milk and a dark lemony thickness with one, thyme and smoked peppered ham with the other.

Just a little later, with quivering fingers, I parted the thin buttocks of the fair one (who seemed much more eager than the shy *bruno*, who initially stood near the edge of the bed, hesitant) and suddenly inserted my tongue deep into that fragrant and savory asshole. The salt was there, certainly, along with the lemon, a sweeter lemon than the mouth, more distilled and assertive. The dairy taste had disappeared, replaced by a delicate vegetal trace, green, but more mossy than leafy, not of the sun but of the soul, nocturnal and secret. I withdrew and rapidly began to flick the tip of my tongue around the rim. He rose up slightly, and I moved my left hand around his thigh to his hairless testes, where I softly cupped and caressed them, feeling them relax and descend. I held one between my forefinger and thumb and rolled it gently around in its sac. His cock stiffened, but I kept my hand away, instead timing the rhythm of my fingertips to coincide with my flicking tongue. He was moist, but I wanted him wet. Dripping, I wanted the luscious nectar from his asshole to coat his perineum, so I let my saliva gather around the center of my tongue, and I began to lick his hole with as much tongue as I could, transferring my spit into and around his anus. One, two, three, four times I ran the length of my tongue over his hole, starting near the base, moving down the body toward the tip, keeping my tongue inflexible and rigidly rocking my entire head from the neck. I like to surprise, and so I quickly stuck my tongue in his hole, as far as it would go. As I rotated it around the inside rim, I could again taste the salt and lemon, with the mossy plant taste more pronounced. There was something new as well, a trace of something yeasty and waxy. I moved my right hand to steady his hip, to provide my mouth better purchase. I drew the tip of my left pointer finger of my left hand lightly from his scrotum to the base of his shaft, where I made an O with that finger and my thumb around his cock.

I slowly, patiently, perhaps cruelly slid my fingers up his reedy shaft, keeping my palm from touching. He tried to slide his hips forward, but the grip of my right hand kept him in place. I reached the base of his glans and tightened my grip ever so slightly, and I could sense his stomach muscles constricting in response. I slowly, slowly, slowly, moved the circle of my finger and thumb over his glans and gently brought my hand over the head and to the tip of his penis. He squirmed and tried to lean his pelvis forward, but I strengthened my grip on his hip and held him in place.

I relaxed slightly, and moved the O back over his glans, slowly, and hesitated at the corona. I made my hand pulsate, so that the ring of my thumb and forefinger quivered on his shaft under his glans. At the same time, I licked down the seam of skin from his asshole to the perineum and sucked the soft folds of the base of his balls. He was completely hairless there, almost mannequin-like, and I was suddenly terrifically aroused by that purity, that unblemished perfection. Later, in the café drinking wine, I asked him about it. He laughed and repeated the words *depilatoria* and *cera* and *baffi mi madre*. I guided him to his knees and maneuvered, with some trouble, so my back was against the mattress, my hands gripping his ass and my cheek and forehead against his cock. I inhaled his sweetness, an odor of wet soil and lichen, my grandmother's garden, and began to nibble the base of his cock out of the side of my mouth. I moved my mouth to the center of the base of his shaft and then softly sucked his right testicle. He rose up on his elbows to draw his penis down into my mouth, but I kept my mouth attached to his sac and arrested further motion with my hands on both of his hips: I wanted him inside of me, my mouth, but not yet, not yet. I searched around with my lips until I located his other testicle, and surrounded both of them gently with my lips. I then began to lick the base of his cock with the tip of my tongue. I noticed a thick blue vein snaking up the underside of his white, thin cock. I heard him moan from deep in his chest. With small catlike licks I moved my tongue up the underside of his shaft until I reached the frenulum. I caressed it with the tip of my tongue and drug my wet bottom lip up the frenulum toward his meatus (such an ugly words for such exquisite geography). I hesitated, one, two, three seconds longer. I kissed the tip with both lips again and again, and with each subsequent kiss I took more and more of him into my mouth: on the third kiss my lips covered his corona, and soon his glans rubbed against my soft palate.

He began to move inside my mouth, back and forth, and I allowed him, encouraged him. His glans slipped to my soft palate and uvula, and as I took more and more of him into me, I again noticed the taste of lemon and moss. I covered my teeth with my lips and used my tongue and hard palate for friction. I found his frenulum with the tip of my tongue and stiffened the pointed tip of my tongue against it as his cock undulated back and forth. I recognized the increased urgency and I tightened the pressure ever so slightly with my lips while slowing his rhythm down with both of my hands on his ass. I felt his quiver begin at the very base of his cock as he exploded into my mouth in a groaning frenzy. I've never been one for the taste of semen, so after guiding his initial spasm deep into my throat, I quickly turned my head to the left and reached around to cradle and point his ejaculating cock with my right hand. I felt a hot ropy string on my left ear and smelled a strong odor of bleach and damp straw. I kissed his smooth belly.

The right page was dominated by a calendar page, *el primero de enero*, in black, with smaller red script below. Maldonado leaned forward, "It's a calendar with a prayer for the day underneath and saints and their days below. January First is Saint Mary's Day." I nodded. I was more interested in the facing page, my left. It was full of small blockish handwriting, not cursive, in various colored inks in different languages. I recognized Latin and Spanish, and Italian. All of these used the same alphabet as English, but there was another alphabet as well, in black ink, near the center of the page. The writing began at the top left corner, continued right to the very edge of the page, and then that continued down until the bottom right corner. There were paragraph breaks and indentations that coincided with changes in ink color. I turned the page. Same thing, although the right page had some writing in the margins, near the calendar date and to the right of the names of the saints, and the left page was dominated by a paragraph in English, in green ink. The paragraph described an encounter with one Cardinal Angelo Sodano and a Roberta Garza at Sodano's villa outside of Rome. Much of the paragraph focused on Sodano and his "easy-going, gracious manner" and how comfortable and luxurious his room was, like "a five-star hotel." Below the paragraph in English were three lines of Hebrew; I recognized the alphabet from college, written in blue ink, set off with wide margins. To the right of this verse was the word "LIES" scrawled diagonally and deeply in black ink.

What the hell was Willem Martinez, drug aficionado and Satire lounge lizard, doing with some cardinal in a Roman villa?

Did the book belong to Martinez, or did he steal it, perhaps from Vidal? Is that why he killed him? And why was it in a safe? And why wasn't the safe locked? I thought of Signelli and his desire for the embarrassing documents: these were likely them. I looked up. "You read this?"

"Yeah."

"Think it's Martinez's or stolen from Vidal?"

"Probably stolen from Vidal. Although see what's written in the margin on the right? Next to *San Basilio el Grande? La concha de tu madre?* That means 'your mother's, er. . .'"

"Cunt?" Maldonado turned a little red, nodded. "Not exactly priestly language, is it?"

"Martinez could have added it later, after he took it from Vidal."

"Look at the handwriting though. It's all pretty much the same. Maybe a little younger here and there, maybe a little angrier, but it's the same writer. The same man who visited Cardinal Sodano wrote 'your mother's cunt' next to Saint Basil." I turned the page back and pointed at a paragraph in Spanish about three-quarters of the way down. "Can you read this?"

"Yeah. 'Yesterday, I went down to the coffee shop to study. I miss my music: I haven't been able to *ensaye*, rehearse, play my trumpet for three days now. This theology is dry, *estéril*, barren. I believe God is not to be found in books but in life. I was happy not to see anyone I knew and was able to finish my Italian and my Old Testament assignments without distraction. I didn't work on any of my Timothy translation because I didn't want to carry that big dictionary and grammar. I'm feeling *inquieto*, restless, fidgety. Maybe it's all the coffee I took at Tito's, but I think it's something else.'"

"That it? Do you recognize that language below?"

"It's not Spanish."

"It's not Italian either. Or Latin. And after that, there's English and then Hebrew; I recognize that. But if we turn the page... we get Latin, then German, then some alphabet I don't recognize, then French, right?" I turned the pages again and noticed a thick fold of white typing paper creased in half and inserted between the pages in the middle of the book. I carefully unfolded the sheets with my gloved fingers.

The sheets contained more of the same: paragraphs in Latin, Spanish, English, French, although all written in the same unhurried hand as the book and all in black ink, with some annotations and revision marks, also in the same hand and ink. I read the English quickly and noticed the name of Marcial Maciel. This tied the sheets to Vidal, possibly, which meant the diary was likely Vidal's as well. But what had Martinez to do with Vidal? Maybe there was a drug connection: Maciel had used and so maybe Vidal had bought from Martinez in the past. That didn't make sense, as Maciel and Vidal were in Mexico City and wouldn't want or need to come to Denver to buy drugs and then take them back over the border. Maybe Vidal bought from Martinez since moving up here. But why kill Vidal? In order to take the book? Then why put the book in an unlocked safe?"

I folded the papers up, placed them where I found them, closed the book and stood. "What else is in the box?"

"Notebooks. I think it's the same kind of thing. Lots of different languages, not much we can understand. It's all the same handwriting as that." Maldonado nodded at the book in my hand.

"Let's say this is all Vidal's." I raised my voice to address the techs in the other rooms. "We don't know where Martinez is. Is there anything here that might help us find him? Have we discovered anything that might tell us where he is? A computer? A cell phone? A notepad? An answering machine? A letter? Anything?" Shoulders shrugged and heads shook. Then one of the techs from the bedroom stuck his head through the doorway. "We are getting prints, Detective. We are getting prints."

His recent actions were displeasing to God. There was no other explanation. He had caused, directly or indirectly, it mattered little, the death of another human being, a priest, Father Vidal, *requiescat in pace,* and God was showing His displeasure by withdrawing. He made the sign of the cross. He would not be granted the shield of faith until he confessed and made the adequate and proper penance for this mortal sin. Alone, without God's armor, he was useless.

God was displeased, as were his superiors. He had been asked to retrieve Vidal's journal, not to murder the man, and both his inability to recover the diary and the scandalous and very public killing could not help but severely disappoint those who had given him the task. He had always been competent and trustworthy, but here he had so far failed spectacularly. He'd have to locate and obtain the journal; that was the only possible way of limiting the damage. If he retrieved the book, much would be forgiven, or if not forgiven, then neglected. Nothing would be forgotten.

Where had he faltered? Where had he gone wrong? This was no time for notes: this was the time to examine his heart. After he had listened to the telephone call requesting that he retrieve the diary Vidal was keeping contrary to his superiors wishes, a diary that might prove damaging to the reputation of the Holy See, he looked carefully at the file that had been emailed. He was not particularly pleased that this involved the Legionaries: he thought that whatever scandal and punishment they might receive well deserved. But that would not color his efforts. He had assumed this to be a simple matter of money or of favor, assuming Vidal's hesitation to provide his journal to be grounded in loyalty, confusion and insecurity—after all, his *patron*, the man whom he had followed for years, had not only just died, but had proven to be a fraud and a *stronzo* of the first order. And money, and perhaps a new position in a comfortable location, would help soothe Vidal's conscience and recover balance. He thought he would fly out, negotiate the adequate sum and then quickly return with the notebook.

A bit later, after his lunch if he was remembering correctly, he was thinking on another matter when he recalled that Father Malachi had retired to a monastery in the American Southwest. In Ireland, more than once Malachi had proven himself tactful, persuasive and discreet. A quick email to Father Grisó confirmed that Malachi was indeed living in Santa Fe, a few hundred miles from Denver. Initially he thought that Malachi could simply provide him with a contact, a messenger to speed the journal's transfer. Experience had taught him that such matters almost never called for delicate negotiations: this was merely a matter of money, and money could be offered, was often best offered, impersonally, at a distance. And later, when he telephoned and spoke to Malachi in person, he was surprise and grateful that Malachi insisted on handling the communication himself. He had assumed, incorrectly, that all would be reasonable here. And this assumption had cost a man his life.

What had he said to Malachi; what words had he used? He would have preferred to speak in Italian or even Latin, but Malachi's Italian was bad, and so he had used English. How had he phrased it? Something along the lines of 'There are those here who might be embarrassed by a journal Father Vidal has kept, and so we need to obtain this book from him.' How had they discussed the money? He did tell Malachi he would be reimbursed for his expenses, but had he not mentioned any figure in dollars? Had he not indicated he was to go as high as ten thousand dollars? Perhaps even twenty? No, he was certain he *did* mention the ten thousand, near the end of the conversation. He said something like 'We can go up to ten thousand, maybe more. Your expenses will be covered separately.' And then Malachi had said goodbye and hung up. He trusted his memory of the conversation.

Could Malachi have misunderstood? This was not the 'Ndrangheta. No murders were ever arranged, either *un tacito accord* or otherwise. No, Malachi did not misunderstand. This was either a foul-up, some miscommunication or Malachi was *rincoglionirsi*. No, not senility: Malachi was *pazza furbo come una volpe,* crazy like the fox. He was playing something, that fox. That peacock. But what? What possible interest did he have with Vidal and the Legionaries?

No, he did not direct any murder. He had no knowledge of it, did not even imagine this thing. But deep down in his heart, he knew that even if he did not direct the killing, even if he had no knowledge or intuition a man would be murdered, he was still responsible in the eyes of God. There was no consent, there was no intention, there was no will or desire, but there was still responsibility. And until he confessed and was absolved of that responsibility, God would remain distant, inaccessible and remote, and he would be ineffective and alone.

He was never sure what constituted perfect contrition and so always depended on the external ritual of *sacramentum poenitentiae*. But to whom would he confess? His confessor, Father Zancredi, was in Rome, and the two American priests he knew and trusted lived in Boston. He would not confess in English and did not want to soil Latin with his language of murder. In Italian he could be both discreet and exact. He would not unburden himself to some child just out of short pants who knew nothing of the world. He looked around at the empty nave: he could inquire here. Perhaps there was someone older, someone forgotten and mostly unused, someone who visited hospitals to murmur the *sanctam unctiónem* to ancient lonely souls in the deadest of night.

No, he would likely have to do without confession and penance and rely on perfect contrition. Perfect contrition was an internal contrition, yes, a contrition based purely on the love of God and hatred of the sin as displeasing to God. Perfect contrition was not moral, it was not social and it could not be made with any sense of gain or of loss. God knew what was in his heart, God knew that he never intended anyone should die and God knew that he understood murder as the most mortal of sins. God understood.

But was he doing this from pure motives, from pure love of God? Did he not want to come clean with God? Did he not want to regain the shield of faith so he could wield again the sword of spirit? Was he not, ultimately, confessing his role in the murder of Vidal so he could obtain the journal and complete his task? He was certain of nothing.

He was alone.

Dear Father B,

Your letter of the previous week has left me in some confusion. I can read nothing in your note but the repetition of secondhand gossip and unsubstantiated rumor. Are there any witnesses other than this single imaginative boy? He has no father, is that correct? It sounds as if this may be a bid for attention or the creation of some sort of revenge scenario. Father G is a valuable and respected member of the clergy and our diocese and deserves to have his name cleared from these groundless and malicious accusations as soon as possible. You need to nip this in the bud, my dear Father B, and prevent the foul tongues of idle gossip from destroying a fine and dedicated priest. Think of your parish, Father, as well as our Holy Catholic Church.

Discretion and vigilance are of the utmost importance here, Father B, as you no doubt realize. Find what you can to prove the innocence of Father G, and report only to me. Communicate with no one else. I will pray for you as well as for God's faithful servant, Father G.

Yours in Christ,

Most Reverend M
Bishop of S

Dear Monsignor P,

It seems G is up to his old tricks again. I received a letter from his parish priest, a Father FB, S.P.M., who relayed the rather thorough accusations of a boy, age nine, regarding sexual activity forced upon him by our smiling Father G. I had hoped counseling at the Springs would help, but I should have known better. I thought that by placing him outside the city, the temptations would diminish, and long walks and physical sports would occupy the body. But I should have known that the farm is as conducive to sin as the street. He even talked himself into youth ministry. It was a mistake to grant him Faculties. I charged Father B to prove Father G's innocence, but that proof is likely nonexistent. We'll have to move him, probably within the month. I'm going to send him back to counseling, at least until we determine where to assign him. Would you please contact Father F at the Springs, tell him Father G is on his way? And if you have time, would you say a small prayer for me? I am weary of this filth.

Yours in Christ,

M

My Dear Father B,

I was most distressed to receive your letter of March 25th. You write that you believe both boys, without doubt. I caution you, Father B, about placing such unshakable confidence in the irreligious, especially the stories of two young, likely confused, boys. Nevertheless, my certainty has been shaken, and perhaps, perhaps, it is possible that Father G may have acted in ways where misunderstanding was imaginable. I know him to be young, energetic and somewhat unconventional in his desire to bring the Gospel of Our Lord to the young, and conceivably this enthusiasm didn't suit the culture of your parish.

Do not misunderstand me, Father B. I do not believe these boys and I do not believe anything untoward has occurred. However, these rumors and accusations have already poisoned the well, and I do not see how Father G can function effectively as a servant to Our Lord, given your parish's prejudices and propensity toward rumor.

I will remove Father G from your parish within the month.

Given the shortage of priests, I am not sure when a suitable replacement will become available.

You are right to impress upon the families the absolute need to keep this within the Church. I am concerned about the father of the second boy, R. His stepfather, yes? Children require two parents, and a mother and a father, to prosper, do they not? Perhaps when they see that Father G has been removed they will understand that the Church can take care of its flock. Do not allow the families to waiver or to be tempted to speak of these unsubstantiated rumors to anyone, anyone at all. I will write again with Father G's reassignment.

Yours in Christ,

Most Reverend M
Bishop of S

NINE

The Thirty-Third Saturday of Ordinary Time, 1983

Thomas Aquinas—*Summa Theologiae Two*

Reply Objection 1: There is nothing written about the negation of the self.

I answer that, With such specialized description, one needs to chose between anatomy and metaphor, and, accomplished at neither, I am forced to indicate or approximate.

The dark one was hesitant, shy, as I've said, and while I was occupied with the light one (I never learned their names, not in that room or at the café later that night), he stood there, perhaps masturbating until, after a while, I felt him sit lightly on the edge of the bed. He then caressed the back of my calf and ankle clumsily, fitfully, with irregular rhythm and roughened fingers. He continued this almost perfunctorily, or at least distractedly, until I turned over on my back, after which he removed his hand completely and repositioned himself on the bed. He moved little: my focus was directed elsewhere, and so it seemed I would enjoy them sequentially rather than simultaneously. As I put the fair one's— no, they need names: I will call the lighter one Romulus and the darker one Remus—as I put Romulus's balls in my mouth, I felt Remus's fingertips gently brushing my left thigh. I stiffened, as if recently awakened.

I wondered what he was going to do. His caresses seemed without purpose, accidental, dutiful, unthought. I could feel him drawing little circles on my upper thigh near my hip, perhaps even tracing words, like a children's game. Maybe he was focusing on my activity with Romulus, working himself up somehow to join the party, although I didn't sense any arousal or tension from that end of the bed. I didn't know what he was thinking sitting there and drawing abstract circles on my thigh while I licked the asshole and balls of his pale friend.

I put Remus mostly out of my mind as I focused on Romulus: his hairless scrotum, the vein bulging on his long thin shaft, his taste of lemon and moss. I vaguely registered Remus removing his hand from my thigh and then leaving the bed altogether, but it was impossible to devote much thinking or speculation to his absence, as my attention was nearly exclusively directed to keeping my teeth away from the glans of Romulus. The glans of Romulus indeed.

As I guided Romulus into my mouth, I felt Remus return: he leaned heavily on one side of the bed and then swung around until he straddled me just above the knees. He then cupped my balls roughly with one hand while he began to spread a thick and almost chilly lotion onto my dick with the other. I instantly became very hard, and he encouraged me by working the cream up and down my shaft, warming it, while still massaging my sac. He brought both hands to work on my cock now, starting at the base and gently gliding up with his rough palms and fingers until releasing at the frenulum, first one hand, then the other, with a steady and delicious rhythm. He repositioned himself and began to rub the tip of his cock against my balls and the bottom of my shaft. He hesitated, then brought our glans together in his well-oiled hand. As Romulus came in my throat, I twisted my face and neck away, and I felt Remus rise up on his knees and work my tip against his scrotum. Remus moved forward and guided me roughly to the rim of his asshole, where he moved my tip back and forth to moisten his opening. He straightened his back and began to insert my cock slowly into his ass. He was extremely tight and still somewhat dry and I thought that maybe he was being too impatient. There was some pain but nothing prohibitive. I remained still to let him guide me. I felt his heat as he leaned forward to adjust the angle. This helped a little, and the lubrication began to spread inside, making the going easier. I was about halfway in now. I looked down, for the first time really, and saw his cock, erect and long, waving freely, perpendicular from his stomach.

Soon I was completely inside him. For a long time, neither of us moved. I looked up at his face and noticed his eyes were looking into mine but focusing behind me somehow. I saw his dick quivering in the air. A drop of sweat rolled down his cheek to his throat, and nestled in the hair below his collarbone. Still we didn't move. He leaned forward very slightly and contracted his rectum. My back arched, and I moved my hands to his thighs. He closed his eyes and contracted his sphincter again, and after he relaxed I began to move gingerly inside him. We slowly, tentatively established a rhythm. The lubrication spread inside him, and while he was still very tight, it felt much more comfortable and safe. He leaned back, and Romulus, whom I'd almost forgotten, moved behind him and caressing his chest, kissed him on the mouth.

He kept our motion deliberate, preventing me from hurrying or abbreviating the long slide of his asshole over the entire length of my cock, from the middle of the glans to the base, back and forth, steady, long, exquisite. I closed my eyes to better focus on his muscular slipperiness enclosing me. I felt my orgasm stirring deep in my lower back. I wanted to keep it there, keep it down, keep it from erupting, but his unvarying and indefatigable rhythm, his taut and lubricious sliding, up and down, up and down, began to bring it to the surface. From my lower back I could feel this flame travel down my spine. My balls tingled in anticipation. Suddenly, I felt his perfect rhythm break. I opened my eyes and saw that Romulus had covered his hands in glistening white lotion and was stroking Remus's thick cock in his pale fist: it was no longer perpendicular to his belly but rose up at an angle. Remus's head was thrown back, his eyes closed and his lips were curled in an expression that reminded me of statues. Romulus nibbled on his ear.

It took awhile, but our rhythm resumed, more jerkily than before. My orgasm, which had returned to the small of my back, now quickly bubbled up to my balls. I closed my eyes. He contracted his sphincter again and again, and my coming burst from my balls and shot out from my dick in countless spasms. I heard him moan and felt him jerk as hot and sticky semen landed on my chest. He kept coming and coming.

Eventually I flopped out of him.

"This book is pretty much all we have so far, yeah?" Maldonado nodded. "And we can't read most of it. Who can translate it?"

"We have some people at HQ who do Spanish and the like, or Japanese or Chinese, different types of Chinese. Lot of times we use interns. We had an intern last year who knew some African languages, and a guy who helped us with that Eastern European smuggling case. If not, we hire out from DU or CU Denver."

"Interns? Jesus. I'm guessing DU or UCD takes time."

"They're usually pretty responsive. It's frequently just so we can question witnesses: we don't often have documents, and if we do they're pretty simple, like manifests or bills of sale."

I had an idea. I moved Maldonado to the corner and lowered my voice. "Is this dusted?" He nodded. "Take this immediately to McCormick. Have him do whatever he needs to do, but I need a photocopy of this. Including the loose sheets. Tonight. This evening. By six. If he gives you any lip, and he might, tell him not to forget what he owes me. If he gives you any more lip, call me right away."

"You want hard copy or email?"

"Email would be quicker but hard copy. Keep it off email. Quickly please."

"You have an idea?"

"I do, but what I have in mind is not SOP. We need to try to figure this thing out quick."

Goddamn phone. I motioned Maldonado to leave as I answered. "Detective Fruscella. This is Lieutenant Clark, from PIO. I've been trying to reach you all afternoon."

"What can I do for you, Lieutenant?"

"We've been approached by a contact, an emissary, from the Vatican in Rome, semi-officially one could say, who'd like a face-to

-face. Captain Schlaf agrees that this might be beneficial, and so we've set up a meeting for tonight at eight o'clock, in Cherry Creek, a private house. I'll text the address. Uniform unnecessary. Please don't be late, Detective."

"You are aware I'm in the middle of a murder case?"

"Yeah, I am, Detective. I'm thinking your team can spare you for an hour and a half. I'm also thinking that the conversation might provide more intel on our vic, you know, which could only help you catch the bad guy. And, to repeat myself, Captain Schlaf agrees. Most enthusiastically, in fact."

Little prick. "Okay."

"I'll need a report."

I clicked off quickly. I was hot, sweaty and pissed. That little punk could kiss my ass. My phone beeped with what I assumed was a Cherry Creek address. It was almost three now, and I would soon have to swing by the office, then go home, shower, change and fight the Denver traffic. Fuck.

I looked around. Martinez's small apartment was buzzing with technicians all brushing, examining, photographing, etc., like a weirdly coherent dance of white-costumed figures, ghosts with the latest instruments of analysis, unreal figures trying to realize the invisible, trying to conjure the sensible from the spectral.

This was wrong somehow. As detective clichés go, this was the most tedious by far, but I couldn't help but feel that the basic premise of our searching was mistaken: we were looking methodically, rigorously, scientifically, technologically, even at the sub-visible level, for the wrong thing. The basic facts of this case, that a priest named Andrea Vidal was murdered by Willem Martinez, who then took Vidal's diaries home with him before he disappeared, were not facts at all but beliefs. And as beliefs went, they were flimsy, more guesswork than anything. I needed to know what was written in the book.

I walked quickly to the bedroom and stuck my head in. "What was in the bottom drawer of the dresser?"

One of the techs read from a thin iPad or something. "Let's see: condoms, three packages, six each latex, Lifestyle brand; two packages, three each, lambskin, Naturalamb; one four pack of Sliquids Organics Sensations Lubricants, with 2.8 ounces each of Natural, Sensational, Silky and O-gel; one Pleasurebound Restraint Kit, unopened; one Sex Fetish Breathable Ball Gag in unopened shrink wrap; one Sexy Slave leather bondage mask, size medium... and, that's the lot."

The drawer of light kink. Mostly unused. Was there anything Martinez wouldn't try? We hadn't found any guns yet. It struck me suddenly that nothing we could uncover here would really surprise me: I had, after all, initially assumed that his wigs were scalps. Body parts in the freezer would give me pause, okay, but other than that, I couldn't imagine anything that would be outside the realm of possibilities for Willem Martinez. I didn't think he was a killer, but it wouldn't shock me if we found bloody knives beneath the baseboards. There was such a freedom here, I could barely imagine. He was what, forty-nine, five years younger, and could act in ways that left me grasping at straws, or squinting, cocking my head, trying to discern the soft melody of his almost incomprehensible actions from another room. I thought of my son, his needs and desires, yes, and my husband and Hector, their needs and desires, then my father and then my mother, my aunts and friends: definitely, such freedom was masculine, barred to women, forbidden perhaps without exception. Maybe except Zemlinsky. Who would be in prison until she died. I needed some air.

He would pray the act of contrition, then the rosary. The *Actus Contritionis* would cleanse his soul, allow him to pray the rosary with a relatively pure voice. And perhaps Mary would intercede for him with God.

He looked across the nave at the altar, with the statue of Our Lady in the center, blue-and-red robes with a golden crown, flanked by an ivory Jesus on her right and darker Paul on her left. The ciborium above the altar featured a fresco of the haloed Holy Mother surrounded by two cherubim and then two larger angels. There was no transept.

American churches often irritated him. They were usually spartanly and blindly decorated, almost protestant compared to a *chiesa romano*, with lonely mismatched plaster statues, overly bright stained glass and bare white walls. There was little to enchant the eye here: a few flowers in pots around the *predella*, tiny figurines of the *Via Crucis* hung too high to see, microphone stands littering a corner. What was more irksome, however, was the sense of hope these churches seemed to encourage, the absurd sense that one's relationship to God was basically transactional. American churches seemed young, adolescent, with a *ragazzo's* naïve belief that one ultimately received what one deserved, all mystery removed. It was true, this belief was Catholic from the beginning, but the European Church had matured out of this mistake, except perhaps the Irish, and God only knew what the Irish believed.

He felt heavy, earthbound and dense. He heard a noise behind and turned. A small woman in a brown habit with a brown veil crossed herself, genuflected and with a quick look at him, moved gracefully into a pew near the front and knelt to pray. He studied her. She was younger than she first appeared, younger than he was used to seeing in habit and veil. He wondered if this was her home church, if she prayed here daily at this time, or if she was a stranger, as he was, wandering in almost accidently, seeking shade and solace from the hot sun and dust. She leaned forward and placed her elbows on the back of the pew in front of her and bowed her head down on her forearms, and he could see a rosary dangling from her clasped hands.

He shifted in his seat and reached in his pocket to extract his old rosary given to him by Father Ciavonne and blessed by His Holy Eminence John Paul I, *requiescant in pace,* sometime during the thirty-three days he lived as pope. Father Ciavonne had presented him with the rosary after he'd completed his first assignment, an investigation into two Boston nuns belonging to the Annunciation of the Blessed Virgin who worked for a family planning association years before they took their vows. He was twenty-nine years old, filled with zeal for the Church, Curia and Pope, a zeal that convinced that contraception was indeed akin to murder, and these women's sins were, if not unforgivable, then excommunicable. He had proceeded tirelessly, vigilantly, pouring over records and interviewing witnesses, compiling dossiers five centimeters thick. *Bravo, Signelli, bravo!* There was nothing possible to recant, and both nuns were released from their vows and excommunicated *latae sententiae.*

No such zeal accompanied him now. He knelt to pray, and immediately his knee and the small of his back complained. He leaned forward on the top of the pew in front, bowed his head and closed his eyes, and began. He licked his lips. His throat was dry. He hadn't taken enough water, had a half a glass only to wash down his horse pills, and this desert air was removing all the moisture from his mouth. *Deus meus, ex toto corde pænitet me omnium meorum peccatorum.* The murmuring calmed. Although the words followed each other automatically, he always recited his prayers aloud, vocalizing audibly from deep within his chest, careful to annunciate. He didn't slur or elide syllables; he concentrated on speaking the words as if someone were listening, as if it were important that he be understood. This often prevented his mind from wandering and gave the words, the phrases he had declaimed hundreds, thousands of times, a reality they might not otherwise have had. The phrases were memorized, surely, but he didn't recite them mindlessly; and while he couldn't quite speak them as if the language was his own, as if he were coming up with the words for the first time, he could give the rote repetitions as much attention as he could muster. The prayers deserved that. This is why he didn't like praying the rosary. Five decades required a great deal of concentration to prevent the recitation from sliding into unthought repetition, into mere sound and rhythm. And four or five chaplets made that focus all the more difficult. He avoided novenas.

Eaque detestor, quia peccando, non solum pœnas a Te iuste statutas promeritus sum. I detest my sins, all of my sins, *sed præsertim quia offendi Te*, because they offend Thee, my Lord. There is no other reason. Not guilt, hope of absolution, desire to enter into Your powerful presence, no, I detest sin simply and only because it offends You, My Lord and God. And the most detestable sin, the transgression that likely causes You the most pain, must be to end the life of one of Your creatures made in Your image. One of Your servants, one of Your holy servants. *Summum bonum, ac dignum qui super omnia diligaris,* You, who are good and great and deserving of all of my love, I am so sorry for having offended Thee with this most violent of sins. You know my heart, dear God, you know my intentions, and You know my guilt in spite of my intentions. *Ideo firmiter propono, adiuvante gratia Tua, de cetero me non peccaturum peccandique occasiones proximas fugiturum*, and with Your divine grace, with Your sweet and mysterious grace, I do promise, I do solemnly promise to rid myself of sin, to remove myself from all temptation, oh my God. I am so sorry, so genuinely sorry for causing Thee pain. *Amen.* As he finished, he heard a small noise in front of him. He opened his eyes.

Dear Z,

I very much appreciate your input into my problem. You, a man of the world, have that rare ability to cut through the fog and smoke and see right into the heart of the matter, whereas I, a man of spirit, who should be able to see through the mundane and superficial, am so easily distracted by the apparent. Perhaps you would have made the better priest and I the better lawyer. We both serve God in our own way.

I have prayed on your advice, Z, for many days (and nights) now. After our original telephone conversation and your helpful letter of the next day, I was prepared to follow your suggestions, to reach out to the families, to offer to meet with them and to agree to involve the police or other secular authorities if that is what they wished. I was initially disposed to "take my medicine," as you phrased it. But after these many days of prayer, the Lord has granted me the opportunity to see this in a new light. And so finally, with much prayer and thought, I believe another course of action would be more beneficial to our Holy Mother Church. I do not presume to suggest that God is speaking through me with this decision: no, this choice is mine, and mine alone, and I make it with full responsibility. I have decided on the following:

1. Neither I, nor anyone from this office, will contact the families in question. Any and all communication regarding this matter will be conducted through the parish priest, Father B.

2. Father B's prime mission in this matter will be to keep all information, whether substantiated or not, within the jurisdiction and control of the Church. This is first and foremost a Church matter, and the Church and only the Church will decide the proper course of action.

3. Father G's faculties have been revoked and he has been placed in the care of the Congregation of the Servants of the Paracletes. No decision has been made regarding either the duration of this care, restoration of his faculties or the place and/or nature of further assignments.

4. The boys in question will be offered professional counseling. I have in mind two fathers from San Francisco: Father C R, SJ, a highly respected youth minister and advocate with a master's degree in psychology and Father X D, C.S.C., a trained social worker. I believe that these expert fathers will provide the boys with exemplary spiritual and psychological pastoral care. This counseling will take place under the auspices of the parish but will be paid for by the S diocese.

5. No financial compensation or admission of culpability will be offered or implied.

I am guessing, Z, that you will think these solutions inadvisable, unfair and unreasonably harsh. It is here, Z, that our points of view unfortunately differ. And since you gave me such detailed and wise advice, I will try to explain why I've decided to chart a different course.

From your perspective, an intelligent, compassionate man of the world, these solutions might indeed seem draconian in their rigor. But your perspective, my dear Z, is limited. You focus on the individuals, the "victims," and think of how the lives of these young boys have been damaged by the sinful behavior of Father G. My concerns are by necessity greater. Rather than focusing on the health of the individual boys, I must focus on the health of the Mother Church. I must take the long view, Z, and ask how best to serve the spiritual needs of my congregation.

Think, Z, if the voracious and vicious press were to gain knowledge of this unfortunate case. Think how they would distort and exaggerate the details, instilling doubt and provoking disgust not only in the general populace—who are so ready to believe anything that besmirches our faith and our Church—but also in our flock, whose faith in the sanctity and holiness of our dear Mother Church would be severely tested. I will not allow the indiscretions of a single, unwell individual to threaten the faith, threaten the very souls, of the members of my bishopric.

I can hear your objections, my dear Z, almost as if you were sitting on the couch across from me now. "Are you suggesting we should sacrifice," you are saying, "the lives of these two young boys for the good of the institution? Is your church so fragile," you continue, your voice rising, "that it cannot withstand justice and a just civil punishment for a most heinous and unholy felony?"

I apologize for putting words in your mouth, but I do believe you would say something close to what I have written. You would use the word sacrifice, and that is exactly what we are talking about here. I do not shy away from the word: I am asking the boys to sacrifice not their lives but merely their innocence. As a Catholic, I am familiar with sacrifice, the original sacrifice of Jesus Christ, the Son of God, to give His innocent life so that all who believe in Him may live. Sacrifice means to make sacred. And so, yes, I am willing to sacrifice the immediate health of these two boys to keep our Holy Mother Church from the vicious scandal that would wound her unmercifully. "What gives you the right to do this, to sacrifice another?" you would ask.

And here, Z, our differences make communication difficult. I need to impress upon you that I am required, by my belief and duty to the Most Holy Catholic and Apostolic Church, to protect the faith and the Church at all costs. I need to see things in the long run. I cannot focus, like you can, on the things, on the *time*, of this world. I need to see, or at least imagine, the Church in all Her glorious past, as well as Her precarious future.

The time of any individual life—yours, mine, the life of the boys— is miniscule compared with the everlasting time of the Church. We are a Church of centuries, of millennia, and our promise is one of *eternal* life, of either *eternal* salvation or *eternal* damnation. And yet you speak of the temporal, the mundane lives of the two boys. And not even of their lives, dear Z, for no one has lost a life. No, you speak of their health, their relative well-being. And I am not insensitive to this, Z, as I will do my utmost to help counsel and heal them, to provide for them the full psychological and spiritual resources of the Church. And all I ask is that they let me help them.

Think if this were to become public knowledge, disseminated unmercifully by the television and newspapers of our day. Would this help heal the boys? To shame them in public? In front of their classmates, teachers, the entire country? And what of the others, the rest of the congregation, both of Parish V, the S diocese and the Holy Church as a whole? What do you think would happen? I'll tell you what would happen: blinded by the secular, souls would leave the Holy Church. They would see the corruption and hypocrisy and ignore the beauty and the truth, and they would leave and denounce our faith and harden their hearts to the one true path to salvation. And so, my dear Z, we would lose souls; we would condemn souls to eternal damnation. And for what? A temporary, mundane idea of justice.

I will not allow this to happen.

Yours in Christ,

Most Reverend M
Bishop of S

TEN

The Thirty-Third Saturday of Ordinary Time, 1983
Thomas Aquinas—*Summa Theologiae Three*

Objection 1, The soul (self), if it is negated (and that is not proven), is only negated superficially and temporarily: the soul ultimately and rapidly returns to itself.

I answer that, My soul, it is true, always returns to itself: it is a resilient and stubborn thing. I can only hope that my project, no—that is not the right word, my life, my dedication, my existence, all these are poor approximations. I can hope that my soul, my very being, can learn from the experience of these disappointments and that eventually, true negation may be achieved.

I wrote the word "grow" and then changed it to "learn." For my soul is already too large, too cumbersome and present. It takes up too much space and speaks much too loudly: it wants and wants and never tires of expressing even its smallest desires. My soul is an infant, a large unruly infant who calls constantly for its God and by such persistent crying repulses the very thing it desires. All of this is poor, inaccurate, an infantile way of expressing my cloudy thinking.

Knowing my soul is immature, not ready, incapable of withstanding His divine presence, God graciously withholds Himself from me, just out of reach. I know He is there—that is never a question—but I also know I cannot reach Him, not just yet. I am too full with the hope of Him to have room to receive Him. But this is not a call to inaction, to quiet and passive contemplation. My ripening will not come by itself—that is true; it will come only through God's help and my prayers, through vigorous faith in Our Lord Jesus Christ. My maturity will be a gift from God. But I must make myself worthy to receive such a gift; I must shed my infantile conceptions and desires. I must do this with my body, my senses and vital powers. I do not know if this is the right way, but I believe, for my soul, that it could be.

How to rid my soul of my soul? That is the problem. I pray to God for help.

Objection 2, Your concupiscence is a sin, and sin cannot lead to God. John I tells us "Whoever is born of God does not commit sin, for his seed remains in him: and he cannot sin, because he is born of God" (3:9). Your path is mistaken and evil, perhaps prompted by the Great Deceiver.

I answer that, The accidental or capricious indulgence of the senses is mere lust, debasing and sinful: it lowers our souls to those of the animals and leads to degradation and attachment, not loss. This concupiscence is indeed love of the world and the self. This is an ego-affirming indulgence not made to negate but sustain, even amplify. My personal acts, however, are not concupiscence; they have a holy purpose in that they are willful and sincere attempts

to shed my ego and myself, to shrink the expansiveness of my being, to prepare the room in my essence to become the Virgin Wife,
stripped of ego and images that Meister Eckhart, in his reading of
Luke 10:38, so beautifully admonishes us to become.

On the contrary, But you are not the Virgin Wife Eckhart speaks
of. Your sensual experiments do not successfully strip your ego
from you, and your recording of these experiments in writing rein-
scribes both the images and the ego you insist you wish to negate
from yourself.

I answer that, I am but a novice at the beginning of my spiritual
journey. As St. Thomas teaches, "We can't have complete knowledge all at once."

It is true: my recent experiments have largely served to make
me more aware of my body, my sensations, my self. The joy and
delight they have provided have granted me only temporary release
from myself, and I have always returned from these experiences, accompanied by the memories of pleasure, with attachment to both
the pleasure and to its memories. It is true that I return with a love
for the others and for myself. Still, I feel I am on the right track.
I do not believe, in my heart of hearts, that these experiments are
primarily sinful: while they may contain small sins, partial sins, the
acts, as a whole, are sincere. Or, to be precise, they may be sins now,
but they will lead to the shedding of sin in the future. I believe God
would correct me if I were to falter for long following a mistaken
path. If I am mistaken, however, He will judge me.

As to the second point, I object that my writing necessarily
recalls the memories of my pleasure to myself. I use writing to try
to expel or negate the images of my memory. For me, writing is a
way of forgetting.

I sit here in my hotel room writing two nights and two days after my acts with the Roman whores, whom I paid double what they asked, and this act of my pen on the white pages in no way resembles my sensations during that afternoon and evening. I can write of Romulus's scrotum, the thick purple vein of his cock and his smell of lemon and moss, but these words are all incomparable to the thing described: they are not the thing, and in this difference lies my possible salvation.

If I did not write, I would become attached to these images, my memories. I would sit and reminisce, attempt to recapture the scent of Remus on my fingertips, the feeling of Romulus's tongue in my mouth, the taste of Remus's thick milky sperm. And these would mix with other memories, other experiments, and these images and memories would fascinate my soul. This would be the real temptation. This would be the real sin: to focus on the images and experiences at the expense of their ultimate purpose. In writing, I observe myself. I detach from my soul and my experiences and memories. I substitute words for the images in order to negate the images. Or so I try.

On the contrary, You are dishonest with yourself: your writing does not solely or even primarily serve to detach you from your memories and images but works as an aid to memory and recall. By writing, you are able to experience your concupiscence again and again. This writing in fact demonstrates, and helps prolong and strengthen, the attachment you feel toward the world of your sensual desires. Your writing is nothing but an act of love toward the world, not a withdrawal from it.

I answer that, I have no answer to this.

I returned to the living room and sat on the loveseat. I was still missing something, some important note to this strange composition. There was something odd about this concept of freedom, something about the almost limitless possibilities Martinez seemed to cultivate and enjoy. This was not simply getting high and hanging out, no, this wasn't the apartment of a dilettante for whom mindless pleasure was the goal. What was the goal, then? And where did he get the money to live like this?

Blackmail. That might explain Martinez's ability to maintain the apartment and various hobbies without steady employment. He and Vidal were roughly the same age, so it was unlikely that Vidal had molested Martinez directly: it was more probable that Vidal was merely the bank, paying for someone else. Like that Father Macial. If Vidal was paying Martinez because of Macial, this would fill in a few bars. It would give Martinez a motive: Vidal had stopped paying. It would also provide some explanation of the gruesomeness of the method—shotgun blast to the face was hard to ignore—as well as the setting—where better to kill a molesting priest, even if by proxy, than in a confessional? It would also explain why Martinez took the diary from Vidal: there were possibly records of payment that might be valuable to others. But why not lock the safe? Maybe he didn't have time?

I looked around the apartment. The childhood molestation might also illuminate the drug and sex interests. I have always tried to avoid easy psychologizing, but it was tempting in this case. Martinez was abused as a child, and so he turned to sex and drugs as an adult. And finally blackmail and murder? But this wasn't the apartment of an elderly rent boy, maladjusted and feral, as there was no sign of anything out of place or anyone out of control. There was an air of something else here, the atmosphere artificial, *studied*—that was the word—hovering about all the drugs, paraphernalia and sex toys. This wasn't the offhand grace of an adept who had been doing this since adolescence, nor was it the manic scattershot of a midlife crisis, wigs notwithstanding. No, here was something planned, something careful and intricate, something deliberate. This was no den of vice or pleasure pad: with written manuals alphabetized, meticulously measured and separated pills, novice shrink-wrapped bondage gear judiciously placed in the bottom drawer. This was a laboratory. I smiled as an old synapse from an undergraduate Wagner seminar fired briefly to life: Martinez was Apollonian, not Dionysian.

And he was no killer. There was not passion desperate enough here to shove a shotgun into the face of another human and splatter his brains on confessional walls. Freedom, perhaps, but not passion. There was an order here, a rigor that was too personal to be murderous.

I looked around the living room at all the techs dusting, measuring, examining. What I was missing was large, big, basic and not to be found in the minutia of fingerprints or fibers. There was something so obvious that I was looking right past it. Forest and trees. It had something to do with the books, with his reading material. And with the book, his notebook. I got up and went back to his bookcase and took out the big *S&M Manual* on the far left. I opened up the front cover. There was handwriting on the second page. It read, in black ink, "Safewords: Me—Gnostic, Apophatic, Metaxu, Areopagite; J—Door, Puppy, Popcorn, Checkbook,

Smileyface; S—Overcoat, Bronco, Streetlight." The handwriting looked vaguely familiar, but I hadn't looked at this book before. Maybe I'd seen some notes or something in the room. The pill boxes maybe. What was I missing?

I called to the tech. "Can you take a picture of this? This cover? Get the handwriting. Thanks. Do you have a cell phone? With a camera? Can you take one with your phone? And email it to me? Thanks."

There was something here.

I needed to know what was in that notebook. I needed it translated quickly. Father Juan. That was my big idea. That wasn't kosher, as far as the department would say, but I'd cross that bridge, etc. Instead of going at it half-blindly, with my college Italian and Maldonado's Spanish, I'd ask the priest to do the whole thing. Quickly. I replaced the Bible, scurried down the stairs and out the door. It was still hot, the air thin and dry, not refreshing, not much help. I walked across the street to the shade. I found the father's card and dialed.

He answered after a few rings. "*Hola?*"

"Father Juan. This is Detective Fruscella."

"Ah, Detective. So nice to hear your voice. My information was helpful, yes?"

"Yes, Father, it was very helpful. Thank you. Father, I have another favor to ask. We found this diary, and it's an important piece of evidence, vital to our case." I sighed, forged ahead. "And the problem is that it's written in all these different languages: Italian, Latin, French, German, Hebrew and others. We need it translated, and I don't think we have the know-how here."

"I see."

One, two, three. "Can you translate it, Father? I think it's the diary of a priest."

"Perhaps. When can I see this diary?"

"I'll try to bring it over before my meeting. Say seven o'clock tonight?"

"Yes, yes, I will remain in my office."

"I'll need it quickly, Father."

"Yes, Detective."

"And, Father, this is between the two of us."

I heard a small chuckle. "Of course, Detective, of course. Until tonight."

The nun who had been praying finished, and rising to her feet, genuflected and crossed herself quickly. She left the pew and began to move toward the back where he was sitting. She looked different: he hadn't noticed the burgundy tunic underneath her habit, and her habit wasn't brown—it was the deepest blue. She had removed her veil and was bareheaded: her dark hair, short and parted in the middle, contrasted almost painfully against her translucent white skin. Was this the same woman? He was surprised to see she wore no shoes. She padded slowly toward him, her bare white feet against the dark red of the carpet. He looked again at her face, and a soft light began to shine down from somewhere behind her head, a light of pure joy, a light that could perhaps obliterate him with its purity and love. He felt his breath leave him, and could see it, watched it as it floated silvery and fragile, almost like a butterfly, soaring up, up into the light. It soon disappeared into the finest, most beautiful and vivid blue, the blue of the Anzio sea, the sky above his dear Provvidenti,

Mary's robe in Fra Angelico's *Annunciation*, a perfect saturated blue that he somehow *felt*, that occupied the very center of his being.

The blue engulfed him, enveloped him, surrounded him with its warmth and beauty. It gradually filled the space of the nave,- from the floor to the firmament of the apse and sharply illuminated the statue groupings—Christ flanked by Peter and Paul on the gospel side and a replica of the *Dei Genetrix Hodegetria* on the epistle—which guarded either side of the chancel arch. The light flowed and flowed in waves akin to the sea over the *antependium* and then the *reredos*, giving them a soft azure glow. The tabernacle too shone with gentle cobalt light, and the ambo looked brighter, almost aflame, with a brilliant lapis radiance.

Never had he seen such beauty, such absolute otherworldly loveliness. He steadied himself against the facing pew as a delicate, efflorescent fragrance familiar from his childhood began to assert itself among the traces of incense and dust. The scent brought him to the edge of a meadow where he would picnic and play football as a child, a grass field bordered on three sides by the large yellow and crimson blossoms of the *pianella della Madonna*, with its curvaceous hollow lip and soft, downy interior, the plants looking like racks upon racks of only minor variations of the same model and butter yellow shade of ballet slipper. It was a delightful perfume, sylvan and subtle, and it mixed with the rough texture of his father's apron crusted with dried bread dough; the tart taste of his aunt's olives; the relief of the shade of the pine tree near the hot road by the quarry; and clang of the hammer of the *coltellinaio Barberessi* to summon his childhood.

She smiled at him, a beautiful, indescribable smile, and he felt such a sublime and perfect delight. As she walked past him, he heard her whisper, "*Omnia condonabuntur, omnia condonabuntur.*" All will be forgiven.

Time stopped.

Just as air departs a glass when filled with wine, all thought was replaced by feelings of devotion and peace. Language and prayer left him. He didn't lose consciousness: he was sure of that. His eyes were open, but the shapes they registered—rectangles, squares, circles, cylinders, cubes—were unattached to recognizable objects. He was filled with the Holy Spirit, filled so that his intellectual comprehension was rendered irrelevant. He had no need for external objects, there were no external objects, there was nothing external to him: he was one with the Lord and with all of His creation. He was *in* love, the *in* a preposition designating immersion and seclusion, within, inside love, surrounded by and filled with love. At the same time he was enveloped and engulfed by love, he underwent a rapid and extreme expansion. He was everywhere, immediately, and everything. He became illimitable, borderless, without end.

When he would try to think about this later, he found it impossible to put any sort of logic or order on to it, to even put it to language in order to communicate or remember. There were impressions he could recall, impressions besides those of the impossibility of language. There was the sense of absolute unity, of being one with God and with God's creatures throughout time. In fact there was no time, time no longer existed, and so he was one with everything in space as well as one with everything in the past and in the future. He no longer had to worry about death. He felt so much at peace, so expansive and unified. He felt he *understood*, but he did not understand this understanding. And there was the sense of forgiveness: he had sinned, yes, but was now and would always be forgiven.

Slowly, gradually, ever so slowly the blue receded and shapes began to return to objects. The circle above returned to an apse, the rectangle and dark brown below to the mensa, the thick lines again formed a crucifix, the various horizontals once more fashioned into the series of pews before him. His body also returned: he became aware of his breathing, the pain in his left knee, the strain in the small of his back. His heart was racing: he felt hot and flushed, his face and chest were moist with sweat, his black cassock clung heavily. He pushed himself up from the kneeler and sat back in the hard pew in some discomfort. He wasn't confused but needed to sit a while, collect himself. He was thirsty.

He looked behind him and then turned back to face the front. He was alone in the church.

He looked up to the barrel vault. It was almost as if he could see through it, see beyond it, beyond the blazing summer sky into heaven. Mary had forgiven him! *Gratias tibi, o dulcis Maria, gratias tibi.*

My name is D O. I grew up in B, in the early sixties. I played sports in junior high, mostly basketball and track, and I had a lot of friends. The first time I was molested, I stayed after basketball practice to work on my jump shot. I stayed about an hour, hour and a half. I used to like that gym, and you could stay as late as you wanted, turn the lights off yourself. I took a quick shower, and I saw Father V sitting on the bench near my locker. It was weird, you know, I had Father V for Latin, but he didn't seem to be the sporty type. He was strict, and kind of mean, knew everything. I had my towel around my waist. I said hi or something, but he stood up and told me to take off my towel. I was surprised, shocked, but he had this voice, this deep voice that made you listen, made you do what he said. So I dropped my towel. He moved toward me, quick like, and began to fondle my genitals. I got hard, and he put me in his mouth. He kept after me for a year, until I graduated. I quit sports, never went to that gym again.

I'm L P, and I was a student at C M from 1980 to 1982. I was always a skinny kid, but I began to develop, you know, breasts, and I didn't really know how to handle all the attention, you know, the looks and smart remarks. That's why my mother put me in C M: no boys. Ironic, huh? Anyway, there was this Father K, a new art teacher from I. He was handsome, blue eyes, black hair and pale white skin, and he had that great accent. Art classes got popular. I was always a good drawer.

After a while, I used to see him all around school, in the hallways and at the hockey field, and at the McDonald's where we'd sometimes go for lunch. I didn't think anything of it, I liked seeing him. He's always smile at me, say hi, and he was good-looking and unavailable, you know, a priest. Anyway, one day, it was early, before second period, I was going from the second floor to the first, and I see Father K walking toward me on the stairs. He stops me and tells me that I'm a terrific artist and asks me if I want to meet him and a couple of girls at the W Museum next Saturday to look at some paintings, a sort of unofficial field trip. He didn't want to ask me during class because he was only going to take three girls and didn't want the whole class to know. He said that we'd have lunch afterwards.

I was, you know, happy, proud to be chosen. I was naïve I guess. But he was a priest, and I was fourteen. So I met him at the museum, and he was alone, and he said that the other girls couldn't make it, did I mind? I don't know, what could I do? I'd snuck out, hadn't told anyone where I was going, and he was a priest. And yeah, part of me was excited to be seen with this handsome man, this handsome safe man. So we went around the museum, and I remember looking at drawings by this guy van Eyck, do you know him? Father K was so smart, telling me about the history and how he would work to get this line just right: it was amazing. If the day had ended there...

We went to the museum café to have lunch. I had a burger and a Coke or something. And he's still talking about van Eyck,and how those drawings reminded him of mine, which even then I thought was total bullshit. But all of a sudden I started feeling bad, sleepy, like I was out of it: I could barely keep my eyes open. But was more than just sleepy. I mean obviously, he drugged me. But I didn't know that at the time. He looked real concerned, and asked if I'm feeling all right. I told him I felt totally out of it, and he said he had a friend with an apartment a couple of blocks away, if I wanted to lie down.

I must have passed out, because next thing I remember was waking up in this bed, naked, sore and bloody. Father K raped me. When I started crying in the bed, he came with a glass of water and he told me not to tell because it was my fault. It was my fault that my breasts and legs, my exquisite beauty had tempted him beyond control. He asked me if I wanted my mother to know, if I wanted my classmates to know. He raped me—we had sex—for about four months after that, five or six times a month, until he disappeared from school. I heard he got sent back to I. It's been hard for me to trust people, you know.

Canon 1387 A priest who in the act, on the occasion, or under the pretext of confession solicits a penitent to sin against the sixth commandment of the Decalogue is to be punished, according to the gravity of the delict, by suspension, prohibitions, and privations; in graver cases he is to be dismissed from the clerical state.

In a four year span, Father Q molested at least twenty-three children, including three toddlers and an eight-month-old baby.

Father H, yeah, don't talk to me about Father H. He was fucking me and my brother, me on Wednesdays and my brother on Saturdays. We were so ashamed. We never talked about it, never mentioned anything to anyone. We slept in the same room all that time and never said nothing. Until those lawyers contacted my mom. I was fifteen; my brother was ten. A year and a half this went on, a year and a half. My brother, he weighs ninety pounds now, a junkie. And look around you: I ain't doing so good neither. Yeah, we got some money, but money ain't everything. I hope that motherfucker burns in hell. I wish I still believed in God just so I could still believe in hell for that fuck.

ELEVEN

The Feast of the Chair of St Peter, Apostle and Martyr, 1993
The Letters of Pseudo-Dionysius
"These things are not for the uninitiated" —Psuedo-Dionysius, *Mystica Theologia*

Dear *Nuestro Padre,*

My soul is troubled, and this is a difficult letter to write. It is very cold here in Denver, grey and somber, and the streets are packed with snow. It is true that the weather is affecting my spirit, and for this I am ashamed. It is also true that my spirit is saddened and disturbed by more than the cold and clouds, and for this I write to you.

I have done all you have asked of me, dear Father. When you asked me to live in Denver for months of the year, separated from you and my dear Legionary brothers, separated even from the holy Church herself, I complied happily, without reservation. When you assigned me specific and intricate tasks and errands, I completed all quickly and efficiently, with joy in my heart. When you asked me to travel and serve as your specific representative, to personally deliver packages, money or spoken messages, I did so without suspicion or hesitation. And when you asked me to obtain certain medicines for you, esteemed Father, I did my utmost to procure the very best. I have served you without question, my precious Father, because by serving you I believed I was serving Christ.

But in your recent letter to me, *Nuestro Padre*, there are two suggestions that trouble me, that roil my previously placid spirit, and so I need to ask you for clarification. Perhaps I am mistaken, perhaps I am misreading your words. If so, please correct me, dear Father, please enlighten this darkened soul! If only I could feel confident that I was erroneous, that I have misunderstood these admonitions and commands, how happy I would be. But I cannot feel that certainty, dear Father, and so I am writing now to ask you to confirm that I have misunderstood, to confirm that your intent and meaning is very different from what I am interpreting and to reaffirm your knowledge and wisdom are infallible and just.

In your letter, you suggested that I "stop being so methodical" in my experiments. You said I needed to "loosen up" and that my trials "seemed joyless and sterile." Dear Father, I cannot help but read this as a fundamental misunderstanding of all I am attempting. Please tell me I am wrong in my reading of your words. Please tell me that this is perhaps haste on your part, a phrase or a suggestion to which you did not give much thought.

Freedom is God's most Holy gift, for it allows us to best determine how to serve Him. It is also His most dangerous gift, for it provides many opportunities to refuse Him, to betray Him, to chose the paths of wickedness and deceit. In order to minimize the possibilities of ignoring God, of acting only or primarily to further my own desires or the desires of Satan, I require a methodical and systematic schedule. I require a rigorous structure, dear Father, to control freedom's temptations. To proceed haphazardly, chaotically, is at best to indulge in mere vice and concupiscence and at worst to succumb to the exhortations of the Archfiend. My project can only have validity if it is sincere, dear Father, and it can only be sincere if it is rigorous and orderly.

I must tell you, my Father, my system brings both joy and suffering. Joy in the feeling that by each failure, I am getting closer to the truth. And suffering in that my failures are indeed failures, that my ego always returns, intact and articulate, conspicuous and imperious, hungry for life. Such failure saddens, but this sadness cannot be "sterility," my Father, not with the tears and blood and other bodily secretions by which I purchase this knowledge. It is true that such suffering is not truly separate from this joy, but neither passions come cheaply, *Nuestro Padre*; both are dear. And both are ever-present, and both are the food of my soul.

Your second request is perhaps even more troubling. You ask that "for personal edification and instruction" as well as the "possible use for the teaching and enlightenment for certain talented and conversant novices" that I send you copies of my diary entries. I do not know where to begin to express my dismay and discomfort with this request. I pray to God that I am misunderstanding, although your words seem clear enough. There are many reasons this request disturbs me, Holy Father, and I will elaborate when I see you in person in three short weeks. For now, I will articulate but two.

First of all, I am not at all convinced that knowledge of my path, my trials and experiments, can be useful for another soul, let alone one young or inexperienced as a novice. My experiments are such that they could, when viewed by someone not practiced in the knowledge of the many possibilities of Catholic faith, seem to be contradictory, ambivalent or even blasphemous. Advanced knowledge given to the immature is like poison, like strong drink given to children. You, as well as a few others, carry the adequate preparation to understand my activities. But to disseminate this knowledge to the uninitiated would be a grave and irresponsible error. My path is personal, and the knowledge I have gained is difficult and obscure, unfathomable to those who might come to it with prejudice or convention, as well as those who bring enthusiasm and fervor. Given the near certainty of misunderstanding by both the reticent and the eager, I do not see any possible benefit to making the record of my experience available to others.

Nor, dear Father, do I wish to share my writings with you. It pains me so to refuse this request: I have never refused you anything before! And I will gladly continue to share my experiences and memories verbally with you in person, perhaps with a small glass of the Camus cognac after dinner on the veranda of your Polanco apartment or even, perhaps, with Cardinal Sodano in his villa at Impruneta outside of Florence. I remember our many conversations well, my dearest Father, and I hope we can return to the intimacy and community such warm and honest fellowship brought us. I recall one conversation, very late, after all the brothers had retired. It was at Impruneta. The bottle was empty, all the bottles were empty, and I was thinking about gathering myself to get up and take a taxi back to my room. You spoke to me then, dearest Father, softly and slowly. You told me that faith was much too important to leave to others and that one's relationship to God was personal. You insisted, and I can still hear your voice in my ear, that faith was the only thing that could not be taken from us and that I needed to protect this faith, this relationship, at all costs. Do you remember this conversation, *Padre*? You told me that you recognized in me a holy solitude, a capacity for being alone with God and that I should respect and nurture this capacity. You told me to block out inappropriate dogma and useless advice and that my pathway to God was my own. Then you told me I would be sent to Denver, that I would be allowed the freedom to grow and become, without the yoke of busybodies, gossips and Sadducees inhibiting my struggle. I could not find the words to thank you, and so I sat there in silence.

I will speak to you about my experiences, my dear *Padre*: how can I keep that from You? But my writing is my own and is meant for no one's eyes but God's and mine.

Yours in Christ,

Andrea.

I went home first, showered and changed, then swung by my office. Maldonado followed me in from the bullpen and closed the door behind me. He handed me what I assumed to be a copy of the notebook in a brown paper bag.

"McCormick says not only does he not owe you anymore, but you've gone way past even and now you owe him. 'Big time,' was the term he used."

"You look at this?"

He shook his head. I removed the book from the bag—McCormick had placed it in a thin clear plastic two-ring binder—and opened it to a random page. I looked down, and the light bulb went on, the angels sang, and the scales fell from my eyes.

"Jesus Christ."

"What?"

"They're the same guy."

"Who?"

"Vidal and Martinez. Same fucking guy."

"What?"

"There's no other explanation: it's the same handwriting."

"Same handwriting as what?"

"There were some notes in one of the sex books. I knew I'd seen the handwriting before. I did, a couple of minutes before." I tapped the page. "Right here."

"You sure it's the same?"

I showed him the photo the tech had sent me on my phone. "Positive."

"Maybe they were brothers or something. Twins?"

"Oh c'mon."

"Maybe he took the priest's book. Maybe the book belonged to Vidal."

"No, Father Andrea Vidal and Willem Martinez are the same person. That's what the handwriting says, that's what the wallet says, that's what the bookcase says, that's what the wigs say, that's what the entire apartment says: they're the same." I sat on the edge of my desk and set the book down. "Nothing else makes sense."

"*That* doesn't make sense. Why would someone go to such an elaborate ruse to be two people?"

"You never heard of priests who like to fuck, huh?" Maldonado blushed. "Wasn't his boss that big-time sleaze, the junkie who whored around? I could see it. Anyway, you don't have to take my word for it. Two to one says the majority of prints in Vidal's and Martinez's apartments are identical. I'm going to call Crime Scene to tell them to compare the prints before they do a database search. Just to set your mind at rest."

I hopped off my desk and pivoted around to the phone, dialed the 4-4-6-8. "Califano."

"This is Detective Fruscella. I'm working on the Vidal homicide. You did your thing at an apartment today, on Humboldt. Who's the lead on that? Is she there? Let me talk to her. Housman? This is Fruscella. You know those prints you pulled on Humboldt? There should be a dominant set. Compare them to the vic's, Andrea Vidal. Soon as possible. I'm in my office. 5575. Thanks."

Maldonado stared down at the book, then looked up at me.

"I don't know. So who killed him—them—him?"

"You double the victims, you double the number of suspects. People who might kill Martinez would never have reason to kill Vidal. And vice versa."

"You can look at it the other way, too."

"What do you mean?"

"Do we even know who the victim was? Was it Martinez or Vidal?"

"Whoever did it shot him in church."

"But that doesn't mean it was necessarily Vidal. Maybe they knew about the double life. Maybe they found it easier to kill him there. Maybe they wanted to throw us off the scent, have us look for Vidal's killer instead of Martinez's."

"You're right. But at least we know that Martinez didn't kill Vidal. This wasn't a suicide. We're no longer chasing our own tail."

"But we're back at square one: if Martinez didn't kill Vidal, who did?"

"We have this. We need to get it translated ASAP." I hesitated. I wasn't sure I wanted to confide in Maldonado in case this somehow blew up. The department was very particular about keeping the chain of custody pure and uncontaminated, and would frown upon stray copies of murder investigation evidence floating around. Although I'd already involved him in securing a rogue photocopy for me, letting him know I was going to hand that copy over to a third and unconnected translator might be a bad idea: it was one thing to make a copy for the lead investigator; it was another level of complicity entirely to make a copy for an outside party. I decided to keep my mouth shut.

The phone rang.

"Fruscella. Same prints. Absolutely sure. Any other prints found? Vidal 98%. Martinez 77%." I looked at Maldonado. "Anything else? Thanks." I put the phone down. "Same prints. Same guy."

"I heard."

Omnia condonabuntur, omnia condonabuntur, Maria spoke those words to him, a poor sinner, a weak and unworthy servant. He had seen Her in front of him, beautiful and sacred, divine in the bluest light, and She had spoken to him in a voice of pure music, omnia condonabuntur. Gratias tibi ago, Maria, Gratias tibi ago, Gratias tibi ago. How can I serve You, oh Maria, how can I serve You? Holy Mother of God, I was close enough to smell the sweetness of Your perfume, close enough to hear You forgive me, close enough to understand. And I pray to You now to thank You. You in all the glory of Your twenty-six names. *Sancta Virgo virginum, ora pro nobis; Mater Christi, ora pro nobis; Mater Ecclesiae, ora pro nobis; Mater Diviniae gratiae, ora pro nobis; Mater purissima, ora pro nobis; Mater castissima, ora pro nobis; Mater inviolata, ora pro nobis; Mater intemerata, ora pro nobis; Virgo fidelis, ora pro nobis; Speculum iustitiae, ora pro nobis; Sedes sapientiae, ora pro nobis; Causa nostrae laetitiea, ora pro nobis; Vas spirituele, ora pro nobis; Rosa mystica, ora pro nobis; Stella matutina, ora pro nobis...*

"Signelli, Signelli." He felt a hand on his shoulder, rough. He opened his eyes. Where was he? He felt strange, disoriented. He looked up at the face looming before him. Who was he? He closed his eyes and tried to return to the litany. Where was he? *Consolatrix afflictorum, ora pro nobis; Auxilium Christianorum, ora pro nobis...*

"Signelli, Signelli." The rough hand returned. He opened his eyes again, slowly, reluctantly. Who was this man with the wild white hair and red face? His knee was painful and his back bothered. When he was praying, the aches of life were unnoticeable, thanks be to God, but as he stared at this red face, his body returned, hurting and insistent. He stumbled up from his knees and sat on the hard pew.

"Look at you, man, look at you. What happened?"

Malachi. He didn't recognize him at first. He looked around again. He was in a small chapel, the front pew, and Malachi was leaning over him. Upset about something. He rubbed his forehead with the fingers of his left hand, then looked up and toward the front at the small *mensa* and *reredos*. The rectory chapel. He was beginning to recognize and remember. He had come here early in the morning, the morning after he had been visited by *Maria, Regina Martyrum*. She had visited him. She had forgiven him. She had spoken to him and She had forgiven him. *Regina sine labe originali concepta.*

"Signelli. Are you with us? Jesus, Mary and Joseph, man, what happened?"

He didn't like being shaken.

He explained slowly and annunciated carefully, as if talking to a child. "I saw Mary. She spoke to me. She forgave me." He dropped his gaze. "Thanks be to God."

"And did she tell you to stop shaving? And to sleep in your white soutane? You look a *raic*. I've been calling you half the morning now, and we need to talk. Whether you be up to it or not."

He wasn't sure how to respond to that. It sounded unimportant. Malachi stared down at him, his face a question, a question Signelli had no interest in. After a while: "Signelli, let me sit now." Signelli slid back slightly: the sooner Malachi would leave, the sooner he could return to his prayers. Malachi buttressed hard against the pew end. He looked at Signelli and shook his head slightly. "I understand your parlay with the police officer wasn't productive. Well, no matter. They have the notebook; that I learned. Seems our Father Vidal had a double life, the *sleeveen*. Seems the good Father enjoyed a wee bit of the *gadge*, he did, as well as your various magic potions and products of the poppy. Not to mention whores of all genders and abilities. Our good Father had an alias, the same as his suspected killer. The *garda* remain befuddled."

Somewhere in Signelli's consciousness a small voice reminded him that never had he heard Malachi speak for that amount of time before. Odd. The time he could not listen to Malachi was the time he spoke the most. Malachi looked at him with his rheumy blue eyes and florid, dappled skin, looked at him as if he was waiting for something. He wished Malachi would go away.

"Are you getting this, man?"

He was getting it. He just didn't care. There was a notebook he was supposed to obtain. And a priest had been murdered. He remembered all that, vaguely. He had been forgiven, forgiven of everything. He needed to thank Maria for that.

Malachi leaned in closer. "As I said, the garda have the notebook. Normally, this would make things much more difficult. But I planned—I planned for that possibility, you see. I have something to trade for the notebook." He scowled, and his twisted face somehow reminded Signelli of the expression on a rooster-shaped wine pitcher Father Gustave was particularly proud of.

"*Del Gallo.*"

"I duuno what you're on about, Signelli." Malachi leaned back and sighed. "Listen, you'll be going back to Rome soon, but you've one last play here. I want you to meet with the detective and offer her this: she gives us the notebook, and we give her the name and location of the killer. With evidence to tie him to the murder. And then you fly back and thank Mary at St. Peter's yourself, eh?"

Malachi waited. He leaned forward again. Maria was so lovely in that beautiful light. He had never seen anything that could even approach that. He closed his eyes in order to better remember it. Malachi shook his shoulder until he opened them.

"Are you with me? We've a couple hours. I'll get Lanzarote to clean ya up, a fresh soutane: can ya shave, Signelli? Look at me, man. All you have to do is offer the killer and his location for the notebook. Can you remember that? I'll provide a telephone number and arrange the exchange: when she provides the notebook, we'll give her the killer's identity and his location. No questions asked. You'll need to impress upon her that speed is of the essence here, and if she don't agree, we'll talk to her boss. And if he don't agree, we'll talk to his boss. You got that? Can you do this, Signelli?" All this talk, all this *borbottio*. It was giving him a headache. He much preferred the quiet Malachi, Malachi the terse. Maybe this was his final task, after which he could pray in peace. Malachi stood and motioned with his right hand. "Lanzarote will help you clean up. And then we'll drive over, and you'll meet with the detective, and soon you'll be back at your prayers."

He was tired, and he wanted to be alone, alone to pray. Perhaps this was the way. He nodded.

As Archbishop of the Diocese of M, USA, I respectfully request permission to proceed with the alienation of property owned by this same archdiocese. The alienation will involve the transfer of assets from the patrimony of the Archdiocese of M to a separate juridic person, an autonomous pious foundation known as the Archdiocese of M Catholic Cemetery Perpetual Care Trust. By transferring these assets to the Trust, I foresee an improved protection of these funds from any legal claim and liability, including any possible awards contingent on the outcome of current legal actions against the diocese. The value of the funds to be transferred was $56,943,983.35 as of December 31, 2006.

Sincerely Yours in Christ,

Most Reverend U V,
Archbishop of C.

My name is R F, but most people call me B. All I want is some kind of closure, some kind of acknowledgment that I was hurt, wounded by this man, this priest, who raped me for a year and a half when I was ten years old. Ten years old. And he was a man of God. I thought that God sanctioned that, those things he did with me. That's what he told me. Imagine what that would do to you at ten years old.

Yeah, I got some money for it. I figured it out: about $15,000 per rape, as far as I can remember. That's just an approximation; I've blotted much of that time out. Drink, drugs, women and men, that's how I blotted it out. I couldn't really keep a relationship after that, couldn't trust anyone. Still can't.

No, money's not closure. People toss around the F-word: Forgiveness. I'm not going to forgive. It might be the Christian thing to do, forgive, but I'm not a Christian any more. How much is that worth? All I want is for someone in the Church to say I'm sorry, we did you great harm, and we want you back.

1. A priest without the vow of a monk who sins with a young girl or prostitute shall do penance for two years.

2. If with a female servant of God or with a male, a fast is added. The punishments shall be increased to five years if habitual.

3. A cleric without the vow of a monk shall do penance for half a year: if habitual, for two years.

4. If anyone has sinned as the Sodomites, ten years penance: if he is in the habit, more must be added.

5. A cleric who commits femoral fornication shall do penance for one year: if he repeats, two years.

6. If he fornicates with an animal or mule, he shall do penance for ten years.

7. Any cleric who commits *sollicitatio ad turpia* shall do penance for ten years and, if a bishop, lose their rank.

Father W L has confessed to molesting thirty-seven boys over a ten year period in hundreds of incidents, in parishes ranging from G to R to D. His victims included triplets, a three-year-old, two boys with learning and cognitive disabilities, a paraplegic, and the seven-year-old son of a parish secretary. He would often prey on the disadvantaged: over half his victims came from one parent or otherwise dysfunctional households, and seven were in foster care at the time they were molested. Two of the boys he admitted to molesting subsequently committed suicide.

He preferred younger boys and found secondary sexual characteristics distasteful. He would shave the pubic area of the boys if necessary and collected their hair in individual bags, which he labeled and kept. He had a diverse collection of pornography that he used to arouse his victims and himself. A favorite ploy was to invite two or three boys on a camping trip to a cabin his family owned in the D Park. He would offer alcohol and gradually molest them as a group. He would often then videotape the boys molesting one another while he directed the action, until he was ready and able to join in again. Victims reported that he became more violent as the sessions wore on, and he would curse and blaspheme "like he was possessed." One victim reported that Father L once forced himself and two other boys to ejaculate on a pile of communion wafers, but this charge has not been corroborated.

Mrs. L D accepted $50,000 seventeen years after the first of the abuse occurred. She refused the offer of counseling, saying she wanted nothing more to do with the C Archdiocese.

Father G is believed to be living in Ireland near Cork.

TWELVE

Visitation of the Blessed Virgin, 2004

Giovanni Pico della Mirandola—*900 Theses*

Nine Theses on the Mistaken Path toward God as determined by Experience

1.0 After forty-five years of attempting to negate myself and bring myself closer to God, I realize I have failed.

1.1 I have failed absolutely.

1.2 This failure was sincere.

1.3 The sincerity of my failure does nothing to mitigate or exculpate the unholy accomplishment of my failure.

2.0 My failure is displeasing to God.

2.1 I have no proof of God's displeasure, other than His silence.

2.2 As I have grown older, and as I have proceeded with my attempts to negate myself in order to prepare myself for God, I have drifted further and further away from God.

2.3 This movement away is not a path towards God.

2.4 As far as I can tell.

3.0 My failure and error in my relationship to God is a sin.

3.1 My fundamental relationship to God is one of sin.

3.2 For this, I am deeply sorry.

3.3 My sorrow is in no way adequate penance for my sin.

4.0 This sin is mine; it belongs to me and no one else.

4.1 This sin is not the fault of God.

4.2 This sin is not the fault of Satan.

4.3 This sin is not the fault of the Holy Catholic and Apostolic Church.

4.4 This sin is not the fault of the Legionaries of Christ

4.5 This sin is not the fault of Father Marcial Maciel Degollado, LC or any of his colleagues or subordinates.

4.6 This sin is not the fault of any other entity or person.

5.0 The overall sin of my life can be broken down into many examples of individual sins. These sins, in turn, can be organized into two main areas: the sins of commission and the sins of impenitence.

5.1 The sins of commission can be further classified into sins of concupiscence and sins of intoxication.

5.1.2 The sins of concupiscence included immoral sexual acts with both women and men. These acts included sodomy, fellatio, cunnilingus, participation in orgies, sadism, masochism and other unclean and debauched activities.

5.1.3 The sins of concupiscence did not and have never included any type of rape or other non-consensual sexual activity.

5.1.4 The sins of concupiscence did not and have never included any sexual activity with anyone under the age of seventeen.

5.1.5 The sins of concupiscence did not and have never included the viewing of any pornographic material featuring children under the age of seventeen.

5.1.6 The sins of concupiscence did not and have never included sexual activity with any animal or beast.

5.1.7 Through my many sins of concupiscence, I debased the Holy Temple of the Lord that is my body.

5.1.8 Through my many sins of concupiscence, I preoccupied my mind with unclean thoughts.

5.2 The sins of intoxication included the deliberate ingestion of chemical compounds and/or organic matter in order to alter my senses and states of consciousness.

5.2.1 This ingestion took the form of oral digestion (pills, capsules, organic materials, "edibles" and liquids), nasal absorption, intravenous injection and pulmonary administration.

5.2.2 Neither chemicals or organic matter were ever sold.

5.2.3 The chemicals or organic matter were never shared with an unwilling or underage participant *to my knowledge*.

5.2.4 The possession and use of these chemicals and substances often involved the breaking of secular laws.

6.0 The sins of impenitence occurred when I did not recognize that my sins of commission were in fact sins.

6.1 Instead of recognizing and repenting these sins of commission, I recorded them.

6.2 I mistook both the commission of sins and their recording as an authentic spiritual journey, as a genuine attempt to prepare myself for God.

7.0 In addition to these major sins of commission and impenitence, I committed many minor sins of procurement, specifically the procurement of intoxicating and hallucinogenic chemicals and organic substances.

7.1 This procurement was for the benefit, and on the instruction, of Father Marcial Maciel Degollado, LC.

7.2 I did not control the use or distribution of these substances once I delivered them to Father Maciel.

7.3 These minor sins of procurement were lapses of spiritual and moral judgment on my part. However, I do not believe they contributed to my straying and likely damnation as the more grievous sins of commission and impenitence.

7.4 These sins of procurement often involved the breaking of secular laws, local, national and international.

8.0 I do not know what penance I can do to possibly expiate the sin that is my life.

9.0 I can only pray for God's mercy.

"Sit, Detective, please sit. Would you like a *pequeño*, a small one? I have some very nice mezcal from Tamaulipas: smoky, but not too harsh."

Juan's office retained that good smell of leather and books. His eyes were small and bright without his glasses. A desk lamp illuminated his desk and little else. I sat and leaned forward. "I'd love one, Father Juan, but once I started I'm afraid I wouldn't stop. Before you know it, the bottle would be gone and I'd be passed out on the couch in reception."

"We'd have an interesting conversation until then, Detective, of that I have no doubt." He studied me, not unkindly. I thought briefly of Signelli, then of the Vidal/Martinez apartment. I felt quite the interloper here, quite the intruder: among such men, books, leather and drink, women were to be at best merely tolerated, at worse utilized for the satisfaction of the insatiable male desire. And I no longer provided satisfaction. Finally, Father Juan rubbed his forehead and placed his glasses on his nose. "You have the book?"

I took it from the bag and handed it across the desk. "There were twenty or so loose pages inside. They're in the front."

He thumbed through it, adjusted the light. "Spanish, ancient Greek, French, German, Hebrew, English, Latin—this shouldn't prove too difficult. Handwriting's legible enough. No Asian languages I can see. No Finnish or Hungarian. I don't foresee much difficulty."

I leaned back. "When can I read it?"

"Four, five days. There are many pages and my German is rusty."

"Day after tomorrow? What would that take?"

He continued rapidly turning the pages, stopping to read here and there. "If I can use an associate, a discreet graduate student, I could likely have it to you day after tomorrow, yes."

"No one can find out about this."

"Of course. As I said, I would use only a discreet student, one whom I trust completely."

I nodded. "I'll have a hard time paying either of you. This task is, should we say, unofficial. I can possibly scare up something, but it won't be for a while."

He didn't look up from his skimming. "A priest was murdered, Detective. It would be churlish, if not sinful, to seek profit from his demise. *Ad maiorem Dei gloriam*, for the Greater Glory of God, Detective, I will do what I can to help you find the man responsible for this terrible crime."

"Thank you. I'll need to know, Father Juan, if there's any mention of sex abuse in there. You cannot hide that. I'm trusting you."

"As much as it pains me to admit it, that is not an unfair request. Concupiscence, pedophilia, is the original sin of Catholicism. Similar as to how slavery is the original sin of the United States, no? Sins not easily exculpated nor eradicated."

"I would argue that misogyny is the original sin of Catholicism. But anything about pedophilia you can see there?"

He continued to turn the pages, reading and skimming. "Not at first glance. Vidal was adventurous, it seems. But I'll need to read the whole thing." He peered over his glasses at me. "Are you sure you don't want that drink, Detective?"

"No, I need to get going."

He picked up the book again and leafed through it. "This will not be easy for you, I'm afraid. I can render the languages into English, but the chronology is uncertain, and some of the theology, at first glance, seems a bit specialized. There are some situations here; they might make us both blush. At first glance I can see transgressions, certainly, against his vows as an ordained cleric, a Catholic and a Christian, but nothing illegal, not as yet. No, not as yet."

I began to gather my things. "Thank you, Father, for everything."

He stood behind his desk and held out his hand. "*De nada*, Detective, *de nada*."

"Day after tomorrow?"

"I am hoping. I will telephone you when we are finished."

He had to concentrate to remember his English. He needed to sit as his left side from his hip up to the top of his ribs was tight and sore, and he wasn't sure of how to make this request known to either the detective or to the shifty child-looking man accompanying her. It would be rude to simply sit without a *ti chiedo perdone*, but he felt shaky, unstable, the opposite of the image he was trying to project. He would be more effective sitting, esteemed but beneficent, *forte*, and above everything, *ragionevole*, reasonable. This was, above all, a reasonable deal—Malachi was not wrong—with both Church and *Commune* receiving what they desired. But he could not present the reasonableness if his *figura* appeared vulnerable or weak. *Salve Regina, Mater misericordiae.*

Maria beckoned, holy and sweet. Roma beckoned, his home. This was a mere job, unimportant, *una mosca, non un elefante,* a small task to be accomplished rapidly. He would do his duty. With Maria's help. With God's help.

To sit. To drink a glass of water, cold water, and sit and wait and let the pain from his side fade and the weakness in his legs withdraw and be able to reasonably focus and reasonably discuss what was reasonably to be done.

They were looking at him, expecting, the *ragazzo* with a lack of respect on his face. He looked back at them and eventually remembered. He knew what he had to do. "*Mi scuzi,* Detective, may I sit?"

She frowned. "Of course. These look comfortable." She moved over to a grouping of tufted leather and chrome armchairs near the center of the room and turned. The room was large, sparsely furnished, with very high ceilings and thin, luminous white fabric billowing from the wall of windows on his right. A ceiling fan rotated lazily above. It was neither hot nor cold. He moved more slowly and sat more heavily than he would have liked. The pain in his side began to dull. She sat to his left, erect on the edge of her seat, her hands folded on her lap. The *scemo* stood behind her, his arms folded like the portrait of young Bernardino Osio without the glasses.

"I did not expect to see you again so soon, Father."

"Nor I."

"And what can I do for you now?"

"The situation has changed since we last spoke." He remembered the rehearsals with Malachi in the car and remembered what he had to say. "You possess property from Father Vidal that belongs to the Church. A notebook, a diary." It was almost as if someone else were speaking. "You may have recovered many volumes, but there is one in particular the Church wishes returned."

"Where did you get this information, Father?" He said nothing. "Assuming we had this notebook, Father, why would we hand over evidence in a homicide investigation?"

He suddenly felt very tired, perhaps not capable of this. He closed his eyes. He needed to return to his prayers. He opened his eyes and stared ahead. He recited, "I have a telephone number. If the notebook is returned, you will be provided with the identity and location of the killer. I am assured he remains in the city. Along with enough evidence to prove his guilt."

Fruscella leaned forward. "Father, if you have information regarding the murder of Vidal, you need to give it to me now."

"I am merely a messenger."

"How do you know about this? Did you or someone you know arrange to have Vidal murdered?" He shook his head and brought his hands together, fingertips touching in front of his chin. He closed his eyes again. Fruscella continued, "Father, listen to me. If you know something, you need to tell me. I can bring you down to the police station: I can question you officially." He wished he was back in the small church and Mary was speaking to him, Maria in Her blue light. She was so beautiful.

Signelli opened his eyes slowly and shrugged his shoulders. He knew what to say. "It will be difficult to question me officially, I am afraid, Detective. I have a Vatican diplomatic passport, and I leave tomorrow for Rome. As for my possible involvement in Vidal's death, I can assure you, I have never possessed any knowledge of his murder at any time. We are not the Knights Templar or the Masons. We do not, cannot, order the death of another human being."

"How will this transfer come about?" from the *ragazzo*.

"I do not know. I will give you this telephone number, and the person will then provide you with detailed instructions."

"Why should we trust you?" again from the young man.

"Please do not assign a role to me that I cannot play. I have been sent here only to offer this telephone number and to make sure you understand that this is a case of extreme urgency. If you do not wish to act on this, we will contact your supervisor. And if your supervisor declines, we will, as you say, go up the ladder. It is my understanding that the person in question is of interest to your FBI as well as Interpol. I am certain that very soon we will find the necessary cooperation. I come to you first primarily as a courtesy, Detective, given our previous conversation. But if you do not wish to be involved, I am certain your superiors will know how to proceed." He hesitated. He was good at his job. "To demonstrate good faith, I was told one of the names this killer has used: Stephen Corr."

That was it. He was spent. Was there anything else he needed to say? He had mentioned the FBI and Interpol and had repeated the fact that he had no more information to offer. He hoped the conversation was over.

He looked at Fruscella. She was looking intently at him. Her assistant behind her was staring down at his hands. He tried to smile.

"This sounds very much like blackmail, Father. And obstruction of justice."

He stood up with difficulty. "I am leaving tomorrow morning. I will likely not return to America. You have one hour to telephone the number. After that, your supervisor will be contacted. In any case, my task is done. The telephone number is 303–564–3434."

As he left, he noticed the young man tapping into a large cell phone.

Aye, killing a priest is extraordinary. But not, perhaps, to me. I've considered it before, won't say dwelt on it, won't say it was a goal of mine, but considered it before, I have, in the past, during the war, and tonight, all these years later, it came to pass. Note the passive. That he was a bad priest, a child-fucker like many, made little difference. They told me he was crap, rotten, a bloody nonce, a sprog molester and they told me he deserved to die, all the shite he caused and the suffering he arranged, they really put it on thick, gave me an earful they did, all so that the costume wouldn't intimidate and the incense wouldn't restrain, and the setting now, the setting wouldn't mollify. They could have all saved their fucking breath.

I still carry it with me, after all these years. I'm not one to forget. And in the war, well, if we held back, or didn't hold back, but we held back more often than not, it was for other reasons, not for whomever a good priest might be fucking. Our disagreements were more profound. So I'm familiar with the conversation, even if what was said and when it was said and who said it is now vague and largely ill-remembered.

This was no surprise to him either. I won't say he was expecting it, because no one expects to lose their beal with a Boss and Co fowler, but he wasn't shocked, not even a wee bit, he wasn't, not at all. Didn't lack for spine, I'll give him that. Looked me in the eye, he did, did his sign of the cross, and, well I won't say he dared me to do it, but he didn't look away. Didn't look down or up, at hell or heaven, he didn't, looked me in the eye straight, and waited for me to oblige him. It was then, when our eyes locked and stayed, that I knew finally he'd not give what I came for. I had no time for the ways of persuasion, and that's never been my line anyway, and if I had to take a punt, it wouldn't be on him giving in, not with those eyes. A quick objection might be made, and I realized it at the time, that in some ways, the tables were turned in that he would gain what he wanted and I would not. Namely death and the book. If I pulled the trigger, that is. I had, and still have, no answer to that. So I pulled one trigger and killed the priest.

I've passed over much, maybe too much to recall. I've always had trouble with time, a sentence that could easily be inverted. I'm indifferent to the future, as she to me, don't give a rat's ass, that we share, and while I don't exactly confuse the present and the past, I don't exactly keep them separate either. So when I stuck the fowler up his dial, I was reminded, to say the least, of thirty years earlier when I could have been doing something similar. Not to him, but to one of his brothers. And, at that time, thirty years earlier, I was a thousand miles away, all these years and miles being now in the past, and now mere words. That'd be a good alibi, eh, I was a thousand miles and thirty years away. Just reminded, not confused, I don't remember ever being confused, perhaps there were times in my life when I'd preferred more information, the possession of, but that's not the same as confusion, not by a long shot. I've always known who and when I am. Not to mention what.

Another objection might be made, or less than an objection, a question really, or maybe less than a question, maybe an insinuation, that perhaps, just maybe, between the two of us, between he and I, or really, more to the point, in me, because, well, his current point of view is now difficult to ascertain, that there was, that I felt, a certain respect for the child-raper. Truth be told, and mark those words, I didn't feel anything then. Just as I don't feel anything now. Not for him anyway.

And a third objection, if it can be called that, again more of a question, or questions, there are more than one really, concern the fact that I carried an expensive and rare weapon, a Boss and Company over-and-under 20 gauge fowler. Why, why would I carry such a rare and, more to the point, singular and therefore traceable weapon? And to that I'd like to say it was gift from my da, but that would be a lie, this was too dear for my father's station in life, and so I have no familial sentiment attached. And I came by this not from a dead comrade, or unfortunate victim, well, let us say I obtained it through the spoils of war, and leave it at that. For appreciating fine weapons, I can thank both the SRR and the Vols for teaching me the difference between bespoke and shite. Any sentiment this fowler engaged is more practical and aesthetic than sentimental. First of all, I carried this particular weapon for this particular job primarily because it's massively reliable, unlike everything else from Albion, mind, with nary a jam or misfire, it's the physical manifestation of cause and effect. And shotguns have no rifling in the barrel, so as long as I tidy the spent shells and wads, they are almost impossible to trace, not that any Wild West American peeler has ever heard of a Boss and Co O/U. And the yoke is beautiful, it makes me feel grand when I carry it, like neither God nor man can touch me. It's a bit intimidating, it is, it gathers attention and grants its wielder a certain gravitas. It's not a subtle weapon, that I give, but please tell me what subtlety is proper to kill a priest within the walls of his church.

I'd followed him about for nearly a week, but he never carried anything, no backpack, briefcase, portfolio, nothing. He really didn't go anywhere either, he'd wander over to the park, or a bookstore, and a couple of times he went to a soup kitchen, but I never saw a book or a parcel that could have been a book. Three days he didn't go out at all. I lost him often, for tracking's not my strength, and it didn't seem to matter, that was clear, to both of us, his hands were always empty and he never wore a coat, it was perhaps as if he had emptied his hands and shed his coat for my benefit, on account of me following him, watching him, small sample that, but he almost seemed to go out of his way to demonstrate that any burden he carried wasn't physical. He never went out accompanied. Come to think of it, I don't remember ever seeing him speak to any of his fellow taigs, not even a how d'ya do, or whatever the fuck they say.

MOTETS
LAUDATE DOMINUM

Feast of Our Lady of Mt. Carmel, 2010

And here I sit writing, always writing. As if I'm trying to write myself to God. No, that's not it. I write to fill the gap left by God fleeing. Writing, fucking, drinking, drugging—all to fill the hole left by the eternally absent. The Great I'm Gone.

And why wouldn't God flee? In horror. His dirty robe raised, his thin dusty ankles scurrying as fast as they can move, away from the absolute gruesomeness of his finest creation.

The present tense bothers, like wearing another's soutane.

I'm sitting at the 'Pec, writing in my original *diario*, waiting for the music to start. I could use some food: my first drink, a Maker's Manhattan, has already gone to my head. That's one thing I fucked up: intoxication. I never understood until recently the absolute holiness of inebriation; the pure sanctity of losing a fraction of control, however small; the untainted pleasure of forfeiting a tiny bit of self; the sheer hopefulness of opening the smallest fissure to let something out. Or something in. The blessed consecrated blood of Christ. I took it for granted, abused its sacred power. And for what? For recreation, for social ease, to loosen inhibitions I never possessed.

I hold the glass up to my face, swirl the deep golden liquid around, the small ice cubes clinking softly. Two maraschino cherries swish around among the ice. I take another sip. The bourbon is a little hot in my mouth, and I swallow quickly. I prefer sweet vermouth, European style, the wine mellowing the rough edges of the American whisky. But I forgot to mention that when I ordered, so this is a Yankee version, the macho whisky unaffected by the effeminate hint of white vermouth.

The mark of the maker.

This high-class Denver whore, escort, Carlene, taught me to drink Manhattans one weekend. I had some really good crystal meth, and we went from whisky bar to whisky bar until we ended up at some loud nightclub on Lincoln where they brought us an entire bottle of Maker's Mark and a bottle of Antica Carpano vermouth. And we made friends.

Carlene would let me pay her with drugs. I wonder what happened to her.

I need to eat something but no one comes here for the food.

I'm Willem tonight: scraggly jeans, a Che Guevara T-shirt, one of my good wigs that's making my forehead sweat. Willem Martinez, drinking a Yankee Manhattan, writing in a notebook about Carlene the call girl. Waiting for the music to start. Hoping no one gives a second glance.

Intoxication—sometimes it doesn't come, no matter how much I drink. Sometimes I just remain: I get sick, dizzy, nauseous, my legs stop working, my mouth stops working. And I'm still here. And then I throw up, but the nausea continues; or I pass out, but the oblivion is temporary, and I wake up on the floor, and I remember.

Even when it does work, I remember.

And I'm still here.

I'm still here. Infinitely or at least significantly corrupted: my original goodness diminished drink by drink, fuck by fuck, pill by pill, until little remains. But what's left is stubborn, tenacious, unmovable if not unlovable, and, despite my many and increasingly desperate attempts to lose it, it endures, living on with the furtive gracelessness and questionable effluvium of that which dies too late.

One crosses the street to avoid Lazarus.

Forever and ever. Amen.

Booze is liquid, and when it works, it makes me feel liquid too. Without form, without the barriers and limitations of my body, I can transcend these walls that encase my soul. Sometimes when I'm drunk the membranes seem permeable, and the possibility of that fissure seems real. That's when I have faith. Or what I thought was faith.

I drink so I can sit alone in the dark.

Dear God, I could never tell if Your withdrawal was disapproval or encouragement.

"No. No way. Fuck no."

Clark slid down into Signelli's chair and leaned forward. He had this stupid grin on his face. "You're going to want to get out in front of this, Detective. Everyone wants this quickly fixed. Schlaf won't say no. And if for some unforeseen reason he does, Peterson will not: she'll be all-in before you can say 'Is the Pope Catholic?' She loves the high profile, loves the FBI and Interpol would make her, well, let's just say it would make her very, very *excited*. Lemme find out who this guy is. Jerry, it's me. Whatya got on a Stephen Corr? Fuck, I dunno, C-O-R-E? C-O-R-R? International, my guess is. Paid killer. POS. Call me back."

"I don't make evidence disappear."

"My guess is that very soon it's not going to be your call. You ever wonder what's in that notebook? Have you looked at it? Curious as to why they're jonesing so bad?"

"Could be a record of other crimes. Like molestation. Vidal was pretty sketchy. As was his boss."

"Could be. Could also be money. Or a combo of both molestation and money."

I shook my head. "I have two questions: first of all, how do they know who killed Vidal? How could they know that? Did they hire someone to do it? I think so. This was not some sort of persuasion gone wrong; this was a hit. Contracted by the Catholic Church. And secondly, how do we do the trade-off? What are the logistics? How do we give them the book and then get the drop on Corr?"

"What do you know about the dude today, Signelli? How deep is he?"

"We had a conversation a couple of nights ago. He looked odd today, distracted, sick, looked like he aged about ten years in two days. I don't know, I don't think he's behind this. I would like to keep him around though."

"That ain't going to happen. I was cc'd on the request to Schlaf. Let me just say he can leave anytime he wants. And he looked kind of cray-cray to me."

I walked over to the large French doors, opened one and stepped through the billowing curtains out onto the balcony. The temperature had dropped, and the clouds had thickened, diffusing the glare into something more pleasing. It smelled like rain.

This rankled. I never liked being bullied, but the fact it was the Catholic Church doing the bullying added salt to my stigmata. Fuck 'em. I had a copy of the notebook, they didn't know that, and maybe the press might be interested. I'd lose my job, okay, but I was sick of smelly men in dresses and their sexist bullshit. There was this local guy, Krupka, at the *Post*, or maybe Clark would introduce me to one of his CNN buddies.

Clark came out to the balcony. "You all right?"

"No, I'm not fucking all right. The fact is, two men, Signelli and Schlaf, are going to take my case away. And that sucks."

"We catch the bad guy, though." He looked at me, then looked away. "Who might get away otherwise."

"Fuck you, Clark." His phone rang.

"Hey, Jerry. Hit me. Okay, Stephen Corr, aka Stephen Kinsey, aka Stevie Nelson, aka Stephen Crown, aka Steven Deadalus okay, okay, that's enough. Former member of the UDA, Ulster Defense Association, and the Red Hand Defenders, what the fuck is that? Paramilitary huh? Wanted by British, Irish, French and Romanian authorities, hmm, suspected in the deaths of three Irish nationals last year, and a French undercover cop the year before. On Interpol's website, yeah? Along with 187 others? Bummer. Okay, send me a file. Later." He clicked off and stared at me. "You might want to inhibit your feels, Detective. This is a bad man who's killed a priest and a cop. Ain't about you."

My rage against Clark was drowning out something I learned in some far-off undergrad Euro history course. "Fuck you again, Clark. What do you know about anything?"

"I know we can get a killer off the streets. With one phone call."

"You don't know a fucking thing." What was it, what was it? Red Hand, Ulster Defense Association, Ulster, Ulster, right. "We're being played. How do we know this guy even did Vidal? You know who the Red Hand is? The UDA? Protestants, asshole. Why would the Catholic Church hire a protestant to kill a priest?"

"Cuz maybe a protestant would be the only one who'd do it?"

I shook my head again. I needed a glass of wine. "You're right, this isn't about me. But there's something rotten here, something really rotten. And if we give the notebook up, we'll never figure out what it is."

"We get a major assassin off the streets, and you get a feather in your hat. Case closed. Win-win to me."

What the fuck was I doing, trying to explain to this frat boy needle dick how angry and small I felt, ground between the wheels of the Catholic Church and the Department and how this grinding began early, with my first prickly experiences with the Church, accused of "inappropriate questions" during catechism, and how this grinding continued all the way from being asked to "stand and smile" by an academy professor to the more recent requests to fetch coffee for Rossman and Miller and couldn't I take a joke? Even Schlaf, by assigning Clark to shadow me—that was demeaning and insulting. Why was I wasting my breath? I needed that glass of wine.

I turned to leave to find the bar.

"Are you going to call, Detective? Or do you want me to?"

He went to the cathedral every morning at four. I shadowed him once to the caretaker's closet, where he pulled out a mop and bucket. I didn't want to follow him into the church proper, a bit sore-thumb that early, but there was an all-night McDonald's across, and I could watch at least the main entrance and side door until a more reasonable hour when I could enter and sit without kneeling in the back. He didn't say Mass, and I never saw him once the party started but noticed the floors were brilliant and the pews smelled nicely of Fiddes.

I met him in the hall the next day, Sunday. I stuck Mr. Boss under his nostrils and whispered steady Where's the fucking book give me the bloody book or I'll blow your Fenian head off and he didn't say anything. He just looked at me funny like he was expecting something. I pulled the hammers back, and some light went on in his eyes, this is cliché I know I went to school, uni in Scotland for a year, amn't one of those eejit yobs from Sandy Row, but he shrugged and motioned with the top of his head and walked past me into the church proper. I followed, stuck the barrels hard in his back, thinking three possibilities here: first of all, he's sick of the whole mess, wants to unburden his conscience, hand over the book after some long to-do, taigs can bore the smile off a pig with their stories of guilt and redemption, and this is how he's going to do it, this was before we face-to-faced, so seven to one and two, he's stalling for time doesn't really know what the fuck he's going to do just wants to get somewhere where he can maneuver ten to one and three he wants to get into the church proper to die maybe right on the altar beneath the bleeding Christ that was even money.

But he kept walking, past the altar and down a couple of steps, and I kept following, what choice did I have, and he kept walking like he had a bus to catch, straight into one of those little rooms off to the side, the confessing booths, and he turned on this dim lamp, flipped down the wee padded kneeler and genuflected himself down, his back to me, like I warn't even there, and started up with his mumbling. And there was no book for sure for sure. So I was standing in the doorway like a culchie from Fintona, the dim light casting my vague shadow against a nearby column, and should I follow and shut the door, the quarters would be close, I didn't think there'd be operating room, what with me, Mr. Boss and the nonce, and I didn't want the light out either, but my shadow projecting behind like some kiddie-time church movie weren't the wisest, so I leaned tight against the doorjamb, got situated and gave him a moment, then a little job in the back of the melon with the Boss, and he turned his head around to look at me but kept mumbling and then turned back you know like I was interrupting well feck all so I gave another jab harder this time and he crossed himself he did and stopped. I need the book I say and this doesn't look like a library. He raised himself slowly, with some effort, like an old man, one of those ancient codgers who tend the graves at Milltown, and he turned, slowly again, and looked me in the eyes, dead in the eyes, and he said nothing, not a word, just looked at me. And that's when the light when on. And his face, it wasn't dead, it wasn't alive exactly either, it was like hadn't given a fuck in so long he'd forgotten what it was like. Most hard men I seen, and I've a few on both sides, most hard men I've seen, well, there's this hope anyway, this hope that there's something that keeps 'em hard, and if you can reach that something, well, then maybe they won't be so hard anymore. Now maybe you can't reach that something, maybe there's not enough time, or maybe you amn't good enough, or maybe that something's just too far away, something past death, but there's still the hope, the belief really, that there is that something. I didn't see that something with this man. This man was beyond hard, and I don't say this lightly.

And it wasn't God, I'd bet my life on that. He wasn't ready to meet his maker, he knew that would likely disappoint as well. There was no impatience there, or acceptance, it was like whatever happened didn't concern him at all. But he wasn't waiting for Jesus, he wasn't, Jesus wasn't with him, Jesus wasn't with us, in that little room. With all that, he was a believer, he was. Not one of those bookie-eyed Fenian fanatics, calculating the sin to penance percentages, the indulgence to purgatory odds. No, this fellow was a believer in that he didn't know, he wasn't sure, that was the strange thing about, that he believed so strong, so strong that it stayed belief, stayed not-knowing, like knowing was besides the point. I can not explain.

So it was obvious to me that he wasn't going to give what I needed, not then not ever. They had made it clear that he needed doing, whether he give me the book or not. You either give me the book or I'll have to shoot you. He didn't say anything to that, just looked me in the eyes, and then made the sign of the cross. I waited a bit, and then shot him. Once was enough.

The blast was loud, but I hoped the wee room contained the noise a slight. The shot lifted him off his feet and slammed him against the far wall. There wasn't much left of his face, and there was a lot of blood splattered on the plaster behind. The blue plastic wad had alighted on his left shoulder, and as I leaned forward to pick it up, I noticed a dark square by his feet, someone's wallet. I looked quickly: it wasn't his, memorized the name and address, put it back on the floor, lifted his feet up against the wall and closed the door. From there it was SOP, I walked quickly over to the side alcove where I had stashed my duffle, put the Boss in, placed the shell casing, wad and me rubber gloves in a plastic bag then in the duffle, and went out into the night on a side street to the west.

When I got back to my flop, I texted the number and got a text in return. An extra £5000 a week to stick around. With the possibility of another job. I decided to think about it. Tomorrow I would get rid of what I needed to get rid of.

"Commander Schlaf wants to see you, Detective. As soon as you get in."

Fuck. They were going to take the case away. They were going to make the deal. Probably already had.

I debated going to my office first, putting my stuff down, having some coffee. I could take my time; there was no longer any rush. Schlaf could wait ten more minutes. The case certainly could. I didn't want to have to walk through the bullpen though, with all those faux sympathetic faces and phony commiserations. Most of those dudes thought I was too big for my boots anyway and deserved to be taken down a notch. And the women, while they might feel some initial sympathy, sure as hell didn't want me fucking it up for them. At least their stink eyes would be genuine. No, I'd see Schlaf first, and if he said what I knew he was going to say, maybe I'd go home, take the day off, listen to something loud. Mahler. Or Hendrix.

"Detective Fruscella, sir. Go on in, he's waiting for you." The express lane. Clark and Schlaf stood as I entered. A bad day just got worse. I saw Schlaf's big ring glint in the light. I couldn't help myself. "I hope I'm not interrupting."

Schlaf missed it. "No, no, Detective, we've been waiting for you. We called your cell."

"I don't use the phone while I'm driving, sir."

"That's smart. You should get one of the devices, Blu-ray or something, lets you talk on the phone without using your hands. I got one in my car."

"Bluetooth," Clark helpfully added.

"Anyway, Detective, I'm guessing you know why you're here."

"No, sir."

"Clark tells me you were offered a deal last night that would go a long way to closing this case. And that you refused."

"I wasn't convinced of the legitimacy of the offer, sir. And I wasn't aware the department was in the habit of bargaining with key evidence in a homicide investigation. Sir."

He looked at Clark, then back at me. They weren't smiling. "You are aware of the suspect's identity and record? You know who this Corr is and what he's done?"

"Yes, sir. I looked him up in the Interpol files last night."

"And you still decided not to proceed?"

"Yes, sir. There's too much that doesn't make sense. Why kill Vidal? Especially like that? Why hire an assassin to retrieve a notebook? And who hired him in the first place? And why rat him out now? And how exactly is this supposed to work? When do we turn over the evidence? Before he's apprehended? After? And what's in the notebook? Is it a record of other crimes? Child molestation, for example. Too may questions, sir."

"Not everyone can afford to be so scrupulous as you can, Detective."

"This is my case."

"No longer. I won't say how, but Homeland Security has gotten involved. They're planning to apprehend Corr sometime this morning. Perhaps they already have. We're cooperating fully, of course. All evidence has been transferred, as have all official files. I'm requesting you to turn over any and all physical evidence you may possess, as well as any other material relating to the case as soon as possible. I'll need your notes, originals and not copies. I'll also need a final report from you at the end of the day."

"So the notebook's been returned? And no one here ever had a chance to read it."

"Someone from IT will look over your computer after you file your report. Do you have any questions?"

"I take it I won't get to question Corr? After he's apprehended?"

"You'll get credit for the collar, Detective. As well as the gratitude of Homeland Security. I was instructed specifically to convey that to you. Clark and I've been talking, and we've decided to recommend you for an MOV. You did a good job with a nasty case, Detective. You've helped to stop an international assassin. That's big league, Detective, big league." He began to fiddle with his ring. "But no, you won't question or have any contact with Corr. As far as we're concerned, there's no longer an open file."

It was time for me to go. Schlaf was staring down at papers on his desk and Clark was checking out his phone. For some reason I kept standing there, not shocked, not obstinate. There was no point I wanted to make, nothing I could change. I just didn't want to go quietly, to disappear. I wanted them to see me: I wanted them to see me leaving.

I wasn't sure that was it either. Maybe I was just tired.

Schlaf looked up at me. Clark did not. "Do you have any questions, Detective?"

All I had were questions. "No, sir."

He smiled. "After you finish your report, you can take the rest of the week off."

REGINA COELI

Feast of Our Lady of Mt. Carmel, 2010

Sex is like drinking, another attempt to fill in the chasm rent by God's escape. The pounding, undulating, quivering, swaying, moaning, coming, the inexorable, inevitable rhythm of that desperate act of tube into tube, piston into cylinder, blade into sheath, that absurd and ridiculous dance of death, nothing but the desire to ejaculate one's soul from the nearest orifice, to leak or drip out into something else or to have something else leak, drip or ejaculate into you. To feel saliva mixing with other saliva, milk with other milk, cum with other cum, blood with other blood, into an undifferentiated and primordial pool... watery and already fading.

The headlong rush into another, followed always by the repulsive withdrawal.

Don't touch me.

The bitter return of the same.

Dear God, I took you at Your word, Your holy and disappearing word. I believed Matthew 16: "Then said Jesus unto his disciples, If any man will come after me, let him deny himself, and take up his cross, and follow me." I took that seriously, took that literally I denied my *self* as best I could. I tried: I took up my cross, if not without pleasure, then certainly without *joy*. I followed You, Oh Lord, into the desert, and as You receded further and further, I tried to lose my self in sex, drink and drugs, not in order to turn stones into bread, not to enjoy my self, but in order to try to disappear once and for all.

So that You would return.

It was never about redemption. Or salvation. I never could abide those banking metaphors. I was never interested in faith of the balanced book.

It was a gift. Of my self to You. I had nothing else.

My cup is empty. Except for the two cherries and some half-melted ice. Remove this cup from me. I could stop now, go back to my apartment, find something to make me sleep. Close the book, put the glass on the bar and walk out into the night.

I signal to the barmaid, a stocky white women with a blond wig much worse than mine, and order a Manhattan with Maker's Mark and red vermouth, red Martini & Rossi, *rosso*. She nods at me like I'm stupid.

Maybe because I'm sitting at the bar, writing.

I still could use something to eat. I'll wait until the music starts.

I used to like to smoke, especially when I was younger. The Cloud of Unknowing, ephemeral and amorphous, transient like breath. But I could never recapture that early ecstasy of the flower smoke, and everything else I burned just made me hungry and sleepy.

'Shrooms and peyote worked, a little too well. But with them I always felt impatient and inauthentic, like I was seeking a shortcut to an audience with someone else's god.

The pills, the shots, the inhalers—they never really attracted. It was all too artificial, the movement more horizontal than vertical. I tried a number of combinations, kept meticulous records—how many milligrams did this, what concoctions did that—but I could never shake the feeling that I was cheating. Even when I was as high as Icarus, there was always, in the back of my mind, some voice that chided me for relying on a *bargain*, a cut-rate ecstasy open to anyone who could swallow, smoke or otherwise ingest whatever it was I was taking.

And heroin, heroin was its own reason, its own deity.

How long has that fucker *Nuestro Padre* been dead? Two and a half years now?

Let's leave him out of this, shall we? I've no time nor interest in determining whether Father Marcial Maciel Degollado, LC bleeds in Malebolge or freezes in Cocytus. He was a minor character at best, and his betrayal, if it can be called that, was slight.

But I want them to know what happened to his money. I keep the letters close.

I followed You, Jesus, into the desert, and I was not tempted. What could Satan offer me? There was nothing there, nothing except denial and resentment. I couldn't even enjoy my own sins. You took away my sin.

For that I will never forgive.

The IT guys were thorough, if slow. After being whisked away to some subaltern vault in the bowels of the NSA, or the Vatican, or both, the entire case files of the Vidal homicide were eventually wiped out, erased, burned to ashes in some electronic fireplace. Father Andrea Vidal was non-existent as far as anyone in the DPD was concerned. The whisking and the burning took all of the morning and most of the early afternoon.

I drank coffee and organized my office.

Around two-thirty there were whispers that Corr had been killed. Some guy knew a guy who knew a guy who saw a bagged and tagged wheeled out and placed in an unmarked van. Tying up all the loose ends.

It was after four-thirty by the time I finished my report. I was careful, detailed and wrote like it actually mattered, like it actually would be read. But I doubted it. After I submitted it, I briefly wondered if I could access it tomorrow or if it already had been burned and whisked, or whisked and burned. I tore the corresponding pages from my notebook, placed them in an envelope and addressed an IO to Schlaf. That was it.

It was the opposite direction from any reasonable drive home. And rush hour was just beginning. I thought I'd leave it to fate, and fate answered unequivocally with a parking space right in front, underneath that big beckoning neon sign. I needed a mixed drink.

It was cool and dark and smelled like it did a couple of days ago. My eyes adjusted to a couple of older guys with dark weathered faces and cowboy hats at the bar and a quartet of college kids sharing a pitcher or two in a booth near the juke. It was quiet, with only the low murmur of college conversation and air-conditioning hum.

"Hey." She smiled from behind the bar. "Where's your girlfriend?"

I was happy to see her. "Not my girlfriend."

"Jimmy's not here. I think he comes in at eight."

"Not here for Jimmy." I slid my ass onto a barstool, looking at the smile and trying not to be too clumsy. My lesbian explorations were rare, limited to undergrad, and had been, without exception, unqualified disasters. And it wasn't really that, as I was old enough to be her etc., etc., but I needed a drink as far away as possible from any male, macho or otherwise. And sipping a cocktail illuminated by that generous smile might make me feel less shitty about my life, less shitty about the entire world.

"You staking us out? You want a Coke or something?"

"Nope. Case closed. I'm here as a private citizen."

She began to cut limes on a cutting board. "Congratulations. Although you don't look too happy."

"A long story. But I could use a drink."

"A long story, huh? Who's got time for that? But lemme guess. You're not really a beer drinker, and you wouldn't come here for wine. It's too hot for scotch or bourbon, and I can't really see you as a vodka sneak. That leaves gin or tequila. So, martini or margarita?"

"You're a better detective than I am."

"The more you know about people, the better they tip. Sometimes." She continued to quarter the limes.

"How about a gin and tonic?"

She looked up from her citrus. "Oh c'mon, you can do better than that."

I chuckled. "You always refuse what your customers order?"

"No. But you need something better than a G and T. Something less ladylike."

I was somewhat taken aback. "Like what?"

She gazed down at her fruit and quartered a lime. Then another. "Something less cliché." She was smiling when she looked up. "I have some very nice tequila, some extra añejo. It's a little smoky, like mezcal, but not as oily."

"So a margarita?"

"No, no, too good for a margarita." She put her knife down and turned to the cabinet of bottles behind her to the right. I felt my phone thrash in my pocket before I heard the ring. Regis University. Father Juan. There was no longer any rush. I put the phone back.

She returned with a brown bottle and two tequila glasses. She removed the stopper and carefully filled the two glasses to the rim. "This one's on me." She set a glass in front of me.

"What should we drink to?"

"That's a good question."

"Then let's just drink."

TOUS LES REGRETZ

Survivors Network of those Abused by Priests
PO Box 56539
Saint Louis, MO 63156

Reverend Father Andrea Vidal
1300 S. Steele St.
Denver, CO 80210

Dear Reverend Father Vidal,

We are delighted to accept the generous donation from your client to our organization. As per your instructions, the donation will be kept anonymous, and both the amount of the gift and the identity of the giver will be kept in the strictest confidence. Should the wishes of the benefactor change, I would be delighted to discuss with you any emendations to our previous agreement.

I have enclosed a receipt for your invaluable contribution, as well as other documents required by law. As you are no doubt aware, SNAP is an organization that depends almost entirely on volunteer labor and donations from generous souls such as yourself. Simply put, we could not exist to do the work we are doing without contributions like yours. Your generous gift will allow us to retain the best of lawyers to put an end to this terrible scourge, as well as to begin to provide adequate counseling, rehabilitation and medical services for the victims and their families, some of whom are as young as eight years old.

Gratefully Yours,

Samantha King

Executive Vice President
Survivors Network of those Abused by Priests

Received by wire transfer from the Bank of Switzerland, June 1st, 2010, the sum of $2,000,000.

BishopAccountability.org, Inc.
P.O. Box 541375
Waltham, MA 02454–1375

Reverend Father Andrea Vidal
1300 S. Steele St.
Denver, CO 80210

Dear Father Vidal,

I write to thank you for your generous donation to our organization. As you know, we are strictly autonomous and independent
and are funded exclusively by donations from private parties such
as yours. Your client's support will allow us to commit to the research, verification and publication of the names of Catholic sex
offenders and those who enable, conceal and support their crimes.
We believe that it is only by the thorough and just documentation
of these crimes that this horrific cancer may be eradicated from
the Holy Church. We thank you again. Sincerely, the workers of
Bishop Accountability dot org.

Received by wire transfer from the Bank of Switzerland, June 3rd,
2010, the sum of $2,000,000.

Associazione Rete L'ABUSO,
via Pietro Giuria 3/28
Savona 17100 Italy

Reverend Father Andrea Vidal
1300 S. Steele St.
Denver, CO 80210
USA

We would like to thank you for your donation. Please be assured that your gift will help us to combat the terrible corruption.

Thank you,

Director and Founder Paulo Massimino
L'Abuso

Received by wire transfer from the Bank of Switzerland, June 1st, 2010, the sum of €950.000.

The next morning, I felt better than I had any right to. I was dehydrated, with a slight headache, but inconvenienced rather than incapacitated. Sally the bartender had arranged to have a friend drive me home in my car. One of the old guys at the end of the bar said he didn't drink, said he was going this way anyway. I was in no shape to argue. Nicholas was out, and Hector was in the shop, so I staggered up the stairs, had two bowls of too-sweet cereal and managed to pee and get undressed and into bed without throwing up. And now I wanted some coffee, OJ, and even eggs.

I checked my phone. Other than the message from Father Juan telling me the translation was ready, there was nothing. Nothing from Schlaf, Clark, Maldonado—not a goddamn thing. Case was closed.

Hector was reading the paper, drinking his big mug of coffee, my empty bowl and spoon still there. I assumed Nicholas was at school. "Early night last night," he stated into the paper. I poured myself a cup of coffee, found the half-and-half and stirred. "We had dinner at seven, then heard you come in not too long after, like eight, eight-thirty. Knocked but no answer."

I sat down. "I was beat. The case is over."

He put the paper down and looked at me. "You catch the guy? The *pendejo* who killed that priest?"

I hesitated. "I guess we did. Yeah."

Hector nodded and went back to reading. I took a long sip of coffee.

Father Juan needed a thank-you and last night's tequila was very good, so I thought I'd stop by Argonaut to see if I could find it. I wasn't sure what it was called, Tears of Lorraine or something, but I was pretty sure I'd recognize the bottle. I could phone up the

Satire, see if Sally was working and ask her, but there was so much wrong with that.

Anyway, I found it: Tears of Llorona for $250. A little more than I was planning to spend, and it wasn't like the book mattered anymore anyway, but he turned it around quickly, and maybe we could use him again. Just in case we had another multi-linguistic priest killed with a shotgun blast to the face.

It was almost eleven when I parked the car in the Regis lot near Juan's office. I was wondering if he'd open it in front of me: what was the etiquette for that? Would he offer a drink? Would I take it? Eleven was too early. But that office was nice, and I had no place else to be. No place at all.

I hid the brown-bagged bottle behind my thigh and nodded to the beehived receptionist (curiously all in black) as I passed and knocked firmly on Juan's door. The noise echoed loudly. There was no sound of movement or response. I knocked again. His message said he'd be in all day. Maybe he'd gone to the bathroom or lunch. I hit redial on my voicemail. "We are sorry. You have reached a number that has been disconnected or is no longer in service." Huh? He just called me from this number last night. Hopefully the receptionist could tell me where he was.

"Excuse me." I kept the bottle down against my leg as inconspicuously as I could: I should have bought one of those ornate wine gift bags instead of this brown paper alkie sack. "Excuse me." She looked up quickly, smiled wanly. "I'm Detective Fruscella and was here the other day. I was supposed to meet Father Juan, but he doesn't seem to be in his office. And for some reason, his telephone isn't working. Do you know when he's expected back?"

She stood up quickly, her mouth forced into this exaggerated expression of surprise and regret. She moved deliberately from her desk to the counter, focusing on not tottering on her high heels. She was indeed wearing a black dress, cocktail length, with dark hose and shiny black pumps with large silver buckles. Her heels and hair combined brought her to six-two, six-three. She steadied herself with her hands on the counter.

I waited while she formed words. I had time.

Finally, "Father Juan, Father Juan has been transferred."

"Transferred? But he tried to call me last night."

She nodded. I waited. "How could they transfer him? What about his classes? His students?"

She nodded. And continued to nod. I wondered about the decisions made, by both her and some supervisor, to place her in a job for which she was so definitely unsuited. "Do you know how to contact him? His telephone seems disconnected."

"He has been transferred. I don't know where. I don't know anything else. He's not regular faculty, and so they can send him wherever." She sighed heavily and closed her eyes. She shifted her weight to her right hip and opened her eyes in some weird approximation of a defiant schoolgirl. One of us was in the wrong opera.

"So that's it? You don't know where he is or how to reach him?" She shook her head no. "Did he leave anything for me? A package, a notebook, anything?"

She nodded yes.

I stood, watching her nod. Eventually, she turned abruptly, retrieved something heavy from her desk in a green Whole Foods tote, moved back to the counter and placed it in front of me. I looked inside. There were two thick folders. The notebook.

I looked at her. "Is there anyway of getting hold of Father Juan? Of thanking him?"

"No."

I put the bottle of tequila in the Whole Foods bag and left.

The shop was cool and dark, closed for lunch. Hector was probably bumping around upstairs. The back studio had a comfortable chair and good light. I rummaged around until I found a plastic cup in one of the drawers underneath the workbench. I turned the lights on in the studio and flipped switches, rotated knobs and pushed buttons until I got some music. Joni Mitchell. "I was an unmarried girl/I just turned twenty-seven." It had been a long time since I'd listened to Joni Mitchell. I liked the voice and the open tunings. I never listened to the words. I turned it down but not off.

I put the tote on the floor next to the center chair and sat down. On something. A paperback. Flannery O'Connor's *A Good Man Is Hard to Find*. Ain't that the truth. I had other reading to do. I slid the paperback across the floor.

I took the translated notebook from the bag and set it on my lap. I poured some tequila into the glass and began to read.

ACKNOWLEDGMENTS

The author would like to thank the following: Marco Breuer, Robert Steiner, Katherine Eggert, Melanie Sheffield, Marcia Douglas, Stephen Graham Jones, Kathleen Woods, Ryan Chang, Loie Rawding, Paul Youngquist, the fine writers of FC2, Patrick Greaney, Francis Greaney, Emmanuel David, Emily Ripley, Mónica de la Torre, Megan O'Connell, Dan Waterman, Lou Robinson, and Tracy Schoenle. Henry Sussman's *The Task of the Critic: Poetics, Philosophy, Religion* got me started down the rabbit hole of negative theology and eventually Catholic mystery, costuming and lore. I would also like to thank Elisabeth Sheffield with all of my soul. I owe her the observations regarding the hysteria of the male characters in the *Incipit* and the original sin of Catholicism in *Lamentations*. The first pages appeared in *BOMB*, Spring 2015: many thanks to the editors.